Sought-after!   £2.00

NEM

Also by Shaun Hutson

SLUGS
SPAWN
EREBUS
SHADOWS
RELICS
DEATHDAY
VICTIMS
ASSASSIN
RENEGADES
BREEDING GROUND

NEMESIS

SHAUN HUTSON

Macdonald

A Macdonald Book

First published in Great Britain in 1989 by W. H. Allen & Co plc.
This edition published in 1991 by
Macdonald & Co (Publishers) Ltd
London & Sydney

Printed and bound in Great Britain by
Redwood Press Limited, Melksham, Wiltshire

ISBN 0 356 20029 9

A CIP catalogue record for this book is available from the British
Library

Macdonald & Co (Publishers) Ltd
165, Great Dover Street
London SE1 4YA

A member of Maxwell Macmillan Pergamon Publishing Corporation

For Belinda

with love

August 15, 1940

They were getting closer.

There was no doubt about it.

The rumbling which filled the subterranean corridor seemed to emanate from every brick, swelling around him like an approaching storm.

George Lawrenson knew that the tunnel which he now hurried along was at least seventy feet beneath the pavements of Whitehall, but still the reverberations rocked him as he walked. Flecks of dust floated from the ceiling every now and then, tiny pieces of plaster, dislodged by the incessant shaking detached themselves and fell like solid snow. Lawrenson wiped some of the dust from his jacket as he walked, looking up as the lights flickered once.

Below ground there was light. On the surface all was darkness.

The peculiar reversal of roles, the dislocation of normality which everyone had been living through for the last few weeks was illustrated perfectly by this particular example, Lawrenson thought. Where there should be blackness there was light. Where street lights should be burning there was gloom.

The only light on the surface was that which came from the fires.

From the incendiary bombs which the Luftwaffe dropped. From the blazing wreckage of houses and factories.

It had been like this every night for the past two weeks

and no one knew how much longer it would go on. The skies above London were full of German planes, pouring bombs onto the capital, transforming it into a gigantic torch which flared with the flames of a thousand fires.

Lawrenson walked on, the file gripped firmly in his right hand. He turned a corner and proceeded down another long corridor. Above him the lights dimmed briefly then flared into life once more.

The bombs were falling on the embankment now.

Coming closer.

How many would emerge from the relative safety of the underground stations the following morning to discover that their houses no longer existed? That the places they had called homes had been reduced to piles of blackened brick.

Every night they poured down the steps and onto the platforms of the stations, there to spend the night sleeping or lying awake listening to the pounding from above. Then, the following morning they would emerge from below ground like a human tidal wave.

Like souls let loose from hell.

Only they were climbing the stairs *into* hell.

Into streets cratered by bombs, littered with human remains and obliterated vehicles.

But, for now, they were below ground like so many rabbits and all they could do was wait and hope. And pray.

Lawrenson thought briefly about his own wife as he strode along the corridor. His home was in the country, about forty miles from the capital. Unlike others, he was reasonably sure she was safe. He spoke to her by phone every evening and she had told him that she had seen the crimson glow which came from the city. She had told him she was frightened. Afraid for his safety. But, every night he told her not to worry then he retreated below ground like some kind of be-suited troglodyte, there to sit out the fury which Hitler's air force unleashed with the coming of night.

The rumbling grew louder and the lights dimmed once again but this time Lawrenson walked on without slowing his pace. He held the file close to his chest, as if protecting it from the tiny pieces of debris that fell from the ceiling.

As he turned the corner the two figures seemed to loom from the walls themselves and, despite himself, Lawrenson faltered.

He nodded a cursory greeting towards the first of the uniformed men then reached inside his jacket for his security pass. He held it up for inspection, allowing the senior of the two men to scrutinise the small photo which adorned the pass. He glanced at the picture then at Lawrenson as if to reassure himself that the man who stood before him was indeed who his pass declared him to be. Satisfied with that fact, the soldier turned towards the door, knocked once then stepped back, ushering Lawrenson through.

On the other side he was greeted by a third uniformed man. An officer.

The military man nodded affably and then returned to the table to his left where he and two other men were gathered around a map which was spread out before them.

Maps covered the wall too. The room was about twenty feet square and it seemed that every single inch of wall space was covered by maps and diagrams. Lawrenson spotted one which showed the British army's withdrawal to Dunkirk.

The room smelt of coffee and cigarette smoke and he waved a hand before him as if to dispel the odour. The men inside the room glanced quizzically at him, those who hadn't seen him before, others who knew him nodded greetings. No one smiled.

Lawrenson brushed a stray hair from his forehead and approached the large table which was set in the centre of the room. Two men stood behind it, looking down at yet another map. As Lawrenson approached they both looked up and the elder of the two nodded deferentially. He glanced at the file which Lawrenson held, watching as it was laid before him.

Others now gathered around the table, as if the file were acting as some kind of magnet, drawing them from all corners of the room. But only the older man sat, rubbing his eyes briefly then re-adjusting his glasses.

Outside, the earth shook as another shower of bombs fell.

Inside the subterranean Headquarters Winston Churchill began to read the contents of the file marked 'Genesis'.

One

The car came within inches of his motorbike and Gary Sinclair swerved violently to avoid being struck by the speeding vehicle.

'You stupid bastard!' he bellowed at the retreating tail lights but, in seconds, the car had disappeared around a bend in the road, swallowed up by the night.

Gary sucked in a deep breath, both shocked and angered by the near miss. Hadn't the driver seen him? Maybe the stupid sod was pissed. Either way it had been a close thing. Another couple of inches and he'd have been off. The bike juddered beneath him as if sharing his apprehension and, instinctively, he glanced down at the fuel gauge. The needle was almost touching red, the tank close to being empty. Gary muttered to himself and eased off slightly on the throttle. Perhaps, he thought, if he took it steadily, he'd get home before the bike packed up on him. When he'd taken it for a couple of test runs he'd been sure that the fuel tank was leaking but his brother, who'd sold him the bike, had assured him there was nothing to worry about.

Nothing to worry about, Gary thought irritably, glancing down once more at the gauge. He had another five miles to go before he reached Hinkston, he doubted if he'd make it.

As if to reinforce his doubts the bike slowed noticeably and refused to speed up even when he twisted the throttle violently. The engine spluttered dismally then died. Gary instinctively allowed his left foot to drop to the ground to steady himself as the Kawasaki came to a halt.

He grunted in annoyance and swung himself off the saddle. Then, propping the bike up against the hedge which ran along the roadside, he pulled his helmet off and glared at the bike. He drew his fingers through his shoulder length brown hair and squatted down beside the 750. Inspections, mechanical or otherwise, seemed somewhat pointless at this stage, he thought after a moment. He was stuck five miles from home. There was nothing else to do but wheel the bloody bike back into town. He pulled a packet of cigarettes from one of the side pockets of his leather jacket and lit one, allowing the smoke to burn its way to his lungs, then he took hold of the handlebars and guided the bike away from the hedge, the helmet hanging from the throttle.

A strong breeze had blown up in the last hour or so and it caused Gary's hair to flap around his face like so many writhing snakes. He pulled some strands from his mouth, cursing his brother once more for selling him the bike. It would take him more than an hour to walk into Hinkston from his present location and the weight of the bike made that journey all the more uncomfortable. He stopped every few hundred yards and drew in a couple of deep breaths.

The wind was keen and he was glad he wore a sweatshirt beneath his jacket. However, pushing the bike kept him warm, it was just his face that felt cold.

On both sides of him trees bowed as the wind grew in strength. The moon had retreated behind a bank of thick cloud. The road was dark, flanked by tall hedges beyond which stood the trees that rattled their branches almost mockingly at him. Low hills rose to his right, masking the approaches to the town of Hinkston, hiding the glow of street lights and making it seem as if he were much further than five miles from the town. He glanced down at his watch and saw that it was almost 12.15 a.m. And he had to be up at six in the morning. He cursed his brother once more. He'd be lucky to reach home before 1.30 at this rate. Four hours sleep if he was lucky – Christ, he'd be wrecked by tomorrow. He thought about ringing in and saying he was ill but he decided against that. The job at the bakery was the first he'd had since leaving school two years earlier. Jobs weren't easy to come by and he couldn't afford to be choosy. An eighteen year old with two CSE's and negligible work experience wasn't exactly an employer's dream.

He guided the motorbike around a bend in the road, kicking several tree branches aside. The wind must have been stronger than he thought. It whistled through the tall hedges, a shrill banshee wail. Gary trudged on, now feeling quite warm from the effort of pushing the Kawasaki.

The car was parked about two hundred yards ahead of him.

There was a kind of makeshift lay-by, little more than a gap in the right hand hedge with a muddy verge before it but the vehicle was standing motionless there, lights on, smoke rising from its exhaust.

Gary smiled thinly to himself. Maybe the driver would give him a lift into Hinkston. He could wedge the 750 into the boot. Surely the bloke wouldn't mind. He increased his pace in an effort to reach the car before it pulled away.

There was something familiar about it.

Something . . .

He was about fifty yards away when he realised it was the same car that had almost forced him into the hedge further back on the road.

Gary felt the anger rise within him briefly but he fought it back. If the driver was willing to give him a lift then the previous aberration could be overlooked. He might mention it in passing, just as a joke. But, he reasoned, why make an issue out of it?

He drew closer to the car and heard the engine idling in the stillness of the night.

Maybe the driver wasn't alone. He might have his girlfriend in there with him. Maybe he'd pulled over for a quick one. Gary chuckled then shook his head. If they were romping about on the back seat the driver wasn't likely to have left his engine running and all his lights on.

The dull purring of the car engine continued to fill the otherwise noiseless night.

The wind had slackened slightly although the tree branches still swayed as if pulled by invisible strings.

Gary rolled his bike up to within twenty feet of the car and peered into the vehicle.

It was empty.

The bloke must have nipped behind the hedge for a slash, he thought, moving closer. He'd just wait until he came back then ask for a lift.

Gary leant the bike against the hedge and walked closer to the car, admiring the sleek bodywork, deciding that he would start saving up for driving lessons. He liked the bike but a car had more class. He walked around it, patting the bonnet as if he were inspecting the car with a view to purchase.

The engine continued to purr.

Gary glanced behind him towards the hedge, wondering where the driver could have got to. He sighed and continued with his tour of inspection of the vehicle, sliding his hand almost unconsciously to one of the handles.

The door opened as he pulled.

He frowned.

This was weird, he thought. It was bad enough leaving all the lights on and the engine running but to leave the car unlocked too? The driver was either very trusting or very stupid. Gary tried the rear door.

That too was unlocked.

He walked around to the driver's side and tried that door as well.

Not surprisingly he found it unlocked.

The car moved.

Only a matter of inches but the motion was enough to startle Gary who took a step back, realising that the handbrake must be off. The car came to a halt a couple of inches further on, engine still ticking over. Gary stepped forward again, reaching for the handle, deciding he'd at least reach inside and pull up the handbrake, stop the car rolling down the slight hill which sloped away ahead of it. He reached for the door.

Hands gripped the back of his head.

He felt uncontrollable force and strength at the base of his skull as two strong hands fixed themselves around his neck, fingers digging into his throat.

Taken by surprise he was helpless, unable to stop himself as the hands forced him forward with incredible speed, slamming his head into the driver's side window of the car.

The impact opened a hairline cut across his forehead and a thin trickle of blood oozed down his face.

As he shouted in pain and surprise, he felt himself being propelled forward a second time, with even more force.

His face was driven into the top of the car door and he felt searing agony fill his head as two of his front teeth were shattered, one of them forced backwards into his tongue. Blood filled his mouth and spilled down his chin as he tried to twist, to fight off his attacker.

But his hidden assailant was taking full advantage of Gary's helplessness and another sickening contact with the car roof splintered two more of the youth's teeth and chipped the bone of his lower jaw. He tried to scream but the pain had already driven him to the edge of consciousness. As the hands relaxed their grip on the back of his neck, Gary Sinclair fell across the bonnet of the car then slid to the ground, his vision clouded by agony. He rolled onto his back on the muddy verge, looking up at his attacker who stood over him for brief seconds then knelt beside him, grabbing a handful of his hair, lifting his bloodied face as if to inspect the damage.

It was then that Gary saw the knife.

The blade was about ten inches long. Slightly thicker than a knitting needle.

Gary opened his mouth, moaning as he felt fresh waves of pain from his smashed jaw. He tried to squirm away from the hand which held him so firmly but it was useless.

The point of the knife actually brushed his upper eyelid and he felt his bowels loosen as fear overcame him.

The wickedly sharp point of the knife punctured the bulging orb of his right eye effortlessly.

It was pushed with no haste. It wasn't driven into the writhing boy's eye, it was *inserted* with a kind of sadistic precision.

And now he did find the breath to scream but the frantic bellow was cut off abruptly as two more inches of the blade disappeared into his eye socket, pushed with an even pressure.

Two inches.

Three.

Four.

Vitreous liquid spurted onto his cheek, mingling with the blood which already covered his skin.

The eye seemed to burst like a water-filled balloon. The white turned red and the orb seemed to collapse in upon itself as the blade was pushed deeper. One final surge of pressure and it punctured the frontal lobe of the brain.

Gary Sinclair shuddered then lay still.

The knife was pulled free then the driver of the car calmly unlocked the boot and pushed it open.

It took only a moment to lift Gary's body and push it

16

unceremoniously into the rear compartment of the vehicle. The lid was slammed down and the driver walked unhurriedly around to the door, slid behind the wheel and guided the vehicle back out onto the road.

Once again, the tail lights were swallowed by the blackness.

Two

It looked as if someone had been shading beneath her eyes with charcoal.

Susan Hacket looked at the reflection which stared back at her from the mirror and sighed. She picked up the brush which lay on the dressing table and swept it through her hair, listening to the static electricity crackling. She fluffed up her shaggy locks with her fingertips then reached for her make-up. She plucked a brush from the hand-shaped container on her left and began applying foundation to the pale visage which confronted her. The brushes and the make-up had been a present for her twenty-fifth birthday, just seven months earlier. But, at the moment, she felt a hundred and twenty-five.

Susan sighed again, tiring of her own efforts to brighten her appearance. She got to her feet, crossed the landing to the bathroom and washed the foundation off, towelling her face dry, glancing at herself in the bathroom mirror this time.

She was grateful that she didn't feel as rough as she looked.

Even the ravages of so much worry, so many sleepless

nights, could not hide her natural attractiveness. She rarely wore heavy make-up. People were always telling her she didn't need it. But, in the last couple of months she had taken to wearing it on these nightly visits. Taken to making an effort. He had always liked her in make-up before, had always complimented her on her appearance. What reason was there to stop? Just because . . .

She splashed her face with more water, dried it a second time then returned to the bedroom where she hastily but expertly applied some mascara and eye-liner. The dark smudges beneath her eyes didn't look too bad she told herself. A few good nights' sleep and they would vanish. Exactly when those nights would come she had no idea.

She pulled on a sweatshirt and jeans, stepped into a pair of short suede boots and headed back out onto the landing once more. The door directly opposite her was slightly ajar. Sue crossed to it and moved silently into the room, careful not to collide with the half-a-dozen mobiles which hung from the ceiling. Snow White and the Seven Dwarfs. Dumbo. Postman Pat. All swayed gently in the slight breeze which wafted through the window. Sue rubbed her hands together, thinking how cold it was turning. She crossed to the window and closed it, pressing a hand to the radiator as she stepped away.

She moved close to the bed and crouched down beside it, pulling the sheet back from the tiny sleeping form cocooned within it.

Lisa Hacket lay still as her mother gently brushed some strands of fine, silver-blonde hair from her face. Then Sue leant across and kissed her four-year-old daughter on the cheek.

'I love you,' she whispered, then slowly straightened up and crept out of the room.

At the foot of the stairs she picked up her handbag and

jacket then popped her head round the door of the sitting room.

'I'm off now, Caroline,' she said, smiling. 'I'll be back in a couple of hours.'

From the sofa, Caroline Fearns turned and smiled. A bright, pretty, sixteen-year-old with uncomfortably large breasts, she nodded and smiled broadly at Sue.

'I really am sorry I had to call you at such short notice,' Sue said. 'But John's got a meeting at the school and I'm not sure what time he'll be back. If he gets back before me could you tell him I've left some food in the oven for him, please?'

Caroline nodded briskly, smiled again then turned her attention back to the TV screen. She enjoyed baby-sitting for the Hacket's. They paid her well and they had a colour TV as well as a video. Her own father refused to buy a colour TV despite the fact that, during snooker matches, he spent the entire time complaining about not being able to figure out which balls the players were trying to pot. But besides the money and the TV there was an added bonus. Mr Hacket always insisted on taking her home in his car after the baby-sitting was over. Caroline found him unbearably sexy (even though he *was* pushing thirty). She wished *her* English teacher looked like him.

She heard the front door close and glanced at her watch. 6.35 p.m.

She'd wait until the soap opera she was watching had finished then she'd make a cup of tea. She stretched out contentedly on the sofa.

As Sue stepped out into the night she shivered. The wind whistled around her and she pulled up the collar of her jacket as she headed for her car, fumbling in her handbag for the keys. She slid behind the wheel of the Metro and started the engine, checking her reflection briefly in the rear-view mirror. Cheerful enough? No cracks in the mask?

She pulled away, making a note to stop off at the garage and get some flowers.

Flowers were so important.

They saw her leave.

Hidden by the darkness, sitting in the car parked about fifty yards down the street, they watched her as she pulled away.

6.38 p.m.

One of them glanced at the house, at the light burning in the front room.

They would wait a little longer.

Three

He heard the thud from above and squinted at the ceiling, as if expecting it to cave in. But no cracks appeared, there was no rending of beams or crashing of concrete. The ceiling remained as unblemished now as it had been ten minutes ago when he'd first fixed his eyes on the spot above his head.

John Hacket draped one arm across his forehead, catching sight of his watch in the process. The ticking sounded thunderous in the relative silence of the bedroom. As even as his own low breathing.

'Penny for your thoughts.'

The voice came from beside him, a slight Irish lilt to it.

Hacket turned his head slowly to look at Nikki Reeves.

20

She was looking at him with those large brown eyes, fixing him in the kind of gaze which had first drawn him to her. There were a thousand clichés for those eyes, for that look. *Come to bed eyes. Hypnotic glances.*

Hacket almost laughed.

How about, *Screw me and to hell with your wife eyes?*

She asked him again, brushing hair from her face.

'What are you thinking about?'

Hacket shook his head dismissively, watching as she raised herself up onto one elbow to look down on him. Her right hand rested on his chest, her index finger tracing patterns across his skin. He could smell her perfume. He knew the smell well. He should do, he'd bought it for her. The delicate aroma mingled with the stronger musky scent of their own post-coital exertions.

'What makes you think I've got something on my mind?' Hacket asked her, raising one finger and gently running it along her bottom lip.

She flicked out her tongue and licked the tip of the probing digit.

'Because you're quiet,' she said, smiling.

He shrugged.

'Be thankful for small mercies.'

Hacket lay still while she continued stroking his chest, only now his eyes were on her, taking in the details of her face and upper body. The sheet had slipped down to reveal her breasts, the nipples still erect. He looked at her face and, again, found himself lost in those eyes. His finger strayed from her lips and he took to stroking her cheek, enjoying the smoothness of her skin. And, all the time he could smell her perfume. It was one of the things which had first attracted him to her. The fact that she was good-looking had seemed almost secondary. Romance begins in many different ways and Hacket could think of a thousand more clichés to describe that particular peculiarity which

21

men and women put so much faith in. But he knew that this was not romance. It was an affair. Pure and simple.

He almost smiled again at the irony of that phrase. There was nothing pure about it and simplicity was rapidly eroded when a man took a lover.

She was twenty-two, eight years younger than Hacket. The affair had been going on for the past three months. Ever since . . .

He tried to push the thought from his mind but it persisted.

Ever since Sue's father had become ill.

Hacket wondered if he was trying to justify his actions to himself. Even trying to shift the blame for his indiscretions onto his wife.

Her father was dying. She was worried. She hadn't enough time for Hacket so he'd found a lover. There, he thought, bitterly, it *was* simple when you thought it through.

Nikki leant across him and pressed her lips to his. He felt her tongue flicking urgently against his teeth then it slipped inside his mouth, stirring the warm wetness. Hacket responded fiercely and when they finally separated both were breathing heavily. He could feel her nipples pressing into his chest, his own erection now nudging her belly as she lay closer to him.

After a moment or two she pulled herself across him and sat on the side of the bed.

'Was it something I said?' he asked, watching as she got to her feet and reached for a baggy T-shirt on the chair nearby.

She smiled and slipped it on, the voluminous folds hiding her shapely figure as she padded towards the door. She paused there, silhouetted by the soft light which was spilling from the sitting room.

'I'm hungry,' she told him. 'Do you want something?'

He shook his head.

'No thanks I'll . . .' He coughed. 'I'm fine.'

I'll have something to eat when I get home. I'll eat the food that my wife has prepared for me, Hacket thought. He exhaled deeply, almost angrily, and sat up, reaching for his cigarettes, pulling the packet from the pocket of his trousers. He lit a Dunhill and sucked hard on it. Sue would be at the hospital by now, he thought, glancing at his watch. The nightly vigil. Christ, why did she torture herself like that? Every single bloody night she was at the hospital. He blew out a stream of smoke watching it dissipate slowly in the air. And how much longer was it going to last? No one knew, no one could tell her. The same way no one could tell *him* how long his affair with Nikki was going to continue. Nagging doubts at the back of his mind told him he should end it now. But the doubts only came when he was at home, when he was away from her. When he was with her the desire to end the relationship wasn't so pressing. He didn't love her, that much he knew, but he felt for her more strongly than he should have done. She filled a gap in his life, a gap which should never have been there to begin with. Was he blaming Sue again? The role of neglected, misunderstood husband didn't suit him particularly well.

How about husband who's feeling sorry for himself?

Hacket took another drag on the cigarette.

How about unfeeling, selfish bastard? That seemed to suit him perfectly.

Hacket's philosophical musings were interrupted by Nikki's return. She was carrying a glass of milk and a plate with a couple of hastily-made sandwiches stacked on it.

She shivered, commented how cold it was in the kitchen then sat down on the bed beside him and took a bite from one of the sandwiches.

'Pig,' he said, watching her as she ate.

'Oink, oink,' she replied, giggling.

He snaked an arm around her waist and drew her closer to him, kissing her ear. She put down the sandwich, kissed him lightly on the tip of the nose then reached for the glass of milk. She took a mouthful but didn't swallow it. Instead she leant closer to him, the white liquid staining her lips. As she kissed him he opened his mouth and allowed her to pass some of the milk to him. When they parted she was smiling broadly. She allowed one hand to drop to his thigh, stroking the hair which grew so thickly there. Then her fingers were exploring higher, her nails gently raking his scrotum before gliding around his stiffening penis.

'I'll have to go soon,' he whispered as she gripped his shaft more tightly, working up a rhythm, coaxing him to full hardness.

'Soon,' she breathed in his ear.

They lay back across the bed, bodies entwined.

Four

The houses in this particular part of Clapham all looked similar. Terraced and semi-detached, inhabited by unremarkable people with unremarkable lives.

People like John and Susan Hacket.

It was their home which the men in the grey Ford Escort had been watching for the last twenty minutes.

As if some kind of silent signal had been given both of them swung themselves out of the car and walked unhurriedly up the path towards the passageway which led towards the back garden of the Hacket's house. The street lamp outside the house was off, and it afforded the two men the cover they needed. The curtains of the houses on either side were drawn. It was too late in the day for people to be peering out checking on callers. A couple of doors down a dog barked but the two men paid it no heed. The first of them, a tall man with what seemed like abnormally long arms, gently lifted the catch on the passage door and opened it.

His companion followed him into the enveloping gloom.

The passage was about fifteen feet long, the floor of chipped concrete. The two men moved cautiously along the narrow walkway, careful not to create any noise as they made their way to the back of the house.

The garden was in darkness.

A rusted tricycle stood close by and the first man pushed it with his foot, ignoring the protesting squeal from its wheels. He smiled broadly and looked at his companion but the other man was already trying the back door, finding, not surprisingly, that it was locked.

The knife he took from his belt was about eight inches long, double-edged and wickedly sharp.

He stuck it into the frame of the window, working the blade expertly up and down until the window lock finally came loose. He nudged it gently and the window opened a fraction.

Peter Walton smiled and nodded to his companion who squatted down, clasping his hands together to form a stirrup. Walton put his foot on the helping hands and allowed himself to be hoisted up onto the window-sill. He paused there for a moment then swung himself inside, the sound of the TV reaching his ears as he eased himself down onto the tiles. He stood in the darkened room, watching as the tall man followed him inside.

Ronald Mills moved with remarkable dexterity for a man of over six feet. He clambered through the window and joined Walton in the kitchen, taking a step towards the closed door. He too could hear the sounds coming from the lounge.

Walton chewed his bottom lip contemplatively. He hadn't expected anyone to be at home. His expression of bewilderment gradually melted into a grin of satisfaction. This was an added bonus.

He looked at Mills and nodded, reaching for the handle of the door.

It opened soundlessly.

Both men stepped into the hall, the staircase to their right.

The sound of the TV was louder now.

Caroline watched the end credits of the soap opera. She even watched the adverts after it had finished. It was like seeing them for the first time watching them in colour. But finally she decided to make herself a cup of tea then check on Lisa. She hadn't heard any noise from the girl's bedroom, she never had any trouble with her, but she thought it part of her duty as baby-sitter, to actually check her temporary charge. Caroline stretched then got to her feet, glancing back at the television, as if reluctant to leave it for too long. She pushed open the door and walked out into the hall, slowing her pace.

It was dark.

And yet, hadn't Mrs Hacket left the hall light on when she'd gone out?

Caroline was actually reaching for the switch when the hand grabbed her by the throat, stifling any attempt at a scream. She was yanked backwards, almost lifted off her feet by the hand which held her.

She felt something cold against her cheek and realised that it was a knife.

Ronald Mills pressed the razor sharp blade against her flesh and whispered in her ear, his voice low and rasping.

'You make one sound and I'll cut your fucking head off!'

August 26, 1940

She wouldn't stop screaming.

Lawrenson had tried to calm the woman, tried to reassure her, but his efforts had been useless.

They couldn't stop her screaming.

'Give her an epidural for God's sake,' snapped Maurice Fraser. 'She's in agony.' He bent close to the woman's face, seeing the pain in her bulging eyes, as if he needed further proof that she was indeed suffering.

'No pain killers,' Lawrenson said, quietly, his eyes never leaving the woman. She was in her mid-twenties but the pain etched on her face gave her the appearance of someone ten years older. Her feet were secured in the metal stirrups by thick straps, her arms also held firmly. Despite the restraining straps though, she jerked and shuddered incessantly as wave upon wave of pain tore through her.

The white gown which she wore had slipped away from her lower body, exposing her swollen belly and, as Lawrenson watched, he could see the sometimes violent undulations from inside her abdomen.

It looked as though the baby was trying to tear its way free.

A particularly violent contraction tore through her and she unleashed a scream which reverberated around the room. Lawrenson felt the hairs at the nape of his neck rise.

'She's losing a lot of blood, doctor,' Nurse Kiley told him, watching the steady flow from the woman's vagina. Several swabs had already been used, unsuccessfully, to

29

stem the outpouring of crimson fluid, they now lay discarded in a metal receiver like thick placental fragments.
Another pint of blood was attached to the drip which fed
blood into the prone woman by way of a twisted tube to
her left, the needle jammed securely into the crook of her
arm.

'Remove the baby, for God's sake, Lawrenson,' Fraser
said. 'Perform a Caesarian before it's too late. We'll lose
them both.'

Lawrenson shook his head.

'It'll be all right,' he said.

Another piercing scream filled the room and drummed
off the walls.

Nurse Kiley, who was standing between the woman's
legs, peered towards the weeping vagina then glanced at
Lawrenson.

'It's starting,' she said.

Lawrenson moved closer, anxious to see the birth.

Fraser gripped the woman's shoulder, trying to offer
some comfort but she continued to scream in pain as the
contractions became more violent. She felt something inside
her tearing, as if part of her insides were detaching themselves then, incredibly, the pain seemed to intensify.

Lawrenson saw the top of the baby's head, the lips of
the woman's vagina sliding back like fleshy curtains to
expose the first couple of inches of the child. The bloodied
lips reminded him of a mouth, trying to expel something
bloated and foul tasting. The labia swelled until it seemed
it must tear, until it appeared that the woman would begin
to split in half. Blood pumped from the widening cleft
which was now opening ever wider to release its precious
load.

The woman began thrashing madly on the bed, so ravaged by pain that she actually managed to pull her left arm
free of the restraining strap. As she waved it before her,

the drip came free and blood spurted madly from her arm and also from the end of the tube. Nurse Kiley hurried to re-attach it.

'Come on,' shouted Lawrenson, watching as more of the baby's head came free. 'Push. It's nearly over.'

There was a soft, liquescent spurt as the woman defecated, the waste mingling on the reeking bedclothes with the blood which still streamed from her vagina.

The head was free now, the child itself twisting from side to side, as if anxious to escape its crimson prison. The woman's labial lips spread ever wider as the child slithered into view. Lawrenson reached for it, ignoring the blood which drenched his hands.

He lifted the child, the umbilical cord hanging from its belly like a bloated snake, still attached to the placenta which, seconds later, was expelled in a reeking lump.

The woman's head lolled back, sweat covering her face and body, her hair matted to her forehead.

Fraser turned to look at the child which Lawrenson held aloft, gripping it like some kind of trophy.

'Oh Jesus,' murmured the doctor, his eyes bulging wide.

Nurse Kiley saw the child and could say nothing. She turned away and vomited violently.

'Lawrenson, you can't . . .' Fraser gasped, one hand clapped to his mouth.

'The child is all right, as I said it would be,' Lawrenson beamed, holding it up, not allowing it to squirm out of his grip. The umbilical cord still pulsed like a thick worm. It looked as if a putrescent parasite was burrowing into the child's stomach.

He held it towards the mother who had recovered sufficiently to look up. Her eyes were blurred with pain but as she blinked the clarity quickly returned and she saw her child.

'Your son,' said Lawrenson, proudly.

And she screamed again.

31

Five

Walton guessed that the girl was seventeen, maybe older. He didn't care.

She stood before him, hands clasped, shuffling her fingers like fleshy playing cards. There were tears in her eyes as she looked back and forth at the two men who stared so raptly at her. One of them, the taller one, kept wiping the back of his hand across his mouth and Caroline was sure he was dribbling. His breath was a low rasping wheeze, like an asthmatic gasping for air.

'You're pretty,' said Walton, touching her cheek with the point of the knife.

Caroline tried to swallow but her throat was dry. She closed her eyes and, this time, the tears did flow, running down her cheeks.

Walton pressed the knife against her flesh, allowing one of the salty droplets to dribble onto the metal. He withdrew the blade and licked the moisture with his tongue. Then he smiled at Caroline.

'Take your blouse off,' he said, softly, still smiling.

'Please don't hurt me,' she said, wiping the tears away with the back of her hand.

'Take the blouse off,' Walton urged, his voice now almost inaudible. He took a step closer to her, his face close to hers. He breathed stale cigarettes and tooth decay over her.

Still she hesitated.

'Take the fucking thing off or I'll take it off for you,' he hissed through clenched teeth.

Caroline reached for the top button, her hands shaking uncontrollably but, slowly, she managed to undo the fastener then repeated the procedure until the blouse hung open. Even through her fear she blushed.

'I said take it off,' Walton reminded her. 'Do it.'

'Please . . .'

'Do it,' he snarled.

She eased first one shoulder then the other out of the flimsy material, allowing it to drop to the floor in front of her. She sniffed, trying to fight back the tears but not succeeding.

'Please don't hurt me,' she whimpered, looking at both men as if expecting to find some trace of compassion. There was none.

'Why are you crying?'

It was Mills who asked the question this time.

He moved closer to her, and rested one hand on her left shoulder, peering at her breasts, which she attempted to cover.

He slapped her hands away and pulled at the strap of her bra.

'You've got lovely hair,' he told her, winding it around his hand, pulling her head to one side, towards his face. 'Kiss me.' He smiled broadly then looked at Walton, who nodded as if to urge his companion on.

'Well, go on, kiss him,' Walton said.

'Please . . .'

She got no further.

Mills pulled her round to face him, pushing his mouth against hers. She gagged as she felt his thick tongue pushing against her lips, his spittle running down her chin.

'A virgin. Never been kissed before?' Mills asked, pressing the point of the knife under her chin, digging it into the flesh gently at first. He watched as tears mingled with his own sputum.

'Take your bra off,' Walton said. 'Show us your body.'

Caroline shook her head almost imperceptibly, sobbing now.

'You said you didn't want us to hurt you,' Mills reminded her, grabbing a handful of her hair once again. He pressed

33

the razor sharp knife against her taut locks and sliced effortlessly through, pulling the handful of hair free. 'Hair today, gone tomorrow,' he chuckled, looking at Walton who merely nodded.

'Take off the bra,' he snapped. 'Now.'

She tried to plead, tried to beg but no words would come. Instead she reached behind her and unfastened the clasp of her bra, holding it for precious seconds before releasing it, pulling the garment free and exposing her breasts.

Walton rubbed his growing erection through his trousers. 'Now the jeans,' he said.

She was crying softly all the time now, tears pouring down her cheeks.

The two men stood a couple of feet back, watching the obscene strip-show with growing excitement.

'Don't kill me,' she sobbed, standing before them in just her knickers. 'I'll do what you say but don't kill me.'

'Take off your panties,' Mills told her. 'Slowly.'

She hooked her thumbs into the elastic and eased them down over her hips and thighs, shrugging them off to finally stand naked before her tormentors. She raised a hand to cover her sandy pubic hair but Mills gripped her wrist, lifting her hand instead to his own crotch, forcing her to touch the throbbing erection he now sported.

'Have you got a boyfriend?' Walton asked, pressing himself against her.

She didn't answer.

'Have you?' he snarled, jerking her head around so that she was looking directly into his staring eyes.

She shook her head, her eyes now clouded with tears, her whole body shaking.

'So you don't know what it's like to be touched by a man?' Walton said, softly. 'You don't know what you're missing.' He chuckled and gazed at her breasts for a second.

34

'Now if you're good we won't hurt you. Are you going to be good?'

She tried to nod but it was as if her body was paralysed. She thought she was going to faint.

'Dance for us,' said Mills, smiling.

'I can't,' she wailed, close to breaking point.

'Come on,' he said, chidingly, pressing the knife to her left cheek. 'Every young girl can dance.'

'You said you wouldn't hurt me. Please . . .'

Walton bent down and picked up her bra on the end of his knife. He dangled it before her like some kind of trophy.

'Dance,' he said.

'Mummy.'

All three of them heard the word.

Mills spun round, a faint smile on his thick lips.

'Who else is in the house?' snarled Walton, grabbing Caroline by the hair.

'It's a child,' said Mills, his eyes blazing.

'Where is she?' Walton rasped.

'Upstairs,' sobbed Caroline.

Again the plaintive call.

Mills moved towards the door.

'Don't hurt her,' Caroline shouted but the exhortation was cut short as Walton clamped his hand over her mouth and forced her down onto the sofa, the knife held against her throat.

'I'll see to her,' Mills said, softly, heading out of the room and towards the stairs.

'He's very good with little children,' Walton informed her, fumbling with the zip of his trousers. 'Now, you just stay quiet for me, all right?'

Mills reached the bottom of the stairs and paused, listening to the calls from upstairs then, slowly, he began to ascend.

He reached the landing and moved towards the door which was slightly ajar.

He saw the child sitting up in bed as he opened the door, his frame silhouetted against the light.

The child was silent as he walked into the bedroom.

'Hello,' he said, gaily.

Lisa looked puzzled by this newcomer. She'd never seen him before but she remained silent as he knelt beside her bed.

'You're a very pretty little girl,' Mills breathed. 'What's your name?'

She told him.

'What a pretty name.' He pushed her gently back into bed, looking down at her, smiling, wiping his mouth with the back of his hand.

Then he reached for the knife.

Six

The ward sister nodded politely as Susan Hacket passed her. She managed a smile in return and walked on up the corridor.

A tall nurse also smiled at Sue. Most of the staff recognised her by now. After all, she'd been coming to the hospital every night for the last six weeks. If was as if she belonged there. As she pushed the door to room 562, she wondered how much longer she would be repeating this ritual.

She paused in the doorway for a moment, closing the door slowly behind her.

The air carried the familiar smell of stale urine and disinfectant, but tonight it was tinged with a more pungent odour. Sue recognised it as the stench of stagnant water. The flowers which stood by the bedside were wilting, some of them weeping their shrivelled petals onto the cabinet. The water was cloudy. It was three or four days since she'd changed it.

She walked towards the bed, aware of the chill in the air. She shuddered involuntarily and noticed that the window was open slightly.

She murmured something to herself then shut it, keeping back the cold breeze which had been hissing under the frame. Then she turned towards the bed.

'Hello Dad,' she said, softly, smiling as best she could.

He didn't hear her.

Over the past two weeks he'd been slipping in and out of consciousness more frequently. Sometimes it was the extra doses of morphine they gave him, at other times his body just seemed to give up, to surrender to the pain and seek release in the oblivion of sleep. Sue reached across and touched his hand. It felt like ice. He had only one blanket to cover him and this she hastily pulled up around his neck, easing both arms beneath it too.

As she leant over him she smelled the stale urine more strongly. As his condition had deteriorated they had fitted him with a catheter and now she glanced down to see that the bag was half full of dark urine. Sue swallowed hard, thinking how undignified they were. It was as if the bag was one of the final concrete illustrations that he was helpless, unable even to reach the toilet. He never left his bed now. When the illness had first struck he had been able to walk up and down the corridor, even take the odd trip into the hospital gardens but, as the cancer had taken a firmer hold, all he had been able to do was to lie there and let it devour him from the inside.

She stood by the bedside for a moment longer gazing at his face. The skin was tinged yellow, stretched so tightly over the bones it seemed they would tear through.

Tom Nolan had never been a big man even when he was in the best of health but now he looked like an escapee from Belsen. His eyes were little more than sunken pits, the lids slightly parted as if he were watching her. Watching but not seeing. She could hear his low rasping breaths, and only the almost imperceptible rise and fall of his chest, accompanied by those grating inhalations, told her he was still alive. His thinning white hair had been swept over to one side of his head, a couple of strands having fallen untidily onto his forehead.

Sue reached into the drawer in the bedside cabinet, took out a comb and carefully ran it through the flimsy hair. As she withdrew she found that her hands were shaking. She stood gazing at him for a moment longer then picked up the vase with the dead flowers and threw them into the waste bin nearby. She then washed the vase in the sink and arranged the flowers she'd bought on her way to the hospital.

As she was replacing the vase she noticed that there was an envelope on the top of the cabinet. Sue opened it and pulled out a card which bore the words 'HOPE YOU'RE SOON FIGHTING FIT'.

Underneath was a picture of a boxer. She flipped it open, her teeth clamped together as if to fight back the pain. Sue didn't recognise the name inside, didn't know who'd written 'Get well soon'.

She tore the card and the envelope up with almost angry jerks of her arm then tossed the remains into the bin with the dead flowers.

'Get well soon,' she repeated under her breath, her eyes fixed on the shrivelled, shrunken shape which was her father. She almost smiled at the irony. You didn't 'Get well soon' when you had lung cancer, she thought. You didn't get well at all. You did what her father was doing. You lay in bed and let the disease eat you away from the inside. You let it transform you into a human skeleton. You let it tear you apart with pain.

The tears came without her even realising.

Every night she saw him, sat by him and, every night she swore she wouldn't cry but, again, the sight of him lying there waiting for death proved too much. She sat on the edge of the bed and pulled a handkerchief from her pocket, wiping her eyes.

Her own subdued whimperings momentarily eclipsed the low rasping sound coming from her father. She clenched her teeth hard together, until her jaws ached, then she blew her nose and sighed wearily. How much longer was this going to go on? How many more nights of waiting? There had been times, especially during the last couple of weeks, when she had felt like praying for his death. At least it would mean the end of his suffering. But when she had thoughts like that she swiftly rebuked herself. Life was so precious that it was something to be grasped, to be retained no matter what the indignities, no matter what the suffering. Life with pain was better than no life at all.

She wondered if her father thought the same.

Sue squeezed his hand through the thin material of the blanket and felt again how thin he was. It was like clutching the hand of a skeleton, hidden beneath the cover she could easily have imagined that no flesh covered the bones and that to exert too much pressure would crush the hand. She held him a second longer then wiped her eyes again, the initial outpouring of emotion now passed. All that was left was the feeling of helplessness, the feeling which always came after the tears. An awful weariness and, at the same time, bewilderment that, after so long watching him wither away before her, she still had tears to offer. Every night as she arrived at the hospital she told herself that she would not cry, that she had become used to his appearance, to the knowledge that she was marking time waiting for him to die. But, every night, when she saw those ravaged wasted features and realised again that he would soon be gone forever, the tears came.

She knew she was the only one who ever visited him. It had been the same when he'd been in his flat in Camden, prior to being struck down with the illness.

Sue had a sister a year older than herself who lived about forty miles outside London, less than an hour's drive but she had visited the hospital only twice, at the beginning. Before the cancer took a real hold. Sue didn't blame her for that. She knew that there were practical reasons which prevented more frequent visits. And, besides, over the last two or three weeks, she had come to feel that the nightly visits were almost a duty. She came out of love but also because she knew she had been the one her father had doted on when she'd been growing up. She was still his 'little girl'. She *had* to be there for him.

She sniffed back more tears and clutched his hand again. He felt so cold, even when she took to rubbing his hand with her own, he still seemed frozen. It was almost as if he were sucking in the chill air and storing it in his waxen skin.

There had been none of this interminable waiting when her mother died. A stroke had taken her nine years earlier. The swiftness of it had been devastating but now, as Sue sat with her father she was beginning to wonder which was preferable. Although she, like everyone else, knew that there was *no* preferable way. Death brought pain and suffering, whichever guise it chose to arrive in. After her mother's death, Sue had realised both the awful finality of it but also how empty it leaves the lives of those who remain. She had seen the devastating effect her mother's death had wrought

40

on her own father. The flat where they had lived for thirty years, where they had raised a family, had become a prison for him. A cell full of memories, each one of which held not joy but pain because he had known that memories were all he had. There was no future to look forward to, only the past to dwell on.

Sue knew that feeling now. There had been good times with her father but, once he was dead, there would be just memories and memories sometimes faded. Even the good ones.

This thought brought a fresh trickle of tears which she hurriedly wiped away with the back of her hand.

She touched his cheek with the back of her hand, stroking gently, feeling the prominent cheekbones, tracing the hollows which had formed in his features. This time no tears came, and she remained like that for the next fifty minutes, stroking his face and hair, clutching his hand.

Sue finally glanced at her watch, saw that visiting hours were over, and heard others leaving, making their way down the corridor outside. Slowly she got to her feet then pulled up the blanket again, tucking it around him to keep out the cold. Then she leant forward and kissed his forehead.

'Goodnight, Dad,' she whispered. 'See you tomorrow.'

She turned and did not look back, pulling the door open and slipping out silently, as if not to disturb him.

Seven

He pulled on his shirt, tucking it into his jeans as he heard the sound of the shower from the bathroom. Through the open door he could make out the blurred silhouette of Nikki behind the frosted glass.

Hacket buttoned his shirt then pulled on his trainers and started tying them. He sat on the edge of the bed, glancing up as he heard the shower being turned off. A moment later, Nikki stepped from inside, her body glistening with water, and Hacket admired her figure for a few seconds before she wrapped herself in a towel. Her hair was hanging in long tendrils, dripping water onto her shoulders as she walked back into the bedroom. She crossed to Hacket and kissed him softly on the lips, some of the water from her wet hair dripping onto his shirt. She slid the bath towel from around herself and began drying her arms and legs. He watched her for a moment longer, still sitting on the edge of the bed.

His eyes were fixed on the gold chain which she wore around her neck and the small opal which dangled from it. Another of his gifts to her. *If you're going to have an affair then do it with style*, he reminded himself. Buy her things. Show her that you care. Hacket almost laughed aloud at his own thoughts. *Care*.

What the hell did he know about caring? If he cared for anyone he'd be at home now, not preparing to leave the flat where his lover lived.

The self-recrimination didn't strike home with quite the vehemence it was meant to. He exhaled deeply, reaching out to touch her leg as she raised it, placed her foot on the bed and started to pat away the water with the towel.

'Do you have to go now?' she asked him.

Hacket nodded.

'Sue will be back from the hospital soon,' he told Nikki. 'I'd better make a move.'

'Won't she wonder where you've been?'

'I told her I had a meeting.'

'Is she trusting or just naive?' There was a hint of sarcasm in Nikki's voice which Hacket didn't care for.

'Do you really want to know? I thought you didn't want to hear anything about my wife,' he said, irritably.

'I don't. You mentioned her first.' She finished drying herself and reached for her housecoat which she pulled on, then she began drying her hair. 'Do you think about her when you're with me?'

Hacket frowned.

'What is this? Twenty questions?' He rolled up the sleeves of his white shirt revealing thick forearms. They regarded each other silently for a moment then Nikki's tone softened slightly.

'Look, John, I didn't mean to sound so bitchy,' she said.

'Well you made a bloody good job of it,' he snapped.

'I want you. I don't want to know about your wife or your family and if that sounds callous then I'm sorry. You chose to have this affair, just like I did. If you've got second thoughts, if you feel guilty, then maybe you shouldn't be here.'

'Do you want me here?' he demanded.

She leant forward and kissed him.

'Of course I do. I want you whenever I can have you. But I'm no fool either. I know this affair won't last. It can't. And I'm not going to ask you to leave your wife for me. I just want to enjoy it while I can. There's nothing wrong with that is there?'

Hacket smiled and shook his head. He got to his feet, enfolded her in his arms and kissed her, his tongue pushing past her lips and teeth, seeking the moistness beyond. She responded fiercely, the towel falling to the floor, her breasts

43

pressing against his chest. When they parted she was breathing heavily, her face flushed. She looked at him questioningly and Hacket was held by the intensity of her stare.

'What do you want, John?' she asked him. 'What do you get out of it? What am I? Just a quick fuck? A bit on the side?' Her Irish accent had become more pronounced, something he always noticed when she was upset or angry.

'You're more than a bit on the side,' he told her. 'Christ, I hate that expression.'

'What would you call me? A lover? Makes it sound more respectable doesn't it? What about a Mistress?'

'A mistress is an unpaid whore,' he said, flatly. 'What do names matter, Nikki? You ask too many questions.' He stroked her gently beneath the chin with his index finger.

She caught the finger, raised it to her mouth and kissed it, flicking the tip with her tongue.

'You spend your money on me,' she said, touching the opal necklace. 'Don't hurt me, John, that's all I ask.'

He frowned.

'I'd never hurt you. Why do you say that?'

'Because I'm scared. Scared of becoming involved, of starting to think too much of you. You might hurt me without even knowing it.'

'It cuts both ways. I can't turn my emotions on and off Nikki. I'm at as much risk as you. And I've got more to lose. If I fall in love with you I've got . . .' He allowed the sentence to trail off.

'Your wife and daughter,' she continued.

'Yeah, wife, daughter and mortgage to support,' he said, smiling humourlessly.

'So we carry on,' she said, pulling him closer. 'Like I said, I want you whenever I can have you. I just have to be careful.' She kissed him.

Hacket looked at his watch then headed for the door.

She wrapped the towel around her again and followed him out to the hall.

'When will I see you?' she asked.

He paused, one hand on the door knob.

'Tomorrow at the school. We can walk past each other and pretend we've never met just like we always do,' he said with a trace of bitterness in his voice.

'You know what I mean. Will you call me?'

He nodded, smiled at her, then he was gone.

Hacket took the lift to the ground floor then walked across to his car. He slid behind the wheel of the Renault and sat there for long moments in the darkness then, he glanced behind him, towards the window of Nikki's flat where the light still burned. He exhaled, banging the steering wheel angrily. He cursed under his breath then, with a vicious twist of his wrist, he started the car, stuck it in gear and drove off.

If the traffic was light he should be home in less than forty minutes.

Eight

The first police car was parked up on the pavement close to the street entrance.

Susan Hacket drove past it, noticing the uniformed men inside it as she drew closer to her house. However, she was almost blinded by the profusion of red and blue lights which seemed to fill the night. On top of ambulances and police cars they turned silently and, with the men around them moving about in relative calm it looked like a scene

45

from a silent film. Sue frowned, suddenly disturbed by the sight of so many official vehicles.

It took her only a second to realise that they were parked outside her own house.

'Oh God,' she whispered under her breath and brought the car to a halt. She clambered out from behind the wheel and hurried across to the pavement where a number of uniformed policemen were standing around in well ordered groups, most, it appeared, guarding the gates of the other houses. Sue could see lights on in the front rooms of the other houses, could see faces or at least silhouettes peering out into the night, anxious to see what was happening.

Uncontrollable panic seized her as she saw two ambulancemen entering her house.

She broke into a run, pushing past a policeman who tried to bar her way.

Two more men moved to intercept her as she reached the front door.

'What's going on,' she blurted, her passage blocked by a burly sergeant. 'Please let me in. I live here. My daughter is inside.'

It was another man, a man in his mid-thirties, dressed in a brown jacket and grey trousers, who finally spoke. He appeared behind the sergeant, eyeing Sue up and down appraisingly as if trying to recognise her.

'Mrs Hacket?' he finally said.

'Yes. What's happening, please tell me?'

The sergeant stepped aside and Sue rushed into the hall.

The smell struck her immediately.

A pungent stench of excrement, mingling with a smell not unlike copper.

The man in the brown jacket now barred her way and, as she tried to push past him, he caught her arms and held her. His face was pale, his chin dark with stubble. Even in such a tense moment Sue noticed how piercing his eyes were. A flawless blue which seemed to bore into her very soul. They were sad eyes.

'Please tell me what's happening,' she pleaded, trying to shake loose of his grip.

'You are Mrs Susan Hacket?' he asked.

'Yes, please tell me what's going on.' She practically screamed it at him. 'Where's my daughter?'

It was then that the ambulancemen emerged from the sitting room and Sue became aware of the smell once more, stronger now.

On the stretcher they carried was a sheet which, she assumed had once been white. It was soaked crimson and Sue realised that the thick red stain was blood. Her eyes bulged madly and she moved towards the stretcher.

The man in the brown jacket tried to hold her back but she wrenched one arm free and tugged at the sheet, pulling it back a few inches.

'No!' she shrieked.

As the ambulancemen hurried to cover the bloodied body of Caroline Fearns, Sue felt the bile clawing its way up from her stomach. In that split second she had time to see that Caroline's face had been slashed in a dozen different places, her lips clumsily hacked off so that only a hole remained where her mouth was. Her hair was matted with blood which had pumped from the wounds which had caused her death.

The man in the brown jacket tried to guide Sue into the kitchen away from the sight of Caroline's body but she seemed to resist his efforts until he practically had to lift her bodily from the hall.

'Where's Lisa?' she gasped, unable to swallow.

'Mrs Hacket, I'm Detective Sergeant Spencer, I . . .'

Sue wasn't interested in the policeman's identity.

'Where's my daughter?' she shrieked, tears beginning to form at her eye corners.

47

'Your daughter's dead,' Spencer said, flatly, trying to inject some compassion into his words but knowing it was impossible.

He held on to Sue for a moment then she shook loose and stumbled back against the table. For a moment he thought she was going to faint but she clawed at one of the chairs and flopped down on it.

'No,' she murmured.

'I'm so sorry, Mrs Hacket,' he said, gripping her hand. She felt so cold.

'Where is she?' Sue demanded, her face drained of colour, her eyes searching Spencer's face imploringly for an answer.

'She's upstairs,' he told her then, quickly added, 'we've been trying to reach your husband . . .'

'I must see her,' she blurted. 'You must let me see her. Please.'

She got to her feet and tried to push past Spencer who, once again acted as a human barrier.

'Let me pass,' she shouted. 'I have to go to her.'

Spencer pushed the kitchen door shut behind him, penning her inside the room with him.

'There's nothing you can do,' he said. 'Your daughter is dead.'

Sue suddenly froze then, with a final despairing moan, she *did* pass out.

Nine

By the time Hacket arrived home there was just one police car parked outside the house. He gave it only a cursory glance as he walked towards the front door, fumbling for his keys, remembering he'd left them in his other jacket. He rang the doorbell and waited, blowing on his hands in an effort to warm them.

The door was opened by Spencer.

Hacket looked aghast at the policeman, standing on the doorstep even when he was ushered inside.

Across the road a curtain moved as the family opposite tried to see what was happening.

'Mr John Hacket?' Spencer asked.

The teacher nodded, finally finding the will to step over the threshold. The front door was closed behind him.

'Who are you?' he said, falteringly.

Spencer introduced himself.

'I don't understand. Why are you here?'

Hacket found himself manoeuvred into the kitchen where another plain-clothes man waited. The second man introduced himself as Detective Inspector Madden. He was older than his subordinate by five years, his hair greying at the temples, a stark contrast to his jet black moustache and eyebrows which knitted over his nose giving him the appearance of a perpetual frown. However, there was a warmth in his voice that seemed almost incongruous to his appearance. He asked Hacket to sit down and the teacher obeyed, finding a mug of tea pushed towards him.

'Will someone tell me what the hell is going on?' he said, irritably. 'Has there been an accident? My wife, is it my wife?'

'Your wife is with your next-door neighbours,' Madden told him, softly. 'She's been sedated, she's sleeping now.'

49

'Sedated? What the fuck are you talking about? What's happening?' His breath was coming in gasps now, his eyes darting back and forth between the two policemen.

'Your house was broken into tonight,' said Madden, his voice low and even. 'We found two bodies when we arrived. One we believe was a girl named Caroline Fearns, the other we think was your daughter. They're dead, Mr Hacket, I'm sorry.'

'Dead.' The word, the very act of speaking it seemed to drain all the anger and irritation from Hacket. His head bowed slightly. He tried to swallow but it felt as if his throat had filled with sand. When he spoke the word again it came out as a hoarse whisper.

'I'm sorry,' Madden repeated.

Hacket clasped his hands together before him on the table, his gaze directed at the cup of steaming tea. He chewed on one knuckle for a moment, the silence enveloping him.

Both policemen looked at each other, then at the teacher, who finally managed to croak another word.

'When?'

We think between seven and eight this evening,' he was told.

Hacket gritted his teeth.

'Oh God,' he murmured, feeling sick, wondering if he was going to be able to control himself. He closed his eyes, squeezing the lids together until white stars danced before him. Between seven and eight. *While he was with Nikki.*

He rubbed his face with both hands, still fighting to control his nausea. His mouth opened soundlessly but no words would come. He wanted to say so much, wanted to know so much but he could not speak. Only one word finally escaped.

'Why?' he asked, pathetically. 'Why were they killed?'

The question had an almost child-like innocence to it.

Madden seemed embarrassed by the question.

'It looks as if someone broke in with the intention of robbing the house,' he said. 'When they found your daughter and the young girl they . . .' He allowed the words to fade away.

'How was it done?' said Hacket, an unnerving steeliness in his tone, despite the fact that he could not bring himself to look directly at either of the policemen.

'I don't think you need to know that yet, Mr Hacket,' Madden said.

'I asked how it was done,' he snarled, glaring at the DI. 'I have a right to know.'

Madden hesitated.

'With a knife,' he said, quietly.

Hacket nodded quickly, his gaze dropping once more.

In the resultant silence, the ticking of the wall clock sounded thunderous.

It was Spencer who finally coughed somewhat theatrically, looked at his superior then spoke.

'Mr Hacket, I'm afraid that your daughter will have to be formally identified.'

Hacket let out a painful breath.

'Oh Christ,' he murmured.

'It has to be done within twenty-four hours if possible,' Spencer continued almost apologetically.

'I'll do it,' Hacket said, his words almost inaudible. 'Please don't tell my wife. I don't want her to see Lisa like that.'

Spencer nodded.

'I'll pick you up tomorrow morning about eleven.'

'Would you like one of my men to stay outside the house tonight, Mr Hacket?' Madden asked. 'It'd be no trouble.'

Hacket shook his head and, once more, the three of them endured what felt like an interminable silence finally broken by Madden.

'We're going to have to ask you to leave the house too, Mr Hacket, until the forensic boys have finished. Is there somewhere you can stay? It'll only be for a day or two.'

Hacket nodded blankly.

'Just let me see it,' he murmured.

Madden looked puzzled.

'Where it happened,' the teacher said. 'I have to see.'.

'Why torture yourself?'

He turned on Madden.

'I *have* to see.'

The policeman nodded, watching as Hacket walked out of the kitchen and through into the sitting room.

The sitting room had been wrecked.

The furniture had been overturned, ornaments smashed, television and video broken, but it was not the wanton destruction which shocked Hacket – it was the spots of blood on the carpet, so delicately covered with pieces of plastic sheeting. He pulled one of the armchairs upright and flopped down lifelessly in it, gazing around the room, his eyes bulging wide, looking but seeing nothing. He sat there as the minutes ticked by, surrounded by silence. Alone with his thoughts. Then, slowly, he hauled himself to his feet and walked towards the hall, pulling the sitting-room door closed behind him.

He hesitated again at the bottom of the stairs, as if the climb were too much for him or he feared what he might find at the top but then, gripping the bannister, he began to ascend.

He faltered again when he reached the landing, looking at the four doors which confronted him.

The door to Lisa's room was now firmly shut, but it was towards that one which he advanced, his hand shaking as it rested on the handle.

Hacket turned it and walked in.

More plastic sheeting.

More blood.

Especially on the bed.

He felt a tear form in the corner of one eye and roll slowly down his cheek. As he turned to step back out of the room his foot brushed against something and he looked down to see that it was one of his daughter's toys. Hacket stopped and picked up the teddy bear, holding it before him for a second before setting it on top of a chest of drawers. Again his gaze was drawn to the bed.

So much blood.

He felt more tears dribbling down his cheeks as he stared at the place where she had been killed.

How much pain had she suffered?

Had she screamed?

He clenched his fists together, each question burning its way into his mind like a branding iron.

How long had it taken her to die?

Does it matter? he asked himself. All that matters is that she's dead.

Perhaps if you'd been here . . .

The thought stuck in his mind like a splinter in flesh. He turned and closed the door behind him, wiping the tears away with one hand, sucking in deep breaths.

★   ★   ★

He undressed swiftly and slid into bed beside her, feeling the warmth of her body against him. She murmured something in her sleep and he gently placed one arm around her neck, wanting to hold her more tightly. Wanting *her* to hold *him*.

She woke up suddenly, as if from a nightmare then, immediately, she saw him and Hacket could see that her face was unbearably pale and drawn. Even in the darkness he could see the moisture on her cheeks.

'John,' she whispered, her voice cracking and now he held her tightly, more tightly than he could ever remember. An embrace more intense than any born of love. She looked so vulnerable. And he felt her tears on his chest as he held her, his own grief swelling and rising once more.

'If only we'd been here,' she whimpered. 'If I hadn't been at the hospital and you hadn't been at that meeting she'd still be alive.'

Hacket nodded.

'We can't blame ourselves, Sue,' he said but the lie bit deep and he finally lost control. Hacket could, and did, blame himself. 'Oh Jesus,' he gasped and they both seemed to melt into one another, united in grief.

September 10, 1940

· The voices outside the room grew louder.

One he recognised, the other he had not heard before.

Garbled, angry words then the door swung open as he rose.

'I tried to stop him, George,' said Lawrenson's wife, Margaret, looking helplessly at her husband who merely smiled and nodded at her.

'It's all right,' he said, eyeing the other newcomer with suspicion. 'You can leave us.'

She hesitated a moment then closed the door behind her. The veneer of civility which Lawrenson had managed to retain dropped sharply.

'Who are you?' he demanded. 'How dare you burst into my home like this?'

The man who faced him was tall but powerfully built, the thick material of his uniform unable to conceal the muscles beneath. He had a long face with pinched features and his cheeks looked hollow, giving him an under-nourished look which was quite incongruous when set against the rest of his physique. He strode across to Lawrenson's desk, a steely look in his eye and, even as the doctor noticed the man's rank, he introduced himself, albeit perfunctorily.

'Major David Catlin,' he announced, stiffly. 'Intelligence.'

Lawrenson didn't offer him a seat but Catlin sat down anyway.

'And to what do I owe this intrusion?' Lawrenson wanted to know.

'I'm here on official business, from the Home Office. It's about project Genesis.'

Lawrenson shot him a wary glance.

'Your work on the project is to stop as of now,' said Catlin, his eyes never leaving the doctor.

'Why?' Lawrenson demanded. 'The work has been going well, I've made great strides. Is someone else being put in charge?'

Catlin shook his head.

'The whole project is being shut down,' he said.

'You can't do that. You mustn't do that, I'm close to finding an answer. There are certain things which need perfecting, I know . . .'

The Major cut him short.

'The project is to cease immediately, Doctor,' he snapped. 'And I can understand why.'

'The Army, the Home Office, everyone was behind me at the beginning,' Lawrenson protested.

'That was until we saw the results,' Catlin said, quietly. 'Lawrenson, listen to me, if the public found out what this work involved there would be massive outcry. No one would stand for it, especially if the press got hold of it. Can you imagine the repercussions if a newspaper managed to get some photos of your work?' He shook his head. 'Work. God, I don't even know if that's the right word for it.'

'The Government encouraged me to perfect Genesis,' Lawrenson insisted, leaning on his desk and glaring at the officer. 'They funded me while I was researching.'

'That funding is also to be withdrawn,' Catlin informed him.

'Then I'll carry on alone.'

'Lawrenson, I didn't come forty miles to *advise* you to stop work on Genesis, I'm ordering you.'

56

The doctor smiled thinly.

'I'm not in your army Major, you can't give me orders,' he said.

The officer got to his feet.

'You are to stop work immediately, do you understand?'

'I've only been working under laboratory conditions for a month, less than that. You can't judge the results as early as this. It's unfair.'

'And what you're doing is inhuman,' snapped Catlin.

The two men regarded one another angrily for a moment then Lawrenson seemed to relax. He moved away from his desk towards the window which overlooked his spacious back garden. In the splendour and peacefulness of the countryside it was difficult to believe there was a war on, that, forty miles away in London, people would soon be preparing themselves for the Luftwaffe's nightly onslaught.

'What is more inhuman, Major,' Lawrenson began. 'The work that I'm involved in, work that could help mankind, or the senseless slaughter of millions in this bloody war we're fighting?'

'Very philosophical, Doctor but I didn't come here to discuss the rights and wrongs of war.'

Lawrenson turned and looked at the soldier.

'I will not stop my work, Major,' he said, flatly.

'Is it that you *cannot* or *will* not see why Genesis must stop now?' the officer asked.

'When I first began work on the project everyone backed me. I was hailed as a saviour.' He laughed bitterly. 'And now, I'm to suffer the same fate as the first saviour, metaphorically speaking.'

'Even you must realise the risks,' Catlin said. 'If details of your work were discovered there's no telling what would happen. That is why you must stop.'

Lawrenson shook his head.

'Tell the Home Office, tell your superiors, tell the Prime Minister himself that I will continue my work.'

Catlin shrugged.

'Then I can't be responsible for what may happen.'

Lawrenson heard the iciness in the soldier's voice.

'Are you threatening me, Catlin?' he snapped.

The Major turned and headed for the door, pursued by Lawrenson.

The officer strode towards the front door, past Margaret Lawrenson, who had emerged from one of the rooms leading off from the large hallway.

Lawrenson caught up with him as he reached the front door.

'Tell them to go to hell,' he roared as the soldier walked briskly across the gravel towards his waiting car. The driver started the engine and the officer slid into the passenger seat.

'You keep away from here, Catlin,' Lawrenson shouted as the car pulled away.

As he watched it disappear down the short driveway towards the road he wondered who the man in the back seat was.

The man who stared at him so intently.

Ten

Christ he needed a cigarette.

Hacket fumbled in his pocket for the fifth time and then glanced across the small waiting room at the sign which proclaimed, in large, red letters, 'NO SMOKING'.

Had it not been for the circumstances he may have found the irony somewhat amusing. Cigarette smoke was hardly likely to damage the residents of this particular building.

He sat outside the morgue, eyes straying to the door through which, minutes earlier, DS Spencer had disappeared. It felt as if he'd been gone for hours. Hacket felt utterly alone despite, or because of, the smallness of the waiting room. It was painted a dull, passionless grey. Even the plastic chairs which lined the wall were grey. The lino was grey. The only thing that wasn't grey was the NO SMOKING sign which he glanced at again, shifting uncomfortably in his seat.

Outside he heard an ambulance siren and wondered, briefly, where it was going. To an accident? A road smash?

A murder?

Hacket tired of sitting and got to his feet, pacing steadily back and forth in the small room. There weren't any magazines to look at to pass the time, no three-year-old copies of *Readers Digest* or *Woman's Own*. For some absurd reason a joke sidled into his mind. A joke about a doctor's waiting room. *Two men talking, one said I was at the doctor's lately, I read one of the newspapers there. Terrible about the Titanic isn't it?*

Terrible.

Hacket fumbled for his cigarettes once more and, this time he ignored the sign and lit up, sucking deeply on the Dunhill. He blew out a stream of grey smoke which perfectly matched the colour of the walls.

He found, when he took the cigarette from his mouth, that his hand was shaking. Neither he nor Sue had slept much the previous night. She was at the house now, still sedated. A neighbour was sitting with her. Hacket wouldn't have wanted her here with him, he wasn't even sure how *he* was going to stand up to seeing his daughter laid out on a slab. For fleeting seconds he wondered if the Fearns family had identified Caroline yet. Had they felt like he felt now? Had they stood in this same waiting room wondering, fearing what they were going to see?

The thought faded, merging into thousands of others which seemed to be whirling around in his head. And yet despite all the apparent activity inside his mind there was a peculiar emptiness. A numbness. He sat down again and almost reached out to touch the chair beside him to reassure himself it was actually there. He was a million miles away, his mind sifting through details with a swiftness that created a vacuum. He took another drag on the cigarette then stubbed it out beneath his foot.

He felt sick and rubbed a hand across his forehead, feeling perspiration. He'd rung the school earlier that morning and said that he wouldn't be in for a few days. No details. A family bereavement he'd said, wanting to keep it simple. He didn't want too many questions asked. They'd find out soon enough when the story appeared in the papers. Then would come the questions, the enquiries, the consoling handshakes. He sighed and looked at the door again.

It opened and Simpson emerged, raising his eyebrows in a gesture designed to beckon Hacket forward.

He'd been waiting for this moment, wanting to get it

over with, but now he would have given anything to sit for a while longer in that grey room in one of those grey chairs. He walked purposefully towards the door and entered.

The morgue was smaller than he'd imagined. There were no rows of lockers, no filing cabinets for sightless eyes. No white-coated assistants wandering back and forth with hearts and lungs ready to weigh.

And there was only one slab.

On it was a small shape, covered by a white sheet.

As he drew nearer to it, Hacket visibly faltered, he felt the colour drain from his face and his throat seemed to constrict.

Simpson moved towards him but he shook his head gently and advanced to within a couple of feet of the slab and its shrouded occupant.'

The coroner, a short man with heavy jowls and a balding head attempted a smile of sympathy but it looked more like a sneer. He looked at Spencer who nodded.

He pulled back the sheet.

'Is that your daughter, Mr Hacket?' the DS asked, softly.

Hacket let out a breath which sounded as if his lungs had suddenly deflated. He raised one hand to his mouth, his eyes rivetted to the small form on the slab.

'Mr Hacket.'

She was as white as milk, at least the parts of her which he could see through the patchwork of cuts and bruises. Her face and neck were tinged yellow by bruises and, across her throat was a deep gash which curved upwards at either side like some kind of blood-choked rictus.

'Why are her eyes still open?' he croaked.

'Rigor mortis,' the coroner said, quietly. 'The involuntary muscles sometimes stiffen first.' His voice trailed away into a whisper.

'Is it your daughter, Mr Hacket?' Simpson persisted.

'Yes.'

The detective nodded and the coroner prepared to pull the sheet back over Lisa but Hacket stopped him.

'No,' he said. 'I want to see her.'

The coroner hesitated then, slowly, he pulled the sheet right back, allowing Hacket to see the full extent of his daughter's injuries.

Her chest and stomach were also covered in dark blotches and deep gashes. The area between her legs was purple and he noticed that the inside of her thighs were almost black with bruising. The contusions continued right down her legs to her feet. Hacket looked on with lifeless eyes, there was no emotion there. It was as if the shock of seeing her had sucked every last ounce of feeling from him. He looked repeatedly up and down her tiny corpse.

'How was it done?' he asked, his eyes still on his daughter. 'Have you done the post-mortem?'

The coroner seemed reluctant to answer and looked at Simpson who merely shrugged.

'I asked you a question,' Hacket said, flatly. 'How was she killed?'

'No post-mortem has been done yet but, from external examination you can see . . . well, I decided that death was caused by massive haemorrhage, most likely from the wound on her throat.'

'What about the bruising,' he pointed to the purplish area between her legs. 'There.'

The coroner didn't answer.

Hacket looked at him, then at Spencer.

'You have no right to keep information from me,' he said. 'She was my daughter.'

'We thought that it would save you any more suffering, Mr Hacket . . .' Spencer said but the teacher interrupted him.

'You think it can get any worse?' he snapped, bitterly. 'Tell me.'

'There was evidence of sexual abuse,' said Spencer.

'Was she raped?' Hacket wanted to know.

'Yes,' the detective told him. 'There was evidence of penetration.'

'Before *and* after her death,' added the coroner by way of thoroughness.

Hacket gritted his teeth.

'Would she have felt much pain?' he wanted to know.

Simpson sighed wearily.

'Mr Hacket, why torture yourself like this?'

'I have to know,' he hissed. 'Would she have felt much pain?'

'It's difficult to say,' the coroner told him. 'During the rape, yes, probably, she may have been unconscious by that time though, she'd already lost a lot of blood before it happened. The cut across the throat would have sent her into traumatic shock. The rest would have been over quickly.'

Hacket nodded and finally turned away from the tiny body.

The coroner replaced the sheet and watched as Hacket strode out of the room, followed by Simpson.

The body was hidden from view once more.

Eleven

The drive from the hospital back to the house seemed to take hours, though Hacket assumed that it was actually less than thirty minutes.

Spencer drove at a steady speed and Hacket gazed aimlessly out of the Granada's side window hearing only the odd phrase which the detective spoke.

'. . . Positive identification of the killers . . .'

Hacket noticed a woman and her two children trying to cross the road up ahead, waiting for a break in the traffic.

'. . . Criminal records as far as we know . . .'

One of the children was only about four. A little girl and she held her mother's hand as they waited for the cars to pass.

'. . . No doubt that two men were involved . . .'

Hacket seemed to see nothing but children during the drive back. It was as if the world had suddenly doubled its population of four-year-olds.

With one notable exception.

'. . . Let you know as soon as we have any information . . .'

'What kind of man rapes a four year old?'

The question took Spencer by surprise and Hacket repeated it.

'You'd be surprised,' he said. 'Men you'd never expect. Fathers like yourself . . .' The DS realised his mistake and let the sentence trail off. 'I'm sorry,' he added.

'What are the chances of catching him?'

'Well, we got good dabs from around the house, blood type we know, approximate height, weight and age. We'll get him.'

Hacket laughed humourlessly.

'And if you do? What then? A ten-year sentence? Out in five if he's a good boy' he said, bitterly.

Spencer shook his head.

'It's not like that, Mr Hacket. He'll go down and he'll stay down.'

'Until the next time,' Hacket said, still looking out of the side window.

Hacket said a brief goodbye to the detective when they reached the house in Clapham and Spencer promised to be in touch as soon as he had any information, then he thanked the teacher for his co-operation, offered his sympathies once more and drove off. Hacket stood on the pavement for a moment then turned and headed towards the front door, letting himself in rather than ring the bell and risk disturbing Sue.

He found her sitting in the kitchen with the next-door neighbour, Helen Bentine. The two women, Sue a little younger, were sitting over a cup of tea talking, and Hacket thought how much brighter his wife looked. Granted she still had dark rings beneath her eyes and she looked as if she hadn't slept for a fortnight, but she actually managed a smile as he entered, rising to make him a cup of tea from the recently-boiled kettle.

Helen beat her to it, handed the teacher his drink then said she'd better go. They both thanked her, listening as the front door closed behind her.

'The doctor said you should rest, Sue,' he said, sipping his tea, loosening his tie with his free hand.

'I'll rest later,' she told him. 'I don't want to keep taking those pills he gave me, I'll get addicted.'

He sat down beside her, touching her cheek with his fingertips.

'You look so tired,' he said, looking at her.

She smiled weakly at him then took a sip of her tea.

Hacket knew she was about to say something but, when it came, he was still unprepared.

'What did she look like?' Sue wanted to know.

He shrugged, unable to think of a suitable answer.

Well, she was cut up badly, she'd been raped and the bastard had knocked her about so much there was hardly an inch of skin left unmarked, but apart from that she looked fine.

'John, tell me.'

65

'She looked peaceful,' he lied, attempting a smile.

'We'll have to tell the family, your parents, my family. They'll have to know, John.'

'Not just yet,' he said, softly, clasping her hand.

'Why did they pick on us?' she asked, as if expecting him to furnish her with an answer. 'Why kill Lisa?'

'Sue, I don't know. Would knowing the answer make it any more bearable? She's still dead, knowing why she was killed isn't going to bring her back.'

'But it isn't fair.' There were tears in her eyes now. 'My Dad's dying – that's hard enough to take – and now this.' She laughed bitterly and the sound caused the hair to rise on the back of Hacket's neck. 'Perhaps God is testing our faith.' She sniffed, wiped a tear from her cheek. 'Well if he is he's going to be unlucky.' Hacket gripped her hand more tightly, watching as the tears began to course more freely down her cheeks. 'God is a sadist.' She looked at Hacket, her eyes blazing. 'And I hate him for what he's done.'

Hacket nodded, got to his feet and put his arms around her. They stayed locked together for some time, Sue sobbing quietly.

'I just wish that I could have said goodbye to her,' she whispered. 'To have held her just one last time.' She looked up into his face and saw the tears in *his* eyes. 'Oh, John, what are we going to do?'

He had no answer.

At first he thought he was dreaming.

The ringing sounded as if it were inside his head, but, as he opened his eyes, Hacket realised that it wasn't make-believe.

The phone continued to ring.

He rubbed his eyes and eased himself from beneath Sue's head. She had taken two of her tablets and been asleep for the last hour or so. He had dozed off as well, the strain of the last twenty-four hours finally catching up with him.

Now he stumbled towards the hall and the phone, closing the sitting room door behind him. He picked up the receiver, blinking hard in an effort to clear his vision.

'Hello,' he croaked, clearing his throat.

'Hello, John, it's me, Nikki. Look, I'm sorry to ring your home.' Her voice was low and conspiratorial.

'What do you want?' he said, wearily.

'I needed to speak to you,' she said. 'Someone at school said you weren't going to be in for a few days.'

'That's right, why is there a problem? Are you keeping a check on my movements or something?' The acidity of his tone was unmistakeable.

'What's wrong?' she asked. 'Are you all right?'

'Look, is this important? Because if it's not will you get off the line now.'

'I said I was sorry for phoning you at home,' Nikki said, both surprised and irritated by his aggressiveness. 'Is your wife there, is that why you can't talk?'

'Yes she is but that's not the reason. You shouldn't have called me.'

'We were supposed to meet tonight, I was waiting . . .'

He cut her short.

'Don't call me here again, all right?'

'I cooked us a meal.'

'Eat it yourself,' he rasped and slammed the phone down. He stood in the hallway, his hand still on the receiver, the residue of that soft Irish accent of hers still lingering in his ears.

He couldn't tell her the truth. How could he?

From behind him in the sitting-room he heard Sue call his name and he turned to rejoin her.

As he did he cast one last glance at the telephone, as if expecting it to ring again.

Twelve

The banks of black cloud which brought the rain also seemed to hasten the onset of night.

Like ink spreading over blotting paper the tenebrous gloom slowly seeped across the heavens above Hinkston. Icy rain came down in sheets, driven by a wind which cut into exposed skin as surely as a razor blade.

Bob Tucker pulled the scarf tighter around his chin in an attempt to protect himself from the elements and looked down into the grave.

The coffin was already hidden beneath a thin layer of muddy earth but the rain was rapidly washing it away, exposing the polished wood beneath. Bob shoveled a few more clods into the hole, paused to light a cigarette, then continued in earnest. The rain quickly extinguished the cigarette and he stuffed the sodden remains into the pocket of his overcoat, cursing the weather, his luck and anything else which came to mind as he toiled over the open grave. He knew he had to work fast. The rain falling on the excavated earth would rapidly transform it to mud. The soil in Hinkston was like clay at the best of times, but when it rained some parts of the town resembled Flanders in 1918.

Bob paused for a moment, straightening up, groaning as he felt the bones in his knees click. His back was beginning to ache as well. Occupational hazard, he told himself. He'd been grave-digger at Hinkston cemetery for the last twelve years. He liked the job too. Bob had never been much of a mixer, he enjoyed his own company and the job certainly gave him plenty of time alone. He had never married. Never wanted to. Approaching his fortieth birthday he was happy alone. He had a couple of friends who lived in the town, men he could share a drink with if he felt the need for company, but most of his time was spent in the small bungalow which overlooked the cemetery. It came with the job. He'd converted one of the sheds in the back garden into a workshop and he did his most precious work there. Carving shapes from lumps of wood he picked up in the cemetery. The thick growths of trees which populated the graveyard offered him plenty of raw material. The walking sticks he made from fallen branches he'd often sold at Hinkston's twice-weekly market. Some had fetched upwards of fifty pounds each, but it wasn't the monetary rewards which interested Bob, it was the craft itself.

He stood at the graveside a moment longer, peering through the rain towards the lights of the town. The street lights looked like jewels twinkling on a sheet of black velvet.

The cemetery was about half a mile from the town centre, on a steep hill designed to help drainage, but some of the older graves had begun to break up and sink and Bob feared that there might be some subsidence. However, the damage to the graves was not all attributable to natural causes.

There had been a spate of vandalism during the last three weeks. Gravestones had been smashed, flowers scattered from new plots, paint sprayed on headstones and, in the worst case, a grave had been tampered with. About two feet of earth had been excavated but, fortunately, the vandals had not dug down as far as the coffin.

Bob wondered what kind of people found pleasure from disturbing the dead and where they rested. The consensus of opinion in Hinkston itself seemed to point to youngsters. Bob had caught a young couple about a fortnight ago, laid out naked on top of one of the older graves but vandalism had been the last thing on their minds. He smiled at the recollection. Of how the boy had tried to run with his trousers round his ankles while the girl screamed and scuttled along beside him waving her bra like some kind of white surrender flag. Bob hadn't reported that particular incident to the police but the vandalism itself worried him. Many nights he'd left his bungalow and walked the tree lined paths through the cemetery in an effort to catch the vandals but his vigils so far had proved fruitless.

He continued to shovel earth into the grave, anxious to finish his task and return to the warmth of his home, to get out of his wet clothes.

The flowers from the funeral lay in a heap to one side of the hole, he would replace those when he'd finished. The rain tapped out a steady rhythm on the cellophane which covered the blooms, running off the clear covering like tears.

Bob shovelled more earth, trying to ignore the growing ache in his back.

The noise came from behind him.

At first he wasn't sure whether or not it was merely the rain pattering through the thick branches which hung overhead but, when it came again he was sure that the sound was coming from beyond the cluster of bushes which gathered around the grave like camouflaged mourners.

Bob stopped immediately and looked round, shielding his eyes from the rain and attempting to see through the darkness to the source of the noise.

He stood and waited but heard nothing.

After a moment or two he continued with his task.

Another foot or so and he would be finished, he thought, thankfully.

The noise came from behind him again, this time slightly to the left.

Bob dropped the spade and spun round, almost slipping on the wet earth.

It could be an animal of some kind he reasoned, taking a step towards the bushes. He'd found squirrels, even a badger during some of his nocturnal strolls through the cemetery. But, it was too early to be a badger. Despite the darkness his watch told him that it was only just 7.30 p.m.

Vandals perhaps? No, surely they'd wait until late, until they were sure no one was around.

He parted the bushes and eased through the first clump, surprised at how high they grew.

No one hiding behind them.

The rain continued to pelt down.

He felt something touch his shoulder.

Bob almost shouted aloud, his hand falling instinctively to the Swiss Army knife in his coat pocket.

The branch which had slapped against him had been blown by the wind.

The lower, leafless, branches were flailing about like animated flagellums and Bob shielded his face from the stinging twigs which whacked into him as he turned back towards the grave.

The figure which stood before him was holding the spade he had dropped.

In the driving rain Bob could not make out the features, he merely strode towards the figure, calling that it was private property and, besides that, to put his spade down.

The figure swung the spade in a wide arc which caught Bob in the side of the face. The powerful impact splintered bone and his left cheekbone seemed to fold in upon itself. The strident crack of bone was clearly audible over his strangled cry of pain. The figure advanced and stood over him for a moment, watching as blood from his pulverised face poured down his coat. Then the figure brought the spade down a second time, this time on his legs.

Both shin bones were broken by the blow and Bob screamed in agony, feeling one of the shattered tibias tear through the flesh of his leg.

He fell back into the mud, the merciful oblivion of

71

unconsciousness enfolding him, but seconds before he slipped away he felt his head being lifted almost tenderly.

Then he saw the long, thin, double-edged knife which, seconds later, was pushed slowly into his right eye.

The figure pushed on the blade until it felt the point scrape bone, then, as easily as a man lifts a child, the figure lifted Bob Tucker's body.

All that remained to show that a struggle had even taken place was the blood on the ground and, as the rain continued to fall, even that was soon washed away.

Thirteen

She looked at her watch and lit up a cigarette, puffing slowly on it, gazing at the phone as if it were a venomous snake sure to bite her the moment she extended her hand.

Nikki Reeves sat for five minutes until she finally picked up the receiver and jabbed out the digits. She waited, taking a last drag of her cigarette and stubbing it out in the ashtray. The tones sounded in her ear. She waited.

'Come on,' she whispered, ready to replace the receiver if necessary.

There was a click and she heard a familiar voice.

'Hello.'

She smiled.

'Hello, John, it's me, can you speak?' she said.

'If you mean is my wife here the answer is no,' Hacket said, irritably. 'I told you not to call me at home again, Nikki.'

'I had to speak to you. I have to know what's going on. You haven't been in to the school, I was worried.'

'I'm touched,' he muttered, sarcastically.

'John, what's wrong?' she wanted to know. 'I'm sorry for calling your home, I can understand you being angry about that.'

'When I told you not to call again I meant it. Not just here but anywhere.'

Nikki sat up, her brow creasing into a frown. She gripped the receiver more tightly.

'What are you saying? You don't want to see me again?'

There was silence at the other end then finally Hacket spoke again, his tone softer this time.

'You said you realised the affair couldn't go on indefinitely. I think it's time we stopped seeing one another.'

'Why the sudden change of heart?' she wanted to know.

'Things have happened that I can't discuss, that I don't want to discuss. It's over between us, Nikki. There wasn't much there to begin with, but I've been thinking and it's best ended now.'

'A sudden attack of conscience?' she snapped. 'It isn't quite as easy as that, John. We both knew what we were getting into. Why can't you talk to me, tell me what's bothering you?'

'For Christ's sake, Nikki, you're not my wife, you're just . . .' The sentence faded as a hiss of static broke up the line.

'Just a quick fuck,' she snapped. 'You don't have the right to just drop me like that. I'm not a tart you picked up in a bar. You didn't pay me. Unless that's what the perfume and the jewellery were.' She touched the onyx almost unconsciously.

'What do you want me to do, stick a cheque in the post?' Hacket said, angrily.

'You bastard.'

73

'Look Nikki, I made a mistake, right? End of story. My wife needs me now.'

'And what if *I* need you?' she said, challengingly.

'It's over,' he told her again.

'And what if I hadn't rung you. What were you going to do, hope that I'd forget what had happened in the last three months? Avoid me at work? You could have had the courage to tell me to my face, John.'

'Look, I can't talk any longer, Sue will be back any minute. It's finished.'

She was about to say something else when he hung up.

She gripped the receiver for a moment longer then slammed it down on the cradle, her breath coming in short gasps. Finished was it? Nikki lit up another cigarette and got to her feet, walking through to the sitting room where she poured herself a brandy, her hands shaking with anger.

Finished.

She fought back her tears of rage.

Finished.

Not yet, she thought.

September 23, 1940

George Lawrenson looked at the file marked 'Genesis' and nodded. The notes, the thoughts and theories contained within that manilla file were the sum of his work over the last ten or fifteen years. Only in the last few months had his ideas actually seen fruition.

And then, once those ideas had become facts, those who sought to control him had ordered him to stop the work which had been a greater part of his life. They had no right to stop him.

They had no understanding.

'Do you think they've changed their minds about the project?' Margaret Lawrenson asked, watching as her husband slipped the file into his small suitcase.

'I won't know until I get there,' he said.

The call from London had come late the previous evening. He had been told to come to the capital for 're-evaluation' (he hated their jargon) of his work. 'First they order me to stop and now they ask for more results.' He shrugged.

Margaret smiled and crossed to him, kissing him lightly on the cheek.

'You take care of yourself while I'm away,' he said, softly. 'Remember, there are two of you now.' He smiled and patted her stomach.

'What if they order you to stop, George?' she asked.

'Do you want me to stop?' he countered.

'I know you believe in what you're doing. *I* believe in what you're doing. Be careful, that's all I ask.'

He locked the suitcase.

'Where are the copies of my notes?' he asked finally.

'Hidden,' she assured him. 'If the originals are destroyed I've got the copies, don't worry.'

'They won't destroy them, they're not that stupid. Genesis is far too important for that and they realise it.' He picked up his suitcase and headed for the stairs. She descended with him, walking to the front door and out onto the drive. He slid the case onto the passenger seat of the car then walked around to the driver's side.

'Call me when you get to London,' she said, watching as he clambered behind the wheel and started the engine. Then she retreated to the front door and watched as he pulled away.

Lawrenson guided the car slowly down the driveway, turning to wave as he reached the end.

It was then that the car exploded.

The entire vehicle disappeared beneath a searing ball of yellow and white flame, pieces of the riven chassis flying in all directions. The concussion wave was so powerful that Margaret Lawrenson, standing more than fifty yards away, was thrown to the ground, her ears filled by the deafening roar as the car blew up.

A thick, noxious mushroom of smoke rose from the wreckage, billowing up towards the sky like a man-made storm cloud. Flames engulfed what little remained of the car, burning petrol spreading in a blazing pool around the debris. Cinders floated through the air like filthy snow and, as Margaret finally pulled herself upright and ran towards the flaming shell of the car she could smell burning rubber and a sickly, sweeter stench.

The odour of burning flesh.

The heat of the flames kept her back, away from the

76

twisted remains of the car which were now glowing white from the incredible heat. But inside she could see what was left of her husband, burned so badly he resembled a spent match, still clutching what was left of the steering wheel with hands that had turned to charcoal.

She dropped to her knees in the driveway, sobbing.

Other eyes had seen the blast.

More professional eyes.

The two figures who sat in the jeep across the road, hidden by trees, watched appreciatively as the car first exploded then blazed.

The first of them smiled, the second reached for the field telephone.

'Give me the Prime Minister's personal aide,' he said, in clipped tones. There was a moment's silence then he continued. 'Tell Mr Churchill that, as of 10.46 a.m. today, Project Genesis ceased.'

Major David Catlin replaced the phone and gazed once more at the flames.

Fourteen

Hacket felt as if he'd been hit with an iron bar. His senses were dulled, his head aching. He moved as if in a trance, stopping to hold on to furniture every now and then as if afraid he was going to fall.

On the sofa, Sue sat quietly, her face pale, her eyes red and puffy from so many tears. She looked exhausted, as if the effort of so much sobbing had sucked every last ounce of strength from her.

She still wore the black skirt and jacket which she'd worn to Lisa's funeral.

Hacket had tried to coax her into changing after the last of the mourners had gone but she had merely shaken her head and remained on the sofa, her eyes vacant. He had wondered a couple of times if she had slipped into shock but, each time he'd touched her she'd managed a smile, even kissed his hand as he'd brushed her cheek.

Now he stood in the kitchen waiting for the kettle to boil, hands dug in the pockets of his trousers.

The day had passed so slowly. It seemed that each minute had somehow stretched into hours, each hour into an eternity. The pain of their loss had become almost physical. Hacket rubbed a hand across his forehead and watched the steam rise from the kettle, just as he had watched it first thing that morning when he'd risen, dreading what was to come.

The arrival of the flowers.

Then the guests. (They had limited those present to his own parents and Sue's sister and her husband.)

And finally the hearse.

Hacket swallowed hard, fighting back tears at the recollection.

The huge vehicle had completely dwarfed the tiny coffin. Hacket had thought how easily he could have carried the box himself, under one arm.

He made the coffee, reaching into the cupboard for an aspirin in an effort to relieve the pain which still gnawed at the base of his skull. He took a sip of coffee, scarcely noticing when the hot liquid burnt his tongue.

And at the cemetery they had watched as the box was lowered into the grave, again so pitifully small. He had feared that Sue would collapse. She had spent the entire service crushed against him, weeping uncontrollably, but he had tried to fight the tears, to be strong for both of them. It had been a fight he had no hope of winning. As the small box had come to rest on the floor of the grave he had surrendered to the pain inside him and broken down. And they had supported each other, oblivious to those around them, to the empty words the vicar spoke. Words like 'resurrection'.

Hacket now shook his head slowly and sighed.

The service had seemed to take an age and finally, when it was over, both he and Sue had been led like lost children back to the waiting car and driven back to the house. The mourners, feeling as though they were intruding, had stayed for less than an hour then left the Hackets alone with their grief.

Sue had slept for a couple of hours that afternoon but Hacket could find no such peace. He had paced the sitting room, smoking and drinking, wanting to get drunk, to drink himself into oblivion but knowing that he had to be there when Sue woke up. She needed him more now than ever before.

Even more than Nikki needed him.

He pushed the thought to one side angrily, picked up the mugs of coffee and headed back towards the sitting room.

Sue had her eyes closed and Hacket hesitated, thinking she was asleep but, as he sat down opposite her she opened her eyes and looked at him.

'I didn't mean to wake you,' he said, softly, smiling.

'I wasn't asleep. Just thinking.'

'About what?' he asked, handing her the coffee.

'About that stupid phrase people always use when someone's died. "Life must go on." Why must it?' Her face darkened.

'Sue, come on, don't talk like that. We have to go on, for Lisa's sake.'

'Why, John? She's dead. Our child is gone. We'll never see her again, never be able to hold her, kiss her.' Her eyes were moist but no tears came. Hacket wondered if tear ducts could drain dry as he watched Sue wipe her eyes. She shook her head, wearily.

So much pain.

'I should go and see my father tomorrow,' she said, quietly.

'No. Not yet. You're not ready.'

'And what if he dies too? What if he dies when I should have been with him?'

Hacket got up, crossed the room then sat down beside her, pulling her closer.

'Your sister could have stayed for a few days, she could have visited him.'

'She had to get back to Hinkston, her husband has to work and they have a child, John. It wouldn't be fair to leave him alone.'

'You do too much, Sue. If ever anything's needed to be done, you're the one who's done it. Never Julie. You take too much responsibility on yourself.'

'That's the way I am.'

'Well maybe it's time you started putting yourself first in order of priorities instead of coming second to everyone else's needs.' He gently held her chin, turned her head and kissed her on the lips. She gripped his hand and squeezed.

'I love you,' she whispered.

'Then prove it. Come to bed, get a good night's sleep.'

'In a while,' she said. 'You go up, I won't be long.' She glanced down at the coffee table and noticed a letter addressed to her lying beside a card offering 'Sincerest Sympathies'. 'What's this?' she asked him, reaching for the letter.

'It came this morning. I figured you'd read it when you felt like it.'

'I don't recognise the writing,' she said, turning the envelope over in her hands.

'Can't it wait until the morning?'

'Just give me a minute, John. Please,' she asked softly and kissed him.

Hacket rose and headed for the hall.

'One minute,' he reminded her then she heard his footfalls on the stairs as he climbed.

Sue put down her coffee, let loose a weary breath then opened the letter. It was just one piece of paper, no address at the top and, as she glanced at the bottom, she noticed it wasn't signed either. She checked the envelope again, ensuring that it hadn't been delivered to the wrong house. Her name was there, the address was correct.

'Dear Mrs Hacket,' she read aloud, her eyes skimming over the neat lettering. 'I know what you will think of me for writing to you but I had a feeling you would want to know what has been going on between myself and your

81

husband, John . . .' The words faded into silence as she read the remainder of the note, her mouth open slightly.

She read it again, more slowly this time. Then, she folded it, gripped it in her hand and got to her feet.

She paused at the bottom of the stairs, looking up towards the landing, then at the crumpled letter.

Sue began to ascend.

Fifteen

'I should have stayed with her for a couple of days,' said Julie Clayton, gazing out of the side window of the Sierra. 'I should have gone to see Dad too.'

'They're best left on their own, there's nothing you could do,' Mike Clayton said, glancing agitatedly at the car ahead of him. He indicated to overtake, saw that the car ahead was speeding up and dropped back again. 'Come on you bastard,' he hissed. 'Either put your foot down or get out the bloody way.'

He looked down at the dashboard clock.

10.42 p.m.

'We're not going to make it back in time at this rate,' he said, irritably. 'I said you should have come alone.'

'Sue *is* my sister, Mike,' Julie snapped. 'She needed me there.'

'Well your own son needs you now,' he reminded her, attempting to overtake the car in front once again. He stepped on the accelerator hard, easing the Sierra out into the centre of the road, ignoring the lights which he saw coming towards him.

'Mike, for God's sake,' Julie gasped, seeing the oncoming vehicle but her husband seemed oblivious to the approaching car. He pressed down harder, the needle on the speedometer touching eighty as he sped past the van ahead of him.

The car coming the other way swerved to miss the Sierra, the driver slamming on his brakes, simultaneously hitting the hooter. The car skidded and looked like crashing but the driver wrestled it back onto the road and drove on.

Mike Clayton, now clear of the van which had been blocking him put his foot down.

They passed a sign which read 'HINKSTON 25 MILES'.

Clayton shook his head, trying to coax more speed from the car.

Julie also glanced at the clock and saw that it was fast approaching 10.47. She guessed it would take another twenty minutes before they reached home, provided there were no more delays.

She swallowed hard and looked across at her husband who was gripping the wheel so tightly his knuckles were white.

She too was beginning to wonder if they would reach Hinkston in time.

She prayed that they did.

Sixteen

'Who is she, John?'

Sue stood in the bedroom doorway, the letter held before her like an accusation.

Hacket looked across from the bed and frowned, not quite sure what was happening. Sue crossed to the bed, standing beside it, looking down at him, a combination of anger and hurt in her eyes.

More pain.

The realisation slowly began to creep over him.

'I had a feeling you would want to know what has been going on between myself and your husband,' she read aloud.

Hacket exhaled deeply, wanting to say something but knowing that whatever words he found they would be inadequate.

'I do not care what you think of me,' Sue continued, reading from the crumpled letter. 'But I felt you had a right to know what has been happening between us.'

'Sue . . .'

She interrupted him.

'I do not like being used,' she read, her eyes still rivetted to the paper. Then, finally, she looked at him. 'Who is she?'

He knew that it was pointless to lie.

At least clear one part of your conscience, eh?

'Her name's Nikki Reeves,' he said, quietly. 'She works at the school.'

It was said. There was no turning back now.

'You had an affair with her?' Sue said and it was a statement rather than a question. 'How long did it last?'

'Three months.'

He watched as she sat down on the edge of the bed, the

84

letter still held in her hand. She had her back to him as if to look at him caused her disgust. He wouldn't have blamed her if disgust was the emotion she was feeling but he guessed it was more painful than that.

'Is it over now?' she wanted to know.

'Would you believe me if I told you?'

'Is it over?'

'Yes. I finished it a couple of days ago.'

She looked at him finally, a bitter smile on her lips.

'All those meetings at school you went to, you were really with *her*.' Her eyes narrowed suddenly. 'You never brought her here did you?'

'No, never.'

'And where did your little *liaisons* take place, John?' she asked with something bordering on contempt. 'In the back of the car? In an empty classroom or office?'

'Sue, for Christ's sake it wasn't as sordid as that. She has a flat . . .'

'Oh, her own place, how convenient. Somewhere to wash away the dirt afterwards.' The last sentence was barbed and it cut deep. 'How old is she?'

'Twenty-two. Is that really important?'

'I thought teachers were meant to have flings with pubescent pupils, nymphomaniac sixth-formers. Still, you always liked to do things differently didn't you, John. Why someone so young? Re-affirming your attractiveness now you're reaching the dreaded thirtieth birthday?'

'Don't be ridiculous.'

'Me? You're the one who had a bloody affair with a secretary at your school, John. I would have thought *that* qualified as ridiculous, wouldn't you?' She glared at him, her eyes moist.

'Don't patronise me, Sue,' he said, irritably. 'I know it was wrong and I'm sorry. If it's any consolation I feel pretty bloody lousy about it as well.'

85

'It *isn't* any consolation,' she snapped.

They sat in uncomfortable silence until Sue spoke again.

'Why, John? At least tell me that,' she said, quietly.

He shrugged.

'I don't know. I really don't know. Whatever explanation I give you is going to sound inadequate, pointless.' He sucked in a deep breath. 'I can't explain it.'

'Can't or won't?' she demanded.

'I can't,' he replied with equal anger, trying not to raise his voice but frustrated in the knowledge that whatever she said she was right. What he had done was indefensible. 'Look, I'm not proud of what I did. It just happened.'

'Affairs don't just *happen*,' she chided. 'What was the attraction anyway? Is she pretty? Got a nice figure? Is she good in bed? Not that you'd have known that until you got her back to her flat though, would you? Well come on, tell me, I'm curious. Did this pretty young thing just fall into your arms?'

He shook his head but didn't answer.

'Tell me,' she snarled, vehemently. 'Is she pretty?'

'Yes,' he confessed.

'*And* good in bed?'

'Sue, for God's sake . . .'

'Is she good? Come on, I'm curious, I told you. Is she good in bed?'

He smiled humourlessly.

'What do you want me to do, rate her one to ten?'

'Just tell me if she was good,' Sue snarled.

'Yes,' he said, almost inaudibly. 'It was only ever a physical thing. I didn't feel anything for her. I never stopped loving *you*, Sue.'

'Am I supposed to be grateful, John? You'll be telling me next that I should understand why you did it. Well, perhaps I ought to try and understand. Tell me why, make me understand.'

'Since your father's been ill . . .'

'Don't blame it on my father, you bastard.'

'Let me finish,' he snapped, waiting until she was looking at him once again. 'Since he's been ill you've been obsessed with him, with what he's got. You've been distant. Perhaps I felt neglected, I know it sounds like a fucking lame excuse but it's all I can think of.'

'Oh I'm sorry, John,' she said, sarcastically. 'I should have realised you weren't getting enough attention, it's practically my fault you had this affair. It sounds as if I forced you into it.'

'That's not what I'm saying and you know it.'

'You're saying that you couldn't have what you wanted from me so you picked up some little tart and fucked her,' Sue spat the words.

'She's not a tart.'

'Why are you defending her, John? I thought you said it was only a physical thing. If you wanted sex that badly you might as well have found a whore, paid for it. I do apologise for having other things on my mind, if only you'd let me know how you were suffering perhaps I could have fitted you in a couple of nights a week.'

'Now you *are* being ridiculous.'

'What the hell do you expect?' she yelled at him. 'Rational conversation? On the day my daughter is buried I find out my husband's been having an affair.' He saw her expression darken, her eyes narrow. Hacket could almost see the thoughts forming inside her mind. That final piece of deduction which would damn him forever. 'You were with her the night Lisa was killed weren't you?'

He didn't answer.

'Weren't you?' she hissed.

He nodded.

'I can't get that out of my mind,' Hacket whispered. 'The thought that if I'd been here it probably wouldn't have happened. You don't have any idea what that's doing to me, Sue.'

'I don't care what it's doing to you,' she said, coldly. 'You killed our daughter.'

'Don't say that,' he snapped.

'You didn't hold the knife but you're as responsible for her death as the man who killed her. Our daughter died for the sake of your bloody affair.'

She lashed out at him, wildly, madly, the suddenness of the attack taking him by surprise. Her nails raked his cheek, drawing blood. Hacket tried to grab her wrists, seeing now that tears were coursing down her cheeks. She struck at him again but he caught her arm and held it, getting a good grip on the other wrist too. She struggled frantically to be free of his restraining hands, wanting also to be away from the touch of his skin against hers. It was as if he were something loathsome.

'Let go of me,' she shouted, glaring at him. 'Don't touch me.'

He released her and she pulled away, moving from the bed, almost falling as she reached the door. Hacket swung himself out of bed and moved towards her but she held up a hand to ward him off.

'Don't you come near me,' she hissed. 'Don't.'

He hesitated, knowing that whatever words or actions he chose were useless. The two of them remained frozen, like the still frame of a film, then, finally, Hacket took a step back. A gesture of defeat.

'Sue, please,' he said. 'Don't shut me out. Not *now*. We need each other.'

She almost laughed.

'Do we? Why do you need me? You can go back to your whore can't you?' She glanced at him a second longer then turned and left the bedroom.

He thought about following her as he heard her footfalls

on the stairs but he knew it was useless. Instead, he spun round and, with a roar of rage and frustration, he brought his fist down with stunning force on the dressing table. Bottles of perfume and items of make-up toppled over with the impact. Hacket gripped the top of the dressing table, gazing at his own pale reflection in the mirror.

The face that looked back at him was despair personified.

Seventeen

The barking of the dog woke him.

In the stillness of the night it seemed to echo inside the room, inside his head and he sat up in bed immediately, glancing to one side, squinting at the clock.

1.46 a.m.

Brian Devlin thought about snapping on the bedside light but hesitated. He rubbed his eyes, the barking of the dog still reverberating through the darkness. The animal could be anywhere on the farm, perhaps even in one of the fields, noise carried a long way in the stillness of such a late hour.

Devlin hauled himself out of bed and padded across to the window which overlooked the main farmyard.

The porchlight which burned offered little by way of penetrative glow and Devlin could see no further than the land rover which was parked just outside his back door. Again he thought about putting on a light, but again he hesitated, reaching instead for the torch which stood on the floor beside the bed.

Then he slid a hand beneath the bed and pulled out the Franchi over-under shotgun. He broke the weapon, thumbed in two cartridges from the box in the bedside cabinet then moved quickly towards the stairs, the torch gripped in one hand, the shotgun cradled over the crook of his other arm.

At the back door he paused to step into his boots, pulling his dressing gown more tightly around him. It was cold and he cursed as his bare feet were enveloped by the freezing wellingtons.

Outside, the dog continued to bark.

Devlin unlocked the back door and slipped out into the night.

He stood still for a moment, squinting into the gloom, letting his eyes become accustomed to the darkness, then he headed off in the direction of the barking Alsatian.

Devlin was sure the sound was coming from the rear of the barn. From the chicken coop. He'd lost nearly a dozen chickens to foxes over the last month or so. This time he'd catch the bastard, blow it to pieces. The woods which grew so thickly on the eastern side of his land were perfect breeding ground for foxes and he had already searched part of them in an effort to track down the vermin, but so far with no success.

Other farmers, on the western side of Hinkston, had reported no such losses of poultry and that, in itself, irritated Devlin. He'd been running the farm for the past twenty years, ever since his twentieth birthday, he didn't have the resources that the farmers on the other side of the town had. His was a small concern built up over the years first by his father and now by himself. The farm was a consuming passion. So much so that his ex-wife had found it impossible to accept that the farm and farm business would always take precedence. Perhaps, Devlin had thought when she'd left him, she didn't like taking second place to a sty full of saddle-backs. He smiled at the recollection. Of how she had tried to play the farmer's wife, milking the cows, even mucking out the pigs but, after a year or so the novelty value had worn off and she'd seen it for what it really was. Bloody hard work. Devlin worked a sixteen-hour day sometimes to keep the farm ticking over. There was no time for a social life. It had been almost inevitable that the marriage should break up. There had been no children though, and consequently no complications. She was only too happy to leave and he was quite content to carry on devoting *all* his time to the farm. If he had one regret it was that they had been childless. The thought that, after his death, there would be no one to run the farm bothered him. But, he mused, when he was six feet under he wouldn't be worrying about anything anyway, would he?

Right now, all that worried him was the barking Alsatian.

He steadied the shotgun in his other hand, ready to drop the torch and fire should he see a fox, but as he drew closer to the barn and the chicken coop beyond a thought occurred to him. Surely the dog's insistent barking would have frightened the would-be predator away by now? Why was the animal still so agitated?

The barking stopped suddenly and Devlin found himself enveloped in the silence. He paused for a moment, waiting for the Alsatian to begin again.

It didn't.

The silence persisted.

Maybe frightened the bloody fox off, Devlin thought, chased it away and now it's going back to get some sleep which is what he himself ought to be doing. He was supposed to be up again in less than five hours.

Nevertheless he advanced towards the barn noticing that one of the doors was slightly open. He muttered to himself and moved towards it.

He was almost there when he tripped over something.

Cursing to himself he flicked on the torch, shining it over the ground around him.

The beam picked out the dead Alsatian.

Devlin frowned as he looked at the animal, leaning closer. From the angle of its head he guessed that its neck had been broken. Its tongue lolled from one side of its mouth and he saw that blood was spreading in a wide pool around its head, spilling from its bottom jaw. The dog's mouth looked as if it had been forced apart, its bottom jaw almost torn off. Devlin prodded it with the toe of his boot, spinning round when he heard a rustling sound from inside the barn.

He was seized by a deep anger. Whoever had done this to his dog was probably still inside.

'Right, you bastard,' he hissed under his breath and blundered into the barn, shining the torch all around. Up to the second storey where hay and straw were kept. The light bounced off the row of tools which were lined up against one wall. The rakes, the spades, the cultivators, the sythes and the pitchforks.

Nothing moved.

'You've got ten seconds to come out,' he shouted, hearing a slight creak from above him.

There was someone up on the second storey.

It was accessible only by a ladder which led up through a trap-door and it was towards this ladder which Devlin now moved, anger at the killing of his dog overriding all other emotions. Whoever was up there was going to pay, one way or another he thought as he reached the ladder.

He paused, one foot on the bottom rung. Then he jammed the torch into the waistband of his dressing gown and gripped the shotgun in his free hand.

He began to climb.

'You're on private property,' he called as he ascended. 'What I do to you is *my* business. You're on my land.'

He was half-way up by now.

'You didn't have to kill my dog, you bastard.'

Devlin slowed down as he reached the trapdoor, pushing against it hard. It flew back and crashed to the floor with a bang that reverberated throughout the barn.

'I'll give you one more chance to come out,' he called, pulling himself through the narrow entrance. 'You can't get past me, this is the only way out.'

Silence.

'I've got a shotgun,' he called.

Nothing.

Devlin took a couple of paces towards where he thought he'd first heard the sound, holding the shotgun in one hand, playing the torch beam ahead of him, over the bales of hay and straw which were stacked like over-sized house bricks.

There were plenty of places to hide, he thought.

The beams creaked beneath his feet as he walked, stopping every few paces to shine the torch behind him, checking that the intruder hadn't tried to slip out through the trapdoor.

Below, the barn door banged shut.

Devlin spun round, running back to the trap door, peering through.

The door swung open again then crashed shut once more and he realized that it was the wind which had caused the movement.

He straightened up and continued with his search of the loft area.

Had his ears been playing tricks on him, he wondered? The loft seemed to be empty. No one hiding behind the bales. No sign of any disturbance. The barn appeared to be empty. Devlin shone the torch back and forth over the upper level once more then shook his head and turned, heading back towards the ladder.

He laid the torch and the shotgun on the rim of the trap door as he lowered himself onto the ladder.

The barn door creaked open again and remained open.

Devlin jammed the torch back into one of the pockets of his dressing gown and, holding the shotgun in one hand climbed down carefully.

He stood at the bottom of the ladder, listening.

Only silence greeted him.

Puzzled and a little disappointed, Devlin made for the door, closing it behind him. He turned, his torch shining ahead of him.

The body of the dog was gone.

There was just a puddle of crimson to show where it had been laying. The dead animal had vanished as if in to thin air.

Devlin sucked in an angry breath.

This had gone too far. If someone was pissing about with him then he didn't find it very funny. He stormed off back across the farm yard towards the house.

Behind him, the barn door opened a fraction.

Devlin pushed open the back door and stormed in, snapping on lights now, putting down the shotgun and cursing to himself.

The figure was standing in the kitchen

Devlin opened his mouth to say something but no words would come. He reached back for the shotgun but it was too late.

The figure lunged forward, driving the pitchfork before it like a bayonet.

The twin steel prongs punctured Devlin's chest, one of them skewering his heart, the other ripping through a lung, bursting it like a fleshy balloon. Blood erupted from the wounds, spraying the kitchen, and the farmer was propelled backwards with incredible force, driven by the sheer strength of the thrust.

He crashed back against the wall, blood spattering the plaster and leaving a red smear as he slid down to the ground, still transfixed by the pitchfork. He tried to scream but his throat was full of blood and, as he tried to move he could hear the air hissing through his ruptured lung, could feel the cold breeze gushing through the hideous rent. While, all the time, blood from his punctured heart fountained into the air as if expelled from a high pressure hose.

As unconsciousness began to overtake him he saw the figure standing over him.

Saw the long, stiletto blade being held before him.

Devlin found some lost reserve of strength and, even with the pitchfork still embedded in his chest, he tried to drag himself towards the open back door.

But the figure merely knelt beside him, like a priest administering the last rites.

Devlin felt his head being cradled almost lovingly in the intruder's hands and then, as he found the breath for one final scream of agony, he felt the knife being pushed slowly into his right eye.

Eighteen

In the days following Lisa's funeral Hacket found himself enveloped by a feeling similar to isolation. Despite his return to work (perhaps *because* of it – the endless chorus of condolence rapidly became tiresome) and the necessity to mix with people once more, he found that Sue was becoming even more distant. He felt like a lodger. She spoke to him as if he was a stranger for whom she existed solely to put food on the table and to offer perfunctory conversation.

Instead of returning to her own job as a secretary at a computer firm she had considered giving up work completely. Hacket had suggested that, under the circumstances, that might not be a very good idea. Something which had only served, it seemed, to push her into resignation more rapidly. The firm had given her four weeks' compassionate leave but Sue felt that wasn't enough.

And she had begun returning to the hospital on a nightly basis to visit her father.

His condition had deteriorated during the past week and it now seemed only a matter of days until the inevitable happened.

As Hacket sat staring blankly at the television screen he heard the door open and realised that Sue had returned from another of her nightly vigils. She closed the front door behind her and walked straight into the kitchen where she made two coffees, returning to the sitting room to set one of them in front of Hacket. He smiled gratefully but received no reciprocal gesture.

She sat down in one of the armchairs and looked, with equal indifference at the screen.

'Is there any change in your father's condition?' Hacket asked, watching as she kicked her shoes off.

Sue shook her head.

'Have they said how long?' he said, quietly.

'They can't be specific. Days, weeks. They don't know,' she told him, still gazing at the TV. She took a couple of sips of coffee then picked up her shoes. 'I feel tired. I'm going to bed.'

'It's only nine o'clock,' he said.

'I said I was tired.'

'Sue, wait. We have to talk.'

'About what?'

'You know what. About us. About what's happened. We can't go on like this.'

'Then perhaps we shouldn't go on,' she told him, flatly.

Hacket frowned, surprised by the vehemence of her words and disturbed by their implication.

'You mean you want us to split up?' he said.

She shrugged.

'I don't know, I haven't thought about it properly. I've got other things on my mind.'

'Listen to me,' he said, trying to control the tone of his voice. 'We've been married for almost seven years. I love you, I don't want to lose you. I want you back, Sue.'

'I want Lisa back but wishing for it isn't going to make it happen is it?' she countered, acidly.

'Lisa's dead,' he said, through clenched teeth and then finally, he raised his voice in frustration. 'Jesus Christ, Sue do you think you're the only one feeling that pain. You haven't got a monopoly on grief you know. I miss her as much as you do. She was my daughter too, in case you hadn't noticed.' His breath was coming in gasps.

Sue regarded him impassively.

'We've got to rebuild our own lives,' he continued, more calmly. 'I'm not saying we should forget Lisa, we should never do that, she was the most precious thing in both our lives. But now all we've got is each other.' He sighed. 'I know you still feel angry about what happened between me and Nikki but it's over now, Sue. I said I was sorry and I'll keep on saying it as many times as you want me to. For as long as it takes for things to go back to normal between us.'

'They can't ever be normal again, John,' she told him with an air of finality. 'We're not talking about just an affair. We're talking about the death of our daughter. A death you *caused* because of your affair.' She eyed him angrily.

'I have to live with that knowledge,' he rasped. 'I don't need you to remind me all the fucking time. Do you have any idea what I'm feeling? What it's like to carry that guilt with me all the time? Do you care?'

'No John, I don't. All I care about, all I know is that our daughter is dead. That you've wrecked our marriage. Don't mention love to me again, you don't know the meaning of the word.'

'So what's the answer?' he wanted to know. 'Divorce? Is that going to make things better? It certainly isn't going to bring Lisa back is it? And if that sounds harsh it's because it hurts me to say it. Hurts me more than you'll ever know.'

There was an uneasy silence, finally broken by Sue.

'I've been thinking it might be best if I go away for a while,' she told him. 'To stay with Julie in Hinkston. We don't see much of each other now. And I need the break.'

'What about your father? Who's going go visit him?'

'I can drive in from Hinkston, it only takes an hour.'

'How long will you go for?'

'As long as it takes.' She got to her feet, shoes in hand, and walked to the door.

Hacket sank back on the sofa, drained. He heard her footfalls on the stairs as she climbed. He stared at the TV screen for a moment longer, listening to the endless catalogue of strikes, accidents, murders, kidnappings and rapes that the newsreader was relaying, then finally he got up and switched the set off.

He sat in silence for what seemed like an eternity then suddenly got to his feet, walked through into the hall and picked up the phone.

'I'd like to speak to Detective Inspector Madden please,' Hacket said when the phone was finally answered.

Madden wasn't available.

'What about Detective Sergeant Spencer?'

The man on the other end of the phone told him to wait a moment.

Hacket shifted the phone from one hand to the other agitatedly as he waited.

DS Spencer was in the office, he was told, but the man wanted to know what the call was about.

'Is it important? I want to speak to Spencer. Just tell him it's John Hacket,' the teacher told him.

There was a moment's silence at the other end, a hiss of static then the other man agreed, announced he was connecting Hacket, and the teacher heard a series of crackles and blips. Then Spencer's voice.

'Mr Hacket, what can I do for you?' the policeman asked.

'Is there any news on the men who murdered my daughter?' he wanted to know.

'We're following several leads. It's still early days . . .'

Hacket cut him short.

'Have you arrested anyone yet?' he snapped.

Spencer sounded somewhat perplexed.

'I told you, Mr Hacket, we have leads which we're following up but no arrests have been made yet. We'll inform you as soon as anything happens.'

Hacket nodded, thanked the DS then hung up. He stood staring down at the phone for a moment then looked up the stairs towards the landing, towards the room where his wife slept.

He clenched his fists until the nails dug into the palms of his hands.

No arrests yet.

And when they did catch the men, what then?

Hacket stalked back into the sitting room, reaching for his cigarettes. He lit one and sucked hard on it.

What then?

The thought had come to him only fleetingly to begin with, but now, as he stood alone in the deserted sitting

99

room, that thought began to grow stronger. Building, spreading like some festering growth within his mind.

And he nurtured that thought.

Nurtured it and clung to it.

May 7, 1941

The contractions had begun almost an hour ago.

Margaret Lawrenson hauled herself out of the chair, her bloated belly almost causing her to topple over. She paced back and forth for a few moments, trying to relieve the awful cramping pains which came so rhythmically. Over the last sixty minutes the contractions had become more frequent and more intense. Each one almost took her breath away and, twice she reeled as if she were going to faint.

She was alone.

No doctor had been called to the house. No doctor *would* be called. Her husband had assured her that the birth would be a straightforward one and she had believed him.

The thought of George Lawrenson made her momentarily forget even the pains of labour.

Her husband had been dead almost nine months now, and since his murder (she had no doubt that he had been killed even though the autopsy and examination of the car had suggested a faulty petrol tank) she had lived in the large house on the outskirts of Hinkston alone. She had become reclusive, venturing into the town itself as little as possible. She had no friends there so no visitors ever came out to the house. But Margaret had preferred it that way. She had remained in the large building like some kind of guardian, her husband's papers, his notes on Project Genesis, safe in her care.

As she struggled towards the lab her legs buckled and she fell heavily, falling on her side. She felt a sudden gush of liquid from between her legs and looked down to see a flux of thin, blood-flecked discharge spreading across the carpet. Margaret grunted and tried to pull herself upright but it seemed the weight of the child she was carrying prevented that action and she was forced to drag herself along the floor, gasping for breath as she drew nearer the lab.

If only she could reach its sterile environment, its pain killers.

A contraction so savage it practically doubled her up caused her to cry out and, for a moment, she stopped crawling. It was difficult enough with the huge weight of the child in her belly, but now the pain was coursing through her as if it were liquid pumped into her veins by some insane transfusion.

Pain killers.

She moaned in agony and felt more warm liquid spilling onto the inside of her thighs. She looked down to see that it was blood.

She was less than ten feet from the door of the lab but it may as well have been ten miles. Every inch took a monumental effort both of will and endurance.

Margaret Lawrenson suddenly surrendered to the pain, rolling onto her back, knowing that she was not going to make it. Excruciating pain seemed to numb her lower body and she gripped the carpet in anguish as she felt the child move, beginning its slow emergence. She tried to breathe as her husband had taught her, tried to think about him standing beside her. Tried to think about anything other than the savage pain which followed her and caused her to cry out.

She screamed as she felt the child's head push clear of her vagina and now she was unsure whether it was being propelled by her own muscular contractions or using its own strength to escape the prison of the womb. Blood

102

spattered onto the carpet and she felt the incredible pressure ease momentarily as the child's head showed. It nestled between her legs, stained with blood and pieces of placental waste. Margaret gripped the carpet in both fists, her jaws clamped together to prevent the escape of another scream. Perspiration beaded on her forehead and cheeks then ran in rivulets down her face.

She pushed harder, her muscles finally expelling the child which lay on the floor beneath her, still joined to her by the umbilical cord.

Margaret tried to sit up, to reach the child and, as she did she felt the remains of the placenta burst from her vagina in a swollen lump. She swivelled round, her body still enveloped by pain and reached for the child. It was coughing, its mouth filled with blood and saliva. She took it into her arms, using her index finger to scoop the thick mixture of crimson mucous from its tiny mouth. It began to cry immediately.

She raised herself up onto her knees, the baby held in her arms, the umbilicus dangling from its belly. It had to be severed.

She laid the child down again then took the slippery coil in both hands and raised it to her mouth.

Ignoring the taste of blood she bit through the cord, bright flecks of crimson filling her mouth and running down her chin. But she fought the need to vomit and swiftly tied the cord, wiping her mouth with the back of her hand.

The child continued to cry and she smiled as she heard the sound. It was a healthy yell to signal its arrival in the world. Margaret looked down at it. At her son. He was perfectly formed, and as she picked him up his sobs diminished slightly. She rocked him to and fro in that cold corridor, her hair matted with sweat, her clothes drenched with blood. The coppery odour of the crimson fluid was strong in her nostrils but she ignored it. All that mattered now was that her son was alive.

The second wave of contractions took her completely by surprise, both because of their intensity and the unexpectedness of their arrival.

She looked down at her belly to see that the flesh was undulating slowly, swelling then contracting.

As the pains grew more severe she realised what was happening.

She screamed in agony as the head of the second child nudged its way free.

Nineteen

The drive to Hinkston took her about an hour due to the heavy traffic leaving London, but as she guided the car down the main street of the town Sue Hacket noted that it was still barely noon.

The sunshine which had accompanied her on the first part of the drive had given way to a cold wind and the promise of rain. She glanced at the shoppers in the high street, noses red from the cold, some walking briskly, others standing and chatting.

Hinkston was a busy little town close enough to London to qualify as green-belt commuterland but also with enough distance to rightfully be called a country town. Its population, she guessed, was around eight thousand. At least that's what it had been three years ago when she and Hacket had last visited.

Sue drove through the town, past a library, and found herself surrounded by houses which were beginning to take on a solid uniformity. She knew she had entered the estate where her sister lived. She found the street then slowed up, looking for the number of the house. She counted them off as she drew nearer, smiling as she saw Julie standing on the front doorstep talking to the window-cleaner. As Sue parked the Metro outside the house, Julie waved and walked out to meet her. They embraced, watched by the window cleaner who nodded affably as Sue approached him, carrying a small suitcase. Julie introduced her and the window cleaner smiled, making some comment about how alike they were and both so sexy. Julie laughed and slapped him playfully on the shoulder. Sue could see his blue eyes lingering on her own breasts, his attention caught by the fact she wore no bra beneath her blouse. She slid past the window cleaner, leaving Julie to pay him.

Sue stood in the hallway of her sister's home and put down her suitcase, glancing around at the entryway.

There was a chain-store copy of 'The Haywain' hanging on one side of the hall, opposite a particularly large cuckoo-clock which looked as though it could have comfortably housed a vulture. Sue noticed that it was almost twelve o'clock and moved towards the sitting-room to avoid the appearance of the noisy bird. Sure enough, the mechanical occupant of the clock duly shot forth on the hour and proceeded to fill the hall with the most unholy din as the hour hand touched twelve.

Inside the sitting-room Sue again glanced around, noting the fixtures and fittings which filled her sister's house. The room was overflowing with ornaments. Perched on every available ledge. On top of the TV, the wall units, the bookcase. There was even a plastic model of the Eiffel Tower on top of the stereo.

'Mike brought that back from Paris for me,' Julie announced, entering the room. 'He was there on business the other week. He doesn't like ornaments himself but he collects them for me whenever he goes away.'

Sue smiled and held out her arms to embrace her sister. The two of them clung to each other for a moment then Julie kissed her lightly on the cheek.

'I'm pleased you came,' she said, softly.

They exchanged pleasantries, chatted about the weather and Julie told her sister about the window cleaner, what a randy sod he was. She chuckled as she poured tea for them both as they sat in the kitchen. Sue listened and smiled

106

when she felt she should but her mind was elsewhere. Something Julie wasn't slow to notice.

'I'm not going to ask you what's on your mind,' she said, finally. 'You don't know how sorry we were to hear about Lisa. I thought what I'd have been like if anything had happened to Craig.'

Mention of her nephew seemed to coax a smile from Sue and she looked across the table at her sister.

'Where is he?' she asked.

'He's across the road playing with one of his friends. It keeps him from under my feet while the school half-term is on. He'll be pleased to see you. I'll fetch him in a little while.'

Sue nodded and sipped her tea.

'Mike's working late tonight, so . . .'

Sue chuckled at her sister's words and Julie looked puzzled.

'I'm sorry,' Sue explained, sighing. *Working late. Meetings.* She thought of John and his lover. The perennial excuse. *I've got to work late.* She finished her tea and began tracing a pattern around the edge of the cup with her index finger.

'What's going on, Sue?' Julie wanted to know. 'When you rang and asked to stop with us it was all *I* need to get away, and *I* can't stand to be in the house anymore. You never mentioned John. He could have come with you, you know.'

'John was one of the reasons I had to get away,' Sue said, raising her eyebrows.

'Why? What's wrong?'

Sue exhaled wearily wondering whether she ought to burden her sister with her worries but knowing that she had to tell someone. She couldn't carry on bottling up her feelings.

'He had an affair, Julie.' The words came out with ease.

She went on to explain what had happened. The letter. The discovery. The row.

How she blamed him for Lisa's death.

Julie listened intently, her face impassive.

'That's why I had to get away,' Sue continued. 'To give myself time to think, to decide where I go from here.'

Julie still didn't speak.

'I don't know if I can ever forgive him,' said Sue. 'I don't even know if I *want* to.'

The two women regarded each other silently, across the table. Sue feeling slightly drained after relaying the revelations of the last few weeks, Julie not sure what to say.

The silence was broken by the sound of the back door being flung open.

Craig Clayton bounded in, spreading dirt over the kitchen carpet as he bounced his football. He was smiling happily, the football strip which he wore covered in mud, just like his face. He saw Sue and bounded towards her.

She held out her arms to grab him, lifting him up onto her knee and kissing his muddy cheek.

Julie could see the tears forming in her sister's eyes.

'How's my favourite nephew?' Sue asked, hugging him.

'I'm all right,' he beamed and slipped from her grasp, heading for the sitting room.

'Boots off, football kit off, and into the bath,' Julie said. 'Look at the state of you. I've told you not to come into the house with your boots on.'

'But Mum, Mark's just as dirty as I am,' he told her as if that information would somehow pacify her.

'Well it's a good job you didn't bring him over here with you then, isn't it. No dinner until you've had a bath.'

He shrugged and looked at Sue as if expecting her to offer assistance but when she only smiled he turned and stalked back outside to remove his football boots.'

'Kids,' said Julie, smiling. 'Sometimes . . .' She allowed the sentence to trail off, feeling suddenly awkward.

'I'm going to change,' Sue told her, getting to her feet. 'I know where the spare room is. You take care of Craig.' She smiled and walked through into the sitting room then beyond to the hall, where she picked up her case and climbed the stairs.

Julie sat at the kitchen table a moment longer then went to see how her son was managing with his football boots.

Outside, the first spots of rain were beginning to fall.

Twenty

She woke with a start, propelled from the nightmare with a force that shook her and left her trembling.

Sue sat still in the darkness, trying to calm her laboured breathing, worried in case she'd woken anyone else in the house. The silence which greeted her seemed to indicate that she hadn't. She lay back down, her heart still beating fast, perspiration glistening on her forehead despite the chill in the room. She shivered then swung herself out of bed and closed the window.

The rain which had begun as a shower had turned into a full-scale downpour with the coming of night and Sue stared out into the gloom for a moment, noticing lights on in other bedrooms in other houses on the estate. Aware suddenly of her own nakedness she reached for her dressing gown and pulled it on, realizing that she would not be able to find the comfort of sleep so easily now. Instead she walked, barefoot, from the bedroom and out onto the landing, passing Julie and Mike's room. She paused to listen for any sounds of movement, any indication that she'd disturbed them.

Silence.

She repeated the procedure outside Craig's room, pushing his door open slightly to look in on him.

Clad in pyjamas with pictures of motorbikes on them, he lay cocooned underneath his quilt, his mouth slightly open, his breathing even. Sue stood looking at him for a moment longer. He was just two years older then Lisa. A healthy, strong boy. Sue carefully pulled his door closed and made her way downstairs.

Craig's eyes snapped open, his mind instantly alert. He heard footsteps on the stairs which he knew didn't belong to his mother or father. He lay beneath the quilt, only his eyes moving.

Sue snapped on the light in the kitchen and sat at the table while she waited for the kettle to boil. When it finally did she made herself a cup of tea and drank it slowly, gazing into empty air, listening to the steady ticking of the clock on the wall behind her. As she got to her feet to return to bed she noticed that it was 3.11 a.m.

She drifted off to sleep after about ten minutes, the pattering of the rain on the window an accompaniment to her steady breathing.

The door to the bedroom opened soundlessly and Craig stepped inside, his gaze never leaving Sue.

He moved to within two feet of the bed, looking at her, watching as she moved restlessly. But even her movements did not prevent his silent vigil. He remained beside the bed.

Julie had heard the movement and eased herself out of bed, careful not to disturb Mike.

Now she made her way down to her son's bedroom and peered round the door.

110

She saw that the bed was empty.

'Oh God,' she whispered, swallowing hard.

She turned and headed for the spare room.

Craig was still standing beside Sue looking down at her, watching the steady rise and fall of her chest.

Julie crossed to him and gripped his shoulder firmly.

He turned round and looked at her, smiling. Then he looked back at Sue.

'No,' Julie whispered, shaking her head, trying to coax him out of the room.

He hesitated then allowed himself to be led away.

Julie glanced at her sister, ensuring that she was still asleep. Then she closed the door and ushered Craig back to his own room.

He climbed back into bed and slid down beneath the quilt.

Julie knelt close by him and once again shook her head.

'No,' she said, quietly. 'Not her.'

Twenty-one

He would kill them.

That was the only answer.

He had lain awake thinking about it, even at work the idea was constantly with him.

Somehow Hacket was going to kill the men who had murdered his daughter. He didn't know how and he didn't know when. All he knew was he was going to kill them.

Of course there was the matter of practicality. If the police didn't know who they were then how was he to find out alone? And, even if he succeeded, what then? What if he found them and actually managed to end their lives? It would mean arrest, imprisonment. No jury in the land, no matter how sympathetic they might feel to his predicament, would be allowed to bring in a verdict of not-guilty once he was tried. But Hacket didn't seem to care about that. The thought that by ending the lives of his daughter's killers he would effectively be ending his own life made little impression on him.

What had begun as a vague wish had begun to turn slowly but surely into an obsession. Scarcely an hour passed that he did not think about finding and killing the men. He considered how he would make them suffer. Plotting and planning ways to rid the world of them. He revelled in his own inventiveness. He rejoiced in his capacity to imagine what he might do to them. Castration.

God, how he would love to draw the knife so slowly around the scrotum of the one who had penetrated his daughter. To slice through that soft flesh and expose the reeking purple egg-shaped objects inside. He would cut them free one at a time then, while the bastard bled to death, Hacket would push the knife into his anus. Split his bowel. And finally he would take the penis, that vile member which had violated his little girl and he would insert the point of the knife into the slit in the glans and he would push. Push until he sliced the organ in two, cutting slowly and carefully, finally severing it at the root.

Jesus, the thought was a good one and, as he lay in bed gazing at the ceiling he smiled to himself.

At first he had been horrified that such thoughts should have found a home within a supposedly educated and civilised mind like his own but then, as the thought of his dead daughter flashed back into his mind more vividly, the sight of her tiny body on that mortuary slab, he had actively pursued the thoughts. Each method of torture and death

112

had been dredged from blacker regions of his mind until he felt as if he were pillaging the thoughts of some degenerate sadist.

He enjoyed the thoughts.

He would destroy their eyes.

The organs with which they had first looked upon his little girl.

Hacket thought how he would take the blade and cut across the glistening orbs, or else he would carve them from the sockets.

He would cut off each of their fingers in turn.

Cut off their ears.

Shatter their knees with an iron rod then methodically break every bone in their bodies.

Make them eat their own faeces.

The thoughts tumbled around inside his mind, each one to be savoured. Punishment for him would be meaningless. Nothing the law could do to him could make him suffer more than the death of his daughter.

And, perhaps, he thought, with vengeance would come forgiveness. When Susan saw what he had done to the killers of their child she would love him again. She would want him back.

He knew now, more than ever before, that his only hope of atonement lay in finding and killing the murderers of his child.

He swung himself out of bed, reaching for the bottle of whisky on the cabinet beside. He drank straight from the bottle, some of the fiery liquid spilling down his chest. The amber fluid burned its way to his stomach and he sucked in a deep breath, holding the bottle before him. He grinned, seeing his own distorted image in the glass.

If madness was a mirror then Hacket was indeed studying his own reflection.

Twenty-two

It all had an appalling familiarity about it.

The flowers in their cellophane wrappers, the empty words of the priest. The tears.

And the grave.

The inevitability of Tom Nolan's death made the event no less traumatic and Hacket found that, even though he hadn't known the man that well, he was fighting back tears as he stood at the graveside beside Sue, Julie and Mike.

Sue stood motionless, gazing down into the grave as if trying to read the brass nameplate. Hacket thought how serene she looked but he realised that what he had mistaken for serenity was something bordering on shock. He felt like waving a hand before her to see whether or not she would blink.

Julie was crying softly, comforted by her husband who kept her in his arms throughout the ceremony.

Grey clouds rolled by overhead, spilling a thin curtain of drizzle onto the tiny band of mourners. There were others standing nearby although they seemed reluctant to move closer to the grave for fear of intruding. Hacket guessed they were friends of Tom's. One or two of them were crying also but their anguished utterances were carried away on the wind which whipped across the cemetery.

When the time came, Sue moved forward and gently tossed a handful of earth on top of the coffin then stepped back to stand beside her husband.

Julie did not move.

The vicar finished speaking, offered his usual perfunctory words of condolence then waddled off back towards the church to greet the next cortège which was just passing through the cemetery gates.

More pain, thought Hacket.

Even death had become like a production line.

'I'm going to take Julie back to the car, Sue,' Mike said, leading his sobbing wife away. He nodded to Hacket who managed a smile.

Sue continued looking down into the grave.

'I know this isn't the right time,' Hacket said, self-consciously. 'But can we talk?'

'Just give me a minute,' she said, without looking at him.

Hacket nodded and turned, walking slowly towards a seat beneath a tree away to his right. He brushed some fallen leaves from the seat and sat down, watching Sue who stood gazing down into the grave. Hacket could see her lips moving and wondered what she was saying. Her father's death didn't seem to have hit her as badly as Lisa's. Perhaps the end of his suffering had been something of a relief to her, he thought although he decided not to mention it. Instead he waited as she walked towards him.

He brushed the seat with his gloved hand and she finally sat down.

'Thanks for taking care of the funeral arrangements, John. I appreciate it,' she said, quietly.

'I knew you wouldn't be in any state to do it. I owed you that at least.'

'It doesn't earn you any gold stars,' she said, a slight smile on her lips but also he saw the tears in her eyes.

He moved towards her, wanting to hold her, she held up a hand as if to keep him at a distance. Hacket clenched his teeth.

'I'll be OK,' she said, quietly. 'What did you want to talk about?'

'I wanted to know when you're coming home.'

'I'm not.'

Hacket swallowed hard. Was that it, he wondered? The final pronouncement on their current state of affairs?

'You mean it's over between us?' he asked, almost incredulously.

'What I mean is I can't come back to that house, John. There are too many memories there.'

'So what will you do? What will *we* do?' he wanted to know.

'I'll stay with Julie for the time being. I know I can't do that indefinitely, but . . .' She sighed. 'Like you said, this isn't the right time to talk about it.' She moved to get up and Hacket reached for her arm, holding it for a moment.

She pulled free from his grip, glancing at him for a second. He saw something akin to hatred in her eyes and lowered his hand.

'Julie needs me,' she said. 'I'll have to go.'

'*I* need you,' he said, trying to control the anger in his voice. 'We have to talk, Sue.'

'But not now,' she repeated, walking away from him. He watched as she strode down the narrow path towards the tarmac area which served as a car park. He saw her climb into the back seat with her sister, then he looked on as the car turned and sped away.

Hacket stood alone for a moment, the wind whipping around him, then he too turned and headed back towards his car. There was so much he had wanted to say to her. To tell her that he would sell the house and move to Hinkston, that they could start afresh if she'd have him back. So much to say. But, more than words he had wanted to hold her, just to feel her in his arms for a moment.

He'd been denied even that simple pleasure and, as he climbed into the car and started the engine, he began to wonder if it was one which was to be denied him forever.

He'd lost her.

Hacket was convinced of it.

First he'd lost his daughter, and now his wife. There

wasn't the appalling finality of loss with Sue that there had been with Lisa but he was still sure that their relationship was over. She might as well be dead.

He sat alone in the sitting room of their house, a glass of scotch in one hand, his head buzzing from the amount he already drunk. Half a bottle remained from the full one he'd opened just an hour earlier.

Hacket looked around the room suddenly realising how much he hated it. Sue was right, it held too many memories. But it held them for him too, couldn't she see that? But he couldn't run from them. He could never escape the memories no matter where he went because the thoughts which tortured him were *inside* him. Eating him away as surely as the cancer had eaten away at Sue's father. And yet still he clung to the hope that revenge would be his salvation.

He took a long swig from the glass, some of the fiery liquid running down his chin.

Hacket let out a roar of rage and frustration and, as he did, he squeezed with even greater force on the glass.

It shattered. Thick shards of crystal tearing into the palm of his hand. Others flew into the air along with a mixture of whisky and blood which spurted from the savage gashes. He dropped the remains of the glass and slowly turned his palm to look at it. Glass had lacerated the flesh in several places and thick crimson fluid pumped from the wounds. A piece of crystal the size of his thumb had punctured the palm and was still protruding from the flesh. Hacket reached slowly for it and pulled it free, holding it before him for a second before tossing it aside.

He studied his bloodied hand then slowly raised it to his face and, with measured movements, he drew the torn and bleeding appendage across each cheek until his face was smothered with the thick liquid.

He sat motionless, like some war-painted Indian brave, the throbbing pain in his hand growing worse but dulled

117

by the amount of whisky he'd drunk. The smell of blood was strong in his nostrils. He could feel the life-fluid congealing on his cheeks, while, by his side, it dripped from his slashed palm.

Hacket smiled then laughed. Stupidly, drunkenly.

And slowly the tears of laughter became tears of despair.

Twenty-three

To say that the dining room of The Bull was small would have been an understatement. It consisted of five tables and, as he pulled his chair out and sat down, Stephen Jennings tried to visualise the place full of diners. He doubted if that ever happened.

The Bull was what people like to refer to euphemistically as 'homely'. In other words it was cramped. A small, family run hotel (even the description seemed rather grand for somewhere as modest as The Bull) in the centre of Hinkston, it was cheap, immaculately clean and friendly. He had stayed in dozens like it and many much worse. Jennings had worked for the past three years as a rep for a company of jeans manufacturers. It wasn't the greatest job in the world but it got him around the country and he had a company car and a reasonable salary. However, now approaching his twenty-seventh birthday, he was wondering if the time had come to move on. Better himself, as his mother always liked to say. She was also fond of saying that he should settle down and marry, something which he had definitely *not* given any consideration to. He'd been in an on-off relationship for the last eighteen months, although

118

his time on the road seemed to ensure that it was more 'off' than anything else. Still, he was too young to settle down, he kept telling himself. Too old to rock and roll, too young to die, he thought, and smiled to himself.

Casting aside his philosophical musings, Jennings picked up the menu and glanced at it for a moment before taking another look at the dining room of the hotel. Each table had a vase of flowers at its centre, every napkin and tablecloth was spotlessly clean. The lighting was subdued to the point of gloom. Perhaps to hide the state of the food when it finally arrived, he thought, returning his attention to the menu.

The choice was small but fairly adventurous for a place of The Bull's modest means. Steak in red wine and mushroom sauce. He glanced at the price. Expensive, but what the hell, it was going on his expense account. He checked the wine list.

'Hello.'

The voice startled him from his considerations and he looked up to see a young woman standing there. Woman was somewhat overstating the fact, perhaps and a quick appraisal told Jennings this newcomer was in her late teens. She smiled at him and he noticed the pad in her hand and realised that she was the waitress.

She was slim, that fact accentuated by the tight fitting black skirt and top she wore. A thick mane of shaggy blonde hair cascaded over her shoulders, framing her thin face from which two eyes like chips of sapphire seemed to shine as if lit from within. She wore no make-up and the freshness of her complexion seemed almost unnatural for a girl in the throes of pubescence. She stood beside the table patiently and Jennings glanced down to see that she was wearing not the flat shoes of a waitress but a pair of high heels. The girl was little short of stunning.

She smiled at him again when she noticed his surprise.

119

'Did I startle you?' she said, happily. 'Sorry. My Dad's always telling me not to sneak up on customers.'

Jennings returned the smile.

'Your dad?'

'Yes, he owns the hotel. Him and Mum have been running it for about twenty years, since before I was born.'

She kept those sapphire eyes on him, also appraising.

'You're new here aren't you?' she said. 'Just arrive today?'

He nodded.

'So, you know all the guests?'

'That's not difficult,' she told him. 'We hardly have any at this time of the year.' She looked more deeply at him. 'At least none like you.' No blushing. No quick glance down at her pad. The remark hadn't slipped out by mistake.

Jennings could not resist a sly glance at her breasts, the nipples pressing gently against the cotton of her blouse.

'Thanks for the compliment,' he said. 'Is that included in the price of the room?' He smiled.

'I had a boyfriend who looked like you,' she said, her gaze unwavering.

He raised his eyebrows.

'*Had*?'

'We split up. I got tired of him.' She smiled. 'He couldn't keep up with me. Not many of them can.'

Jennings coughed, trying to disguise the laugh which threatened to escape him. She wasn't flirting with him, she was practically propositioning him. About as subtle as a sledgehammer. But then again, as he looked at her face once more, the laugh faded. No doubt about it. She was stunning.

'I'd better order something,' he said, looking at the menu.

'Am I making you nervous?' she asked, brushing a speck

120

of dust from her skirt with exaggerated slowness, pulling the material tight at the top of her thigh to ensure he saw the outline of her suspenders through the skirt.

'No,' he told her, rather enjoying the game. 'But I don't think your Dad would like it if he walked in and heard the way you were talking to me. He'd probably ask me to leave the hotel.' He winked at her. 'Then what would I do for the night?'

'Dad doesn't care what I do,' she said, still gazing at him. 'Nor does Mum. So why should it bother *you*?'

He shrugged, again drawn to those blazing eyes. Jennings ordered then handed her the menu, watching as she walked away, unable to keep his eyes from her legs. She disappeared through into the kitchen leaving him alone in the dimly lit dining room.

'Would you like a drink while you're waiting, Mr Jennings?' Tony Kirkham called from behind the bar. 'I see Paula's taken your order.'

Another five minutes and she'd have taken my bloody trousers, Jennings thought with a smile.

He ordered a pint of bitter, retrieved it from the bar and returned to his table. Paula returned a moment later with his starter which she duly set down before him.

'Thanks. By the way,' he said, spearing a couple of prawns with his fork, 'is there any nightlife around here. I was planning on going out after I'd eaten.'

'There's a cinema down the street, a couple of discos,' she shrugged. 'Not much. We have to make our own entertainment.'

He smiled.

'I thought that's what you'd say. Maybe I'll wander down to the pictures. Thanks.' Jennings wasn't sure whether or not to continue the little game. A glance at her persuaded him. 'It's a pity you're working. You could have showed me around.'

'I still can,' she whispered. 'Later.'

He nodded.

'I'll keep that in mind.'

She turned and left him alone.

He finished his meal, drank a couple of brandies, then decided to venture out and sample Hinkston's somewhat limited nightlife.

As he stepped out of the hotel the wind whistled around him and he pulled up the collar of his jacket. Then, hands dug deep in his pockets, he set off down the street.

Hidden by the darkness of the bedroom, Paula Kirkham watched him disappear out of sight.

Twenty-four

'No'.

'He has a right to be told.'

The two men faced each other across the small office, cigarette smoke floating lazily in the air like a grey shroud.

'I said no,' DI Madden snapped, stubbing out the Dunhill and pushing the overflowing ashtray towards the edge of his desk.

'Why can't we tell him?' Spencer wanted to know.

'Because we'd be breaking the rules.' There was a note of sarcasm in the senior officer's voice.

'To hell with the rules,' Spencer rasped. 'Hacket's daughter was butchered by this fucking maniac.' He held up the arrest sheet, brandishing it before him as if it were some kind of accusation.

'We can't prove that, yet,' Madden reminded him, getting to his feet. He lit up another cigarette.

'Then why did we even bother pulling him in? Was that *procedure*?' Spencer glared at his superior. 'We can hold him for twenty-four hours and then we have to charge him. Only we've got nothing to charge him *with*. So what happens?'

'He walks,' said Madden, flatly. He sucked hard on the cigarette then wearily blew out a stream of smoke.

'Call Hacket,' Spencer insisted.

'What good would it do?' Madden wanted to know.

Spencer continued to gaze at his companion, his expression challenging.

Madden shrugged then, slowly, pushed the phone towards Spencer.

Twenty-five

The man was tall, powerfully built, larger than Hacket. Subduing him had been difficult. The wounds on the side of his face and his scalp testified to the number of blows from the hammer it had taken to finally batter him into unconsciousness.

Now Hacket stood over the man who was beginning to come round, his eyes rolling in their sockets like the reels of a fruit machine. He blinked hard, trying to clear his blurred vision and, finally, he looked up at Hacket.

The man tried to straighten up but found that his arms were secured by rope, tied so tightly that the hemp bit into his flesh when he squirmed to escape the bonds. His ankles too were similarly secured. He was spread-eagled on the floor of what looked like an abandoned warehouse.

And he was naked.

Hacket held the claw hammer in his right hand and took a step closer to the prone figure, then he twisted the tool so that the steel prongs of the claw were facing his captive. With a blow combining incredible power with uncontrollable rage, Hacket brought the hammer down onto the right knee-cap of the bound figure.

The claws shattered the patella, tearing through the cruciate ligaments at the back of the knee and almost ripping the knee cap itself off. Blood from the hideous injury ran freely from the site of the damage and the man on the ground screamed in agony as he felt Hacket trying to pull the hammer free. The claws had wedged behind the knee cap and, with each tug on the shaft, the flat piece of bone rose a few more millimetres until Hacket realised he was levering it free. The sound of tearing ligaments was almost audible above the man's insane screams. Hacket put more weight behind the hammer, determined to lift the patella free.

It came away with a vile, sucking sound, the shattered bone skittering across the floor, pieces of it dangling on the end of tendrils formed from ripped muscles and ligaments.

The man on the floor writhed in uncontrollable pain and Hacket looked at his face, wanting to see the agony register.

But the man *had* no face.

Where the features should have been there was just smooth skin.

No eyes. No mouth.

The screams seemed to be coming from inside Hacket's head as he stood over the man, the hammer dripping blood.

No face.

Hacket began to laugh, the sound joined by the faceless man's terrible screams. And by a new noise.

124

By the strident ringing of the telephone.

Hacket sat up in his chair, his face bathed in perspiration, his cut hand still throbbing madly.

Momentarily disorientated, he looked around him, looking for the claw hammer. For the faceless man.

Neither was present and, as the phone continued its monotone screech, he realised that he'd been dreaming. All that *was* real was the pain in his hand. He winced as he dragged himself out of the chair, wrapping a handkerchief around the swollen appendage.

The phone continued to ring.

Hacket staggered across the room, towards the hall wondering why his face felt so stiff but then remembering the congealed blood which caked it. He scratched at one cheek with his index finger and saw some of the dried, mud coloured mess come away beneath his nail.

He blundered through the doorway to the hall and snatched up the phone.

'Yeah,' he panted. 'Who is it?'

'Mr Hacket?' the voice asked.

'Yeah.'

'It's Detective Sergeant Spencer. I'm sorry to disturb you but you did say you wanted to know if there were any developments in your daughter's case.'

Hacket gripped the phone more tightly.

'And?'

'We've got a suspect in custody. We think he might have been involved in your daughter's murder.'

Twenty-six

It was almost 10.30 when Jennings returned to The Bull. He'd decided to by-pass the cinema in Hinkston. The idea of sitting through the umpteenth cinematic episode of 'Star Trek' hadn't appealed to him. He'd eventually ended up in a pub a couple of streets away called 'The Badger's Set.' There he'd spent a couple of reasonably diverting hours with a couple of the locals discussing topics ranging from the possibility that Margaret Thatcher was a man to Liverpool FC's latest trophy-winning exploits.

Now he pushed open the door which led into the reception area of The Bull and withdrew his hands from his pockets, feeling the welcoming warmth.

Irene Kirkham was behind the desk. A rotund woman in her early forties who still had a pretty face. Perhaps Paula inherited her looks from her mother, thought Jennings with a grin. He wondered who she'd inherited the sexual precocity from but decided it had been nurtured rather than inherited. He crossed to the desk and asked for his key and an alarm call for the morning.

'Is there any chance of something to eat?' he asked. 'Just a sandwich would be fine, thanks.'

'You go to your room and I'll take care of it,' Mrs Kirkham told him, handing over the key.

He thanked her and bounded up the stairs to the first floor, the boards creaking beneath his feet as he entered his room. He closed the door behind him and pulled off his coat, throwing it onto the bed, then he flicked on the TV and wandered into the bathroom to relieve himself.

He was half-way through draining his over-filled bladder when there was a knock on his door. He finished then hastily zipped up his jeans, cursing as he caught a pubic hair in the metal teeth. Re-adjusting himself he crossed to the door and opened it.

Paula stood there holding a tray which bore a plate of sandwiches and a glass of milk.

She had changed from earlier. Now she wore a pair of faded jeans which bit into her crotch so deeply he could practically see the outline of her labia. It was obvious she wore no panties. Just as she still wore no bra, a fact attested to by the prominence of her nipples which strained against her white T-shirt. She was barefoot.

'Room service I presume,' he said, smiling, stepping back to allow her entrance, his eyes flicking admiringly over her bottom as she wiggled past.

'Where do you want it?' she asked, raising her eyebrows.

Ha, bloody, ha, thought Jennings. More games.

He decided to play.

'On the bed?' he chuckled then shook his head and motioned to the dressing table. She set down the tray and looked at the various toiletries on show. There was some anti-perspirant, some after-shave. Paula unscrewed the lid of the bottle and sniffed it.

'Well,' she said. 'How did you enjoy Hinkston's nightlife?'

She sat down on the stool which faced the dressing table, one leg drawn up beneath her.

Jennings hesitated a moment then closed the door of the room. She smiled as he crossed to the dressing table and picked up a sandwich. As he stood before her she reached up and ran one hand gently across his thigh, allowing it slide higher towards his penis.

Game on. Your move, Jennings told himself.

He swallowed the remains of the sandwich and looked down at her. She didn't attempt to stop her firm stroking and, despite himself, Jennings felt a tightening in his groin.

Paula smiled up at him, those chips of sapphire pinning him again in that electrifying gaze.

'What about your parents?' he said, quietly, his erection now painfully constricted by his jeans.

'I told them I was going to bed after I'd given you your food. They won't check on me.' She began to rub more firmly over the bulge in his jeans, outlining his stiffness with her thumb and index finger then she loosened the popper on his waistband and, slowly eased his zip down.

Jennings sighed as the pressure was relieved, that sigh of relief turning to one of pleasure as she eased his pants over his hips exposing his throbbing erection. She bent forward and closed her lips around the bulbous head. He moved closer as she flicked her tongue around the glans, allowing her fingers to trace a pattern across his tightened scrotum. He began to thrust gently in and out of her mouth as she covered his throbbing member with her saliva, still sucking greedily at it.

He slid his hands through her hair, amazed at the fineness of it. Then his hands slipped to her shoulders then down to seek her breasts which he kneaded through the material of her T-shirt, coaxing the nipples to even greater stiffness.

She pulled away suddenly, allowing his penis to slip from her mouth. Then, with a grin on her face she pulled the T-shirt off and moved swiftly across to the bed. Jennings stepped out of his jeans, tugged his socks off then removed his shirt, watching mesmerised as she shrugged off her own jeans, undulating and writhing on the bed, peeling them off like a snake sloughing its skin.

Naked, they were joined on the bed.

He cupped her left breast in his hand and squeezed, his tongue flicking over the stiff nipple, teasing it between his teeth before repeating the procedure on the other. Her hand found his shaft and she enveloped it in her fingers, beginning a rhythmic motion which brought him immense

128

pleasure. He twisted round so that his face was between her legs, nuzzling his way through her tightly curled pubic hair until he found her swollen vaginal lips. He flicked his tongue along each in turn before seeking her clitoris, drawing back the fleshy hood with his teeth, feeling the firmness against his tongue.

Her cleft wept moisture into his mouth as he brought one hand around and began softly stroking the inside of her thighs. Her breathing became deeper.

Then she rolled over, pulling him onto his back, lowering herself onto his face, pressing her wet pubis against his mouth for a moment longer before sliding down his chest, leaving a moist trail. She straddled him taking his penis in one hand, guiding it towards her wetness, rubbing his swollen glans against her clitoris. Using him to stimulate her further. If this was still a game then he was playing by *her* rules now.

'Fuck me,' she gasped, insistently and lowered herself onto him, enveloping his penis with her cleft so that it felt as if he was being seized by a slippery glove which tightened more as he thrust up to meet her downward movement. She gasped and ground against him harder, moaning as he rubbed her swaying breasts, knowing that he was close to orgasm himself.

Paula leant forward and kissed him, her tongue pushing into his mouth, flicking across his lips as she rode him faster. She sucked his tongue into her mouth and he felt it against the hard edges of her teeth. Felt her own tongue retreat to allow *his* to probe deeper.

Felt her front teeth closing on his tongue.

Felt the uncontrollable agony as she bit through it.

Blood burst from the tumescent appendage, filling his mouth and hers, spilling over his chin to stain the sheets beneath.

She sat back, swallowing the tongue with one huge gulp

then she bent towards him again, still riding his now shrinking penis, still feeling the uncontrollable pleasure building within her as he bucked beneath her.

Her orgasm came as she tore off his top lip.

She took it between her bloodied front teeth and bit deep, pulling. Shaking her head from side to side until it came away. She chewed once and swallowed that too.

Her pleasure was limitless now.

The shattering power of her climax sent what felt like an electric charge through her body and, as blood from his severed tongue spilled down her naked torso, she rocked back and forth on top of his writhing body, her arms holding him down with surprising strength.

He tried to scream but the blood flooded back into his throat.

She slid off him, reaching for the vase on the bedside table, bringing it down with terrifying force on his head.

The vase shattered, the blow opening another savage gash on his forehead.

His eyes rolled upwards in the socket as she clambered back onto him, like some unsatisfied lover in search of gratification.

She used the jagged, broken edges of the vase to open his stomach, the muscles and flesh splitting like an overripe peach.

She thrust one hand inside the reeking cavity, her fingers closing around a length of intestine. It felt like a throbbing worm, bloated and slimy but, undeterred, she pulled hard, ripping the bulging length free. Paula raised it to her mouth and bit into it ignoring the blood which poured down her arms and torso. It trickled through her pubic hair like crimson ejaculate and she slid back and forth in the reeking mess, her eyes closed in ecstasy. Her mouth bulging as she filled it with the dripping entrails, chewing happily.

130

Jennings had stopped moving. Even the muscular spasms which had racked his body having ceased.

He was dead by the time she began peeling pieces of skin from his face, pushing them into her mouth with a gourmet's fervour.

It was as she reached for his eye that the door opened.

Twenty-seven

'Who is he?'

Hacket's voice sounded like gravel as he sipped at the coffee, gazing through the two-way mirror into the interrogation room.

The room was bare but for a table, two chairs and three men.

A uniformed sergeant. Detective Inspector Madden and a third man.

'His name's Peter Walton,' said DS Spencer, looking down at a sheet of paper fastened to the clip-board which he held. 'Age thirty-two, no fixed abode. Eleven previous convictions. All small-time stuff though. Handling stolen goods, mugging, that kind of thing.'

'You call mugging small-time?' said Hacket, his eyes never leaving Walton. He studied every inch of the man's face as he sat toying with an empty packet of cigarettes. The lank hair, streaked with grey here and there. The sallow complexion, sunken eyes. Unshaven. His lips were thick and puffy, as if he'd been chewing the bottom one repeatedly until it swelled. He had a dark birthmark on the left side of his neck, just below his jaw. Hacket noticed with disgust that there was some hardened mucous around one nostril. When he tired of playing with the cigarette packet, Walton began picking at that particular nostril, examining the hardened snot before wiping it on his trousers.

Spencer had not expected the school teacher to drive to the police station after the phone call. He was even more surprised by his appearance. Hacket's hand was crudely bandaged, the blood still seeping through. His hair was uncombed and the dark rings beneath his eyes made him look as though he hadn't slept for a week. Spencer noticed the smell of whisky on his breath but made no comment. Instead he had shown the dishevelled man straight through into the office which looked onto the interrogation room, watching as Hacket sat down, his eyes never leaving Walton. As if he were trying to remember every single detail about the man.

Hacket himself had washed his face when he'd finished speaking on the phone to Spencer, scrubbing the dried blood away. The he'd bandaged his hand, pulled on a jacket and driven to the police station. The cold night air combined with the news he had just heard had served to shock him out of his stupor even though he was still aware of the smell of drink on his breath.

Now the two men sat in the small room gazing through the two-way mirror as if they were watching fish inside an aquarium.

'We picked him up in Soho,' said Spencer. 'He was trying to sell some videos. Cassettes which had been stolen from your house.

'You said that there were lots of fingerprints in the house when Lisa was killed.'

'There were. Unfortunately, none of them match with Walton's.'

Hacket exhaled deeply.

'You must be able to hold him on something,' the teacher rasped.

'Apart from receiving stolen goods, there's nothing.'

'You mean you're going to let him go?' Hacket snarled, turning towards Spencer for the first time. The DS saw the fury on the teacher's face. 'He killed my daughter. You can't let him go.'

'We can't prove that, Mr Hacket. Not yet. And, until we can, we can only hold him for forty-eight hours. After that he's free.' Spencer shrugged. 'I don't like it any more than you do but it's the law. *He* has his rights, regardless of what you or I think.'

'And what about my daughter?' Hacket muttered through clenched teeth. 'What about *her* fucking rights?'

'Look, I told you that we thought two men were involved well, perhaps Walton can lead us to the other man. To the one who really murdered your daughter.'

'How do you know it wasn't him?'

'Because his blood group is different to that of the man who raped your daughter.'

Hacket swallowed hard and turned away, his attention returning to Walton. He could see the man nodding or shaking his head as Madden asked him questions. He didn't seem very concerned. At one point he even smiled. Hacket gripped the arms of the chair until his knuckles turned white. What he wouldn't give for ten minutes alone with the bastard.

Forty-eight hours and he would be free again.

Hacket closed his eyes tightly, as if hoping the rage would vanish but, when he opened them again Walton was still there. The rage was still there.

The pain.

And the guilt.

He got slowly to his feet, wiping one hand across his face.

'What did you do to your hand?' asked Spencer, nodding towards the bandaged appendage.

'Just an accident.' Hacket turned towards the door.

'One of my men could drive you home, Mr Hacket.'

The teacher shook his head, pausing with his hand on the door knob.

'You let me know what happens. Please,' he said, without looking at Spencer. 'If you manage to hold him. If he spills the beans on his . . . partner. You'll let me know?'

'Yes,' said Spencer, watching as Hacket left.

The schoolteacher paused a moment on the steps of the police station, sucking in deep lungfuls of night air. As he stood there a police car pulled up and two uniformed men got out, running past him into the building.

Another emergency?

Hacket walked to his car and climbed in, sitting there for a moment before starting the engine. As he twisted the key it purred into life.

'Peter Walton,' he said under his breath.

He had a name and he knew what the bastard looked like.

It wasn't much but at least it was a start.

He pulled away, guiding the car out into traffic.

Twenty-eight

Her fingernails were deep inside his eye socket.

Like hooks, ready to pull the orb free of his skull but, as she heard the door open, Paula Kirkham turned, her blood spattered hand falling to her side. She chewed slowly

134

on a portion of Jennings small intestine, pieces of it sticking to her chin. Her torso was smothered in his blood. The room smelled like a slaughterhouse. Crimson had soaked the bed itself, elsewhere it had sprayed up the walls as if directed by a hose. Some of it had even spattered the sandwiches which Jennings had asked for.

Paula swallowed what was left of the intestine and looked blankly at her parents.

Tony Kirkham slipped inside the room, pulling the door shut behind him. Irene crossed towards the bed, towards Paula and the mutilated remains of Stephen Jennings. She smiled benignly at her daughter and held out a hand, watching as the young girl slid from Jennings' torn body. Irene wrapped a blanket around her then gathered up the clothes which lay in an untidy bundle on the floor, some flecked with blood.

Paula smiled lovingly at her parents and, as she passed him, she paused and kissed her father softly on the cheek.

He smiled and touched her hair. Hair that was matted with blood.

Irene led her from the room and Tony was left alone with the remains of Jennings.

He wasted little time.

First he wrapped the body in the sheets and covers from the bed, cocooning it. Then he reached into his jacket pocket and pulled out the string he carried, wrapping long lengths around the bloodied corpse to keep the covers in place. The stench was appalling but he continued with his task, fetching Jennings' small suitcase from the wardrobe. Into it he pushed the dead man's clothes, his shoes, and anything else he could find which gave the appearance that someone had stopped in the room. He moved through into the bathroom, scooping up the rep's toothbrush and razor. Those too he tossed into the suitcase.

The mattress was sodden with blood, Tony made a

mental note to burn it later. The large wood-burning stove in the basement of the hotel would be more than adequate for that task.

He would dispose of Jennings' body in there too. And his clothes.

As for his car, that could wait. He would drive it out into the countryside in the small hours and dump it. Even when it was found there would be nothing to connect it to the hotel, to the Kirkham family.

To his beautiful daughter.

Tony smiled as he looked down at the blood-drenched parcel of bedclothes which formed a shroud for Stephen Jennings. Some blood was beginning to seep onto the carpet. He would have to move fast before it left too indelible a stain.

The crimson which had spattered the walls would also need to be washed off.

He left the room for a moment, hurrying along the corridor to a utility room from which he took a mop, bucket, several cloths and dusters. By the time he returned to the room, a puddle of thick red fluid was beginning to spread out around the corpse. Tony muttered to himself, knelt down and lifted the body. He was a strong man and the weight bothered him little. He carried Jennings into the bathroom and dumped the corpse unceremoniously in the bath, looking down at it for a moment before returning to the bedroom.

As he picked up one of the cloths to wipe down the dressing table, the door of the room opened and Irene walked in.

'How is she?' he asked.

'She's sleeping now. I cleaned her up first then put her to bed.' She surveyed the blood spattered room indifferently. 'How long will you be?' she wanted to know.

'Give me an hour,' he said.

136

Irene nodded and glanced at her watch.

11.57 p.m.

She turned and left Tony to his task, hurrying down to reception. She ran her finger down the guest register and found Jennings' name. Then, with infinite care she changed the date of which he was due to leave. If anyone came looking for him, which was doubtful, they would say that he didn't stop the night, that he had to leave suddenly. That he hadn't left an address where he could be contacted.

That task done she scuttled back upstairs to her husband who was washing down the walls.

'What about the body?' she asked.

'I'll take care of it in a minute,' he said, calmly. 'There's no rush.'

No rush. No fuss.

They were used to the ritual by now.

12.57 a.m.

He'd said an hour and he'd been right.

The body was gone, all of Jennings' belongings were gone.

Irene Kirkham looked at her husband, who nodded.

She reached for the phone and dialled.

Twenty-nine

The house was large. An imposing edifice with a mock-Georgian front, its stonework covered by a creeping blanket of ivy. The windows peered from beneath this canopy like questing eyes, gazing out into the darkness. During the hours of daylight it was possible to see over most of Hinkston from the main bedroom of the house. The building set, as it was, on one of the many hills which swelled around the town.

A gravel drive curved up towards the house from the main road which led down into the town. Hedges which had once been subject to the complex art of topiary had been allowed to merge into one and now formed a boundary along the bottom of the spacious lawn and also on either side of the curving drive.

There was a pond in the centre of the lawn but it was empty of fish. A couple of weatherbeaten gnomes stood sentinel.

The house boasted eight bedrooms but, at present, only one was used. Downstairs there was a sizeable library, a sitting-room which again looked out over Hinkston itself, and a kitchen.

The surgery had been installed over twenty-three years ago. It had been constructed from two other rooms, one turned into an office, the other a waiting room.

It was in the surgery that Doctor Edward Curtis sat, his jacket off, his sleeves rolled up.

He was cradling a glass of gin in one strong hand, massaging the skin above his eyebrows with the other.

Curtis was a tall, lean man in his late forties. His brown hair was cut short, his skin smooth apart from the moustache which covered his top lip. He turned the glass slowly in his hand, looking down into the clear liquid and telling himself that he would go to bed when he'd finished his drink.

He'd said that after the first two. Now, gazing at his fourth, he determined to keep to his word. He took a sip of the gin.

The house was particularly quiet at this time. Not even the creak of settling timbers disturbed the solitude. Curtis

138

enjoyed silence. He was grateful that the house was set outside the town itself, more than half a mile. Of course a frequent bus service brought his patients to him during surgery, those who didn't drive. But, apart from his work, Curtis was rarely disturbed. He was on call, naturally, twenty-four hours a day, preferring not to employ a locum as the surgeries in town did. Many of his patients called him by his first name and he had found that his rapport, carefully cultivated over the years, helped them to relax. Perhaps, he reasoned, private practice offered more time than that available to his overworked colleagues working for the NHS but it was something which Curtis found both rewarding and necessary.

He had been practising in Hinkston for the last twenty-one years, ever since his return from medical school and he was now a well established member of the community, his skills sought by both old and young, not just in Hinkston but also further afield. There was one woman on his books who came from London to see him, such was her faith in him.

Curtis employed just two people, both on a part-time basis. A receptionist and a housekeeper, although it would be more appropriate to call her a cleaner. But he disliked the term, finding it demeaning to the woman who performed such a necessary task. She cleaned both the surgery and the house itself.

But not the cellar.

The subterranean part of the house was the private domain of the doctor. He had installed a simple but sophisticated store of machinery and equipment which allowed him to perform some fairly complex tests. His ability to test for diseases such as diabetes and various renal problems, to name but two, removed the need for patients to travel to hospital and so cut down the time they had to wait for results. He even had a small X-ray unit down there. Blood tests and urine tests could be analysed on the spot, the patient able to know the results before they left the surgery.

Most of the money to set up the surgery, and certainly to install the equipment, had come from his parents. Now both dead, they had left him not only the house but a sizeable amount of money which Curtis had invested wisely. His fees were more than reasonable and, living alone, he had minimal overheads. Just the wages of his two staff and his everyday living requirements.

He took another sip of the gin and glanced at his watch. 1.36 a.m.

He rubbed his eyes and yawned.

The door to the surgery opened and Curtis looked up as the newcomer walked across to the desk and sat down opposite him.

'Join me?' Curtis asked, pushing the bottle and a glass towards the other occupant of the room.

He filled the glass, watching as his companion drank.

'Sorry if I woke you,' he said.

The other merely shrugged.

'I had to go into Hinkston. An emergency,' he explained, finishing his drink.

The figure also drained the glass and pushed it towards Curtis, who promptly re-filled it.

'I'm going to bed,' Curtis announced, yawning again. He got to his feet, picked up his jacket and headed for the door that led through the waiting room and beyond to the stairs.

The remaining occupant of the surgery sat drinking, only the sound of low, rhythmic breathing breaking the deathly silence.

Thirty

She guessed she'd slept less than three hours all night.

Sue Hacket splashed her face with cold water, dried it then wandered back into the bedroom to apply some make-up. She inspected the dark rings beneath her eyes before adding eye-liner and a touch of lipstick. She rubbed her cheeks, noting the paleness of her skin and finally gave in to the temptation of touching on some rouge.

Downstairs she could hear the sound of the radio, the vacuous ramblings of the DJ periodically replaced by the even more vacuous music he played. She slipped out of her housecoat and pulled on jeans and a sweater, stepping into her shoes before she made her way downstairs.

'Well, come on then,' she said to Craig who was sitting at the kitchen table trying to fasten the laces on his shoes. 'You've got to show me the way and we don't want you being late do we?'

'I won't be late,' he assured her, jumping down from the chair and rushing into the sitting room to retrieve his satchel.

'Thanks for taking him to school, Sue,' said Julie who stood at the kitchen sink, her face looking distinctly haggard. 'Mike would have stayed off work but he says they've got a big contract to finish . . .'

Sue held up a hand to silence her.

'Leave the washing up, I'll do it when I come back,' she said.

'No. I'd rather keep myself occupied. It stops me thinking about Dad,' Julie told her.

'I know what you mean.'

'I'm ready, Auntie Sue,' announced Craig, appearing in the doorway like a soldier ready for inspection. Sue smiled and heard the front door open as he rushed out to the

Metro to wait for her. She turned and looked at Julie then followed him out.

Craig sat in the passenger seat beside her, well strapped in, happily telling her directions to his school, pointing at friends he knew as they passed them on the journey.

Sue saw mothers with younger children and her expression hardened.

The emotion she was feeling was something close to resentment. That others should be enjoying the simple pleasure of walking their children to school while she would never know that joy. Was it resentment she asked herself? Envy or jealousy? It all amounted to the same thing.

'That's Trevor Ward,' Craig announced pointing to a tall, thin child with glasses who was crossing the road ahead of them. 'He picks his nose and eats it.'

'Does he really?' Sue answered, deciding that kind of personal detail didn't interest her too much.

'His Mum and Dad can't afford a car,' said Craig with glee.

'Not everyone is as lucky as *your* mum and dad, Craig,' she told him, the merest hint of rebuke in her voice. Some people aren't even lucky enough to have children she felt like adding, administering a swift mental slap for the feelings of self-pity she felt surfacing. But, surrounded by children as she was, it was difficult not to feel the resentment which Lisa's death had brought. Sue suddenly felt very weary.

She brought the car to a halt outside the main gates of the school and leant across to unlock the door for Craig.

He told her he'd get a lift home with a friend of his. His mum always picked him up. Sue told him to get a teacher to ring if there was any change of plan. He nodded happily, unfastening his seat belt and pushing open the door.

'See you later,' she said, smiling. 'Don't I get a kiss goodbye?'

He looked at her and chuckled, as if it were something he'd meant to do but it had just slipped his mind. She turned her face slightly to allow him to kiss her cheek.

Craig took hold of her chin, turning her face back towards him then, kneeling on the seat, he kissed her full on the lips, pressing his against her own for what seemed like an eternity.

Then he pulled away and jumped out of the car.

Sue watched him run off into the playground, still shocked at his response, still able to feel the pressure of his lips against her own.

She raised two fingers to her mouth and gently ran them across her lips.

As she did she saw that her hand was shaking.

Thirty-one

Hacket stared down at the black marble stone and glanced at the inscription, feeling the tears begin to prick his eyes. He sniffed them back, holding the small bouquet of violets in his hands. The right one was still heavily bandaged and, even with the benefit of pain killers, he could feel a dull throbbing pain coming from it.

The sun was out but it was cold, the light breeze occasionally intensifying into a chill wind which caused him to shiver. The flowers which already stood in the small pot on Lisa's grave had wilted, some shedding their withered petals, and it was these petals that the wind scattered like discarded confetti.

Hacket stood for a moment longer looking down at his

daughter's grave then he knelt and began removing the old flowers from the pot, laying them on the wet grass.

The sunshine and the Sabbath day had coaxed a number of people to the cemetery and he glanced around to see others performing tasks similar to his own. Replacing flowers, pulling unwanted weeds from plots. He saw an elderly woman cleaning a white headstone with a cloth. Not far from her a man in his early forties stood, hands clasped before him, gazing down at a grave. Hacket wondered who the man had lost. A wife? A mother or father? Perhaps even a son or daughter like himself. Death held no discrimination for age, sex or creed.

Hacket began placing the new flowers in the pot his mind full of thoughts. Of Lisa. Of Sue.

Of the phone call he'd received earlier that morning.

DS Spencer had phoned about ten a.m. with the news that, due to lack of evidence, Peter Walton had been released.

Hacket had barely given him time to finish speaking before angrily slamming the phone down.

Released.

The bastard had gone free, just as Spencer had warned.

So, now what?

Hacket continued pushing flowers into the pot, the question eating away at him.

Did he go looking for Walton? Try to trace him? Spencer had said that his address had been unknown so where did Hacket begin? He had no doubt of his own ability to kill Walton should he find him but his first, main problem, was actually hunting the bastard down. And Hacket was no detective. Where did he start? He exhaled wearily. In films it was so simple. The avenging angel always knew where to find his intended prey. Everything always went according to plan. Only this *wasn't* a film, this was real life with all its attendant complexities.

144

Hacket had no doubt he could kill Walton.

No doubt?

He had fantasised about it, dreamt of the most elaborate ways of inflicting pain on the killer of his child and yet, if the time came would he have time to make Walton suffer as he wished him to? Would Walton kill *him*?

And Spencer had also said that another man could be involved.

What then?

What? If? How? When?

Hacket turned and hurled the dead flowers into the nearby waste bin. He turned back and looked at the grave, massaging his forehead gently with one hand. He could feel the beginnings of a headache, the pressure building slowly but surely. Just as it was building within him until all he wanted to do was scream and shout. Anything to release the pent up emotion which swelled like a malignant tumour. Only *this* cancer was eating away his soul.

He looked down at the grave and thought of Lisa.

Of Sue.

Hacket had never felt so lonely in his life.

He turned and walked slowly back towards the car.

Thirty-two

The crying awoke her.

Michelle Lewis sat up quickly, rubbing her eyes as she heard the howls from the bottom of the bed.

Beside her, Stuart Lewis grunted and swung himself out of bed.

'The joys of parenthood,' he said, smiling thinly.

Michelle also clambered out of bed and moved towards the cot which held their child.

Daniel Lewis was crying loudly, his face creased and red.

'He looks like a bloody dishcloth,' said Stuart, yawning, looking down at the screaming bundle which his wife carefully lifted into her arms.

'You probably looked like that at six weeks,' she told him, rocking the baby gently back and forth.

'Thanks,' he muttered, watching as she unfastened her nightdress and eased one swollen breast free, raising the child to the nipple it sought.

He had been a large baby, over nine pounds at birth, but Michelle had been fortunate. The delivery had been an easy one. She had always had what Stuart referred to as 'child bearing hips' which was his way of saying she needed to lose a little weight. But she had already begun her exercise classes to lose the pounds she'd gained while carrying Daniel and she was confident she'd soon have her figure back. After all, she was only just past her twentieth birthday, her body was still very flexible.

'I'm going to make a cup of tea,' said Stuart, running a hand through his hair. 'Do you want anything?'

She didn't answer, merely hissed in pain as Daniel chewed rather over-enthusiastically on her nipple, coaxing the milk from the large bud and gurgling contentedly. However, after a moment or two, Michelle removed him from her left nipple, noticing as she did how red it was. The baby yelled for a second but soon quietened down as she lifted him to the right nipple, allowing him to close his mouth over that. He began sucking vigorously, his eyes darting back and forth as he accepted her milk.

'It's a pity *you* can't do this,' said Michelle, smiling.

Stuart rubbed his chest and shrugged.

'Sorry, love,' he said. 'Empty.'

146

They both chuckled.

Daniel continued to suck with ever increasing vigour.

'I'm sure he's getting some teeth,' Michelle observed, feeling the soreness beginning around her nipple.

'He's too young for that isn't he?' David asked, deciding not to bother with the tea. Instead he sat down on the edge of the bed beside his wife, watching as she nursed the baby. He remained there for a moment longer then got up and wandered along to the bathroom where he urinated gushingly.

Michelle held the baby to her breast, aware of a growing pain around her nipple.

The child had gripped the mammary in both tiny hands and was clinging on like a leech, his mouth still sucking hard. She was sure that he had some teeth, he must have. His jaws continued to move up and down, swallowing the milk greedily. Another minute or so and she'd move him back to the other nipple again, the right one was becoming painfully sore. Besides, he should have had enough by now.

She held him gently, frowning as she felt the pressure on her breast increase. His tiny fingers raked across the flesh leaving four red lines and she winced.

'I think you've had enough, young man,' she said, and prepared to transfer him back to the other nipple, if not to terminate the feed there and then. She lifted him gently.

He did not release her nipple.

'Daniel,' she said, softly, easing him away.

The child continued to suck.

Michelle took hold of one of his tiny hands and tried to pull him away but he wouldn't budge.

She felt a growing pain in her breast as he continued to suck.

'Daniel, that's enough,' she said, more urgently.

He seemed to be nuzzling against her with renewed vigour, pushing his head against the mammary, closing his

147

jaws even more tightly over the protruding nub of flesh and muscle.

She let out a yelp of pain as she felt a sharp stab around her nipple. As if he were biting her. Using his teeth. Teeth which, by rights, he shouldn't have.

Michelle for some inexplicable reason felt suddenly worried. The child would not let go of her nipple and as she tried to pull him free she felt the skin stretching, most of it still held in his mouth.

The pain was growing.

'God,' she hissed as Stuart re-entered the room and looked at her.

He saw the baby pushing hard against her breast, saw the skin of that breast being pulled taut, saw the pain on Michelle's face.

Then he saw the blood.

It trickled from the baby's mouth, mingling with the overflowing milk to create a pink dribble which dripped onto the bed.

'What's wrong?' he said, worriedly, taking a step towards the bed.

Michelle didn't answer, she merely continued to tug at the baby who was now hanging on grimly, using both hands to anchor himself.

The pain spread across her chest until it felt as if her entire torso was ablaze and, finally, unable to bear it any longer, she pulled the child hard.

As she did, Daniel bit through her nipple, severing it.

Blood jetted from the swollen tissue, spraying the child and the bed, soaking into the sheets.

The baby swallowed the nipple with one gulp, blood and milk dribbling over its chin.

Michelle screamed and looked down at her torn breast, a flap of skin hanging over the lacerated mammary. Blood was pumping furiously from the wound and she hastily laid the baby down and tugged the sheet to her chest, pressing it against the wound which bled profusely.

Daniel lay contentedly on the bed, his eyes still as bright and alert.

'Oh Jesus,' gasped Stuart, moving towards her. 'I'll get an ambulance.'

He looked once more at his child, its face soaked in blood, still chewing on a piece of skin which had come free with the nipple. Then he dashed for the phone.

'No,' Michelle called. 'Not the ambulance. Not yet.' She was pressing the sheet to her mutilated breast, trying to stem the flow of blood as best she could. 'You know who you've got to call.'

He hesitated a second longer then stabbed out the digits.

Behind him on the bed, the baby gurgled contentedly.

Thirty-three

Stuart Lewis looked at his watch and then continued gazing out of the front window. Every few moments he would step back to take a drag of his cigarette but then anxiety would force him back to his vigil.

He checked his watch again.

5.46 a.m.

He had made the phone call more than twenty minutes ago.

'Come on, come on,' he whispered, agitatedly, his face pressed to the glass of the window again.

Finally the car swung round the corner and came to a halt outside the house. Stuart moved towards the front door

149

and unlocked it, opening it as the occupant of the car clambered out.

Doctor Edward Curtis strode up the path and through the front door.

'Upstairs,' Stuart said, and the doctor followed the younger man as he bounded up the narrow flight, hurrying towards the bedroom where his wife waited.

As Curtis entered the bedroom he was struck by the strong smell of blood.

The sheet which Michelle Lewis held against her breast was soaked in the crimson fluid, some of it beginning to congeal on the material. There were spots of it on the wall and carpet. It looked as though she was wearing red gloves.

The child lay beside her, its shawl similarly dotted with crimson, its face and hands stained dark with its mother's blood.

It was the baby that Curtis approached first.

'How long ago did this happen?' he asked, unfastening the black bag which he carried.

Stuart told him.

'And you haven't called an ambulance?' Curtis wanted to know, smiling relievedly when Stuart shook his head.

Curtis reached into his bag and took out a syringe. He quickly took it from its plastic wrapping then pulled out a bottle full of almost colourless liquid. He upended it, jabbed the needle through the top and drew off 50ml then he gently took hold of the baby's arm, found a vein and ran the needle into it.

The child didn't murmur as Curtis pushed the plunger, expelling the liquid into its veins.

He waited a moment then withdrew the syringe, dropping it back into his bag. Only then did he turn to Michelle who was still holding the sheet to her chest in what looked like an exaggerated attempt at modesty.

150

'Let me look,' said Curtis and she lowered the blood spattered sheet.

Not only had the nipple been torn off but a piece of flesh as large as the palm of Curtis's hand had also been pulled from the breast. He could see muscles and vein networks exposed. Blood was still oozing from the wound, dribbling down Michelle's stomach.

Curtis reached into his bag once again, this time pulling out some gauze and bandages.

'I'll dress the wound as best I can,' he said. 'You'll need to go to the hospital, you've lost a lot of blood.'

Michelle nodded obediently as Curtis pressed a gauze pad to the place where her nipple used to be then hastily wrapped bandages around to keep it in place.

'Tell them whatever you have to,' he said. 'Whatever you can think of. The child will be fine now. But he's not to be left alone for a while.' The doctor looked at Stuart who nodded. 'He'll sleep now.'

Curtis got to his feet and headed for the door.

'Wait five minutes then call the ambulance,' he said. They heard his footfalls on the stairs, the sound of his car engine as he drove off.

Both of them looked into the cot where the baby lay, already beginning to drift off to sleep.

They smiled down at him then Michelle wet the tip of her finger and wiped some blood away from his mouth.

He was really such a beautiful child.

Thirty-four

She had hesitated for a long time before finally deciding to call him.

It had been over a week since her father's funeral and she hadn't spoken to him since then, but now Sue Hacket sat beside the phone looking down at it as if expecting the digits to reach him without her having to touch them. She hadn't even been sure at first if she *wanted* to speak to him but she had found that loneliness is a truly contagious disease and Sue was finding it creeping into her life despite being surrounded by Julie and the family. She had tried rehearsing what she should say to her husband, even got as far as lifting the receiver once but then replaced it and resorted to pacing the floor of Julie's sitting room surrounded by the dozens of ornaments.

Julie was out shopping. Craig was at school and Mike at work. She was alone with only her thoughts for company.

Finally, almost reluctantly, she lifted the receiver and slowly pressed the numbers which would connect her with Hacket's school.

The connection was made, she heard the dial tone.

'Can I speak to John Hacket, please?' she asked when the phone was finally picked up.

The woman at the other end apologised but Mr Hacket had taken a week's holiday. She could leave a message if she wanted to, the secretary had his home number.

'No thanks,' said Sue and replaced the receiver, looking down at it for a moment before lifting it to her ear and jabbing out the digits of her home number.

Home. The word seemed curiously redundant.

The phone was answered almost immediately.

'Hello.'

She recognised his voice and, for a second, thought about putting the phone back down.

'Hello, John, it's me.'

'Sue? How are you?'

'I'm OK I rang the school, they said you were off for a week.'

'Yeah, I can't seem to concentrate. It's not fair on the kids if I'm not giving it a hundred per cent, besides I've got things to do around the house. I put it on the market, there's been three or four prospective buyers round already.'

'Any interest?'

'One couple seemed fairly keen until they found out what had happened here.' He was quiet for a moment. 'Some bloke came just *because* of what happened here, morbid bastard. I haven't heard anything from the others yet.' There was another awkward silence. 'You say you're all right, you sound tired.'

'I am. I haven't been sleeping too well.'

More silence.

Christ, it was excruciating, as if each was trying to think of something to say. They were like strangers.

'How's Julie and Mike?' he asked.

'They're not so bad.'

'And the boy?'

'He's all right too.' She didn't mention the incident in the car, having since tried to dismiss it from her mind.

'Good,' he said, wearily. 'So everyone's OK'

'Listen John, I had to speak to you. It's about you and me. I told you I couldn't come back to that house and I can't.'

'I understand that but things might not be that cut and dried. I mean, it's not just the house you're avoiding is it? It's me.'

She swallowed hard.

153

'I might *just* have managed to forgive you for the affair, John,' she said. 'But I'll *never* forgive you for what happened to Lisa. And, yes, I still blame you. I always will.'

'You phoned to tell me something I already knew?' he said, trying to control the irritation in his voice. 'How do you think *I* feel? I can't forgive *myself*, I don't need you to remind me all the time. It's me who's living in the house now. I'm closer to the memories. You're the one who ran away from them, Sue.'

'I didn't run away. If I hadn't got out I'd have gone crazy.'

'I know the feeling.'

There was another silence.

'John, the real reason I rang was to tell you that one of the schools down here in Hinkston has a vacancy for an assistant headmaster. Apparently there's a house included with the job.'

'Why Hinkston?'

'Because I don't want to live in London anymore, I told you that,' she snapped.

'And the two of us? If I got this job would you be willing to start again? A new environment, a new life perhaps?' He sounded hopeful.

'Maybe. We couldn't start from the beginning, John. Things would never be the same between us again.'

'We can try for Christ's sake,' he insisted. 'I still love you, Sue. I need you and I think you need me, whether you admit it or not.'

She sat in silence for a moment, knowing there was some truth to his words.

'It'll take time, John.'

'I don't care how long it takes.'

She gave him the address and number of the school.

'Let me know how it goes,' she told him.

154

'Maybe you could meet me when I come down for the interview.'

There was a long silence. For a moment he thought she'd gone.

'Yes, I will,' she said, finally.

'Sue, if you're not sleeping, love, it might be an idea to take something. Go and see a doctor. You've got to take care of yourself.'

'I was thinking of seeing Julie's doctor actually.'

Another long silence.

'I'd better go, John,' she said. 'Call me when you're coming down for the interview.'

'Sue, thanks for calling.'

'I'll see you soon.'

'Sue.'

'Yes?'

'I love you.'

She gripped the receiver tight for a second.

'See you soon,' she said, softly then put the phone down.

It was as if the conversation had drained her of strength. She sat back, looking down at the phone, feeling as if she'd just run a marathon. It was fully five minutes before she got to her feet and wandered into the kitchen. He was right, perhaps she should see a doctor. A few sleeping pills wouldn't hurt her. there was a small booklet lying on the kitchen table with a picture of a smiling cat and the legend 'Important People' embossed on it. Another of Julie's organisational aids. The address book contained numbers for everyone from the Gas board to the local vet. All in alphabetical order. Sue flicked through until she came to the 'D's'.

She found the name she sought almost immediately.

DOCTOR'S SURGERY.

And beneath it:

Doctor Edward Curtis.

Thirty-five

It was a feeling Hacket thought he'd forgotten and he smiled as he drove, glancing out at the scenery which sped past him. The sun was high in the sky as if its emergence were purely to mirror his state of mind.

He hadn't felt this way for many months, years even. It was something like anticipation only it was more heightened, more acute. There was anxiety there too, naturally but, he actually felt reasonably happy and that particular emotion was one which had been intolerably absent from his life of late.

As he drew nearer to the outskirts of Hinkston and houses began to appear in greater abundance, he thought what his prospects were. If he could secure the job at the school and the house which Sue had told him went with it then he had a chance of rebuilding his marriage too. Hacket felt the surge of adrenalin once again and realised that it wasn't anticipation it was, in all senses of the cliché, a ray of hope.

He'd rung the school immediately after he'd finished speaking to Sue and had been surprised to find that they were prepared to interview him the following day. He'd expected a wait of a week at least but apparently they were anxious to fill the post, and consequently wanted to begin seeing applicants as soon as possible.

Hacket was also glad to be out of the house for a day. He hadn't felt like being surrounded by people, that was why he'd taken the week off work, but being imprisoned in the house, alone with just his thoughts, had proved almost as intolerable. The trip to Hinkston and the possibility of a new job had lifted his spirits a little. He'd even found it possible to face some music and had jammed a cassette into the machine as he drove. However, as he drove further into the town he switched the cassette off and contented himself with glancing around at the buildings which were beginning to form more regular patterns on either side of him.

As he paused at traffic lights, Hacket checked the location of the school on the piece of paper he'd written it down on. He wasn't far away now, he realised.

He felt nervous, though not about the interview. He knew his own capabilities, knew he was as able, if not more so, than most to fill the post but his anxiety grew from knowing that if he didn't get the job then his chance of rebuilding his marriage was also in jeopardy. He could stand to lose the job but not to lose Sue.

The lights changed and Hacket drove on. He guided the car through the town centre, looking around at what appeared to be a bustling community. There was an open market in the paved square, the awnings fluttering brightly in the light breeze. He could hear the shouts of traders as they vied for custom.

The school was on the other side of town, about five minutes' drive from the centre, and he finally spotted the iron railings which rose from the concrete like rusted javelins. The playground was empty but past a large red brick building he could see beyond to a playing field where a number of children were kicking a ball about. Hacket swung the Renault into the car park and switched off the engine. He glanced at his reflection in the mirror, running a hand through his hair, then he climbed out and strode through the main doors of the school in search of the headmaster's office.

A young woman in her mid-twenties passed him and smiled and, for fleeting seconds, Hacket caught himself gazing at her shapely legs as she passed him.

A little like Nikki?

He sucked in an angry breath, mad with himself for even

157

thinking about her, but her image would not fade from his mind as quickly as he would have liked. He walked on and finally came to a door marked: D. BROOKS. HEADMASTER

He knocked and walked in, finding himself in an outer office.

A tall woman smiled at him, trying to shovel the final piece of a Kit-Kat into her mouth, chewing quickly enough to ask him what he wanted. Hacket smiled and spared her the trouble.

'My name's John Hacket. I've got an appointment at ten about the deputy Head's job.'

She continued chewing furiously, nodding vigorously as she swallowed the pieces of biscuit.

'Excuse me,' she said, wiping chocolate from her lips. 'I'll tell Mr Brooks you're here.' She smiled again and knocked on the door behind her, walking in when called. Hacket was left alone in the outer office.

He glanced around at the diagram of the school which covered one wall, the paintings which adorned another. Each one had a small plaque beneath it which Hacket read. The paintings had been done by pupils, each one a prizewinner in a different age group.

One of the paintings showed an owl perched in a tree holding something small and bloodied in its claws. Hacket leaned closer, unable to make out the shape.

'If you'd like to come through, Mr Hacket,' the tall woman called, interrupting his inspection of the painting.

'Thank you,' said Hacket, taking a final look at the painting.

As he moved away from it he finally realised what the small bloodied shape was in the painting. He frowned.

In its talons, the beautifully painted owl held a torn and bleeding human eye.

Thirty-six

The heat inside the office was stifling.

Hacket felt his skin prickling as he walked in, and he was aware of his cheeks colouring from the warmth.

The man who faced him across the wide desk, by contrast, was pale and, as he shook Hacket's hand, the younger man noticed how cold the others' touch was.

Donald Brooks was in his early fifties, his immaculate appearance spoilt only by a few flakes of dandruff on the collar of his grey suit. He was an imposing-looking individual despite his pallid appearance, and the eyes which looked out at Hacket from behind spectacles were an intense green. His handshake was firm, his smile friendly. He invited Hacket to sit down, noticing the scarlet tinges on the younger man's cheeks.

'Sorry about the heat in here,' Brooks said. 'I'm a little anaemic and I tend to feel the cold more than most.'

'I'd noticed,' Hacket said, smiling.

'My wife's always complaining about it at home,' Brooks went on. 'Even in the summer we have the central heating turned on.' He shrugged almost apologetically. He asked Hacket if he wanted a coffee and the tall woman in the outer office entered with one a moment or two later. He thanked her and she left the two men alone once more, allowing Brooks to flick through the two-page CV which Hacket had passed to him. The younger man sipped his coffee while Brooks nodded approvingly, reading the qualifications and commendations that Hacket had acquired over the last ten years.

'Very impressive, Mr Hacket,' he said, finally. 'Your qualifications are excellent and you have some very useful experience behind you. I see the school you teach at presently has over 900 pupils – that can't give you much opportunity for personal contact.'

'I'm afraid it doesn't. It's an occupational hazard I suppose, working in London schools. What's your pupil to teacher ratio here?'

'We average about twenty to a class, usually less. Most of the sixth-form classes have only three or four pupils.'

Hacket nodded approvingly and the two men talked for some time about the school, about Hacket's background in teaching and his desire for the present position.

'Are you married, Mr Hacket?' Brooks asked.

'Yes.'

'Any children?'

He hesitated a second, as if the word itself brought pain.

'No,' he said, sharply, reaching for his coffee and taking a sip, wincing when he found it was cold.

Stone cold. As cold as the grave.

As cold as Lisa.

'Have you had many applicants for the position?' Hacket asked, anxious to steer the conversation onto other things.

'You're the fourth,' Brooks told him. 'And, I must admit I'm impressed. When could you start if you were given the job?'

Hacket shrugged.

'Next week,' he said. 'There's details to finalise about selling our house in London, but a week should be plenty of time.'

'Excellent,' said Brooks. 'Then I think it's time I showed you around the school. You ought to see where you're going to be working.'

Hacket smiled broadly, got to his feet and shook the older man's hand, again feeling the coldness of his skin but this time he ignored that small detail. He followed the Headmaster out of the office, pausing again to look at the painting of the owl which hung in the annexe beyond.

160

'Quite a talented artist,' Hacket said, nodding towards the painting, glancing at the name on the plaque beneath.

Phillip Craven.

Brooks glanced at the painting then walked out of the annexe without speaking.

Hacket followed.

The tour of the school took longer than Hacket had anticipated. The facilities were extensive and impressive and he thought that the school must be one of the few State-funded seats of learning not to have been decimated by Government cut-backs in the past few years.

He and Brooks walked past the red brick building Hacket had seen when first arriving at the school and the teacher was informed that it was a gymnasium. A class of girls were playing hockey on the nearby pitch, a shrieking horde supervised by a mistress who had thighs like a Russian shot-putter and shoulders slightly broader than Hacket's. He grinned as he watched her hurtling up and down the pitch, whistle clamped in her mouth.

'You may be asked to take on some of the duties of the Games masters,' Brooks said. 'I noticed in your CV that you'd done that at your last school. Are you a sporty man, Mr Hacket?'

'I played rugby and football for my school when I was a kid. I wish I was as fit now as I was then. But I can manage. No heart attacks, I promise.' He smiled.

Brooks looked at him as if he didn't understand the joke, then he shivered and turned away from the hockey match and strode across the playground with Hacket beside him. The sun was still out but Brooks looked frozen. His skin had turned even more pale and he kept rubbing his hands together as if to restore the circulation.

'As you're aware, there is a house with the position,' he said. 'I'll show you around that too.'

161

It was a white-walled building hidden from the school grounds by a high privet hedge which was somewhat sparsely covered for the time of year. But it was enough to offer protection from any inquisitive eyes within the school. There were a couple of willow trees in the front garden which had been allowed to get a little out of hand. The grass was about six inches long and there were weeds poking through cracks in the path which led to the front door but it was nothing which couldn't be put right in a weekend, thought Hacket.

As for the house itself, it looked in good repair, all the slates were on the roof. At least the ones he could see. The paintwork was good for another six months at least. The only thing which did stand out was the newness of the front door. It hadn't yet been painted the same dull fawn as the window frames and looked as if it had been affixed only days earlier.

Brooks fumbled in his pocket for the key and opened the door, ushering Hacket in.

The hall was narrow, leading to a flight of stairs carpeted with a rusty coloured shag-pile.

'How long has the house been empty?' Hacket wanted to know.

'About two weeks.' Brooks told him, pushing open the door to the sitting room.

There was no carpet on the floor in there and Hacket's feet echoed on the bare boards. There were, however, still some framed prints on the wall and a couple of armchairs.

They were covered by dust sheets.

'The teacher who lived here before,' Hacket began, glancing around the room. 'Why did he leave?'

Brooks rubbed his hands together again and shrugged, partly in answer to the question, mainly as a gesture to indicate how cold he was. He patted one of the radiators as he passed it as if hoping it would begin pouring forth some heat.

'It was very sudden,' he said, sharply and moved through into the dining room.

This room was also carpeted and Hacket wondered why just the sitting room should have been left bare.

There was more furniture, too, also covered by dust sheets.

'What was he like?' Hacket wanted to know.

'He did his job,' Brooks answered, as if that was enough.

'He left a lot of furniture behind. He *must* have left in a rush.'

They wandered through into the kitchen then back through the dining room to the hall and up the stairs to look into the three bedrooms.

'Did he have kids?' Hacket asked.

'He liked to keep his affairs private, Mr Hacket. I don't pry into the private lives of my staff,' said Brooks, stiffly.

'I only asked if he had kids,' Hacket said, somewhat bemused.

Brooks turned and headed for the stairs.

'Have you seen enough? I have to get back to work.'

'I understand,' Hacket said, shaking his head.

As they reached the front door once more Brooks locked it, pressing on the wood to ensure it was properly fastened.

'The teacher before you did what I believe is called a moonlight flit. I don't know *why*, Mr Hacket. I just hope you're more reliable.' He stalked off up the path, leaving Hacket standing on the front step.

'A moonlight flit, eh?' Hacket muttered to himself.

His thoughts were interrupted by the sound of a bell. The signal for lunch.

Within minutes, the playground was filled with children, the sound of their voices swelling the air.

163

Back in his office, Brooks pressed himself against the radiator, the colour gradually coming back to his cheeks. He stood there while Hacket thanked him for the tour of the school and the house then they said their goodbyes and Hacket left, weaving his way through the throng of children in the playground in order to get to his car. Only then did Brooks leave the radiator and move across to the window, watching as the teacher eased the car through the gates and onto the main road.

'I gave him the job,' said Brooks as the tall woman entered the office.

'Did he ask many questions?' she enquired.

Brooks nodded.

'He wanted to know about the teacher who was here before him, wanted to know why he left so suddenly.'

'What did you tell him,' the secretary asked.

'I didn't tell him the truth, if that's what you mean,' Brooks said, rubbing his hands together. 'I'm not *that* stupid.'

Thirty-seven

Hacket parked his own car behind Sue's Metro and then slid from behind the steering wheel. He glanced at the house, hesitating a moment before walking up the path to the front door. He rang the bell, feeling peculiarly nervous. Like a boy on his first date, afraid that no one will answer. He waited a moment then rang again.

The door swung open.

'Hello, John,' beamed Julie and kissed him gently on the cheek. 'How did it go?'

'Fine,' he said, stepping in past his sister-in-law. 'Is Sue here?'

'Go through into the kitchen,' Julie told him.

Sue was drying some dishes. She turned as Hacket entered the room, her smile rather thin.

He thought how beautiful she looked. It seemed like years since he'd seen her, not days. Even longer since he'd held her.

'I got the job,' he told her.

'That's great,' she said, her smile broadening a little.

Julie joined them, aware of the atmosphere. She filled the kettle and prepared three cups while Hacket sat down at the kitchen table. He told Sue about the school, about the job, the salary. The house.

She seemed pleased and even managed to laugh as he mentioned Brooks' obsession with the cold. They gazed at each other long and hard, Hacket searching for even a hint of emotion in her blue eyes. Some sign of love? Was that what he sought?

'Are you going back to London tonight?' Sue asked.

He nodded.

'I've got no choice. I'll have to arrange the move and there are people coming to view the house tomorrow. Why?'

She shook her head.

'Just curious.'

'If you two want to talk . . .' Julie said.

'No, don't be silly. You stay here,' Sue told her sister.

Hacket was a little disappointed but hid his feelings adequately.

'I'd like you to see the house next time I come down Sue,' he said.

'What did the headmaster say about the teacher who lived there before?' Julie asked.

Hacket grunted.

'Very little.'

Julie nodded almost imperceptibly and gazed down into her mug.

'Why?' Hacket asked, noting her expression.

'Perhaps I shouldn't say anything but I think he should have told you. Anyone from around here would have told you. It was all over the local papers at the time. Big news. The police never did find out why he did it?'

'Did what?' Sue wanted to know.

'One night, he must have gone crazy or something. He got a shotgun, killed his wife and his son and then stuck the barrel in his mouth and shot himself.'

Thirty-eight

Elaine Craven sat alone in the waiting room of the surgery.

Shafts of sunlight flowed through the wide windows illuminating the room, making it seem as if the white walls were glowing. Elaine glanced around her, smiling each time she caught the eye of the receptionist.

She was in her late thirties, dressed in a black skirt and a navy blouse, the left sleeve of which was rolled up to reveal a bandage which stretched from her wrist to her elbow. The limb was held stiffly across her chest and, each time she moved she felt a twinge of pain from the arm. Elaine glanced up at the wall clock above the receptionist's desk and noticed that she still had another five minutes before she was due in to see Curtis. She tried to move her

166

left arm slowly in an effort to minimise the pain but it didn't work and she winced once again.

'What did you do to your arm?' asked the receptionist, noticing Elaine's obvious distress.

'A stupid accident,' she said, dismissively, and shrugged, but even that movement caused her pain.

The two women exchanged perfunctory conversation about the weather while they waited for Curtis to call Elaine in. Then, tiring of that particular topic the receptionist tried a different subject.

'How are your family? It's just the one boy you've got isn't it?'

Elaine nodded.

'Yes, Phillip. He's fine. My husband is fine. It's only me who goes around having stupid accidents.' She motioned towards the bandaged arm as if to remind the receptionist why she was here.

There was a loud beep from the console in front of the receptionist and she flicked a switch.

'Send Mrs Craven in, please,' said Curtis, his voice sounding robotic as it filtered through the intercom.

Elaine got to her feet and smiled at the receptionist once more as she passed through the door ahead of her marked 'Private'. It opened onto a short corridor which led down to another door. She knocked and entered.

Edward Curtis smiled as she entered his room. He invited her to sit down, his eyes drawn immediately to the heavy bandage on her arm.

'I hope your family are in better shape than you, Elaine,' he said, getting to his feet and walking around the desk to her. 'What have you been doing?'

'It was an accident,' she told him. 'It should never have happened.' She looked up at him and Curtis saw a flicker of something behind her eyes.

It looked like fear.

'Let me have a look,' he said, and she extended her arm until it was resting on his desk. With infinite care, Curtis began to unfasten the bandages, unravelling them as cautiously as he could, apologising when Elaine hissed with the pain. Finally he pulled the last piece free and exposed two large gauze pads which covered her forearm. He reached behind him, into a small tray on his desk, and retrieved a pair of tweezers. Then he took one corner of the first pad between the ends of the metal prongs and pulled gently.

'Good God,' he murmured, exposing the forearm more fully. 'How the hell did this happen?'

The skin which covered the forearm had been removed in several places. Not sliced or scraped but torn off.

The area around the first deep laceration was red and swollen and Curtis could see the first watery deposits of pus nestling beneath the torn flesh.

The second wound was even worse.

He pulled the gauze pad free and could not resist wincing himself at the damage which had been inflicted on the arm. Part of the flexor muscle closest to the ulna had been severed and the bone was showing clearly through the mass of twisted flesh and muscle. There was more pus forming on the extremities of the wound, this time thicker and more noxious. Some of it was already leaking into the savage gash.

He looked sternly at Elaine.

'When did it happen?' he said, harshly.

'Two nights ago,' she told him.

'Why didn't you call me?' he snarled. 'Was anyone else hurt?'

She shook her head, glancing down at the wounds which looked like dog bites, only made by some ravening animal unlike any ordinary pet. She gritted her teeth as he used sterile pads to clean the gashes.

168

'It was my fault, I know,' she said. 'I knew it was close to the time, I know I should have contacted you but he seemed all right.'

Curtis wiped away the pus, dropping the swab into his waste bin.

'The treatment must be kept up at regular intervals, you know that,' the doctor told her, repeating the procedure on the smaller gash. 'How *is* the boy?'

'Restless.' It was the only word she could think of.

'Bring him to me tomorrow, before this happens again.' He jabbed an accusatory finger at the two wounds.

Elaine nodded, watching as he re-dressed the torn forearm. When he was finished she got to her feet, pulled her coat carefully over her injured arm and turned towards the door.

'Tomorrow,' Curtis reminded her and she nodded, thanking him.

Thirty-nine

The sun was already bleeding to death as he left Hinkston. By the time he reached the outer suburbs of London the vivid crimson of the sky had given way to darkness.

Hacket was feeling a strange mixture of feelings. Anticipation, excitement and anxiety had all fused together inside his mind. Those three emotions were to do with the job and with the possibility of starting afresh with Sue but he also felt something else.

Suspicion? That wasn't the right word.

Unease seemed to better suit his mood.

169

Why had Brooks been so secretive about the previous occupant of the house? Granted, it wasn't the sort of thing which you told a man who was about to work for you, at least not in so many words. Hacket could understand how the headmaster had feared telling him about the double murder and suicide which had taken place inside the house. But why lie about it?

But, it wasn't Brooks' lies that bothered Hacket. It was the reason *why* the previous occupant had murdered his family then killed himself.

He pulled up at traffic lights, the thought tumbling around inside his head.

Pressure of work? That seemed a bit extreme.

Perhaps he didn't like her cooking, Hacket smiled grimly.

Maybe he'd had an affair and couldn't face her any longer. A bit of a kindred spirit, eh?

Hacket tried to push the last consideration from his mind as the lights changed to green and he drove on.

As he drew deeper into the heart of the capital a curious but not altogether unexpected weariness began to close around him. Like some kind of cloying, unwelcome blanket, he had felt its folds slip from him as he'd left the city that morning, but now, as he drew closer to home he felt their invisible weight enfolding him again.

Perhaps it was the thought of returning to so many bad memories.

' . . . *But the night goes by so very slow* . . . ' came from the car radio.

' . . . *and I hope that it won't end though. Alone.*.' Hacket switched it off.

He was less than five miles from home now and he glanced down at the dashboard clock.

8.38 p.m.

He yawned and drove on, slowing down as he came to a

Zebra crossing. A woman pushing a pram piled high with boxes crossed first then a young couple holding hands. Then, finally a tall, thin man who glanced at the car as he sauntered across.

In the light of the headlamps Hacket could pick out certain details of the individual.

The lank hair, the pale complexion, the sunken eyes.

There was something familiar about this man and Hacket felt his chest tighten, the hairs at the back of his neck rise.

It was then that he saw the dark birthmark on the side of the man's neck and, finally, he was in no doubt who the individual was.

Hacket gripped the steering wheel until his knuckles turned white, his eyes rivetted to the man.

To the man who had murdered his daughter.

Peter Walton sauntered past him.

Forty

Hacket was out of the car in seconds.

He hurled open the driver's door and scrambled out, pointing at Walton.

'You, stop,' he bellowed.

Taken aback by the shout, Walton didn't wait to find out who this madman was, he simply turned and ran up the street, bumping into people as he fled. He ran not even knowing why he ran, but he had seen the expression of pure hatred on Hacket's face and it had been enough to convince him that this man, whoever he was, was best avoided.

Hacket slammed his door and, ignoring the blaring horns of the cars behind him, ran after Walton.

Hacket didn't see the figure that followed *him*.

'Walton,' he roared as he pounded after the fugitive.

People on the pavement who saw him coming stepped aside, those who didn't were buffeted aside as the chase continued up the road to a junction.

Walton looked behind him and saw Hacket still hurtling after him. Without checking the traffic he ran into the road, a speeding Volvo narrowly avoiding him. A taxi coming the other way banged on his hooter as he also came close to hitting the running man. But Walton made the other side of the road safely and ran on, glancing over his shoulder to see that Hacket was still in pursuit.

The teacher also ran into the road without regard for the traffic.

A Capri slammed on its brakes and skidded to a halt just in front of him. Hacket leapt up onto the bonnet and slid off the other side while the driver yelled at him.

He hit the tarmac in time to avoid an oncoming mini which swerved, striking the pavement as it narrowly missed Hacket. He sucked in a deep breath and hurtled on, worried he might lose his quarry on the crowded street.

Up ahead, Walton dived to his left, into a cafe, pushing past the customers, bumping into a table and spilling the drinks that were there. One of the customers jumped up to challenge him but Walton merely pushed him aside and burst through the door which led to the kitchen.

Seconds later, Hacket entered the cafe, following his prey, also ducking through into the kitchen where he heard the cook yelling obscenities as he and Walton raced through and out the back door.

The cool air was a welcome change from the stifling heat of the kitchen but Hacket was already sweating profusely,

172

the salty fluid running down the side of his face. However, he didn't slacken his pace.

Walton found himself in the alley which backed on to the café and he bolted down it as fast as he could, overturning dustbins in his wake. Anything to delay his pursuer, but Hacket merely hurdled the obstacles and ran on, desperate to catch his foe.

And when he did catch him? What then?

The thought faded as he stumbled over a box, almost falling. He shot out a hand to steady himself, tearing some skin from his palm on the brick wall of the alley.

Then suddenly, he and Walton were free of its confines, back on another street, amongst people again.

Walton slammed into a young lad, knocking him to the ground but he didn't stop, merely glanced round to see that Hacket was still after him. Walton saw a bus coming down the street and he ran into the road, running alongside it for a few yards before launching himself up onto the running platform.

He laughed as he saw Hacket running after the bus.

Up ahead, the traffic lights were about to change to red.

Stay on red, Hacket thought as he hurtled after the bus.

They did.

To Walton's horror the bus began to slow down and he looked ahead to see the glaring red light then back to see that Hacket was almost upon him.

Walton jumped from the bus, shaking loose of the conductor who tried to grab him. Then he jumped into the road and scurried back onto the pavement, the breath now searing in his lungs. His legs felt like lead weights and he didn't know how much longer he could run for.

Hacket was feeling the same. He could hardly get his breath but he ran on, his head spinning from lack of oxygen. Gulping in huge lungfuls of air in an effort to keep himself going. His heart was thudding against his ribs, threatening to burst but still he found more energy to continue the chase.

Walton looked up and saw what might be his sanctuary.

The neon sign for the Underground station glowed like a beacon in the darkness and he bolted across the road towards the entrance.

Hacket followed.

'Get out the fucking way,' shouted Walton, elbowing a passage through the gang of people emerging from the stairway. He battered his way through, slipping as he was five steps from the bottom. He toppled over, landing heavily on the dirty tiled floor.

Hacket ran on, taking the steps two at a time, ignoring the stench of stale urine and sweat which rose to greet him from the subterranean cavern.

Walton hauled himself upright and looked around, seeing the automatic barriers which led to the trains. He ran towards them, scrambling over, ignoring the protests of the man collecting tickets.

Hacket too vaulted the partition and hurtled after his quarry who was now heading for the escalator that led even deeper into the bowels of the earth.

Walton, scarcely able to walk now, staggered along on legs that felt like lumps of lead, struggling down the metal steps of the escalator, pushing past those who stood in his way.

Hacket followed, still unaware of the figure that pursued him.

He was panting madly, his throat dry and parched from sucking in breath, his muscles crying out for rest but he knew that if he could catch Walton on the platform he had him. There was nowhere for him to hide. No further he could run.

Hacket stumbled half-way down the escalator but steadied himself, seeing Walton reach the bottom and bolt to his right.

Over his own laboured breathing, Hacket could hear the rumble of an approaching train and a further realisation struck him.

Should Walton board a train before him then there was no way he'd catch the man.

The teacher forced what little reserves of strength he possessed into his screaming muscles and ran on.

There were about two dozen people on the platform, most of them moving forward as they heard the train drawing closer.

Hacket looked to his right and left, sweat now pouring from him.

There was no sign of Walton.

The train was emerging from the tunnel, its lights like the glowing eyes of some massive, fast-moving worm as it slid from the tunnel.

Hacket raced down the platform, looking frantically for Walton, glancing back over his shoulder as the train came to a halt and its doors slid open. Those already on the train watched with detachment as he ran back and forth up and down the platform, his face coated in sweat, his eyes bulging as he tried to get his breath.

Where the hell was Walton?

He heard the familiar whirring noise which came just prior to the doors shutting and, in that split second he saw the man he sought dive for the carriage at the far end of the train.

He got in just as the doors were sliding shut.

'No,' roared Hacket and leapt for the nearest door, jamming his hand into it, ignoring the pain, knowing it would force the doors to open fully once again. As they did he slipped inside.

Seconds later the train pulled away again, picking up speed as it entered the tunnel at the far end of the platform.

Hacket began making his way along the train towards the carriage where he knew Walton to be.

As he came to the door marked 'ONLY TO BE USED IN AN EMERGENCY' worried travellers watched him force the handle up and down until the door opened. He squeezed through, feeling the warm air inside the tunnel buffet him as the train sped along, threatening to shake him from his precarious perch. He struggled with the next door, anxious to get into the safety of the carriage, balanced on just the coupling which held the compartments together.

He almost had the door open when his foot slipped.

Hacket yelled in terror as he felt himself falling.

He shot out a hand and managed to grab the door handle which promptly twisted in his grasp.

The door flew open and he fell into the carriage, sprawling on the floor, watched by the other travellers but Hacket wasn't bothered by their stares. He dragged himself upright and struggled on, realising that they were only moments away from the next station. Once the train pulled in he could run along the platform to the carriage where Walton hid then he had him.

The train escaped the blackness and Hacket pressed himself to the sliding doors, ready to bolt out the minute they opened.

The train slowed down, came to a halt.

He was out in a flash, hurtling towards the front of the train.

Towards Walton.

His quarry, as if realising Hacket's plan, came flying from the foremost carriage, knocking a woman to the ground in his haste. He ran across the platform, through a narrow walkway and towards some stairs which led to a bridge across another track. Hacket followed, taking the stairs two

176

at a time, his lungs now feeling as if someone had filled them with hot sand, his legs throbbing.

Walton looked round to see his pursuer was still there, still on his heels.

He jumped the last three steps, landing heavily on the concrete as Hacket ran on, now only yards from his quarry.

Walton turned to his right, onto another platform.

It may have been rancid ice cream, it may even have been a puddle of vomit left by one of the many drunks who frequented the underground complex. But, whatever it was, Walton didn't see it.

His foot slid in the slimy mess and he skidded, stumbled. Then, with a despairing scream, he pitched forward, arms flailing in the air for interminable seconds.

He toppled off the edge of the platform, onto the rails.

Hacket dashed to the edge as he heard the loud crack and the hiss of thousands of volts as Walton's body was scorched by the incredible electrical charge. His flesh was turned black in seconds, the blood boiling in his veins, and his body jerked uncontrollably as the current continued to course through it.

Hacket reached the platform edge and looked down.

Walton's body resembled a spent match.

With a gasp, Hacket sank to his knees, eyes rivetted to the blackened corpse which lay across the lines.

The stench of seared flesh and ozone was overpowering, and for a moment he thought he was going to be sick, but the feeling passed and he knew only the terrible ache in his muscles and the pain in his chest.

Somewhere down the platform a woman was screaming but Hacket didn't seem to hear it.

He looked down once more at the body of Walton and smiled.

He was still unaware of the figure who watched *him*.

Forty-one

Edward Curtis pushed another log onto the open fire then sat back in the high-backed leather chair, watching the flames dancing in the grate.

His face was set in hard lines and he reached for the brandy glass on the table beside him, sipping it, not taking his eyes from the leaping flames. His mother used to tell him that you could see shapes in fire, but the only shape that Curtis could see was the outline of Elaine Craven's mutilated arm.

'I think it's getting out of control,' said Curtis, quietly.

'You're the only one who can do anything about it,' said the other occupant of the room, seated on the other side of the hearth. But the other figure's eyes were fixed not on the fire but on Curtis.

'There have been too many incidents lately,' Curtis said. 'The Kirkham girl at the hotel. The Lewis baby and now this business with Phillip Craven.'

'They knew the risks, Edward, you can't blame yourself.'

'Blame isn't the right word. I don't feel any guilt for what has happened, for what is going to happen. As you say, they knew the risks. But that doesn't stop me feeling a little helpless. There's still too much I don't know.'

'Are you saying you want to stop?' the other said, challengingly.

Curtis looked at the figure and shook his head.

'There's too much at stake to stop now. Besides, I've gone too far to stop.' He sipped his brandy. 'We both have.' He re-filled his own glass and then the glass of his companion.

'It's what they would have wanted,' the other said. 'We owe it to them to carry on.'

Curtis watched as the figure got up and crossed to the

large bay window which opened out from the sitting room. Drink in hand the other pulled back one curtain and looked out over the lights of Hinkston which lay below.

'You make it sound like duty,' Curtis said. 'Saying we owe it to them.'

'Not duty, Edward. Love.' The figure swallowed a size-able measure of the brandy. 'And something stronger.'

'Like what?' Curtis wanted to know.

The other figure did not look at him, merely kept on staring out at the lights of the town. The words were spoken softly.

'Like revenge.'

Forty-two

'What the bloody hell did you think you were doing?'

Detective Inspector Madden bellowed the words at Hacket who sat at the desk, his hands clasped around a paper cup full of black coffee.

'You're not a vigilante. This isn't New York,' Madden continued.

'Look, he fell . . .' Hacket began, but was cut short by the DI.

'Lucky for you he did. Also you should be thankful that there were plenty of witnesses on the platform to testify to that fact. We could have been forgiven for thinking you threw Walton on the line.'

The office inside Clapham police station was small, its confines filled with a thick haze of cigarette smoke. All three men were smoking. Hacket was sitting on a plastic chair in front of Madden's desk. The DI himself was pacing the floor agitatedly, and DS Spencer was leaning against the desk looking down at the teacher, a Marlboro jammed in one side of his mouth.

Hacket took a sip of the lukewarm coffee and winced.

'How long are you going to keep me here?' he asked.

'For as long as it takes,' Madden rasped.

'Takes for what?'

'As long as it takes for you to see sense. To keep your nose out of police business and stop acting like fucking Charles Bronson. Like I said to you you're not a vigilante and this isn't *Death Wish*.'

'I told you, Walton slipped. You know that. Why can't you just let me go?' Hacket asked.

'You're lucky we're not charging you,' Madden informed him.

Hacket spun round in his seat to look at the DI.

'Charging *me*?' he snapped, incredulously. 'With what?'

'Disturbing the peace. Causing an affray. Would you like me to carry on?'

'That bastard killed my daughter,' snarled Hacket getting to his feet. 'You couldn't do anything about it so I did.'

'You don't even know if Walton was the one who killed her,' Spencer interjected. 'There were two men involved in the murder.'

'Great. One down, one to go then.'

'I'm warning you, Hacket,' the DI said, sternly. 'You keep away from this case.' His tone softened slightly. 'I'm sorry, we're all sorry about what happened to your daughter but let the law take care of it.'

Hacket nodded.

'Let the law take care of it,' he echoed. 'And if you catch him, what then? He's not going to be punished is he? A few years in prison isn't enough for what he did to my little girl.'

180

'That's as maybe but he'll serve a *proper* sentence for his crime, proposed by a judge in a *proper* court of law. The Fearns family lost a daughter too didn't they? If you stop to remember that Hacket, two people died in your house that night. I haven't had any trouble from Mr Fearns wanting to be judge, jury and executioner.'

'If he can live knowing that his daughter's killer isn't going to suffer the way he should then that's up to him. I can't.'

'You've got no choice. I'm not *asking* you to keep your nose out of this case, Hacket, I'm *telling* you,' Madden snapped. 'The last thing I need is some self-styled avenger running around London. *We'll* take care of it.'

Hacket shook his head and took a final drag on his cigarette, grinding it out in an ashtray already overflowing with dead butts.

And what would you have done if it had been *your* child?' he said. 'Would you have accepted the judgement of a court?' His voice was heavy with sarcasm. 'Don't tell me you wouldn't have wanted to see the bastard suffer because I won't believe you.'

'And what if you'd caught up with Walton tonight?' asked Spencer. 'What would you have done? Killed him? That would have made you no better than him and you'd be in the cells now, under arrest.'

'Five minutes' satisfaction isn't worth ruining your life for,' Madden echoed. He took another drag on his cigarette then hooked a thumb in the direction of the door. 'Go on, go home before I change my mind and charge you with breach of the peace.'

Hacket paused at the door, turning to look at the two policemen.

'You know,' he said, smiling. 'I'm still pleased he's dead. I just wish he'd suffered more.' Hacket slammed the door behind him.

Madden dropped the cigarette on the floor and ground it out with his foot.

'Do you know the worst thing about all this, Spencer?' said the DI nodding in the direction that Hacket had gone. 'I agree with him.'

Spencer nodded slowly.

'Join the club.'

Forty-three

He stood outside the door for what seemed like an eternity. His eyes riveted to the doorbell, his hand wavering as he reached for it. Hacket wasn't sure if he was trying to summon up the courage to press it. Courage wasn't the word. Right now he didn't know what the word *was* and, what was more, he didn't give a fuck.

He pressed it and waited.

And waited.

He finally heard movement from the other side of the door.

'Who is it?'

He managed a thin smile as he heard the soft Irish lilt to the voice.

'It's Hacket.'

Silence.

'What do you want?' she finally said.

'I've got to talk to you,' he said.

Another silence then he heard the sound of a chain being slid free, of bolts being drawn back. The door opened.

Nikki Reeves stood before him in a long T-shirt which

was so baggy it managed to hide the smooth contours of her body. Her eyes were bleary with sleep and she rubbed them as she looked at Hacket, blinking myopically.

'Do you know what time it is?' she asked. 'Nearly midnight.' She remained at the door, leaning against the frame.

'Can I come in?' he asked, and as he spoke she smelled the whisky on his breath.

'What's wrong, all the pubs shut and your supply of booze run out at home?'

He looked at her but didn't speak. She sighed and stepped aside, motioning him into the flat. He wandered through into the sitting room where he sat down on the sofa.

'Make yourself at home,' she said, sarcastically. Nikki sat down in the chair opposite him, the T-shirt riding up over her knees, exposing a greater expanse of her shapely legs.

Hacket gazed at them for a moment then looked at her face.

'You've got a bloody nerve coming here, John, after what's happened,' she said, sternly.

'I wanted to talk to you,' he said.

'I thought you'd said all you wanted to say over the phone.'

'I just thought you might like to know that your *little note* had the desired effect. My marriage came close to breaking up, I'm still not sure it'll last.'

She merely shrugged.

'I told you not to use me like a doormat. I was hurt. I wanted to hit back at you and it was the only way I could think of.'

'You heard what happened to my daughter?'

'Yes. I'm very sorry about that.'

'Well your *little note* arrived the day of her funeral,' he

183

rasped. 'It didn't take Sue long to figure out that I was with you when Lisa was murdered.'

'Have they caught the killer yet?' she asked, conversationally.

He merely smiled humourlessly.

'One of them is out of action, to coin a phrase,' he chuckled, glaring at her once again. 'What you did was unnecessary, Nikki. If you wanted to hurt someone then you could have had a go at me, not Sue. She didn't ask to be involved in this.'

'It's not my fault your daughter's dead, John. I told you I didn't mean to be vindictive. I'm sorry for what happened.'

'Sorry,' he grunted. 'Really? Well, you're right about one thing, it isn't your fault Lisa's dead, it's my fault. My fault for being here with you when I should have been at home with *her*.'

'And you came over here tonight to tell me that? What is this, confession time?'

He sat on the sofa looking at her, smelling the booze on his own breath as he exhaled.

'Do you want a coffee?' she asked, almost reluctantly. 'You look as if you need one.' She got to her feet and padded into the kitchen. Hacket waited a moment then got up and followed her.

'Sorry I called so late,' he said. 'I mean, you might have had someone here. I wouldn't have wanted to interrupt.'

'By "someone" I gather you mean another man?'

He shrugged.

'Why not? You're a good looking girl. I'm surprised there *isn't* anyone here.' There was a vaguely contemptuous tone to his voice which she wasn't slow to spot.

'Is that how you see me?' she asked. 'In and out of bed with any man I find?'

'It didn't take you long to sleep with me. Three dates it

184

took, didn't it? Pretty fast going, Nikki.' He smiled, again without a trace of humour.

She made his coffee and shoved the mug into his hand.

'Drink that and go will you?' she snapped, walking back into the sitting room. He followed her once more.

'What did you hope to achieve by writing that letter to Sue? Just tell me that. Did you want to break up my marriage?'

'Just remember who started the affair, John,' she snarled. '*You* chased *me*, not the other way round. You knew the risks. We both did.'

'But you had to have your little bit of revenge, didn't you?' he said, bitterly.

'I don't like being treated like some kind of whore,' she rasped. 'You can't just pick me up, use me then throw me away when you feel like it.' She glared at him. 'Now drink your coffee and get out of here.'

Hacket put the mug down and got to his feet.

'Sue called you a tart and I defended you,' he said, shaking his head. 'I think she was right.'

'Get out, now.' She pushed him towards the door. 'Is that why you came here, tonight, John? For the same reason you wanted me in the first place? Because you still can't get what you want from your wife?'

Hacket spun round and lashed out, catching her with the back of his hand.

The blow was powerful enough to knock her off her feet and, as she fell to the floor, Hacket saw the ribbon of blood running from her bottom lip. She glared up at him then touched the bleeding cleft which was already beginning to swell up. She looked at the blood on her fingers and her eyes narrowed.

'Get out you fucker,' she hissed. 'Go on,' the last two words were shouted.

Hacket moved towards the door, pulled it open and

185

looked back at her. She still sat on the floor, legs curled up beneath her as she dabbed at her bottom lip with the end of her long T-shirt. Blood blossomed on the material. He hesitated a moment longer then walked out, slamming the door behind him.

He rode the lift to the ground floor and walked out into the chill night air, standing beside his car for a moment, looking up at the window of Nikki's flat. Then he slid behind the wheel, twisted the key in the ignition and drove off, glimpsing the block of flats in his rear view mirror. Then he turned a corner and it was gone.

Out of sight, out of mind, he thought, wondering why that particular cliché had come into his head.

He wondered if it would be as easy to forget Nikki.

Forty-four

She knew she was going to be sick.

She knew it and, what was worse, she knew there was nothing she could do to stop herself. Amanda Riley gripped the edge of the sink, ducked low over the porcelain and vomited. As she stepped back, moaning, she almost over-balanced. It felt as if the floor was moving beneath her although she couldn't be sure if that apparent undulation was due to her own inebriation or the pounding of the music from downstairs.

She ran the taps, washing the mess from the sink, glancing at her own haggard reflection in the mirror. She groaned again as she caught sight of the apparition which stared back at her. Pale skinned, eyes black from too much smudged

186

mascara. Her hair, so carefully prepared before the party, now hung limply around her face. There were stains on her red blouse and also on her tight white skirt. She shook her head but even that minor act of disapproval caused her to reel once more. She had no idea how much she'd drunk, or even what she'd drunk. The party had begun four or five hours ago, she thought, but now she wasn't even sure of the time. Amanda glanced at her watch but it seemed to dissolve before her eyes. Her drink-clouded vision refused to clear and she sat down heavily on the toilet seat, feeling the vomit beginning its upward journey for the second time that night. She clenched her teeth together and the feeling passed momentarily. It felt as if her head was spinning around on her neck like some bizarre kind of top. She gripped the edge of the toilet seat for fear of falling off.

Amanda was beginning to wish she had never agreed to come to the party. She didn't like loud music, she didn't know many of the other guests and, ordinarily, she didn't drink much. Perhaps someone had spiked her drink, she pondered, rubbing her stomach with one shaking hand. Whatever the answer was she knew she couldn't stand another night of this purgatory. She felt her stomach contract suddenly, struggling to her feet just in time to reach the sink. She hung over it, waiting for the inevitable but the spasms passed and she began to straighten up. Again she caught sight of her reflection. God, she thought. She looked about fifty instead of nineteen.

There was a bang on the bathroom door.

'Amanda.'

She barely recognised the voice.

'Amanda. Are you all right?'

She blinked hard, trying to clear not only her vision but her head too.

Outside the door, Tracy Grant exhaled wearily and banged once more. She was beginning to wish she hadn't invited Amanda. If she threw up on any of the carpets there would be hell to pay. If her parents discovered she'd had the party in the first place while they were away for the weekend she'd be in big enough trouble but, if they came back to find puddles of puke everywhere then she may as well pack her bags and leave home. It would save them the bother of throwing her out. She banged again and repeated Amanda's name.

'Are you all right, I said?' she shouted, forced to raise her voice over the sound of the music thundering away downstairs.

There were a series of raucous cheers from below her and, despite her anger, she managed a smile as she heard the chugging rhythm of AC/DC's 'You shook me all Night long' and realised that her brother was more than likely engaged in his duckwalk dance.

Tracy heard the sound of a bolt being slid back and the door opened.

'You look awful,' she said as she saw Amanda swaying uncertainly before her.

'I *feel* awful,' the other girl told her. 'I'm going home.' She took a step forward, almost overbalancing.

Tracy grabbed her.

'Not in that state you're not,' she snapped. 'What have you been drinking anyway?'

Amanda could only shrug.

'I'll get Carl to drive you home,' Tracy told her. 'He's about the only one who's still sober.' She snaked an arm around Amanda's waist and the two of them struggled down the stairs. As they got to the hallway Amanda clenched her teeth together once more and put a hand to her mouth.

Tracy muttered something under her breath and dashed to the front door, pulling it open in time to allow Amanda to get her head out and retch violently into a rhododendron bush which Tracy's father had so carefully nurtured.

'You stay there,' said Tracy irritably and stalked off into the sitting room where the music was reaching ever more deafening proportions. Amanda gripped the door-frame as best she could, supporting herself while her stomach somersaulted, finding yet more fluid to expel should she lose control. A moment or two later Tracy returned with a tall youth in his early twenties, his face pitted around the chin from the ravages of acne. But, apart from that he had strong features and piercing green eyes which immediately focused on Amanda's backside and legs. He smiled appreciatively.

'Carl's going to drive you home,' Tracy announced.

'I don't want her throwing up in my car,' Carl Dennison said, suddenly realising the state of his intended passenger.

'Drive with the window open,' Tracy snapped, supporting Amanda with both arms as Carl scuttled along the path to his waiting Capri. He'd bought it off a friend about a week ago and the last thing he wanted was some boozed up bitch spewing up all over his mock-tigerskin seats. Still, he thought as he looked more closely at his drunken passenger, she should be all right until he got her home. It was after midnight, the roads in Hinkston would be quiet. He could make it in less than twenty minutes if he put his foot down. Carl slid behind the wheel and started the engine, glancing across at Amanda who had already wound down the window and was leaning out, trying to suck in lungfuls of air. As the car vibrated the girl felt her stomach turning more forcefully and, only by a monumental effort did she manage to retain its contents.

Carl drove off, seeing Tracy in the rear-view mirror. She stood there for a moment then disappeared back inside the house.

Carl looked across at Amanda who was groaning quietly as he drove. The wind was whistling through the open window, blowing her hair away from her face. She had her eyes closed. He took his eye off the road momentarily to

189

glance down at her legs. She'd kicked off her high heels and one leg was drawn up beneath her on the seat. Carl turned a corner, saw that the road was deserted and slowed down slightly.

As the needle on the speedometer dropped to below thirty he reached across with his left hand and touched her knee, feeling the soft material of her stocking beneath his fingers. He grinned.

Amanda moaned and slapped feebly at his hand but there was no strength in the rebuff, she was more concerned with holding down her drink.

Carl's hand slid higher, towards her thigh.

She mumbled something and drew her head back inside the car for a second, glancing wearily at him.

He withdrew his hand, aware of the erection which was beginning to uncoil inside his jeans, pushing painfully against the denim as it became harder.

As Amanda put her head back out of the window he let his hand slip back onto her thigh, but, this time, he pushed it higher, allowing his fingers to brush against the sleek material of her panties.

Again she tried to slap his hand away but this time he hooked two fingers into the top of her knickers, feeling her tightly curled pubic hairs. Amanda shook her head.

Carl smiled triumphantly and pulled his hand away just long enough to unzip his own jeans and pull out his erection. He grabbed her right hand and wrapped the limp fingers around his stiff shaft. What the hell, she was so pissed she wouldn't even remember what she'd done in the morning.

She pulled her hand away but he closed his own over it, forcing her back to his penis, guiding her, using her to masturbate him.

Amanda grunted in disapproval, not sure whether she was more disturbed by the vomit rising in her throat or the fact that she was an unwilling partner to Carl's approaching gratification. She turned in her seat, her hand still clasped around his shaft, his own fist wrapped around hers moving it rhythmically.

'Go on, do it,' he urged, his breathing now becoming more heavy. He was staring ahead at the empty road, aware of the sensations building in his groin.

Amanda finally lost her battle.

She leaned towards Carl and vomited into his lap.

He yelled in rage and disgust as his jeans, the car seat and his throbbing penis were all covered in the copious regurgitation.

He slammed on the brake and leant across, pushing open the car door, digging his elbow into Amanda's side, shoving her from the seat.

She fell heavily onto the grass verge at the roadside and Carl himself felt his stomach spinning as the stench of her vomit filled his nostrils. It covered him like a sticky yellow blanket.

He shouted something at her then drove off, leaving her lying on the damp grass.

Amanda tried to rise, tried to call him back but her protests dissolved into a flood of tears. She thought she was going to be sick again but the feeling passed. Finally she managed to rise, aware that her shoes were still in the car, now disappeared into the night. She felt the dampness soaking through her stockings as she walked.

She had no idea where she was, not even which part of Hinkston. There was a garage about a hundred yards down the road, the forecourt in darkness. But, beyond it there were houses. If she could reach one of those she could use a phone, call her parents. They'd be mad at her. Furious. But she didn't care. She just wanted to get home to bed, to drift off to sleep and shut out this terrible feeling once and for all. Amanda began to walk, her gait shambling, as if her legs would not obey her brain. Twice she stumbled, almost falling. The second time she fell against a hedge, the leafless twigs snagging her stockings and scratching her skin. She moaned, her head still spinning, her plight, it seemed, intensified by the chill night air. She felt as if her head had been stuffed with cotton wool.

She glanced towards the petrol station again and something caught her eye.

A figure moved on the forecourt.

Perhaps it was someone walking their dog. Someone who could help her. She tried to quicken her pace.

The figure stepped back into the shadows at the side of the main building and disappeared.

A second later she saw car headlights lancing through the blackness. The vehicle swung out of the forecourt turned and moved unhurriedly towards her.

It slowed down as it drew level with her then it stopped, the engine idling.

Amanda couldn't see the driver, he was hidden by the gloom inside the vehicle.

She staggered towards it, both surprised and relieved when the passenger side door was pushed open as if to welcome her.

'Help me please,' she slurred, fighting back the nausea as she stuck her head inside the car.

The stench in there almost cleared her head.

She jerked upright still unable to see the driver, appalled by the smell, aware that it was going to make her vomit.

She tried to step back but a hand shot forward and clamped across her mouth, forcing back both the seething hot bile and her scream.

The long, double-edged stiletto blade darted forward and buried itself in her right eye.

Amanda was dragged into the car, the door slammed behind her.

192

The car moved away, the driver indicating thoughtfully as he turned a corner. Only then did he speed up.

Forty-five

She heard the thunderous blows on the front door as he tried to batter his way in.

Sue Hacket stood in the hallway for long seconds, mesmerised by the incessant pounding, her eyes fixed on the door which seemed to bow inward an inch or two with each successive impact.

Another second and he would be through.

She thought about screaming but realised that it would do no good. The house stood at least thirty yards from its closest neighbour, even if they should hear her cry for help it was doubtful if they would reach her in time.

He was nearly through the door.

Perhaps they had heard the banging, perhaps the police were already on the way.

Perhaps . . .

Sue spun round and caught sight of the phone on the stand behind her.

The thunderous blows on the front door seemed to increase and her eyes widened in horror as she saw the first split appear in the wood. It zig-zagged across the paintwork like a crack in a sheet of ice.

If she could reach the phone. Call the police.

Would they arrive before he got in?

Before he reached her?

She had one hand on the phone when one panel of the door was smashed inwards.

Sue screamed, dropped the phone and hurtled up the stairs as fast as she could, stumbling on the fifth step. She whimpered under her breath, glancing around to see his hand reaching through the pulverised wood, feeling for the lock and chain which secured the door.

He freed it and kicked the door open.

Sue screamed again and hauled herself upright, running for the landing, towards the bedroom as she heard him career into the sitting room. Then out into the hall once more, his footfalls pounding on the stairs.

She slammed the bedroom door and stood with her back against it, her breath coming in gasps.

He would find her.

He didn't even need to hurry. There were only four rooms on the first floor of the house. He would be able to move at will from one to the other until he found her and then she knew what would happen.

Just like the woman who had lived in this house before her she would die.

Slaughtered like an animal by the man who supposedly loved her.

The last occupant of the house had been a schoolteacher just as the new occupant was. Only this new occupant was her own husband.

It was John Hacket who prowled the landing stealthily, the double-barrelled shotgun gripped in his bloodied hands.

She heard him kick open the door of the bathroom, then the other two bedrooms.

She heard the creak of the floorboards as he stood outside the room where she hid. There was only three inches of wood between her and her husband.

Her and the shotgun.

Sue crossed to the window and tried to open it but the

194

old sash frame had been painted over and the emulsion secured it as if it had been nailed shut. Through the glass she could see the school beyond, its tall buildings rising into the night sky as if supporting the low clouds.

Hacket drove his foot against the door and the hinges groaned protestingly.

Sue spun round, knowing there was nowhere else to run. Knowing that this was the end.

She had just one comforting thought.

She would soon be with Lisa again.

Strange how, when death is near, the human mind clutches at even the most ridiculous notions to ease its fear.

Hacket roared with rage and drove his shoulder against the door.

It swung back, slamming into the wall and he stepped across the threshold, raising the shotgun to his shoulder, aiming at her head.

He was smiling.

Sue screamed.

Hacket fired and the scream was lost in a deafening crescendo of blazing lead as both barrels flamed.

The scream catapulted her from the nightmare.

She sat bolt upright in bed, perspiration covering her like a translucent shroud.

In the darkness of the bedroom she blinked, trying to readjust to the gloom, to push the nightmare from her mind, not sure for fleeting seconds what was real and what was a residue of the dream.

Like the figure which stood at the foot of her bed.

She blinked, expecting it to vanish.

It didn't.

Standing at the bottom of her bed, his eyes pinning her in an unblinking stare, stood six-year-old Craig Clayton. His body was quivering from head to foot.

Forty-six

Sue looked at the child through the darkness, barely able to make out his features, illuminated as they were by the thin shaft of light from the landing.

He seemed to be swaying gently back and forth at the bottom of the bed but, throughout the strange motions, his eyes never left her.

She pulled the sheet around her, aware of her nakedness and strangely uncomfortable beneath the unflinching stare of the boy.

'Craig?' she said, softly, as if trying to break his fixed concentration. To distract him from that piercing stare. He seemed almost trance-like.

She pulled her house-coat on hurriedly and swung herself out of bed, blinking hard to clear her vision.

As she approached him the door of her bedroom opened and Julie walked in.

Sue saw the look of shock on her sister's face as she looked at the boy and she motioned for Sue to stay back.

'I thought I heard him get up,' Julie said.

'When I woke up he was just standing there,' Sue explained.

'Come on, Craig,' Julie said, sternly, taking the boy by the shoulders as if to drag him forcibly from the room. 'You've disturbed your auntie now.'

'He didn't disturb me . . .' Sue began but then hurriedly closed her mouth as Julie shot her a withering glance.

'Craig, come on. Back to bed,' Julie snapped, pulling him with even greater urgency.

The boy wouldn't move. He shook loose from Julie's grip, his eyes never leaving Sue.

'Is he all right, Julie?' she asked, seeing the boy's expression darken.

Julie didn't answer, she merely gripped the boy by the shoulders and pulled.

He tore himself free of her hold, spun round and punched her in the side, his eyes blazing.

Sue looked on in shocked dismay.

'You'll have to help me,' Julie gasped, making another grab for the boy who was now facing his mother, his hands twisted into claws, as if ready to strike at her should she try to touch him again. Julie moved forward and Craig backed off, his back touching the wall. He glanced at the two women and Sue almost recoiled from what looked like pure hatred in those eyes.

'Mike, come here,' Julie shouted, rousing her husband.

She lunged forward and grabbed Craig, holding one of his wrists, but he gripped her hand, tugging at the skin on the back of it until his nails drew blood. Julie yelped in pain and withdrew her hand, the bloody furrows weeping red fluid onto the carpet. He looked at Sue as if daring her to approach him. She could see the first clear dribblings of sputum beginning to seep through his clenched teeth.

Mike Clayton entered the room, pushing past the two women, making straight for the boy, a look of determination on his face.

'Come on,' he snarled, grabbing Craig around the waist, lifting him into the air.

The boy writhed madly in his father's grip, trying to shake himself free, scratching at Mike's face.

'Get the doctor, now,' Mike hissed, struggling back through the door with the boy. 'Do it,' he snapped as Julie hesitated.

Sue, still bewildered by the tableau, followed Mike and his maddened son out onto the landing. Julie scuttled downstairs to the phone and frantically jabbed out the number, glancing behind her to see Mike carry the boy into his bedroom.

197

Watched by Sue, he threw the boy onto the bed then leapt on beside him, pinning the boy's arms to the mattress, using all his superior strength to prevent his son from moving.

The boy hawked loudly and spat into Mike's face.

Sue put a hand to her mouth, watching as the mucus dripped from Mike's cheek like a thick tear. But he didn't attempt to wipe it away, he seemed too concerned with restraining his son. The boy continued to twist and turn like an eel on a hot skillet.

'The doctor's coming,' shouted Julie, making her way back up the stairs, pushing past Sue, who could only look on in bewilderment.

'I hope to God he's quick,' Mike rasped. 'I can't hold him for much longer.'

Craig seemed to have found an energy and strength quite disproportionate to his age and size. A strength which took every ounce of his father's muscle to hold him down. Sue saw the veins standing out on Mike's forehead as he struggled to keep the boy pinned down.

Julie ushered her out of the room.

'There's nothing we can do until the doctor gets here,' she said, her face ashen.

'Whatever's wrong with him, Julie?' Sue asked, a note of fear in her voice. 'Is it some kind of epileptic fit?'

'Yes, that's right,' Julie said. 'A fit. He doesn't get them very often. I've never mentioned them to you. We thought he'd grow out of them.'

'But he's so strong.'

'He'll be all right when the doctor gets here,' Julie said, dismissing the observation.

Sue was about to speak again when she heard a deafening shout from the bedroom.

From Craig.

She felt the hairs on the back of her neck rise.

She felt suddenly afraid.

Forty-seven

The needle came free and Curtis quickly wiped the puncture in the crook of Craig's arm with a swab, pressing the pad of cotton wool to the tiny hole for a second.

The boy winced and moaned slightly but Curtis merely pressed the palm of his right hand to the child's forehead. He could feel beads of perspiration there but at least the spasms had stopped. Craig let out an exhausted sigh and his whole body seemed to go limp. Curtis covered him with a sheet, watching the steady rise and fall of his chest.

Mike Clayton looked down at his son then glanced at the doctor who had slipped the hypodermic back into his bag.

'Will he be all right now, doctor?' Mike asked.

Curtis nodded slowly and headed for the door.

'We've heard things,' Mike continued, falteringly. 'Rumours. About the others.'

Curtis turned and looked at him, expressionless.

Mike swallowed hard, as if intimidated by the doctor's unfaltering stare.

'What's been happening to them?' Mike asked.

'I don't discuss other patients, Mr Clayton,' Curtis said, dismissively. 'Your sister-in-law, does she know about the boy?' He nodded in Craig's direction.

'No,' Mike said, hastily. 'She saw what happened tonight. We found him in her room.'

Curtis shot the other man a worried glance.

'Nothing had happened,' he reassured the doctor. 'Julie

told her he suffered from epileptic fits. I think she believed it.'

'Good.'

He made for the landing, followed by Mike. They both descended the stairs, the doctor heading for the sitting room where Julie and Sue sat sipping cups of tea.

Julie stood up as Curtis entered but he motioned for her to sit once more.

'Is Craig all right?' she asked.

'He's fine. He's sleeping now.'

Julie looked relieved.

Curtis glanced at Sue and smiled and she returned the gesture, struck by the firmness of his features, the intensity of his eyes. Despite the late hour he looked perfectly groomed, as if he'd come from a dinner-dance instead of having been dragged from his bed by the emergency call. Julie performed a quick introduction and Curtis shook hands with Sue, gripping her hand in his own. She felt a pleasing mixture of strength and warmth there. She looked at him as he sat down, grateful for the cup of tea which Julie offered him. He seemed relaxed, almost at home in the sitting room. As if he'd visited it many times before.

'Do you live in Hinkston, Mrs Hacket?' Curtis asked.

Sue shook her head, unable to take her eyes from Curtis, her mind relaying facts back and forth as she tried to estimate his age.

'Not yet,' she said. 'We . . . I have a house in London but I'll probably be living in Hinkston soon.'

'Any family of your own? I see you're married,' he smiled and nodded towards her wedding ring.

'No,' she said, quickly. For fleeting seconds it occurred to her to mention Lisa but the memory was painful enough locked away inside her mind without exposing it to conversation. She contented herself with a sip of her tea.

'If you don't mind me saying, Mrs Hacket, you look a

200

little pale.' Curtis chuckled. 'An occupational hazard of being a doctor I'm afraid, I see everyone as a potential patient.'

Sue smiled too.

'I haven't been sleeping very well lately,' she told him.

'Well, if you do move to Hinkston then please feel free to come and see me. Your sister has the address of my surgery. Whereabouts in the town are you moving to?'

'My husband's a teacher. He's due to start work next week at the Junior school about half a mile from the town centre. You know the one? There's a house next to the school, it comes with the job.'

Curtis nodded slowly, his expression darkening slightly.

'I know the one,' he said, quietly. 'Well, the best of luck with your move.' He finished his tea quickly, as if the hospitality of the Clayton's was suddenly something he wished to be away from. He got to his feet and headed for the sitting room door.

'Don't forget, Mrs Hacket,' he said. 'Come and see me.'

'I will,' she assured him.

Julie and Mike followed him out into the hall.

'Thank you,' Julie said as he stepped out onto the front porch.

'Be careful,' Curtis said, looking at each of them in turn. 'Watch the boy closely for the next two or three days. Get in touch with me immediately if he suffers anything *like* a relapse. We were lucky this time.' He turned and strode off down the path towards his car, watched by the Claytons, who waited until he'd driven off before stepping back into their house and shutting the door.

Sue finished her tea then announced that she was going to bed. She left Julie and Mike sitting downstairs.

As she reached the landing she paused by the door to Craig's room. Hearing nothing she pushed the door slightly and peered in.

The boy was sleeping, his face peaceful. A marked contrast to the twisted mask which it had become only thirty minutes earlier. Sue closed the door and wandered across to her bedroom where she slipped off her house coat and climbed into bed.

As she lay there in the gloom she gazed up at the ceiling, waiting for sleep to come but knowing that it would not. She heard Curtis's voice inside her head.

'Come and see me'

She closed her eyes, seeing his face more clearly, remembering that mixture of warmth and strength in his grip. The penetrative stare.

Sue allowed one hand to slip beneath the quilt, to glide across her breast, the nipple already stiff and swollen. It was joined by her other hand which she pushed with exquisite slowness over her flat belly and into the tightly curled triangle of hair between her legs, her index finger probing more deeply until she found the bud of her clitoris. She began to stroke it gently, the moisture between her thighs increasing.

'Come and see me.'

She pushed one finger into her slippery cleft, her eyes closed now, the vision of Curtis' face filling her mind.

'Come and see me.'

Forty-eight

He had killed Hacket's daughter and now he would kill Hacket.

Ronald Mills had decided on his course of action with

ease. Ever since he'd seen Hacket pursue Peter Walton through the streets of London, ever since he'd seen his friend fall onto the tracks of the tube train. Mills had watched it all.

An eye for an eye, they called it. His mother had told him that came from the Bible. His mother had always quoted him lines from the Bible, and most of them he'd remembered. Like the one about suffer little children.

Mills chuckled.

God wanted little children to suffer did he? Well, if that was the case then God would love Ronald Mills. God would have looked down on him and Lisa Hacket that night and he would have smiled. He would have seen Mills clamp one hand across the little girl's mouth as he cut away her nightdress with the point of his knife. He would have watched it all. Watched as Mills climbed onto the bed beside her and unzipped his trousers.

Suffer little children.

Afterwards God would have watched as Mills cut the child repeatedly. He used the knife with almost surgical skill, pushing it easily through her flesh until the bed was soaked in blood, until she stopped writhing beneath him, until his penis was hard with lust again and he penetrated her warm but lifeless form for the second time that night.

Mills giggled again and inspected his hands. They were rough, calloused. The left one still bore the remnants of a tattoo but it hadn't taken properly and the skin had turned septic. In place of a snake coiled around a knife blade Mills sported a scab curled around a septic boil. He picked at the scab, pulling some pieces of hardened flesh off.

Mills and Walton had lived in the flat in Brixton for the last ten months. Neither of them had a job but they had made a living dealing in various illegal practices. Mills in particular had found a lucrative market in child pornography. He had become friendly with a couple of dealers and this little sideline had the added bonus of pandering to his own tastes too.

Walton had worked as a pusher around King's Cross, even done a little pimping.

It was on those proceeds that they'd bought the gun.

It was a .38 Smith and Wesson revolver and Mills gently stroked the four-inch barrel as he sat at the table occasionally glancing at the brown mess on his plate which, according to the box, was liver and onion. It certainly didn't look like the picture on the box. In fact, it looked as if someone had defecated on his plate. He prodded the cold food with the barrel of the pistol then wiped it on the makeshift tablecloth. Piled up on the other side of the table were some of the magazines he'd been intending to sell the following day. Every one featured photos of children, some as young as two years, engaged in various acts with both men *and* women. He had heard that one of his dealers could get hold of stuff which actually showed men and babies. Real, new born babies.

Mills smiled again, the stirring in his groin becoming more pronounced.

Suffer little children.

He picked up one of the magazines and leafed through it, his thick lips sliding back as he surveyed the pictures. Many were bad quality, grainy black and white shots taken by amateurs. Probably by those who participated, thought Mills, his erection now pressing uncomfortably against his trousers. But they served their purpose. He finished looking through the magazine and dropped it back onto the pile, picking up the gun again, turning the empty cylinder, thumbing the hammer back then squeezing the trigger.

The metallic click echoed around the small flat.

It had been lonely since Walton's death. Mills didn't enjoy being alone. Apart from Walton he had no friends and he felt as if Hacket had taken from him the one person he really cared about.

He would make him suffer for that.

As he'd made his daughter suffer.

Suffer little children.

God would be watching him again. God was on his side.

He would kill Hacket and God would be pleased with him for upholding his word.

Mills raised the gun and sighted it, thumbing back the hammer again.

'An eye for an eye,' he said, smiling.

Forty-nine

Birth, marriage and moving house.

Hacket was sure that was how the cliché went. They were the three most traumatic things in life. As he sat in the sitting room of the house, perched on one of the many packing cases that filled the place like an oversized child's building bricks he'd come to the conclusion that the former two paled into insignificance alongside the third. It had taken him more than three days to pack the cases, working for anything up to fifteen hours a day. Well, he had nothing else to do. It was better than sitting around in the old house with just memories for company. At least he didn't have to worry about selling the house in London before he could move into the one next to the school. No chain, no mortgage worries. The rent for the house was deducted from his salary every month. Once the house in London was sold the money would be straight profit. It was an enticing prospect.

The thought of the money together with the possibility of starting afresh should have left Hacket feeling elated but, as it was, he sat wearily on the packing case, holding a mug of tea and staring around the room his thoughts jumbled and confused.

He thought about Lisa.

About the deaths that had occurred in *this* house.

From one place of pain to another.

There was always pain.

And he thought about Sue.

He'd called her the previous night to let her know roughly what time he and the accumulated trophies of their life would be arriving but so far she had not turned up. He was beginning to wonder if she would. There was a phone box just across the street. Hacket glanced at his watch, decided to give it another fifteen minutes, then call her.

There was a knock on the door and the teacher jumped down from the box and hurried to the front door, a smile already beginning to form on his lips.

At last, now he wouldn't need to call her.

He felt his spirits lift as he fumbled with the catch.

Donald Brooks stood on the doorstep, immaculate as ever apart from the flakes of dandruff on his collar. The headmaster smiled at Hacket who just about managed to return the gesture, fighting to keep the disappointment from his face.

'Glad to see you arrived safely, Mr Hacket,' said Brooks. 'I won't come in. I just thought I'd say welcome and that I hope you'll be happy in your new home. You and your wife.'

'Thanks,' murmured Hacket, almost grudgingly.

'What does your wife think of the house?'

'She likes it.

'I won't disturb her, I'm sure she's busy unpacking. I'll go now. I look forward to seeing you on Monday morning.'

Hacket nodded and closed the door as the headmaster walked back up the path. The teacher sighed and wandered back into the sitting room. Perhaps he should phone Sue now. He glanced at his watch again. Give it another five minutes? He drummed agitatedly on the top of the nearest crate then the front door bell sounded again. This time he moved with less speed, pulling the door open wearily.

Sue smiled thinly as she saw his face.

'I was going to call you,' he beamed, stepping aside to allow her in.

She stepped over the threshold almost hesitantly, moving through into the sitting room, glancing around at the crates and packing cases.

'We'd better get started,' she said, rolling up the sleeves of her sweatshirt.

They worked in separate rooms, pulling the lids from the boxes and crates, unwrapping the contents as if they were Christmas presents. Sue worked in the kitchen while Hacket attended to the sitting room. He had ensured that the stereo was not left to the tender attentions of the removal men. He had transported that particular item himself on the back seat of the car. It had been the first thing he'd rigged up before unpacking and music filled the house as they worked.

Hacket had no idea of the time, surrounded by empty and half-empty packing cases, his ears filled with the music, his thoughts wandering aimlessly. He wiped his hands on his jeans and wandered across to the stereo, flipping the record before continuing his task.

Sue appeared in the doorway, her sweatshirt and jeans also covered by a thin film of dust. She had some dirt on one cheek and Hacket crossed to her to wipe it away.

She smiled thinly but pulled away and completed the task herself.

'There's a cup of tea in the kitchen,' she told him and walked across the hall.

'. . . *But it was only fantasy. The wall was too high as you can see..*'

sang Roger Waters from behind him.

Hacket wiped his hands again and wandered into the kitchen. He sat down opposite Sue and picked up his mug of tea.

'I've just about finished in here,' she told him. 'I'll do upstairs next.'

'There's no rush,' he told her. 'We've got plenty of time.'

'I want to get it finished, John. I don't want the house looking like a bomb site for too long.'

He nodded.

'Do you remember the first place we ever moved in to?' Hacket asked, a thin smile on his face.

She raised her eyebrows.

'The flat. Trying to lug furniture up three flights of stairs past the snooker hall, wondering if the blokes inside were going to rob us as soon as we got settled in.' She almost laughed. Almost.

'Listening to them playing bloody snooker all night. It kept us awake at the beginning didn't it.'

'As I remember we didn't mind being kept awake.'

Hacket smiled.

'It was a nice place,' he said.

'Apart from the noise,' she added.

'And the damp.'

'And the cold.'

'Yeah, a great place.' He chuckled. 'It doesn't seem like six years since we left there.' He put down his tea. 'Unpacking today it made me think about the flat, about our first place. It could be like that again, Sue. This house is new. Things don't have to change.'

'They already have changed, John. *We've* changed. Circumstances have changed. It can never be the same between us.' There was an appalling finality in her voice. 'I still love you but a part of that love died with Lisa. Because her death could have been avoided.'

'I don't need reminding, Sue. Do you think there's a day goes by that I don't think about her? About what might have been? I made a mistake and I'm sorry. God knows I'm sorry. Sorry for the affair, sorry for Lisa's death, sorry for the way I hurt you and damaged our relationship. I know I can't put those things right and I don't expect you to forget. But if you could find a little bit of forgiveness, Sue . . .' He allowed the sentence to trail off.

She took a sip of her own tea and shivered slightly.

'I feel cold,' she said. 'Is the heating on?'

Hacket sighed wearily.

'I'll check it when I've finished my tea.'

She got to her feet and headed out of the kitchen. He heard her footfalls on the stairs.

'Shit,' he murmured, also getting to his feet. He wandered back into the sitting room to be greeted by the music once more.

He began opening another case, noticing that there were several photos laid on the top of the other items. Framed pictures. He unwrapped the first of them and found that it was a photo of Lisa. Hacket smiled and set it down beside him, reaching for the next one. It was Sue, dressed in a low-cut black dress, taken about a year ago at a party. She looked stunning.

The music behind him was building to a crescendo.

He took out the last photo.

A young couple on it happy and smiling.

Their wedding photo.

209

'. . . . *When I was a child I caught a fleeting glimpse, out of the corner of my eye. I turned to look but it was gone, I cannot put my finger on it now.*.' Hacket frowned down at the picture. '*. . . The child has grown, the dream is gone . . .* '

The glass had shattered, two long thin shards had cut deep into the picture.

Fifty

She didn't know how long she'd been lying there listening to the slow, steady breathing of Hacket and the monotonously regular ticking of the clock. All Sue did know was that she was no closer to sleep now than when she'd first slid between the covers. It had been a tiring day, she had expected to be enveloped by sleep almost immediately, but it was not to be.

She lay still, hearing the house creak and groan as the timbers settled. After a moment or two of this she finally swung herself out of bed and crossed to the window, peering out into the darkness and the school beyond. She could just make out the shapes of the buildings in the gloom and she pressed her hands to the radiator, aware of a chill which had settled upon her. She had pulled on her house coat as she slipped out of bed, but the chill was present nonetheless.

Behind her, Hacket stirred, his hand reaching across for her. He opened his eyes slowly when he could not feel her next to him. The teacher sat up and saw his wife gazing out into the night.

'Sue,' he said, softly. 'What's wrong?'

'I can't sleep, as usual,' she told him, still continuing with her vigil.

'Come back to bed,' he urged.

She finally relented, sliding in beside him.

'John, it's cold in this house,' she said. 'I know the heating is on. It isn't that kind of cold. It's . . . well . . . as if there was some kind of atmosphere because of what happened here.'

Hacket sighed.

'I know what you think about things like that,' she went on, 'the eternal sceptic – but I can't help it. I felt like that in our house after Lisa . . . They say houses carry a residue of sorrow don't they?'

'Do they?' Hacket said, a note of irritation in his voice. 'It sounds like a line from a bad romantic novel. I can't feel anything, Sue, honestly.'

She shivered again.

'Relax,' Hacket said, sliding closer to her.

She flinched almost imperceptibly as she felt his arm glide across her stomach, around her waist. He pulled her to him. As their bodies pressed together she felt the beginnings of an erection beginning to press into her thigh. Hacket kissed her gently on the lips, his shaft growing stiffer.

Sue tried to move away but he held her more tightly, his hand now straying to her breast which he squeezed, thumbing the nipple.

'Not now, John,' she said, gripping his wrist.

But Hacket would not release her. He tightened his hold on her breast, kneading the flesh so hard that she almost cried out from the sudden pain.

'John, please,' she snapped, again trying to squirm away from him.

'I want you, Sue,' he said, raising himself up on one

211

elbow. He straddled her, his erection pointing towards her face, his hands gripping her wrists, pinning her to the mattress. She struggled but could not move him.

'Get off me,' she shouted, angrily.

In one swift movement his hands had left her wrists and fastened around her throat.

Her eyes bulged as he began to squeeze, his thumbs digging into her flesh.

'I want you,' he breathed, squeezing more tightly.

She tried to swallow but couldn't. Her head felt as if it were swelling and, all the time, the pressure on her throat seemed to intensify. She looked up into his face, her eyes blurred with pain and fear. She felt her body beginning to spasm, the muscles contracting violently.

Sue tried to scream but his vice-like grip prevented that action.

She bucked beneath him, trying to dislodge him, already growing weak but, finally, with one last reserve of strength she brought her knee up into the small of his back.

The grip was released and, in that split second, she found the breath to scream.

Hacket twisted round in bed as he heard the scream.

He saw Sue sitting upright, massaging her throat, perspiration beaded on her forehead and upper lip.

'What's wrong?' he asked, shocked by her appearance. He put out a hand to touch her but she drew back, as if frightened of his touch.

Her breathing was harsh and rapid, her eyes bulging, glazed.

Only gradually did she regain her senses as the last vestiges of the dream faded.

It was then that she began to cry.

Fifty-one

He felt the gun in his pocket.

As Ronald Mills stood looking at the 'FOR SALE' sign outside the house he gently traced his fingers over the .38.

There were no lights on in the house. Perhaps Hacket was in bed, he reasoned. After all, it was past midnight.

Mills walked past the house on the far side of the road, reached the bottom of the street crossed then walked back again.

Should he just knock on the front door? Wait until Hacket opened it and shoot him down on the doorstep? It would be simple but hazardous. Although he doubted that he would be caught. God had views about revenge too, Mills remembered.

Vengeance is mine saith the Lord.

He smiled as he remembered the quote from the Bible.

God would not allow him to be caught, after all, he practically had God's blessing for what he was about to do.

He glanced behind him, noting that the street was empty. Mills paused a moment then walked up to the front door of the house.

He didn't knock. Instead he pushed the letter-box open and peered through into the gloom beyond. He could see and hear nothing.

He moved along the front of the house to the bay window. Cupping a hand against the glass he looked through.

The sitting room was empty.

Something finally clicked inside Mills' rather dull mind and he glanced again at the 'FOR SALE' sign. He hurried around the side of the house, down the passageway which he remembered so well. He smiled as he thought of his last journey along this cramped stone corridor.

Smiled at the recollection of finding the child inside the house.

This time, however, it was not to be.

He peered through the rear windows only to have what he'd already surmised confirmed. The place was empty. Quiet as a grave. He smiled thinly, amused at his joke but angry that Hacket was not there. Mills scuttled back up the passageway, his hand touching the revolver in his pocket once again. He had intended to press the barrel to Hacket's neck or to his stomach, make him die slowly. Even shoot his eyes out. But now he had been cheated.

And so had God.

God wanted him to take revenge for the death of Walton. He knew that. He was only upholding God's law by killing Hacket. *His Will be done*.

Mills headed for the street, stopping beneath the sign again. This time, however, he pulled a piece of paper and a pencil from his coat pocket. Resting the paper in the palm of his broad hand he wrote: JEFFERSON ESTATE AGENTS, then the phone number.

Hacket may have left the house but he could be traced, thought Mills.

This wasn't over yet.

Fifty-two

The sun was doing its best to force a path through the clouds and, every so often, a shaft of golden light would lance into the kitchen, bouncing off Hacket's knife as he ate.

Sue sat opposite him as he ate, chewing indifferently on a piece of toast. She dropped the bread and ran a hand through her hair.

Hacket saw how dark she was beneath the eyes.

'How are you feeling?' he asked.

'Tired,' she told him. 'I'm going to the doctor this morning, see if he can give me something to help me sleep.'

'Be careful,' he said, guardedly.

'Careful of what?' she asked.

'Doctors like to give out prescriptions for sleeping pills and drugs like that. It's easier than talking to the patient about their problems.'

'I'm not going to him to talk about my problems,' she said acidly.

'If you're not careful you'll need a shopping trolley to carry the tranquillisers and anti-depressants.'

'Have you got a better idea, John?' she snapped. 'It's all right for you. You start a new job today. I'm the one who's going to be stuck in a new house with nothing to think about but my problems.' She took a sip of her tea. 'I'm seeing the doctor and that's all there is to it.'

'All right, I'm sorry. I'm just suspicious of doctors, you know that.'

'Well this one is good. He's Julie's doctor. I met him the other evening.' She explained briefly about Curtis' visit to the Clayton's home, deciding not to expand on Craig's condition.

Hacket listened dutifully, nodding occasionally. When she'd finished he looked at his watch.

8.30 a.m.

'I'd better go,' he said, standing up.

'I'll finish tidying up the house when I get back,' Sue told him.

'There's no need. We can carry on tonight.'

'I need something to occupy me, John. Now, go on or

215

you'll be late.' She brushed a hair from his collar, looking into his eyes briefly.

'Wish me luck,' he said, hopefully.

She smiled.

'You don't need it.'

He kissed her lightly on the lips and headed for the front door. She heard it close behind him then sat down at the kitchen table again, finishing her tea. She washed up, listening to the increasingly loud noise coming from the playground just beyond the tall hedge at the bottom of their garden. Then when nine o'clock came she heard the bell sound and the noise receded into silence again. Sue dried her hands and moved into the hall. There she found the number she wanted, lifted the receiver and pressed the digits.

It was answered almost immediately.

'Hello. Yes, I'd like to make an appointment for this morning please,' she said. 'I'd like to see Doctor Curtis.'

Fifty-three

The match made a dull hissing sound as it was struck, the yellow flame billowing from its head.

Phillip Craven held it before him for a second, then slowly lowered it towards the boy spread-eagled across two desks.

The boy shook his head, staring up at Craven with pleading in his eyes, but the other lad was interested only in the match, which he now held close to the chest of his helpless companion.

Four children held Trevor Harvey down, making sure that he couldn't squirm away from the approaching flame as Craven waved it over his pale, white chest. He suddenly lowered it onto Trevor's left nipple and the boy shrieked loudly.

Craven and the others watched mesmerised as the delicate skin turned first pink then bright red under the fury of the heat. He held the match against Trevor's chest until it went out. Then he lit another.

And another.

He pressed both of them to Trevor's stomach this time, below his navel, watching as the skin rose in a red welt, already blistering.

Trevor didn't shout so loudly this time. He merely grunted and tried to pull away from the others who held him down.

'Oh come on, Harvey, scream for us,' said Craven, grinning.

The rest of the class, girls and boys, all the same age as Craven, looked on with the fascination most children of thirteen display toward the suffering of others. Most were glad they were not the one being burned but many looked on the whole tableau as a diverting exhibition and Craven as a master showman.

He lit three matches and pushed them towards Trevor's right eye.

The boy's eyelashes had actually begun to smoulder when a shout from outside the room caused him to withdraw the matches.

Another boy came dashing into the classroom, almost falling over in his haste to get behind his desk.

'He's coming,' he said, and the four holding Trevor also bolted for their own places leaving Trevor to ease himself off the desks. He swayed uncertainly for a minute then a rough push from Craven sent him crashing into a nearby chair. He sprawled on the floor amid the cheers and laughter of the other class members.

Hacket heard the rumpus as he strode up the corridor, finally finding the room he sought. He swept in, smiling, closing the door behind him.

'You are form 3A, yes?' he asked.

'Yes, sir,' they answered in unison.

Trevor sat hunched over his desk, his shirt still unbuttoned, his eye streaming from the effects of the match. Still, he thought, wistfully, it could have been much worse.

It could have been like it was last week.

Hacket introduced himself to the class, still smiling broadly, told them where he was from, what they could expect from *him* and what he expected of *them*. Finally he walked to the centre of the room and, standing in front of the blackboard, looked around at the expectant faces.

'I want to get to know all of you so could you each stand up in turn and tell me your names, please? We'll see how many I can remember.' He rubbed his hands together theatrically. The gesture was greeted by good-natured laughter.

One by one the class obeyed and Hacket eyed each member. There were less than twenty of them, mostly sat in groups, apart from Trevor who sat alone at the front of the class, his head still bowed.

The list of names grew until there were just a couple left.

'Phillip Craven, sir.'

The boy sat down.

Hacket snapped his fingers, the name ringing bells of recognition in the back of his mind.

'The artist,' he said, smiling.

Craven looked bemused.

'I saw your painting in the annexe outside the headmaster's office. The one of the owl. It is you isn't it? There aren't *two* Phillip Cravens in the school?'

218

The rest of the class laughed, Craven turned scarlet and smiled.

'I was very impressed with the painting. A bit gory though, as I remember.'

'Life isn't always pretty, sir,' said Craven, his smile fading slightly.

'A philosopher too?' Hacket mused.

He looked at the last boy in the class. Trevor remained seated, his head still bowed.

'Your turn,' Hacket said.

The boy looked up at him but didn't move.

This one is either the comedian or the trouble-maker, Hacket thought. There was one in every class.

'Just stand up and tell me your name, please. It's quite simple.' He smiled.

'So is he, sir,' said Craven and the rest of the class laughed.

Hacket looked around at them and the noise died away.

Trevor rose slowly to his feet, his shirt undone, his hair untidy. There were stains around his crotch and, even from a couple of feet away Hacket could smell the odour of stale urine. The boy was a mess.

'What's your name, son?' the teacher asked.

'Trevor Harvey, sir,' he mumbled.

Hacket didn't hear and Trevor repeated himself.

'He's the village idiot, sir,' Craven called and the class broke out into a chorus of laughs and jeers once more.

'That's enough, Craven.' Then, to Trevor: 'All right, sit down.'

As the boy did so his shirt billowed open and Hacket winced as he caught sight of the red and pink welts on his skin. Some were purple, where scabs had formed over wounds only to be scratched off once more. He saw bruises too, and some cuts.

'What happened to you?' Hacket asked, shocked by the boys appearance.

'Nothing, sir,' said Trevor, trying to button his shirt. But Hacket stopped him, inspecting a burn on his chest more closely.

'Who did this?'

Silence had descended like an invisible blanket, all eyes on the teacher and the boy.

'Trevor, tell me who did this to you,' Hacket said, quietly.

The teacher caught a slight movement out of his eye corner, just enough to see Craven hurl a large eraser. It struck Trevor in the face but he didn't react, merely sat down.

Hacket spun round and glared at Craven.

'What do you think you're doing, Craven?' he snarled, angered by the look of defiance on the boy's face. 'Do you know anything about Trevor's injuries?'

'Why should I, sir?' the boy said. 'He probably did them himself and he's too stupid to remember.'

Trevor was busily buttoning his shirt.

Hacket looked at both boys in turn, aware still of the slight smirk on Craven's face. He held the boys's stare, a little unsettled when the youth didn't look away.

'This isn't a very auspicious start to things is it, Craven?' he said.

'I'll try to do better next time, sir,' the boy said.

Hacket nodded slowly then glanced at Trevor once more.

'Are you OK? Do you want to visit the nurse, get those wounds looked at?'

Trevor shook his head, pushing some strands of hair from his face.

Hacket glanced around the class once more then picked up the chalk and began writing on the blackboard.

The bell was the signal for a mass exodus from the class-room. Hacket dismissed the children, watching as they trooped past him. Craven avoided eye-contact this time as he passed.

Trevor was the last to leave, wiping his nose with the back of his hand.

'Trevor, wait a minute,' Hacket called.

The boy hesitated but didn't turn.

'Listen to me,' the teacher said, quietly. 'Those marks on your body. If you want to tell me who did it, if you want to talk to me then you know where to find me. Do you understand?'

Trevor nodded and sniffed back some more mucus. Then he turned and headed for the door, closing it behind him.

Carter exhaled deeply and wiped chalk dust from his hands.

As he looked up he saw Craven's face peering at him through the classroom window.

The boy was smiling.

Fifty-four

Gravel crunched beneath the wheels of the Metro as Sue Hacket brought the car to a halt. She switched off the engine and looked up at the house which towered over her like some kind of ivy-covered giant. It certainly looked more imposing than the usual doctor's surgery, she thought, as she climbed out of the car. The leaded windows and the hanging baskets which adorned the oak front door made the place look more like a country hotel than a place of healing. She wondered how much it must be worth, set, as it was, in about half an acre of its own grounds. Separated by wide lawns and immaculate hedges from the main road which led into Hinkston. Private medicine obviously *did* have its advantages for those who practised it, she mused.

The large oak door opened easily when she pushed it and Sue stepped into what looked like a hallway. To her left was a dark wood door, to her left a white one marked 'SURGERY'. She walked in.

The waiting room was empty apart from the receptionist who smiled with genuine warmth, and not the practised response which Sue had seen so many times before in women of the same profession.

They exchanged pleasantries and Sue gave her name then was told that doctor Curtis would be able to see her in a minute or two. He, she was informed, would complete a form with her help in order to register her as a patient.

The door behind the receptionist opened and Curtis appeared.

He smiled at Sue and beckoned her through.

Once inside the surgery Curtis sat down behind his desk and invited Sue to take a seat opposite. She slipped off her jacket and draped it over the back of the chair.

Curtis smiled at her once more and, again, Sue was aware of the combination of strength and warmth which flowed from his gaze. She looked at him, not wanting to make it too obvious that she was taking in details of his appearance. As with their first meeting she was struck by the youthfulness of his features. His smile was reassuring. Inviting even. As he folded his hands across his lap she noted how powerful his hands were, his fingers long and slender, the backs of his hands covered by thick dark hair. There was more than the power of a healer in them she thought.

Sue felt strangely light-headed, as if being with Curtis

were somehow intoxicating, his very presence a kind of drug.

An aphrodisiac?

She was aware that her nipples were beginning to stiffen. A welcome warmth began to spread between her legs as she continued to look at Curtis.

She tried to control the feelings, both puzzled and . . .

And what? Ashamed?

'Would you like a coffee while we talk?' asked Curtis.

'What about your other patients?' she asked.

'I don't have another appointment for an hour. That's one of the advantages I have over the National Health Service. I don't have twenty appointments an hour.' He smiled and buzzed through to the receptionist on the intercom.

'I'll just have to take some personal details if you don't mind,' Curtis informed her. 'Date of birth, medical history. That kind of thing.' He smiled that hypnotic smile once again and Sue answered his questions. The coffee arrived and the receptionist retreated back to the waiting room. Sue sipped from the bone china cup, watching as Curtis wrote on a pink sheet.

'If I recall, you were having trouble sleeping,' he said finally. 'Is that still the case?'

She nodded.

'Even when I do manage to get a few hours I seem to get woken up by nightmares,' she continued.

'What kind of nightmares?'

'The usual stupid things that make no sense in daylight,' she said, sipping her coffee as if anxious to avoid the subject.

'Have you any idea what's caused the disruption of sleep, Mrs Hacket?'

She put down her cup, avoiding his gaze for a moment.

'Trouble at home perhaps?' Curtis continued.

223

She took a deep breath, as if trying to summon up the courage to tell him.

'When we first met you asked if I had a family, any children and I said no. Well, I did have, *we* did have. A daughter. Lisa.' The words were coming with difficulty, as if she were learning some kind of new language. 'We used to live in London. A nice house. Respectable.' She smiled bitterly. 'Our daughter was murdered.'

It was said. Simple really.

'A few weeks later my father died of cancer, he'd been ill for months. The two things together were too much for me, especially with what happened to Lisa . . .' She found she could go no further.

'I'm very sorry,' Curtis murmured.

'Around the time of my daughter's murder, my husband was having an affair.' Again she chuckled but there was no humour in the sound. 'This sounds like a hard luck story doesn't it? Perhaps I should be telling an agony aunt instead of you.'

'A doctor should care for his patients' psychological welfare as well as their physical condition.'

'Everything seemed to happen at once. That was why I left London. If I'd stayed I'd have gone crazy.'

'That's understandable.'

Sue smiled at him, aware of how easily she was speaking. Secret thoughts which she had kept locked away were spilling out almost wantonly. And, as she spoke she felt a numbing weariness envelope her, as if talking about what she felt were draining her. It was like a criminal unburdening himself of guilt, glad to be given the chance to confess.

Was this what John had felt like when he'd confessed to the affair?

But it wasn't guilt she was purging herself of, it was an accumulation of misery.

She felt the tears forming in her eyes and pulled a tissue

from the pocket of her jeans. A couple more deep breaths and she had regained her composure.

Curtis looked on silently, his eyes never leaving her then finally, sitting forward in his chair he leant towards Sue.

'Have you thought of having another child?' he asked.

'I can't,' she told him. 'I mean, I want one but, after Lisa was born there were complications. My fallopian tubes were infected. I can't have children.'

This time when she looked at him she made no attempt to wipe away the tears.

'You don't know how much I want another child,' Sue continued. 'Lisa could never be replaced, you understand that. But I think her death hit me harder because I knew I couldn't have another baby. It made things even more final.'

'And does your husband feel the same way? Would he have wanted more children?'

She smiled wearily.

'John always wanted another daughter. We used to laugh about it. You know, how men are supposed to want a son to carry on the family name. Not John. He wanted another girl.' She sniffed.

Curtis was already writing out a prescription.

'Sleeping pills,' he announced, handing it to her. 'Only a week's supply. They can become addictive. I could have given you tranquillisers but they only help you live with a problem they don't remove its cause.'

'Then how can I ever go back to normal?' she wanted to know. 'I know what my problem is. I want another child but I can't have one. It's an insoluble problem.'

'How badly do you want it?'

'I'd give anything,' she said, flatly. 'Anything.'

Curtis smiled benevolently.

'Promise me you'll come back in a few days, even if you feel better. Just to talk.'

She nodded.

'You've been a great help, Doctor. Talking about it helps.'

'So you'll come back?'

'Yes.'

She got to her feet and slipped on her jacket. Curtis showed her to the door and opened it for her. He shook her hand and she felt the warmth in his grasp. He smiled once more and then she was gone.

As Curtis closed the door and turned back into the surgery his smile vanished abruptly. He crossed to the door to the left of his desk which was already opening.

'You heard that?' he asked as the other occupant of the house entered the office. 'She said she'd give anything for another child. Anything.'

'Did you tell her?' the other wanted to know.

Curtis shook his head.

'She's got to be handled carefully but I think she's at the right stage emotionally. She seems particularly receptive.'

'When will you speak to her again?' the figure wanted to know.

Curtis heard the sound of Sue's car pulling away.

'Soon,' he murmured. 'Very soon.'

Fifty-five

Hacket felt the air rasping in his lungs as he inhaled. He hadn't realised until now quite how unfit he really was. As he ran back and forth across the rugby field, following the play he could feel his heart thumping protestingly against his ribs. As a younger man he'd played both football and rugby for his school but that had been more than ten years ago. He might only be twenty-nine, but he felt as if he had the lungs of an eighty-year-old.

The mud-spattered boys who swarmed over the field with him did so with more urgency, as befitted their age. There were those, as there always were, who struggled to keep up, who were constant targets of abuse from their fitter, more athletic colleagues. They too plodded through the mud puffing and panting.

Hacket watched as a boy he knew as Lee Vernon received the ball and began to run with it.

He'd got less than twenty yards when Phillip Craven came hurtling at him.

Vernon tried to avoid the tackle but Craven caught him just above the waist, slamming his shoulder into the other boys solar plexus with something akin to relish. They both went down in a muddy heap and Craven rose quickly, smiling as he looked down at Vernon who had had the wind knocked from him. He lay in the mud wheezing, trying to suck back the air which had been blasted from him by Craven's crunching tackle.

Hacket ran across to the boy and helped him up, bending him over and patting his back in an attempt to re-fill his lungs. The boy gasped, coughed then began to breathe more easily but pain still showed on his face. Hacket asked him if he was all right and he nodded and trudged back into position.

The match re-started and this time it was Craven's turn to catch the ball. He gripped it tightly and ran, barging past a couple of half-hearted tackles, ignoring the boy who had run alongside him to support.

Two opponents came at him and Craven struck out a hand, catching one in the throat. The other was less fortunate.

227

Craven's hand connected with his nose with such force that the appendage seemed to burst. Blood spilled from both nostrils, pouring down the front of the boys shirt, staining it crimson. He moaned and fell forward into the mud while Craven ran on to score.

Hacket blew his whistle to halt the game, running across to the boy with the bleeding nose. It looked bad and the teacher could see that the boy was struggling to keep back tears. It might even be broken. There was certainly enough blood.

'Put your head forward,' Hacket instructed while a number of the other boys gathered around.

Streams of blood ran from the boy's nose and dripped into the mud between his legs. The sight of his own life-fluid draining away made him feel sick and he went a sickly white colour. Hacket thought he was going to faint, but the boy retained his grip on consciousness.

Craven trotted over, grinning.

'A hand-off is supposed to be with the *flat* of the hand, Craven,' he snapped. 'Not a fist. You do that again and you're in trouble.'

'It's not my fault if he can't take it, sir,' said the youth, defiantly.

'Are you all right, Parker?' Hacket asked the injured boy. He pulled a handkerchief from the pocket of his track-suit and held it to the boy's nose. 'Go back to the school, see the nurse. You go with him,' the teacher said, pointing to another boy who seemed only too delighted to escort his companion off the field. At least it meant *he* was out of the action too.

Hacket watched them leave the field then re-started the game again.

The ball was lofted high into the air and it was Craven who caught it, running at speed towards the opposition. Hacket saw him pass two of them but a third, a powerfully

228

built lad called Baker ducked low, beneath Craven's straight arm rebuff and gripped the other boy's legs. Hacket couldn't resist a slight smile as Craven went crashing to the ground, the ball flying from his grip.

'Good tackle, Baker,' shouted the teacher.

Craven tried to wrestle free of his captor, digging his boot into Baker's chest in the process. The other youth reacted angrily and, before Hacket could reach them, Baker had thrown a punch.

Craven jerked free and, instead of rolling away, he threw himself back at Baker, fastening his hands round his throat, bringing his face close to Baker's.

'Stop it,' bellowed Hacket, racing towards them, pushing past the children who had stopped to watch the fight.

Craven closed his teeth around the top of Baker's left ear and, as Hacket watched in horror, he bit through the fleshy appendage.

Baker screamed as the top of his ear was sheared off.

Blood spurted from it and ran down Craven's chin.

'Craven,' Hacket yelled, trying to reach the boy.

Baker continued to scream, looking up to see the portion of his ear still gripped in Craven's teeth.

He held it for a second then swallowed it.

'Jesus Christ,' murmured Hacket, finally reaching the struggling pair.

He hauled Craven to his feet, seeing the blood on the boy's face, the pieces of flesh between his teeth.

The grin on his face.

Baker had curled up into a ball, both hands clasped to his ear, or at least what remained of it. Blood was pouring down the side of his face, oozing through his fingers.

And he shrieked in pain.

'Go and get help,' Hacket roared at a boy close to him, still gripping on to Craven.

The boy ran off.

Another youth took one look at the bleeding mess which had once been Baker's ear and vomited.

Not only had the top half been severed, most of the remaining ear had been torn. The entire appendage was hanging, held to his head only by thin pieces of skin and muscle.

Hacket dragged Craven away.

Behind him, Baker continued to scream.

Fifty-six

'Don't you think you're over-reacting a little, Mr Hacket?' said Donald Brooks, apparently more concerned that mud from the teacher's boots was dropping onto his office carpet.

'Over-reacting?' Hacket gaped. 'The boy is a lunatic,' he hissed, trying to control his temper. 'I saw what happened. If you don't believe me then go and look at Baker, he's in the medical room now waiting for the ambulance to arrive.'

Brooks raised a hand as if to silence the younger man.

'I didn't say I doubted you,' he said. 'But it was an accident.'

'Craven bit Baker's ear off. He swallowed it for God's sake. Are you trying to tell me that's normal?' Hacket snarled. 'What does he do for an encore, pull the heads of babies?'

'Now you *are* over-reacting,' Brooks told him, irritably. 'What do expect me to do with the boy? Call the police? Have him locked up? I've already called his mother, she's coming to pick him up. I've decided to suspend him for a couple of days until all this blows over.'

Hacket shook his head wearily and brushed a hand through his hair.

Brooks huddled closer to the radiator as if fearing that Hacket's presence in the room was somehow sucking the precious warmth from the air.

'Have there been incidents like this before involving Craven?' Hacket wanted to know.

'Nothing,' Brooks told him. 'The boy is a good worker, a highly intelligent child.'

Hacket was unimpressed. He walked to the door of the Headmasters office and peered out. Craven was sitting in the annexe, looking at his own painting. He was smiling unconcernedly.

The teacher glanced at the boy then closed the office door again.

'He seems to be the dominant one in his class,' Hacket said.

'Intelligent children usually are. I don't have to tell you that, Mr Hacket.'

'What about a boy called Trevor Harvey? Craven was picking on him this morning. Is there some kind of antagonism between them that I should know about?'

'Harvey is a little *slow*, for want of a better word. Again, you know that children like that are usually the butt of jokes. You can't accuse Craven of persecuting Harvey as well. You seem to have taken a dislike to this boy, Mr Hacket and it appears to be clouding your judgement.'

'It's got nothing to do with judgement. I'm not talking about character references, for Christ's sake, I'm telling you what I saw today. And I don't like it.'

The two men gazed at each other for a moment, their concentration broken by a knock on the office door. Brooks' secretary popped her head around the door and coughed rather theatrically.

'Mrs Craven is here,' she announced.

Brooks smiled and instructed the secretary to show the woman through.

She was dressed in a loose fitting tracksuit and trainers. Hacket saw that part of a bandage showed beneath the left sleeve of the track-suit top. Her hair was long, jet black and tied in a pig-tail. She bustled into the room, smiling at Brooks then at Hacket. The headmaster greeted her then introduced her briefly to the younger man. Brooks offered her a seat but she declined.

'There's nothing wrong with Phillip is there?' she asked.

'There's been an accident, Mrs Craven,' said Brooks. 'Involving your son. A fight.'

'Is he hurt?' she asked, anxiously. 'I saw him sitting outside the room.'

'*He's* not hurt,' Hacket interrupted. 'But another boy is. Phillip injured him badly and I'm sure it was intentional.'

Brooks shot the younger man an angry glance.

'There was a slight fracas, Mr Hacket is right,' the headmaster said. 'We thought it best if Phillip stayed at home for a couple of days.'

'What happened?' Elaine Craven wanted to know.

Hacket told her.

She looked at him for a moment then turned to Brooks and smiled politely.

'I'll keep Phillip at home, if that's what you think is best. I hope the other lad is better soon.' Then she turned back to Hacket. 'I think you're a little too eager to blame my son for what happened.'

'I saw him do it, Mrs Craven.'

'He could have been provoked,' she said, defensively.

'Provoked into biting a boy's ear off?' Hacket shook his head.

She pulled up her sleeves and shrugged her shoulders, a gesture which signified defiance. Hacket caught sight of the heavy bandage which encased her left arm from wrist to elbow.

'I think it'd be best if I left now,' said Elaine. 'I'll take Phillip with me.' She turned and headed for the door, followed by the headmaster who waved Hacket back into the office. He waited there, listening to the mutterings coming from outside then he heard the door of the outer office close and, a second later, Brooks re-entered the room, making straight for the radiator. He pressed himself to it.

'Satisfied, Mr Hacket?' Brooks said. 'I believe you have a class to take.' He glanced at his watch. 'I trust there's nothing else you wish to discuss.'

'As a matter of fact there *is* something on my mind,' the teacher said. 'I'd like to know why you didn't tell me the truth about the previous occupant of my house.'

Brooks looked vague.

'The teacher who shot his wife and child then committed suicide,' Hacket continued.

'It's not something I like to talk about,' said Brooks rubbing his hands together.

'I had a right to know before myself and my wife moved in. Why did he do it?'

Brooks shrugged.

'You're asking me to give you answers I can't give now, Mr Hacket,' the headmaster said. 'Who am I to see into a man's mind? I had no idea he would do something like that. He may have been unbalanced. There were no outward signs. I'm a teacher not a psychiatrist.'

Hacket was silent for a moment, his gaze never leaving the headmaster.

'You should have told me,' he said finally.

'Would it have changed your mind about the job? Would you have decided not to live there if you'd known all the facts?'

Hacket shrugged.

'I don't know. It's a bit late for that now though isn't it? The main thing is, you should have told me.'

Brooks looked at his watch again.

'Your class, Mr Hacket,' he said, sliding his hands along the radiator.

Hacket hesitated a moment longer then turned and headed for the door.

Brooks turned his back and gazed out of the window. He could see Elaine Craven driving along the short driveway that led past his office.

Phillip sat in the back, a slight smile on his lips.

As Hacket passed through the annexe he paused for a second and looked at the painting of the owl on the wall.

The owl holding the eyeball.

Phillip Craven's painting.

Perhaps it would have been more appropriate if the owl had been holding an ear, he thought bitterly.

All around him bells sounded, signalling the beginning of another lesson.

Hacket looked at his watch.

1.30 p.m.

It was already turning into a long day.

Fifty-seven

As he pushed open the front door the smell of stew greeted him.

Hacket inhaled deeply, the mouth-watering aroma a most welcome one. He dropped his briefcase and sports-bag in the hall and wandered through into the kitchen.

Sue was standing by the cooker stirring the contents of a large saucepan.

'How did it go?' she asked, cheerily and Hacket was pleasantly surprised by the lightness of her tone. She was wearing a pink T-shirt and pair of faded, tight-fitting jeans. Both items of clothing served to highlight both the shapely curves of her figure and the fact that she wore nothing beneath the outer garments. She turned to Hacket and smiled.

He wondered if he'd walked into the wrong house.

It was as if time had somehow been reversed.

Her hair had been washed and, beneath the lights in the kitchen it seemed to glow. She wore just a hint of make-up on her eyes and her face looked as if it had been purged of any lines or shadows. She looked closer to twenty than twenty-five. And when she smiled at him he felt the breath catch in his throat.

It was like finding a long-lost possession again.

He moved towards her and kissed her, surprised when she stopped stirring the stew and, instead, snaked both arms around his neck, drawing him closer to her. Their lips brushed together and he felt her tongue flicking urgently against his teeth, pushing deeper to stir the moistness of his mouth. He responded fiercely, allowing one hand to fall to her bottom, squeezing its firmness. She ground herself against his groin, pulling away for breath, smiling as she felt his penis beginning to stiffen against her.

'The stew will burn,' she said, touching his lips with her index finger. Hacket backed off and sat down, a little bewildered.

Why the sudden change?

He looked at her and smiled.

'I asked how the day went?' she repeated.

He told her, deciding to skip details about Craven's antics on the rugby field. She listened intently, dishing up the

235

dinner, sitting down opposite him as he spoke. Occasionally he would look up at her and, sometimes would find her gaze on him. Hacket's bewilderment at her change in attitude was rapidly overtaken by his joy and relief.

Was this the turning point?

'What about you?' he asked. 'What sort of day have you had?'

'I finished tidying up,' she told him. 'Things actually look respectable in the bedrooms now. I put your clothes away. There's just some stuff that needs to go up in the loft and that's about it.'

'And the doctor? How did *that* go?'

'Fine,' she told him, getting to her feet and scraping the remains of the stew into the waste-bin.

'Did he give you any pills?'

'Sleeping tablets. And don't worry, I won't get addicted.' She smiled.

Hacket looked at her for a moment then he reached out, pulling her to him. She didn't resist but instead allowed him to lift her onto his knee. She put her arms around his neck, feeling the strength in his grip as he held her. He wanted to speak, wanted to say something to her, to tell her how she'd changed. Tell her how much he loved the change. But the words wouldn't come. Hacket was worried that if he spoke to her about her change of mood then she would revert to the way she'd been before. He was both elated and frightened by this new face she was showing.

Face or mask?

She kissed him and he felt sure that it was with genuine warmth.

Had he been forgiven?

He doubted it but he didn't question, he merely enjoyed the moment, savoured the sensations he was feeling.

He wanted her badly.

236

When he felt her hand gliding across his groin he knew the feeling was reciprocated.

She stroked the inside of his thigh then trailed her fingers across his penis, squeezing it through the material of his trousers, coaxing its stiffness. She took one of his hands and raised it to her breast, anxious to let him feel her own excitement. He kneaded her breast gently, feeling her nipple stiffen and swell. She moaned softly and they kissed, deeply, wantonly. She slid from his lap onto the floor beside him, unzipping his trousers, easing his penis from the confines of the material. Then she leant forward and took the bulbous head in her mouth, slowly lowering her head until more of his stiff shaft disappeared into the warm orifice.

Hacket gasped as he felt her tongue lapping around his glans while, with her free hand, she gently rubbed his testicles. He unfastened his trousers and eased them down, not wanting to disturb her then, as she continued sucking he reached down and pulled at her T-shirt, easing it over her head.

She kneeled beside him, moving back slightly, allowing him to reach her breasts, to squeeze them in his eager hands, to tease the hard nipples between his thumb and forefinger.

She stood up and unzipped her jeans, wriggling out of them until she stood naked in front of him.

Hacket stood too, slipping out of his trousers and pants, allowing Sue to unbutton his shirt and tug it free.

Naked, they embraced and he felt her hand close around his shaft, urging him towards her slippery cleft, demanding that he penetrate her.

She moved back, her shoulder blades against the wall, raising herself up onto her toes as he took his place between her spread thighs.

His penis nudged the entrance of her vagina for a moment

237

and she gasped as it rubbed her hardened clitoris then, with a grunt, he slid into her.

It was a pleasure he'd almost forgotten.

She raised one leg, snaking it around the back of his calves, allowing him deeper penetration, gripping his buttocks, unable to stand the torment any longer. He began to drive into her, long slow strokes which caused them both to gasp. Hacket bent his head to her breasts taking each nipple between his lips in turn, flicking his tongue over the hardened buds. Licking the mounds until they glistened with his saliva.

Sue looked into his eyes, her own eyes glazed as if she were in a trance, aware only of the thrusting of his penis and the sensations which were building between her legs.

She pressed her head against his shoulder as he increased the speed of his movements. Looking beyond him her eyes opened for a second.

'Come and see me'.

She knew that this was her husband who held her but she felt another.

'Come and see me'.

Curtis.

She mouthed his name as her ecstasy grew. Mouthed it but did not speak it.

And as the orgasm grew in intensity she closed her eyes, saw Curtis driving into her. Felt him bringing her to the brink.

She heard her name whispered but it seemed vague, muffled.

She cried out as she climaxed, reaching down to squeeze those swollen testicles.

Hacket felt her body trembling with the exploding pleasure, heard her moan her joy. Then, as her hand grasped him gently he too felt the beginnings of his orgasm. He thrust harder into her until he poured his thick fluid into her.

She groaned once more as she felt him come.

The image of Curtis filled her mind. It was *his* penis which throbbed inside her. *His* semen which filled her.

'*Come and see me*'.

Hacket slowly withdrew, his breath coming in gasps. Both of them were covered in perspiration but, even as he tried to pull away she gripped him hard, pulling his face close to hers, kissing him deeply.

Then she leant forward, licking his chest, lowering herself slowly, her tongue flicking over his belly until it reached his flaccid organ, now wet with secretions. She took it into her mouth, tasting herself on him. She licked, sucked, coaxed.

She demanded him again.

And Hacket responded, surprised at his own recuperative powers. He felt the stiffness beginning to return.

She led him, almost dragged him, towards the sitting-room and there they loved again. More slowly this time but with as much intensity.

Hacket felt as if the night had blurred into one long bout of glorious copulation.

Nothing else seemed to matter. He found reserves of strength he didn't know he had, spurred on by Sue's insatiability. She was tireless.

'I love you,' Hacket whispered as she lay with her head on his chest, licking the beads of perspiration from his flesh.

Her eyes were open, her breathing low. She didn't answer him.

All she could think of was Curtis.

And it began again.

Fifty-eight

It had all been so easy.

Much easier than he'd anticipated.

Ronald Mills sat at the table in the flat, smiling, looking down at the objects which lay before him.

At the .38 and its ammunition. The knife. The pad which bore the one word: HINKSTON.

Walton had always done most of the thinking when he'd been alive. Any deals to be worked out, they had been Walton's province. Any financial connivings, Walton had sorted them out, but now Walton was dead and Mills had to think for himself.

He spun the cylinder of the .38 then snapped it back into position, raising the gun so that he was squinting down the sight. He aimed at a dirty vase which stood on top of the sideboard and squeezed the trigger.

The metallic click sounded loud as the hammer slammed down on an empty chamber.

He put down the gun and picked up the knife, holding it almost lovingly in his hand. The hand which still festered from the tattoo. He grunted and picked a piece of the scab off, rolling it between his fingers for a moment before dropping it onto the floor. Then he reached for the sharpening stone, and began carefully drawing the blade back and forth across it, pausing every now and then to press his thumb to the edge.

After nearly five minutes of this task he pressed his thumb to the blade once more.

The knife split the skin effortlessly, opening the pad of Mills' thumb from the nail to the first joint.

He held it before him for a second, watching as the blood welled from the split and ran down his hand. Then he pushed the digit into his mouth, tasting the salty crimson fluid as it flooded onto his tongue. He sucked it as a child would suck on a nipple, coaxing more fluid from it.

Finally he lowered his hand, lowered the knife, his gaze drawn once more to the pad.

He had rung the estate agents and asked about Hacket's house. Said that he wanted to put in a bid for it. And they had believed him. Those fucking idiots who only cared about their commission, who only cared if they sold the house or not. They didn't care who bought it, who enquired, as long as there was the possibility of some money at the end of it all.

'Easier for a camel to pass through the eye of a needle than for a rich man to enter the kingdom of God,' chuckled Mills.

He didn't want money. He didn't care about money.

He wanted revenge.

He wanted Hacket.

The estate agent had tried to arrange a meeting with him, to show him round the house but Mills had hesitated. He had asked to speak to Hacket personally, he wondered if he would be willing to take a smaller offer.

The estate agent thought it might work.

Mills had smiled.

He had asked for a way of getting in touch with Hacket.

The estate agent had given him a phone number and an address in a place called Hinkston.

Ask and ye shall receive.

Mills looked at the word written on his pad then at the gun and the knife.

And at his bleeding thumb.

He knew where Hacket was, all he had to do was find him.

Slowly, Mills wiped his thumb across the pad, leaving a thick red stain.

It was just a matter of time.

Seek and ye shall find.
He began to laugh.

Fifty-nine

The frost crunched beneath his feet as he walked from the back door of the house.

Curtis made his way across the large lawn at the rear of the building, moving slowly, inhaling deeply. The early morning air smelt clean and unpolluted. When he exhaled his breath clouded before him. A watery sun was dragging its way up into the sky but, with dawn having broken scarcely fifteen minutes earlier it seemed to be finding the climb difficult. It wasn't yet strong enough to melt the frost.

The silence in the back garden, indeed all around the house, was almost total.

It was too early for any traffic to be either leaving or entering Hinkston, and the house was set sufficiently far back from the road to mask the sound even if some early morning traveller *was* passing.

The only sounds which Curtis heard as he made his way across the back garden were those of birds singing in the trees around him. Just two or three of them. A sparrow paused in its early morning song to peer quizzically at him as he passed beneath the branch where it sat.

Curtis drew closer to the bottom of the garden, towards the high, perfectly cropped privet hedge which towered a good nine feet.

There was a wrought iron gate set into it, supported on

a wooden frame, the paint of which was blistered and peeling in places. Curtis opened the gate which squealed protestingly on its hinges as he walked through.

The area beyond the hedge was roughly twelve feet square. Surrounded by more hedges, these not quite as well cared for. They were neat but not immaculate. The grass which grew within the shaded square was that little bit longer than that of the lawns, not as neatly cropped. Weeds were poking through it in places. Curtis administered a swift mental rebuke as he surveyed the square because this was caused by *his* neglect. *He* was responsible for the care of this part of the garden.

The gardener wasn't allowed through the gate.

Curtis stood by the gate for a moment, looking around at the tall hedge, also covered by a thin coating of frost. The privet grew three feet taller than him here too. It sheltered the square perfectly.

He walked slowly towards the middle of it, towards the piece of stone which lay there.

The stone was cracked in places due to the ravages of the years and the weather. Moss had begun to grow on it here and there, infesting the cracks in the stone like gangrene infects a wound.

Curtis looked down at the name on the stone.

Below the name was a rose bowl, flecked with rust and, from this he took half a dozen dead stalks of flowers, gathering them up in one hand.

He replaced them with the fresh flowers which he held in his other hand, arranging them so that the red roses seemed to glow against the dull background of the stone.

They looked like a splash of blood on the grave.

Curtis straightened up, walked to one corner of the sheltered green square and dropped the dead flowers into the metal incinerator that stood there, then he brushed his hands together and returned to the graveside, gazing down once again at the name on the stone.

He stood there for what seemed like an eternity, his mind at peace, all thoughts banished. Again, the only sounds he heard were those of birds, his meditative state uninterrupted by nature's extraneous sounds.

Then he heard the footsteps beyond the gate.

Beyond the hedge.

Heavy footfalls which broke the blanket of frost.

Curtis turned his head towards the gate as the footsteps drew closer.

He heard the latch of the gate rattle, then the dull clank as it opened.

The figure walked through to join him.

Curtis turned back to the grave, hands clasped before him once more.

'I heard you leave the house,' said the figure, standing at his side.

'Sorry, I didn't want to disturb you.' the doctor said, softly, almost reverently, as if to raise his voice would have been to defile the sanctity of this very private area.

The two of them stood silently for long moments, both gazing down at the stone.

And the name it bore.

'I've never thought this was right,' said Curtis nodding towards the grave. 'To lie here, even though it *is* our home.'

'Better here than with the others,' said the figure, defiantly.

Curtis nodded in agreement.

'Have you made up your mind what to do about the woman?' the other wanted to know.

'Mrs Hacket?'

'Yes.'

Curtis smiled thinly.

'Yes I have,' he said, his eyes still on the gravestone.

'She's due to visit me again today.' His smile broadened.
'I think the time has come.'

Sixty

The woman was struggling with the books as she climbed the stairs, and Hacket could see what was going to happen.

As she reached the top step he saw the first of the heavy textbooks begin to topple from her hands. Five or six more followed it, landing with a thud on the floor. She muttered something under her breath and began retrieving them. Hacket scuttled up the stairs beside her and began picking up books too.

He glanced across at her as she shrugged and smiled.

She was very attractive. In her early twenties he guessed. Shoulder length brown hair and wide grey eyes. A nice figure too.

A little like Nikki?

He pushed the thought to the back of his mind, angry that it had even surfaced.

'You look as if you could do with some help carrying these,' he said, picking up half a dozen of the books himself.

'If you've got a fork-lift truck handy, it'd be most appreciated,' she told him, smiling. 'You're new here aren't you?'

He nodded.

'The new boy. Yes.' He extended his free hand, balancing the pile of books on the crook of his left arm. 'John Hacket.'

She took the offered hand and shook it.

'Josephine Milton,' she told him. 'But please call me Jo.'

She scooped up the rest of the books and they began climbing the stairs towards the second landing.

'What do you teach?' he asked.

'Biology. I dissect things,' she chuckled. 'What about you? English isn't it?'

'English *and* games,' he told her. 'I've got the strained muscles to prove it.'

She laughed.

'Of course, you took over from Ray Weller didn't you? I suppose you know the story?'

'About him killing his family then committing suicide. Yes.'

'Isn't it creepy living in a house where someone has died?'

'You get used to it,' said Hacket sharply. *Especially when you've lived in the house where your own daughter was butchered. It's a piece of cake.* 'How much did you know about Weller?'

She shrugged.

'Not much. Not enough to know why he should want to murder his family if that's what you mean. He was a nice guy. About your age, easy to talk to. He never struck me as a lunatic.' She raised her eyebrows. 'I haven't really been much help have I?'

Hacket smiled.

'It's probably not important,' he told her, pushing open a set of double doors to allow her through. Four classrooms led off from the landing they stood on.

'My little darlings are in there,' said Jo, nodding towards the door ahead of her. 'If you wouldn't mind just helping me in with these books.'

Hacket watched as she walked to the door and opened it, trying to keep his eyes away from her shapely legs and tight buttocks but he lost the battle, content instead to admire them. She pushed open the door, expecting to be greeted by the usual cacophony of sound but there was only silence. The twelve girls in the class looked up as she entered.

All except one.

Emma Stokes remained at the bench, looking down at the white mouse which lay before her.

Its paws had been swiftly and effectively nailed to the bench, spreadeagling it.

Its stomach had been slit, the raw edges peeled back to reveal the network of intestines within.

It was these small tendrils of entrail which the girl was teasing from the ruptured belly of the mouse much as she might pull threads from a torn piece of material.

Hacket, close behind Jo, noticed with revulsion that the animal was still alive. Its head jerking back and forth, its small body quivering as the girl pulled ever longer lengths of intestine from it.

'What are you doing?' Jo snapped, dropping the books on the desk. She moved towards Emma who finally looked up from the eviscerated mouse and pinned the teacher in an unblinking stare. 'Give me that scalpel,' hissed Jo, holding out her hand to take the lethal blade from the girl who Hacket guessed was about twelve.

Emma hesitated.

'Give me that scalpel now,' Jo said, angrily, her attention flicking momentarily to the mouse.

Emma jabbed it towards Jo's outstretched hand.

The razor sharp blade cut effortlessly through the ball of her thumb and she hissed in pain as blood spurted from the cut.

She pulled the scalpel from the girl, dropping it onto her own desk. Hacket dragged a handkerchief from his pocket and passed it to Jo who pressed it against the wound, watching as blood soaked through the material.

'I'm all right, John,' Jo said. 'I can handle it now.'

247

He hesitated, looking first at the teacher's bleeding hand then at the girl who merely looked back indifferently at him.

He thought for a second he caught a hint of a smile at the corners of the girl's mouth. Not unlike that he'd seen on Craven's face.

The rest of the class remained silent.

Time seemed to have frozen.

Emma Stokes sat over the dying mouse, her face impassive.

Jo stood before her, blood soaking through the handkerchief.

Hacket hesitated a second longer then touched Jo's arm.

'Are you sure you're OK?' he murmured.

She nodded.

'You go. I'll take care of it.'

Hacket glanced around the class once again then walked out, closing the door behind him. He paused, peering through the small piece of meshed glass in the door, watching the tableau he'd left behind.

'Now Emma,' he heard Jo say. 'You tell me what you're playing at.'

He didn't wait to hear the answer.

He had a class of his own waiting for him.

Sixty-one

'John, I want another child.'

At first Hacket thought he had misheard, or perhaps that his hearing was playing tricks with him. Lying on his back,

248

pleasantly drained by their lovemaking, he heard Sue speak the words but it was as if they wouldn't register. She had her head resting on his chest, running one index finger up and down his belly, twisting the hairs around his navel.

The ticking of the clock beside the bed was the only noise in the room apart from their low breathing. No, he was sure now, he hadn't misheard.

'Sue,' he raised his head and began to speak but she looked up at him and pressed a finger to his lips to silence him.

'I know what you're going to say. I know what you're thinking,' she told him. 'But that's what I want. I *need* another child, John.'

Hacket exhaled deeply as she slid up the bed so that they lay face to face. He took her in his arms.

'Sue, it's impossible, you know that. After you had Lisa, after the infection, they told you there couldn't be any more children.'

'I know what they told me,' she said, a little more forcefully.

'Then why torture yourself like this?' he asked, softly. 'Why even think about it?' He stroked her hair softly then brushed her cheek with the back of his hand.

'I went to see doctor Curtis again today,' she informed him, rolling onto her back.

Hacket propped himself up on one elbow, looking down at her.

'I told him how badly I wanted another child,' Sue continued.

'Did you tell him what the other doctors had said?' Hacket wanted to know.

'Yes I did. But it doesn't matter, John,' she said, smiling. 'He said that I *could* have another child. That there *was* a way.'

Hacket frowned.

'How?' he demanded. 'He has no right to tell you things like that, to raise your hopes.'

'I believe what he said and he says I can have another child.'

'It's not possible,' Hacket said, defiantly. 'I don't understand how he can tell you it is, not when half-a-dozen other doctors have said you can't. *You* know you can't. What makes you believe him?'

'Because I'm not the first. He's treated other women who were thought to be infertile, barren, not able to have children. Call it what you like. He's treated women in Hinkston and outside and those women have had babies.'

'Treated them how? He's a GP, Sue, not a surgeon. Your problem particularly is a surgical one. An *irreversible* surgical problem. How can he hope to treat a condition like yours?' There was a trace of anger in Hacket's voice.

'One of the women he treated was Julie,' she said, flatly.

'Your sister?' Hacket muttered, incredulously.

'She and Mike were told that they couldn't have children. But after doctor Curtis had treated her she had Craig. You know how healthy *he* is.'

Hacket shook his head.

'He's offering us hope, John. Can't you see that?' she demanded.

'I don't know what I can see.' He stroked his chin thoughtfully.

'I want to try, John. I have to. I know another child could never replace Lisa, could never wipe out the memory of what happened but we have to at least try. Don't deny me that.'

Hacket saw the tears forming in her eye corners.

'What about you? Don't you want another child?' she wanted to know. 'What have we got to lose?'

He struggled for the words but none would come. The idea seemed simultaneously ridiculous and inviting.

Another child, if it were possible might well bring them together again. It might go some way to helping them re-build what they'd lost together.

But if it failed.

The pain would be unbearable.

So much pain.

'What have we got to lose?' she repeated.

The words hung in the air like stale smoke.

Sixty-two

The petrol tank was full.

He'd have plenty of fuel to reach Hinkston *and* complete the return journey to London.

Ronald Mills glanced down at the fuel gauge and smiled. He'd anticipated having to fill up during the drive but he'd been lucky. The car he'd stolen had a full tank. He'd probably dump it in Hinkston.

Once he'd found Hacket.

Dump it then steal another to return to the capital.

The .38 was in the pocket of his jacket.

The knife jammed into his belt.

He drove with his lights on full beam, ignoring those drivers who flashed their headlamps at him when he dazzled them.

Fuck them.

There wasn't that much traffic leaving London, but stre-ams of it moved through the night towards the capital.

A car overtook him but Mills hardly gave it a second glance. He was in no hurry. He had plenty of time.

He smiled to himself, glancing briefly down at the map on the passenger seat. He had ringed Hinkston with a large biro circle. The drive would take him about an hour he guessed.

There was no need to rush.

Ahead of him he saw the lights of a service station. The neon figure of a chef beckoned him from the road and he swung the car into the slip-road without checking the rear view mirror. The driver behind banged on his hooter as Mills cut across but he ignored the irate motorist and guided the car into the carpark of the service station.

A dog in the back of the vehicle he parked next to began to bark at him as he clambered from behind the steering wheel.

Mills stood looking at the animal for a moment, smiling as it barked and snarled, unable to reach him. Then he raised his hand as if to strike at the dog, driving it into an even greater paroxysm of anger. It threw itself against the glass in its efforts to reach him but Mills merely grinned and walked off, the dog's barks dying away behind him.

The service station restaurant was relatively quiet.

Half-a-dozen lorry drivers, a couple of families, one or two suited men. They were the only customers. None paid him any attention as he sat down and flicked through the menu, wiping the tomato sauce from one corner with his finger.

The waitress ambled over, stifled a yawn and asked him what he wanted.

He ordered then sat back in his seat, glancing around him.

One of the families sitting about twenty feet from him had two children. A boy and a girl. The girl was no more than eight, he assumed. Pretty. Long plaited hair.

Mills clasped his hands together, leant his elbows on the table top and fixed his stare on her.

She was sucking milkshake through a straw, swinging her legs beneath her seat.

Pretty.

He smiled thinly as he watched her, feeling the beginnings of an erection pressing against the material of his trousers. His gaze travelled from her face to her torso, then down to her legs, which were encased by woollen tights.

So easy to cut those tights away.

To feel her skin.

His erection grew more prominent and he slid one hand into his pocket, rubbing it.

'Here we are, sir.'

The voice startled him and he looked up to see that the waitress had returned with his order which she set down before him.

He took it without thanks, eating as if he was ravenous. She turned and walked away, glancing back at him as he shovelled food into his mouth, his eyes still straying back to the little girl every now and then.

When he'd finished he crossed to the pay desk, put down the exact amount and walked out.

Back inside the car he sat, watching the restaurant exit, watching for the little girl.

She and her family emerged ten or fifteen minutes after him and Mills watched them climb into a Volvo and drive off.

He looked down at the map, tracing his route with one index finger.

About thirty miles and he would be in Hinkston.

He started the engine.

The dog in the car next to him continued to bark.

Sixty-three

Hacket smiled as he watched Sue cross to the front window and pull back the curtains, peering out into the night.

'Sue, he'll be here,' said the teacher. 'Don't worry.'

She looked back at him, shrugged and moved away from the window.

'You're like a kid on Christmas Eve, waiting for Santa to appear.'

They both laughed.

Hacket beckoned her to him and she sat beside him on the sofa, moving closer as he snaked one arm around her shoulder.

'I know how much this means to you,' he said, quietly. 'I feel the same way. If there is the possibility of us having another child then I'd be as happy as you.' He sighed. 'I just don't want you to raise your hopes.'

'Doctor Curtis wouldn't have told me about the treatment if he'd thought there'd be any doubt about its success, John,' she said, confidentially.

'What exactly *did* he tell you about the treatment?'

She shrugged.

'He didn't give any details, I suppose that's why he's coming to see us here, to explain it to both of us.'

Hacket was unimpressed.

Sue heard a car pull up and got to her feet again, crossing to the window. This time she saw Curtis walking up the front path. She felt that familiar shiver run through her as she watched him. He was dressed in a pair of dark trousers and a dark jacket.

She hurried to open the door, releasing the latch before he'd even knocked. Hacket heard them exchange greetings, then Curtis entered the living room.

Sue made the introductions and Hacket shook the doctor's hand, impressed by the firmness of the other man's grip.

Curtis declined Hacket's offer of a drink, settling instead for a cup of tea. The three of them finally sat down, Curtis aware that the eyes of the other two were on him.

'Well, I won't waste your time,' he said, smiling. 'Mr Hacket, I don't know if your wife has mentioned anything about our conversation the other day.'

'She said that you told her she might be able to have children again,' Hacket explained.

Curtis nodded and sipped his tea.

'That's right. She told me about your daughter. I'm very sorry.'

'Thanks,' snapped Hacket.'Can you get to the point? Please satisfy my curiosity.'

Sue glared at her husband for a second, annoyed by his abruptness. Then she returned to looking at the doctor, enraptured both by his words and his appearance.

Christ, it was like some schoolgirl crush, she thought, barely suppressing a smile.

'My wife, as I'm sure you're aware, was told that she couldn't have any more children. Several doctors told her that,' Hacket continued.

'But you want another child?' Curtis said.

Hacket opened his mouth to speak but the doctor continued.

'*Both* of you?'

'Yes,' Hacket said, quietly, meeting the doctors gaze.

'I've treated a number of women successfully over the past seventeen or eighteen years, Mr Hacket. They too had been told they couldn't have children, also by other experts.' There was a hint of sarcasm in the last word.

'Whatever it takes, we want another child,' Sue interjected.

Curtis smiled benignly at her, as a parent might smile at a child.

Hacket held up a hand, his eyes still on Curtis.

'Just a minute. Excuse my scepticism, doctor. It's not that I doubt your methods or your expertise but I'm concerned for my wife. If the treatment doesn't work then it could do her untold damage psychologically.'

'Don't talk about me as if I'm not here,' snapped Sue. 'I know the risks. I'm prepared to take them.'

'Please,' Curtis said. 'I didn't come here to start any arguments. I can see both points of view. If you'll just listen to what I've got to say.'

'I apologise for my husband, Doctor,' Sue said and, this time, it was Hacket's turn to feel the anger.

'You want to know about the treatment,' Curtis said.

Hacket nodded.

'I can't see how you can achieve anything without the use of surgery,' the teacher said.

'That is the advantage, Mr Hacket. The treatment can be completed at my own surgery. There is no need to involve a hospital or any other outsiders.'

'Why are you so anxious to exclude outside help? What's so special about this treatment?'

Curtis wasn't slow to pick up the note of challenge in Hacket's voice.

'Because it's *my* treatment, Mr Hacket. This is *my* project. I've done most of the work on it, I don't intend to let others start sticking their noses in where they're not wanted.'

'*Your* treatment. You've worked on this alone then?'

'Yes, for as long as I can remember. Ever since I qualified. It's been mine. My theories, my work. I've seen the results. I know it's successful. You can see the results for yourself, here in Hinkston. Some of them at your school.'

Hacket frowned.

'What do you mean?' he wanted to know.

'I said I'd treated a number of other women over the years. Some of the children they gave birth to are at the school where you teach.'

Hacket sat forward in his seat, his hands clasped together.

'Like who?'

'Phillip Craven. Emma Stokes.'

'Jesus,' murmured Hacket under his breath.

Craven. And he knew that other name too. *Emma*. What the hell had been her surname? *The girl who had been pulling the entrails from the mouse. The one who had slashed open Jo Milton's hand with a scalpel.*

'How old is the girl?' he asked.

'About twelve. A pretty girl. Long black hair,' said Curtis smiling.

Hacket nodded. It *was* her.

'Who else have you treated?' he wanted to know.

'A young couple, recently. Stuart and Michelle Lewis, they have a baby now. The Kirkhams, the couple who own The Bull in town, the hotel. They have a daughter, Paula, thanks to my work. And, as well as the Cravens' and the Stokes' families, there are a number of other children at your school whose mothers I treated. And of course there was Ray Weller.'

Hacket felt the colour draining from his cheeks.

'The man who lived here before us? The one who killed his wife and child then shot himself?'

Curtis nodded.

'A tragedy,' he said, wistfully, a faint smile on his lips. 'She really was such a beautiful child.'

Hacket felt the hairs at the back of his neck slowly rise.

Sixty-four

'Why did he do it?' Hacket wanted to know. 'Why did Weller kill his family then himself?'

'I'm not a psychiatrist, Mr Hacket,' Curtis said, finishing his tea and setting the cup down. 'I thought you wanted to know about the possibility of your wife having another child, not about the misfortunes of this building's previous occupant.'

Hacket looked coldly at the doctor for a moment then nodded.

'Yes, I do,' he said, wearily. 'We both do.'

'When could the treatment start?' Sue wanted to know.

'As soon as you agree to it.'

'You still haven't explained exactly what this treatment is,' Hacket reminded him.

Well, without going into too much technical and biological detail, it involves an injection into the wall of the uterus,' said Curtis. 'It's as simple as that. There isn't necessarily any need for a local anaesthetic. The whole process is over in less than fifteen minutes.'

'But Sue's fallopian tubes were blocked, how can the egg travel from the ovaries?'

'It doesn't have to.'

Hacket frowned, his look of incredulity turning to one of near mocking.

Curtis continued.

'A hormone is injected into the wall of the uterus, it stimulates growth. The foetus gestates in the womb as normal but the fallopian tubes become unnecessary.'

'So it's a kind of artificial insemination?' Hacket said, quietly.

'No. In the case of insemination, sperm is introduced directly into the ovaries. The egg grows there then travels

258

along the fallopian tube to the womb where it grows naturally. As I said earlier, this process eliminates the need for that part of the cycle.'

Hacket shook his head.

'So how is the egg fertilised?'

'By your sperm, within the vagina, as in normal intercourse. The egg is already removed, again by drawing it off using a needle, then replaced in the uterus where it is *then* fertilised. Gestation is accelerated by the second injection which initiates growth.'

'What do you mean "accelerated"?' Hacket said, warily.

'The gestation period is shortened. The time varies according to the individual subject and how well they respond to the drug.'

'It's not possible,' Hacket murmured.

'On the contrary, Mr Hacket, it's not only possible but it works. You can see the examples for yourself. The Craven boy, Emma Stokes and the others I've mentioned to you.'

Silence descended as Hacket struggled to come to terms with what he'd heard and Curtis sat back almost smugly, glancing first at the teacher then at Sue who returned his smile warmly.

Hacket stroked his chin.

'I don't know what to say,' he muttered. 'If this process works then why haven't you done more with it? Brought it to the attention of the medical authorities? It could benefit women all over the country if it works.'

'You still continue to say '*if*', Mr Hacket,' the doctor observed. 'What will it take to convince you? Won't you believe it until you're holding your own child in your arms?'

Hacket swallowed hard.

'I suppose I'm frightened to believe it,' he said, quietly. 'It sounds too easy. *Too* simple. What are the risks to the child?'

'No more than in normal pregnancy.'

259

'I said I'm willing to take those risks, John,' Sue said, defiantly.

'Well I'm not sure *I* am,' Hacket said, flatly.

Curtis glared at the teacher for a moment.

'You still haven't told me enough.'

'It isn't only your decision,' Sue said, angrily. 'It's me who's got to carry the baby. I'm the one who's got to give birth. I told you, I *need* that child.'

Curtis got to his feet.

'I think it would be best if I left now,' he said, making for the door.

Sue hurried after him. Hacket sauntered to the door where he shook hands with Curtis once more.

A chill breeze blew in through the open front door and Hacket felt his skin rise into goose-pimples.

'Take your time and think about what I've said,' Curtis told them, but his eyes were on Hacket when he spoke. 'It's a chance to start again, Mr Hacket. Not many people get that.'

He said goodnight to Sue then turned and headed down the path to his waiting car.

Hacket stepped back inside the house, Sue stood on the step watching as the car disappeared into the night.

When she entered the sitting room, Hacket was sitting in front of the electric fire warming his hands.

'You were rude to him, John,' she said, irritably. 'Like he said, he's offering us another chance. We have to take it.'

Hacket inhaled, held the breath for a moment then let it out in a long sigh.

'Sue, it might be coincidence, maybe I'm overreacting but the kids he's treated . . .' He struggled to find the words. 'There's something strange about them.'

'And what about Julie's son, Craig? Is he strange too?' she snapped, choosing to ignore the night Curtis had been

260

called to the boy. 'It's not you that's overreacting, John, it's your imagination. Perhaps you've been a teacher too long, reading books too long. The name of this town is Hinkston not Midwich. These children aren't the children of the damned, they're not artificially created by some mad doctor.' She was angry, the anger mixed with scorn. 'They're the last hope for their parents. Just like Curtis is *our* last hope. She got to her feet and made for the door. 'I'm going to bed, John. If you want to sit up and think then fine, but just think about one thing. I'm having this child whether you want me to or not. And I won't let you stop me.'

Sixty-five

Curtis drove slowly through the streets of Hinkston, only speeding up slightly when he reached the road that led towards his house.

The massive building was almost invisible in the gloom but for a couple of lights burning in one of the rooms on the first floor. However, as he drew nearer the outline of the house became visible against the black velvet backdrop of night.

The doctor swung his car into the driveway, brought it to a halt before the front door and switched off the engine. He sat for a moment, head bowed, then he swung himself out of the car, locked it and headed for the house.

His footsteps echoed on the polished wood of the hall floor as he entered and, as he made his way towards the sitting room he slowed his pace, glancing towards the stairs.

Listening for any sign of movement from above.

There was none.

The house was silent.

Curtis entered the sitting room, feeling the warmth from the dying embers of the open fire. They still glowed red in the grate and he moved across towards them, warming his hands close to the coals. In the red light which they cast it looked as though his face had been splashed with blood.

'What did she say?'

The voice came from behind him, from the high-backed leather chair which stood close to the fire. Curtis hadn't seen the figure sitting in it when he'd entered the room and the words startled him momentarily. He exhaled deeply, looking at his companion for a moment before once again turning his back and warming his hands.

'The woman is enthusiastic,' he said. 'She *has* been from the beginning. It's her husband who's resisting.'

Curtis got to his feet, crossed to the ornate drinks cabinet and poured himself a whiskey. He raised a glass, inviting the other occupant of the room to join him.

The figure nodded and Curtis handed him a drink.

'How much does he know?' the figure asked.

'He knows about Weller,' Curtis announced, then he swallowed a large measure of the whiskey.

'You expected him to, didn't you? A murder and a suicide in a small town like this are bound to be common knowledge.'

Curtis raised his eyebrows quizzically.

'Murders but not disappearances?' he mused.

'Hacket knows that Weller killed his family,' the figure said. 'What he mustn't find out is *why*.'

Sixty-six

He stood beside the bed for what seemed like an eternity, watching the steady rise and fall of her chest as she slept.

Finally Hacket undressed and slipped into bed beside Sue. He lay back, one arm across his forehead, gazing at the ceiling, listening to Sue's shallow breathing.

Could what Curtis said really be true?

Was it even feasible?

Hacket exhaled deeply and rubbed his face.

He knew that the child was important to Sue. No, important was the wrong word. It had become an obsession. He wondered if he could stop her from undergoing Curtis' treatment now even if he wanted to.

But did he want to?

He knew the child meant everything to her and he also knew that it did offer their only chance of returning to anything like a normal existence. To be given the chance to start again. It was a chance which *he* dare not forego either.

But the risks.

Small compared to the joy which would come with the birth of the child.

What exactly was the treatment?

Curtis had described it. A form of artificial insemination. Only this was less clinical, less mechanical.

The foetus grows at an accelerated rate. Why?

Hacket sat up in bed and looked down at Sue. He reached across and gently pulled a strand of hair away from her mouth.

The thought of the child meant everything to her. He had no right to deprive her of that joy.

The children born because of Curtis' treatment were violent.

Only the ones you know about, he told himself. *Just two out of possibly dozens. It could be coincidence.*

It *had* to be coincidence.

'Oh God,' he murmured, irritably. The questions and queries could torment him forever if he thought about them. The only thing that mattered was that they had a glimmer of hope.

The chance of another child.

The risks . . .

'To hell with it,' he whispered to himself and swung out of bed.

It was then that the phone rang.

Hacket glanced down at the clock.

11.56 p.m.

He looked at Sue but the persistent drone of the phone didn't seem to have disturbed her.

It kept ringing.

Hacket got to his feet and padded down the stairs, shivering slightly from the cold as he reached for the receiver.

'Hello,' he said, quietly.

Nothing.

'Hello,' he repeated, wearily.

Silence.

Hacket put down the phone and shook his head.

Wrong number no doubt he thought as he turned and ascended the stairs once more.

He was half way up when the phone rang again.

'For Christ's sake,' he muttered and retraced his steps, snatching up the receiver once again.

'Yes,' he hissed.

No answer.

'Look, if this is a joke.'

His angry protestations were cut short.

'John Hacket?' said the voice at the other end of the line.

It was the teacher's turn to stand there in silence.

264

He didn't recognise the voice, hardly surprising, really, from the utterance of just two words.

'Is that John Hacket?' the voice repeated.

'Yes, who is this?'

Click.

The line went dead.

Hacket held the receiver away from his ear as if it were some kind of venomous reptile then, slowly, he replaced it. He stood looking at the phone for a moment, as if expecting it to ring again. When it didn't he made his way slowly back up to bed.

Sixty-seven

The smell reminded Sue of a hospital. The strong odour of disinfectant. A scent that was both reassuring and repulsive.

Sue thought of her father, lying alone in that hospital room, waiting to die. It was this smell which must have filled his nostrils for so long.

The memory came unexpectedly, all the more painful for that and she tried to push it from her mind. She sat in the waiting room of Curtis' surgery, nervously clasping and unclasping her hands, glancing alternately up at the wall-clock above the receptionist's desk and at the door which led through to the surgery.

She seemed to have been waiting hours, although she knew that barely five minutes had slipped by since she'd arrived and the receptionist had retreated into the surgery proper to tell Curtis of her arrival. Sue wasn't sure what was making her more nervous, the thought of the treatment or the nagging doubt that it would fail.

She brushed the hair from her face, noticing as she did that her hand was shaking.

Hacket had wanted to come with her but she had assured him she would be fine alone. She trusted doctor Curtis. Felt safe in his hands.

'*Come and see me*'.

The door to the surgery opened and the receptionist ushered her through, finally leaving her alone in the office. Although it looked different from the other times she had visited. For one thing there was no sign of Curtis. Sue saw a door leading out of surgery and she heard footsteps approaching that door. A second later the doctor entered. He was wearing a white lab coat over his clothes but that was the only item of protective clothing in evidence. He greeted Sue warmly and invited her to follow him through the door which she did.

It opened onto the cellar.

The white-washed walls almost glowed so dazzling bright were they painted. In the centre of the room was a couch, covered by a white sheet and, beside it, a trolley which sported a dizzying array of surgical implements.

Sue swallowed hard as she saw them, and glanced anxiously at Curtis, who merely smiled and led her to the lower level.

It was unexpectedly warm down there and she could hear an almost monotonous drone of something which she guessed might be a generator. Access to it though was hidden by a series of screens which surrounded the couch.

'How are you feeling?' Curtis asked, smiling warmly, and Sue, once again, was captivated by his eyes. She felt as if she were drowning in them. Floating.

'A little nervous,' she confessed.

'Then the sooner we get started the better,' the doctor

266

said. 'Are you warm enough? I want you to be comfortable. The procedure doesn't take more than about five minutes.' He touched her arm softly. 'And I'm sure you'll find it worthwhile.'

She smiled, relaxing visibly at his touch.

'If you could undress for me,' he said, quietly.

Sue nodded almost imperceptibly. The words were spoken slowly, almost tenderly. The words of a lover, not a physician. He handed her a white gown from another of the trolleys which she laid on the couch. Then she began unbuttoning her blouse, glancing at Curtis as she did, surprised that she didn't feel the slightest twinge of embarrassment.

Curtis turned his back as she pulled the blouse free of her jeans. He bent over the trolley, inspecting a number of syringes which were laid out, it appeared, in descending order of size. The largest was over eight inches long, the smallest no bigger than his index finger.

'Is your husband still opposed to this treatment?' Curtis wanted to know, his back still to her.

'He wasn't really opposed to it,' Sue informed him, unhooking her bra. 'He was worried because he didn't know all the details.'

'I told him as much as I could.'

'I know that.'

'Does it worry you?' Curtis asked, turning round.

Sue stood before him, naked from the waist up but she made no attempt to hide herself. Instead she stood facing the doctor, almost willing him to inspect her breasts, aware of the tightening and swelling of her nipples.

'I want a child,' she whispered, removing her shoes. 'I don't care what it takes.' As she spoke she began to unfasten the zip of her jeans, easing them down over her slender hips until she stood before him in just her panties.

The droning of the generator continued, a low hum which matched Sue's increasingly deep breathing.

As Curtis turned away from her for a second she was aware of the tingles running up and down her spine, of the growing excitement which was spreading through her body. As she prepared to remove her panties she felt the wetness between her legs.

Completely naked she swung herself up onto the couch.

Her breathing was coming in shallow gasps, her chest heaving almost expectantly.

'Slide your bottom forward to the edge of the couch and open your legs,' Curtis said, softly, laying one hand on her thigh to aid her in that simple manoeuvre. As he moved between her legs he could smell the musky odour of her sex. She shuffled around, gyrating her hips slightly, trying to slow the pace of her breathing.

'I'm going to give you a local anaesthetic,' he told her, quietly. 'Just relax.'

She eased her legs further apart, inviting him to move closer. Sue was gazing at the ceiling, she didn't see Curtis reach for one of the smaller syringes.

With infinite care he parted her outer labial lips, already swollen and red, slick with the moisture of her excitement. They had parted like the petals of a flower and he saw her stomach muscles contract as he gently moved the needle closer to her vagina.

The steel point slid easily into the tumescent flesh and Sue sucked in a deep breath as it penetrated her, holding that breath as Curtis pushed on the plunger, emptying the contents of the shaft into her. Then he withdrew the glistening needle carefully and laid it on the trolley.

'You might feel a little groggy,' he told her. 'If you do just let yourself fall asleep. There's nothing to worry about.'

She smiled.

'I know,' she whispered, closing her eyes, waiting for the next, deeper penetration.

'This time,' Curtis breathed and brought the largest of the syringes closer to her slippery cleft, pushing the needle inside until he felt it press against the spongy tissue of her endometrium. Sue arched her back slightly as the syringe was pushed deeper into her uterus and she felt fluid filling her. Felt a warmth spreading up from her thighs and across her belly. Her nipples ached, such was their stiffness, and she brushed one breast with her hand, suppressing a gasp as her fingers raked against the hard bud.

Curtis remained between her thighs, squeezing the last drops of fluid from the thick container, finally withdrawing it carefully.

Sue let out a long breath, her eyes flickering shut.

Curtis looked down at her and smiled.

'It's done,' he told her, watching as a smile spread across her face.

He reached for the gown and gently laid it over her.

'Rest for a little while,' the doctor said, standing over her until he saw that she was slipping off to sleep. Then he pulled off the rubber gloves he'd been wearing and tossed them into a nearby waste bin, washing his hands in the sink at one corner of the cellar.

He had his back to the door when it opened.

Curtis only heard the footsteps behind him, moving towards the couch.

Towards Sue.

He turned slowly to see the other figure standing over her.

They exchanged glances and Curtis merely nodded, a silent affirmation of what the other wondered. Like the mute answer to an unasked question.

The figure reached for the gown and pulled it up, inspecting Sue's body, gazing at her full rounded breasts, flat

269

stomach and the small triangle of light hair between her legs. Legs which were still slightly parted.

Curtis, still drying his hands, joined the newcomer, who was still looking appreciatively at Sue's naked body.

'It won't be long now,' Curtis said, quietly.

The other nodded.

Sixty-eight

'That's about the tenth time you've checked your watch and we've only been out here for ten minutes,' Jo Milton said, smiling.

Hacket shrugged and dug his hands in his pockets as they walked.

'I promise not to look again,' he said, smiling.

All around them the sound of children playing, shouting, arguing, laughing and sometimes fighting merged into one endless cacophony of noise. Break-time, twenty minutes in which to unleash the furies built up during class, thought Hacket looking round at the children.

A group of boys were kicking a ball against a wall to his right. To his left three or four girls were standing around peering at a magazine. One of them looked at Hacket as he passed and smiled. The others dissolved into a chorus of giggles.

'Seems you've got an admirer,' said Jo, chuckling.

Hacket shrugged.

'Catch them young, that's my motto,' he told her. 'What about you, Jo? Any entanglements?'

'A boyfriend you mean?' She shook her head and sipped the tea she was carrying. 'Nothing serious.'

Hacket glanced at her, struck, as he had been at their first meeting, by her good looks. Her face was full but not fat, her pointed chin making her look much more thin-featured than she actually was. Her high cheek bones accentuated the look.

Was this how it had started with Nikki? A casual conversation?

Hacket tried to push the thoughts aside, but they persisted. Jo was very attractive indeed, and as she looked at him he found himself gazing deep into her eyes, stumbling through the clichés to find one that described them.

Inviting eyes?

He'd played this game before.

Come to bed eyes?

He forced himself to look away from her, glancing around the playground once again at the noisy throng of children.

'How long have you been married, John?' she asked.

'Five years,' he told her, again avoiding her eyes.

'Happy?'

'What makes you ask that?'

'It's an innocent enough question isn't it?' she said, defensively.

Well go on then, tell her, his mind prompted. *Tell her you're happily married. It's just that you wouldn't refuse if she was available would you?*

Or *would* you?

'Jo, can I ask you something,' he said. 'In your official capacity.'

She smiled.

'That does sound grand, John. What is it?'

'Is it possible for a foetus to gestate inside the womb without having travelled along the fallopian tubes?'

271

'Is that a trick question?' she chuckled. 'What's the next one? Who won the FA cup last year?'

'I'm serious. You're a biologist.'

'I *teach* biology, there's a difference.'

'But is it possible?'

'Through certain forms of artificial insemination yes.'

'You mean that the egg is planted directly into the womb?'

She nodded.

'Is it fertilised first?' he wanted to know. 'I mean, the egg couldn't be placed in the womb then fertilised by normal means?'

'No,' she said, flatly. 'There are certain nutrients and proteins found in the ovaries and the fallopian tube which are essential to the development of the foetus.' She looked hard at him. 'If you don't mind me saying, John, this is a little *deep* for this time of the day isn't it? We're doing playground duty not "Mastermind".'

'Just humour me will you? What about the growth rate of the foetus, is there any way it could be speeded up? To cut the gestation period for instance?'

'Well, theoretically, yes.'

Hacket looked at her, stopped walking and gripped her arm.

'How?' he wanted to know.

Some of the children nearby saw him grab Jo's arm and turned to look but the two teachers moved on after a moment or two.

'How could it be done?' he repeated.

'Growth is regulated by the pituitary gland. Too little causes dwarfism, too much causes the opposite and disfiguring disease called acromegaly. The gland secretes the hormones that regulate growth.' She looked puzzled. 'I don't know what you're getting at, John.'

272

'Could the gestation period be altered by these pituitary hormones?' he wanted to know.

'Yes, but no one has ever done that.'

Hacket sucked in an almost painful breath.

'Why do you ask?' Jo persisted.

Hacket didn't answer.

All he was aware of were Curtis' words ringing in his ears.

'This is *my* project, Mr Hacket. *My* treatment.'

Sixty-nine

He pulled a piece of the scab from his hand, picking away at the crusted flesh until it came free.

His eyes, however, did not leave the playground.

So many children, thought Ronald Mills, smiling.

They ranged in age from eight up to about fifteen, he thought, watching as they cavorted noisily around in the school yard.

A tall privet hedge formed a boundary between the school field and the road on one side but Mills could see easily over this barrier as he walked along, glancing at the children as he did.

Groups of boys were playing football, girls were skipping or chasing each other or merely standing around talking.

Mills stopped as he caught sight of two young girls no more than nine years old. The first of them had gleaming blonde hair, so pure it looked almost silver. It reached to the middle of her back and, as she stood talking to her friend, she would occasionally toss the mane of hair with one hand. Her companion was slightly darker and a little taller.

Mills smiled as he gazed at them, feeling the first stirrings in his groin. He slipped one hand into his pocket, rubbing his stiffening penis.

Across the road from the school there was a row of houses, each one painted white with tedious uniformity. It was from the bedroom window of one of these houses that a woman watched Mills.

He stood staring at the children for a moment or two then moved on, looking behind him as he did so.

He saw the woman standing at the window.

She froze as she realised he'd seen her, attempting to duck back behind her curtain, but Mills merely stood gazing up at the window, as if challenging her to re-appear.

She didn't.

After a moment or two he moved on, glancing one last time at the two children in the field beyond.

It took him less than fifteen minutes to wander around the entire perimeter of the school and he came to the gates where he had begun his vigil earlier. There he lit up a cigarette and continued gazing into the playground.

He recognised Hacket immediately.

The teacher was with a woman, walking slowly, talking to her.

Mills sucked hard on his cigarette and watched Hacket with the same determined intent as a predator watching its prey.

He didn't know how long he stood there, but finally the sound of a bell disturbed his observations.

The children flooded towards the school buildings, Hacket and the woman were caught up in the flow and, in moments, they too were gone.

The playground was empty again.

Mills finished his cigarette then turned and headed back to his car.

He was smiling as he slid behind the wheel.

Seventy

The house was in silence when he entered.

Hacket paused by the front door, listening for any noise from within but, upon hearing nothing, he gently closed the door and walked into the sitting room.

Sue was lying on the sofa, her eyes closed.

Hacket looked at her worriedly and immediately crossed to her, kneeling beside her, shaking her gently to rouse her. She opened her eyes, looked up at him and smiled.

'Are you OK?' he asked, softly.

She nodded and sat up, rubbing her temple.

'Just a bit of a headache,' she told him.

'How did it go this morning?' he wanted to know. 'With Curtis? I thought you might have phoned when you got back.'

'I didn't want to disturb you. Besides, there was nothing out of the ordinary. Everything was fine. I *feel* fine.'

'How long did it take?'

'I was back home within two hours. Doctor Curtis told me to take it easy so I did. I must have dropped off.' She began to rise. 'I'll get the dinner.'

'No, Sue, leave it. Just sit,' Hacket told her, crossing to the drinks cabinet. He poured himself a large whisky and Sue a Martini. Then he sat beside her on the sofa, easing one arm round her shoulders.

'What happened?' he wanted to know.

'It was simple, just like Curtis said it would be.' She told him what had happened. The injection. The period of sleep which followed. Hacket listened intently, sipping his drink occasionally.

'Did Curtis say anything more about the nature of the treatment? What it involved?'

'He told us about it the other evening, John,' she said, wearily.

'He didn't tell us everything,' Hacket protested.

'You're never satisfied are you?' she snapped. 'Why do you need to know so much? Surely the most important thing is that we can have another child.'

'I don't like the idea of you being used as a guinea pig.'

'Don't be ridiculous. You speak as if I'm the first he's treated. We know the treatment works.'

'Yes, we just don't know what the treatment *is*.'

She shook her head.

'I've been thinking about it,' Hacket continued. 'I was talking to one of the other teachers today.'

'About *this?*' Sue blurted, angrily. 'It's *our* business, John.'

'Calm down, Sue, I just needed to know a few things. I think I might know what Curtis is doing. What some parts of the treatment are. One of the biology teachers, Jo, she said . . .'

'*She?*' Sue interrupted. 'It's always a woman isn't it? You always seem to get on better with women, John. Is it easier to talk about your problems to a woman than another man?'

He knew where this was leading.

'She was better qualified to answer my questions,' he said, irritably.

'Well, a teacher is a step up from a secretary isn't it?' said Sue, acidly.

'For Christ's sake.'

276

'A little talk. Is that how it started before? With the other one?'

Hacket glared at her, his anger mixed with the guilt which still plagued him. He resented Sue for making him feel that guilt again. He got up and poured himself another drink, his back to her.

'Are we going to talk about this or not?' he asked.

'What? You mean about what your lady friend told you today? Or about our baby? Except you seem to be more interested in your little chat.'

Hacket turned slowly.

'I don't want to argue, Sue. Especially when we've nothing to argue about. I just want you to hear what I've got to say.'

She exhaled deeply.

'Go on.'

'The treatment which Curtis perfected, from what he told us, it sounds like some kind of growth drug. He said the foetus would develop at an increased rate. I think I know what he's doing. What he's using.'

Sue looked on impassively.

'The drug must contain some traces of pituitary secretion in order to cause that acceleration.'

'So what if it does?' she said, flatly.

'The baby could be affected by it. If the dose was wrong it could be too small, perhaps even deformed.'

'And your *friend* told you this, did she?' said Sue, her voice heavy with sarcasm.

'I mentioned it to her, she gave me her opinion,' he said.

'I don't care, John. I knew the risks, we both did. Do you honestly think that a man of Curtis' expertise is going to give me the wrong dose? He said himself he'd treated other women. He's not some mad scientist from a bloody horror film, he's a trained doctor and I don't care what

277

your friend says. I'd trust Curtis with my life. Mine and our baby's.'

'Just try to see my point of view,' he asked. 'I love you. You're all I have since Lisa died. I don't want to lose you too.'

Sue got to her feet and headed for the hallway.

'If you don't want to lose me, then don't stand in my way,' she said. 'Let me have this baby.'

He heard her footsteps as she climbed the stairs.

Hacket waited another moment then poured himself some more whisky, downing the contents of the tumbler in one gulp.

He suddenly felt very alone.

Seventy-one

Ronald Mills pulled the .38 from beneath the pillow and flipped out the cylinder, turning it slowly. Then he snapped it back into position and pushed the gun back out of sight.

Whenever he left the hotel he would take the gun with him, stuffed into the pocket of his jacket. The knife he would slide into his belt but now, he didn't intend leaving The Bull for the rest of the evening so he left the weapons beneath the pillow.

He crossed to the window which looked out onto the main street of Hinkston and peered down at the dozen or so people passing by. It was late, almost 10.30 p.m., the cinema down the street had emptied out about fifteen minutes earlier and the disco didn't open during the week, so the street was quiet.

Mills glanced across at the phone beside his bed.

There was a knock on the bedroom door and he opened it.

Paula Kirkham stood before him holding a tray.

She smiled broadly, shaking her head gently, allowing her long hair to cascade over her shoulders. She wore no bra beneath her T-shirt and Mills noticed that her nipples were straining against the material.

He stepped back to let her into the room, watching as she set the tray of food down on the bedside table.

'Will there be anything else?' she asked, smiling.

'No,' said Mills, holding the door open, as if to emphasise the fact that he wanted her out.

She looked most put out and wiggled past him, glancing briefly at him. He closed the door and she heard him lock it.

Paula hesitated outside the door, ear pressed close to it.

The man didn't seem attracted to her.

He'd been a guest at the hotel for the last five days, keeping himself to himself, ignoring the other guests and her own advances. She didn't think too much of him. Ugly bastard really.

But, he was single.

Alone.

He was a perfect choice.

Just like the man before him.

She struggled to remember his name.

Jennings, that was it. She smiled as she remembered.

The ones before Jennings she could *not* recall.

There had been too many.

She stood for a moment longer outside the door then slowly made her way along the corridor to her own room.

Mills heard her footsteps as she wandered away, only then did he turn his attention to the plate of food which she'd brought him. He nibbled at one of the sandwiches, his eyes flicking back and forth towards the phone every now and then. Finally he pushed the remains of the sandwich into his mouth and reached for the receiver.

Pulling the number from the pocket of his jacket he dialled.

And waited.

'Come on you fucker,' he murmured, listening to the purring at the other end.

The phone was finally picked up.

It was a woman's voice on the other end.

Mills sat listening to her, his breathing subdued, the smile spreading across his face.

'Who is this?' she asked.

He put the phone down.

Another five minutes and he called again.

This time he recognised Hacket's voice.

'Who's there?' the teacher snapped.

Mills sat on the edge of the bed, the phone held slightly away from his ear.

'Can you hear me?' Hacket rasped.

Mills put down the phone.

He chuckled, the grin slowly fading.

The game was nearly over.

Hacket's time had come.

Mills held the knife up before him.

And then there was the woman.

Paula Kirkham stood naked outside the door, her breathing low and rapid, like an animal in the heat.

She glared at the door as if trying to see through it to the man beyond.

To Ronald Mills.

She pressed herself close to the cold wood, feeling her nipples stiffen as she rubbed herself gently against the smooth paintwork, feeling the moistness between her legs.

Her mouth hung open, streamers of sputum dripping from it as she salivated madly.

She wiped her mouth with the back of her hand and smiled.

Seventy-two

She heard movement on the landing.

Julie Clayton sat up, her ears alert for the slightest sound.

Footsteps on the carpet.

She swung herself out of bed, jabbing her husband as she did so.

Mike rolled onto his back and groaned, rubbing his eyes.

'What is it?' he croaked, seeing Julie pull on her dressing gown. He glanced at the clock and saw that it was almost 3.36 a.m. 'Shit.'

'Mike, hurry,' she said, moving towards the bedroom door.

The expression on her face told him how frightened she was. He hauled himself out of bed, following her out onto the landing.

She was approaching Craig's room, aware of the sounds coming from within.

'Oh God,' murmured Mike. 'Not again.'

Stuart Lewis stood over the baby, looking down, his eyes fixed to the blazing stare which seemed to pin him as surely as light draws a moth. He could not look away from his son.

The baby was gurgling loudly, rocking itself back and

forth in its cot frenziedly, grasping at the sides with its tiny fingers.

Michelle joined him, reaching for the baby but Stuart put out an arm to hold her back.

'He needs me, Stuart,' she protested but her husband merely remained where he was, looking down at his child, watching as the boy suddenly stopped thrashing about and lay still, gazing up at his parents. His eyes flicking back and forth from one to the other.

Lewis shook his head slowly.

'It's not *us* he needs,' he said, quietly.

And she understood.

Elaine Craven picked up the phone immediately it rang. Despite the fact that it was so early in the morning she knew who it would be, and she was not wrong.

The voice at the other end belonged to Patricia Stokes.

It was her daughter, Emma, she said.

Elaine said she understood.

Patricia wasn't sure what to do.

Elaine tried to reassure her, touching her own bandaged arm as she spoke.

Upstairs she could hear the shouts and snarls.

She spoke calmly and slowly to Patricia who seemed to relax a little, the longer the conversation went on. Finally she said goodbye and returned to her own problem.

To her Emma.

Elaine waited by the phone a moment longer then she took a deep breath and made her way back up the stairs.

It had happened so quickly this time.

The shouting continued.

As she reached the landing she had to steady herself against the bannister, noticing that her hands were shaking.

She thought she had become used to it by now, but, somehow, the fear still remained.

Seventy-three

She hadn't mentioned the pain to Hacket.

Hadn't thought it worth talking about the silent twinges which she felt around her vagina, especially during their lovemaking.

But now, as Sue Hacket reached for the can on the shelf before her, she sucked in a deep breath, reacting as if she had been punched. The pain was sudden and severe. She gripped the shopping trolley for a second, waiting for the discomfort to subside, which, thankfully, it did. A woman passed and glanced at her, noticing the look on Sue's face and, for a moment, Sue thought the woman was going to stop, but she merely smiled and carried on with her own shopping.

Sue dropped the can into her trolley and walked on, parading up and down each aisle, filling the trolley, trying to ignore the stabs of pain telling herself that they were lessening.

Curtis had said nothing about side-effects. Nothing about pain. If she still felt as bad when she reached home she would call him. Visit him if necessary.

However, as she reached the check-out the pains did indeed seem to be diminishing in severity. Sue ran a hand across her belly almost unconsciously as the woman ahead of her packed her groceries into a succession of carrier bags. Sue shuffled uncomfortably as she waited her turn, brushing a speck of dirt from the leg of her jeans.

She waited for the pain to return.

It didn't.

She began unloading her shopping onto the conveyor belt.

If she'd mentioned the pains to Hacket he would have panicked, she thought to herself. He would have started complaining about the treatment again. Why couldn't he just be happy in the knowledge that they were to have another child? Why all the questions and doubts?

She packed the groceries away then paid the cashier, using the trolley to transport the goods out to the car.

As she unlocked the back of the car the pain struck her once more.

A deep burning sensation between her legs and she gripped the trolley for a second until it subsided.

Sue put the groceries in the back of the car then turned to return the trolley.

The man seemed to loom from thin air.

He was carrying an armful of shopping which promptly fell from his grip as he collided with Sue.

'I'm sorry,' she said, dropping to her knees to help him gather up the spilled groceries.

Her own handbag had also fallen in the collision and she scrabbled to retrieve its spilled contents.

'It was my fault,' said the man, shoving tins back into the shopping bag. 'I wasn't looking where I was going.'

The combination of food and the contents of her handbag had rolled for several feet around the car, some beneath it, and it took about five minutes to pick up everything. Everything except a couple of squashed peaches which had fallen from the man's bag. He looked down at them and shrugged.

'I was eating too much fruit anyway,' he said, wistfully.

Sue smiled, the expression twisting slightly as she felt more pain.

'Are you OK?' the man asked, seeing her wince.

She nodded.

'Thank you, yes. I'll be fine.' She managed another smile. 'Sorry again about . . .' she motioned to his squashed fruit.

'No problem,' he told her, smiling as she climbed into the Metro and started the engine.

284

He was still smiling as she drove off.

He watched her turn a corner and disappear and, as she did he slid a hand into his pocket and pulled out the prize he'd taken from her handbag in all the confusion.

The purse looked small in his large fist.

Ronald Mills wondered how long it would be before she realised it was gone.

Seventy-four

It was happening too fast.

It was as if someone had pressed the fast-forward button on life, and now events were moving at break-neck speed, faster than he could comprehend.

The ambulance, its siren blaring loudly, took the corner so fast it almost overturned.

Hacket gripped one edge of the stretcher to steady himself, with the other hand he held onto Sue's outstretched fingers. Her face was milk white, a thin sheen of perspiration covering her. She had her eyes closed tightly, her forehead wrinkling as each fresh spasm of pain racked her body.

'Isn't there anything you can give her?' Hacket asked the ambulanceman who rode in the back of the vehicle with them. But the uniformed man merely shook his head and looked on impassively.

'We're almost at the hospital,' he said, flatly, glancing at his watch.

Sue gripped Hacket's hand more tightly and he felt helpless to comfort her. All he could do was to wipe the sweat from her face with his handkerchief.

'It won't be long now,' he murmured. 'Hold on.'

Jesus, he felt so fucking useless. There was nothing he could do to ease her suffering. Nothing to stop the pain.

So much pain.

Her body stiffened then relaxed, as if someone were jabbing her with a cattle prod. The spasms became more frequent, more severe until finally she shouted aloud from the pain which raged inside her swollen belly.

Hacket pulled the sheet down and looked at her stomach. It was bloated and, as he watched, he could see the skin gently undulating.

'How much further?' he rasped, glaring at the ambulanceman.

'Not far,' the man said, also glancing at Sue.

'John.' Her voice rose in volume, dissolving into a scream of pain.

Hacket saw the first droplets of blood dribble from between her legs and she stiffened, her body jerking every few seconds.

She began to breathe rapidly and loudly, holding Hacket's hand so tightly it seemed she would break his fingers.

'It's starting,' she gasped, raising her legs and opening them.

'Help her,' Hacket snarled at the uniformed man, his face pale as he saw a steady flow of crimson beginning to pump from Sue's distended vagina. The outer lips seemed to swell and open like a blossoming flower and the sheet beneath her was stained by her life fluid as the contractions became more savage.

The ambulanceman struggled towards the far end of the vehicle, almost overbalancing as it took another corner doing over fifty. He retrieved some oxygen and stuck the plastic mask over Sue's face, but she merely pushed it away, beyond help now, knowing that there was no turning back.

A searing pain filled her lower body and she felt an incredible pressure building between her legs.

Hacket held her hand, his eyes rivetted to her swollen vagina.

A moment later he saw something white appear between the folds of flesh. Something white and bulbous.

The baby's head.

Pieces of placenta were draped over the skull like bleeding streamers, some of which dangled from Sue's vagina as the child fought to free itself.

The head burst free.

Hacket sucked in a deep breath, watching as the torso began to emerge.

'Nearly finished,' he said. gripping Sue's hand even more tightly. 'Nearly . . .'

The words trailed away and he felt the bile rising in his throat, felt his eyes throbbing in their sockets.

The child had a large hump on its back, just below the nape of its neck.

A hump large enough . . .

Hacket shook his head in horrified disbelief as he saw the child emerge.

Sue was still contracting her muscles, as if anxious to expel the child from her body.

The ambulanceman looked on, his face also pale, his eyes wide.

The hump on the child's back wasn't skin and muscle.

It was bone.

Thick bone.

A second head.

The eyes had formed but where the mouth should have been was a gash. No lips, just a rent across the lower face. But the eyes were open, blinking away the blood and fragments of placenta which coated it.

And, in that brief instant before he finally surrendered

to his revulsion and vomited, Hacket noticed that the obscene hole which passed for a mouth was curling up at either side.

The eyes fixed him in a blazing stare.

The second head was smiling at him.

He sat bolt upright in bed, his breath coming in gasps, his heart thudding madly against his ribs.

He turned to look at Sue, surprised to find her sitting up looking at him.

She was smiling.

Seventy-five

Hacket wiped a hand across his face and sighed, the last vestiges of the nightmare gradually slipping away.

'Jesus,' he murmured. 'I had a bad dream. About you and the baby.'

She held his gaze for a moment then slowly leant across and kissed him, her tongue flicking against the hard edges of his tongue before sliding into the warm moistness beyond. Hacket responded, feeling her arms glide around his shoulders. He lay down beside her, raising one knee so that his thigh was rubbing against her vagina. She was already wet and he felt her moisture dampen his leg as he ground it against her, his own movements matched by her slow rhythmic thrusting. She moaned in his arms as he allowed one hand to find her right breast, teasing the nipple between his thumb and forefinger, then kissing the swollen bud for a moment before transferring his attention to her left breast.

Sue reached down and cupped his testicles, rubbing gently, grazing the base of his shaft with the nail of her index finger.

Hacket felt a familiar warmth beginning to spread around his groin.

Sue arched her back as he slid down the bed, his tongue flicking across her nipples while his probing fingers gently outlined the edges of her vaginal lips, parting them, spreading the tumescent flesh like the petals of a musky flower.

'Love me,' she murmured, her eyes closed.

Hacket felt her hands on his back. Felt her nails raking his skin.

'Jesus,' he hissed as she pulled her nails hard across his shoulder.

She raised the hand before her and saw the tiny pieces of his flesh hanging from her nails. She smiled down at him and Hacket looked into her eyes.

He could feel the grazes on his shoulder.

The tiny dribble of blood from the four places she had scraped him.

He slid back up the bed, kissing her breasts again, this time returning to her mouth. They kissed feverishly, his tongue plunging deep into her mouth.

She took his bottom lip between her teeth, sucking gently, then chewing.

She bit hard.

'Sue, for Christ's sake,' he hissed, drawing back. He put a finger to his lip and found that there was blood dribbling from it.

'Please, John, just love me,' she gasped, a note of pleading in her voice, 'Like you were doing before.'

Hacket hesitated a moment then slid down her body once more, blood from his cut lip staining her breasts and belly as his tongue flicked over the warm flesh. He probed inside her navel with his tongue, slowing his pace as he drew nearer to the spot he sought. The tightly curled hair between her legs through which his fingers were already gliding. He withdrew one from her vagina, drawing a glistening trail across her belly with her own moisture. She gasped and pushed him further down towards her burning desire.

Hacket licked her belly again, tasting her wetness which he had smeared there.

The skin of her stomach rose a fraction beneath his tongue.

At first he thought it was a muscular contraction but, when it happened a second time he sat up, looking down at her belly.

'What's wrong?' she said, quietly. 'Don't stop now.'

Hacket rubbed the palm of his hand gently over her stomach.

He felt the movement beneath his palm.

Like..

Like what?

Like the first movements of a growing child?

'It's impossible,' said Hacket, as if in answer to his own thoughts.

'John, what's wrong?' she wanted to know, watching as he moved away slightly, his eyes still on her stomach.

Was this another dream?

'I felt something,' he said. 'Like..' He was struggling for the words, aware of how ridiculous it sounded. 'Like a baby moving.'

'Isn't it wonderful?' she beamed.

'Sue, it's not possible,' he snapped. 'Curtis treated you two days ago.'

'*Accelerated growth.*'

Hacket shook his head. No, this wasn't real. The foetus

290

couldn't possibly have developed at such incredible sp
He had imagined it. Yes, that was the answer. He
imagined it.

Her stomach moved slightly again.

Sue pressed her fingers to the spot and smiled.

'Aren't you happy, John?' she said, smiling broadly. 'I
am.'

'This isn't normal, Sue. I don't know what Curtis has
done to you but it's not right . . .'

She cut him short.

'I'll tell you what he's done,' she snapped. 'He's given
me what you never could give me. He's given me hope.'

'At least let another doctor examine you,' Hacket pleaded. 'There could be complications. Something could have
gone wrong.'

'That's what you want isn't it?' she snarled. 'You want
something to go wrong. You want me to lose this child
don't you?'

'Don't be ridiculous, Sue. I'm worried about your
health.'

'No you're not. You just don't want me to have another
child. Well I'll make sure I don't lose this one. It was your
fault Lisa died,' she hissed, hatred in her eyes. '*You* killed
her.'

'Sue,' he said, his own anger building.

'If it hadn't been for you she'd still be here now.'

'Drop it,' he told her.

'If not for you and your whore.'

'I mean it,' he said, angrily. 'Shut up.'

'You killed our first child, I won't let you kill this one.'

'SHUT UP.'

He acted instinctively, not even realising what he was
doing.

Hacket struck his wife a stinging back-hand blow across
the face.

291

She fell back on the bed, glaring up at him.

Despite his anger he felt the remorse immediately.

'Oh God, I'm sorry,' he whispered, moving towards her.

'Get away,' she roared. 'Leave me alone. Leave me and my baby alone.'

Hacket looked at her. The blazing eyes, her hair coiled around her face and shoulders like damp reptilian tails. She looked like some modern-day Gorgon.

'What's happening to you, Sue?' he asked, quietly, his voice cracking. 'I'm losing you again and I don't want that.'

'Then stay out of my fucking way,' she snarled, getting to her feet. She tugged a sheet from the bed and wrapped it around her.

Hacket could only watch as she padded towards the door.

He heard her cross the landing then heard the door of the spare room slam shut.

Alone, he knelt on the bed, head bowed.

As if in prayer.

Seventy-six

It was almost noon when she heard the knock on the front door.

Sue frowned and got to her feet, lowering the volume on the stereo as she passed.

It was too early for Hacket to be back for lunch. For one thing he hardly ever left the school during the lunch hour and, also, he had his key. He'd have no need to knock. She wasn't expecting Julie until later that afternoon.

She reached the front door and opened it.

The man who stood there looked vaguely familiar to her.

'Mrs Hacket?' he asked.

She nodded, somewhat tentatively.

'Yours I believe,' said the man and held out his hand.

Sue smiled as she saw her purse cradled in the palm of the visitor.

'You dropped it the other day when we bumped into each other,' said Ronald Mills, smiling. 'I'm afraid I looked through it in the hope of finding your address. I wanted to return it to you.'

'You're very kind,' said Sue, beaming. 'I thought I'd lost it.'

Mills shrugged, smiled even more broadly and handed her the purse.

As he did, Sue noticed the tattoo on his hand. The rough design, the discoloured flesh and the raw skin beneath where the scab had been picked away. He turned to leave but she stopped him.

'Look, I really am grateful. I don't know how to thank you,' she said. 'Would a cup of tea be enough? It doesn't seem like much of a reward, but . . .'

'That would be ample reward, Mrs Hacket,' said Mills, holding up a hand. 'Thank you.'

He followed her inside, his smile fading briefly as she turned her back on him.

The knife felt heavy jammed into his belt.

They exchanged pleasantries about the weather. He told her his name was Neville, that he was visiting relatives in Hinkston.

As he sipped his tea he glanced around the sitting room.

A photo of a little girl on the sideboard.

A little girl he recognised.

He felt the beginnings of an erection at the recollection of how close he had been to that girl. How close. How he'd held her.

He remembered using the knife on her.

The same knife which was now stuck in his belt.

'Your husband is out at work then?' he said, gazing at Sue.

'He's a teacher,' she said. 'He works in the school here,' she hooked a thumb in the direction of the building which backed onto their garden. 'That's why we moved here.'

'Your children must like it here,' he said, smiling, picking at the scab on his hand with his nail.

Sue smiled thinly.

'Your little girl, what's her name?' he asked.

'Lisa,' Sue said, quickly, then, trying to change the subject. 'Where abouts in Hinkston do your relatives live?'

'Lisa,' said Mills, ignoring her attempts to steer the conversation along different lines. 'How pretty. She's pretty too.' He got to his feet, crossed to the picture and picked it up. 'You don't mind do you?' he said, almost apologetically, regarding the photo carefully. 'Such a lovely child.'

With his back to Sue his smile faded once again.

So lovely.

'I can't thank you enough for bringing my purse back, Mr Neville,' Sue said, clearing her throat. 'I thought it had been stolen.'

'There are so many dishonest people in the world today, Mrs Hacket. You're lucky that it was me who found it. It could have been a criminal who picked it up.' He chuckled.

Sue found that his eyes were upon her once more, his stare unblinking.

'More tea?' she asked, anxious for the chance of a respite from those piercing eyes.

'Very kind,' he said, handing her the cup.

She took it and headed for the kitchen, aware of Mills behind her.

'You have a lovely house,' he said, stepping into the kitchen, watching as she poured him another cup of tea.

294

She thanked him.

'Lovely house. Lovely child.' He ran appraising eyes over her slim body. The tight jeans, the blouse which she always wore for housework, paint stained and threadbare in places. Her hair had been washed that morning and hung past her shoulders in soft waves. 'And you're lovely too if you don't mind me saying.'

She handed him his tea, beginning to feel a little uncomfortable. She sat down at the kitchen table.

Mills sat down opposite her, his eyes fixed upon her.

As he reached into his jacket pocket for his cigarettes his hand brushed the handle of the knife.

'You don't mind if I smoke do you?' he asked, lighting up. He offered her one and she declined, explaining about the baby. 'You are lucky. I love little children myself,' he said, grinning.

Sue shuffled uncomfortably in her seat, watching him as he sucked slowly on the cigarette. It seemed to take him an eternity to smoke it. Then, finally, he got to his feet and said he would have to go. Sue breathed an almost audible sigh of relief.

He followed her to the front door, standing behind her as she opened it.

She thanked him again and watched as he walked up the path, stopping half-way to smile courteously.

'Perhaps we'll see each other again,' he said. 'When we're shopping.' He chuckled.

Sue nodded, waved and shut the door.

She let out a deep breath, standing with her back to the door for a moment, listening for footsteps, almost as if she expected him to return.

He didn't.

She rebuked herself for feeling so uncomfortable in the man's presence, for being so jumpy.

Never mind, she told herself, he was gone now, *and* she had her purse back.

'Perhaps we'll see each other again,' she said, remembering his words. 'No chance,' she thought aloud.

It was then that the phone rang.

Seventy-seven

Doctor Edward Curtis glanced at the list of names written on the pad before him. He sighed as he ran his finger down the neatly written names. Finally he sat back in his chair, hands pressed together before him as if in some meditative gesture.

He was still sitting like that when the door opened and his receptionist popped her head round.

'Your next patient is here, Doctor,' she said.

Curtis nodded and sat forward, some kind of acknowledgement of the receptionist's presence. She retreated back to her own outer office and Curtis pushed the notepad bearing the names out of sight under a pile of papers.

He ran a hand through his hair and waited for the knock on his door.

It came a moment later and Sue Hacket walked in.

They exchanged greetings and she felt a peculiar pleasure from the fact that Curtis seemed genuinely pleased to see her.

He asked how she was feeling.

She mentioned the pains.

Always pain.

'I'd better check you over,' said the doctor, smiling. 'We can't be too cautious at this stage.' He motioned her towards the couch in the corner of his room and Sue paused beside it.

'Do you want me to undress?' she asked, her eyes never leaving his.

'Yes please,' he said, quietly.

She began unbuttoning her blouse.

Curtis, for his own part, turned to a tray of instruments covered by a sterile gauze sheet. As he lifted it up Sue saw two or three hypodermic needles lying there.

She pulled the blouse off and began unfastening her jeans, simultaneously kicking off her shoes.

'Did you tell your husband about the pains you were getting?' Curtis asked.

'No.'

'Why not?'

'He seems worried enough already, I didn't see the point in making things worse.' She pulled her jeans off and stood before him in just her bra and panties.

Curtis smiled at her and asked her to climb up onto the couch, which she duly did.

'Just relax,' he told her, his hands settling on her stomach. He began to knead the flesh gently, pressing occasionally, his fingers moving lower until he was brushing against the top of her knickers, stirring the silky strands of pubic hair which were in view.

'Show me where the pain was,' he said.

Sue took his hand and guided it between her legs, allowing him to rest against the warmth of her crotch. He pressed and stroked gently along her inner thighs and across her mound. She breathed deeply, her eyes closing. Keeping one hand on her warm vagina he took his stethoscope and pressed it to her belly.

Then moved it across. And down.

'Are you still getting pain,' he wanted to know.

'Only occasionally,' she breathed.

'The baby is fine, as far as I can tell. There's nothing to worry about,' he said, softly.

'When is it due?' she said. 'I know it's probably ages yet.'

'It needn't be,' Curtis said. 'If you want to accelerate the growth there is a way. If you're willing. It involves another injection though.'

'Do it,' she said, flatly. 'Now.'

Curtis smiled.

Sue hooked her thumbs into the sides of her panties and began to ease them over her hips, exposing her silky hairs and her vagina.

Curtis reached for the hypodermic, drew some fluid off from a bottle on the tray then eased the steel point past her outer lips.

She felt the steel penetrate her and it made her gasp. But there was little pain and, as he withdrew, she was smiling.

She dressed again slowly, almost reluctantly, then sat down opposite him at the desk.

'If you have any more trouble let me know,' Curtis said. 'Come and see me anytime.'

She thanked him and got to her feet, ready to leave.

'You don't know how much this means to me, doctor,' she said, pausing at the door. 'I don't know how I can ever thank you.'

Curtis smiled benignly.

Sue closed the door behind her and he heard her footsteps echoing away up the corridor.

His smile faded rapidly and he reached for the pad once more, his eyes skimming over the names he'd looked at a dozen times already that morning. The calls had all come in during a ninety-minute spell earlier that morning.

Calls from Elaine Craven. From Julie Clayton.

Stuart Lewis had rung. So too had Patricia Stokes.

All had been frightened.

Even the call from The Bull had sounded more urgent than usual. Could he come and see Paula, Mrs Kirkham had asked. It was very important.

Curtis knew it was important.

And he knew why.

He sighed as he re-read the list once more.

Had the time come again so soon?

Seventy-eight

Hacket prodded his dinner with his knife then looked across the table at Sue.

She was eating heartily, unaware of his stare.

'What else did Curtis say?'

Hacket finally broke the silence, dropping his cutlery on to the plate.

'He said the baby was fine,' Sue informed him. 'He said there was nothing to worry about.'

'And you believe him?'

She sighed.

'I have no reason to *disbelieve* him. John, I feel fine. I'm fine and the baby's fine. The only one who seems to have any problems is you.' She regarded him coldly for a second. 'He *did* say that the baby would be born earlier than we'd first thought.'

'How can that be possible?' he demanded.

Sue finished chewing the mouthful of food she had then put down her knife and fork.

'He gave me another injection,' she said, quietly.

'Jesus Christ. What of? More of his miracle fucking treatment? We don't know what's happening, Sue. Haven't you stopped to think about this? To think about what's happening to *you* as well as the baby?'

She didn't answer.

'You're changing, Sue,' he told her. 'Your attitude. Your temperament. Even your character, and it's all down to this fucking treatment.' He hissed the last few words through clenched teeth. 'You're blind to what it's doing to you. The only thing you can think about is that damned baby – you don't seem to care that Curtis could be doing you harm.'

'And all you seem to care about is yourself,' she countered. 'I thought you'd be pleased to think that we could have another child. You were the one who said you wanted to start afresh, a new beginning. And when that chance comes along all you do is criticise and complain.'

'I'm worried about you, can't you see that?'

'I can see your jealousy, John.'

'What the hell are you talking about.'

'You're jealous of Curtis.'

'Don't be so bloody ridiculous,' he snorted.

'It's *him* who gave me that hope. Is that what really hurts you? Is *that* why you're so opposed to this child?'

Hacket didn't answer. The muscles at the side of his jaw throbbed angrily and he pushed himself away from the table, getting to his feet.

'You don't understand do you?' he snapped, heading towards the sitting room.

Sue followed, watching him pour himself a large measure of whiskey. He downed most of it in one gulp and re-filled the glass.

'Are you going to get drunk now?' she asked.

'No. I'm going to have one more then I'm going to see Curtis,' he said, flatly.

300

The look on her face changed from anger to surprise.

'What for?' she wanted to know.

'I want to talk to him about a few things. Like what this treatment really is. What exactly he's been injecting into you and the other women he's treated. What is it that can make a child grow at five times its usual rate?'

'You can't just go barging into his house, John,' she said.

'Can't I?' he said, defiantly.

'This is because of that girl isn't it?' said Sue, acidly. 'That other teacher you spoke to. Until then you were as happy as I was about the possibility of having another child. But since you spoke to her you've changed your mind.'

'That's bloody stupid. It's got nothing to do with what she said.'

'Hasn't it?'

'You don't have to be a genius to figure out that things aren't quite right here. I don't like all the mystery surrounding what Curtis is doing.'

'There is no mystery.'

'He didn't tell us everything. He told us what he wanted us to know. Nothing more.'

Hacket finished his drink and slammed the glass down.

'Well, now I'm going to see what he's got to say.'

'No,' she hissed, blocking his path, her eyes narrowed in anger.

'Sue, get out of my way.'

She spread her arms so that he couldn't pass her.

'Come on,' Hacket said, quietly, a little unsettled by the look in her eye. 'You see what this is doing to *us* too. I told you, you're changing.'

'It's always me isn't it? Put the blame on me. As long as you don't have to face up to your own guilt. It's a wonder you didn't blame my father for Lisa's death. I mean, if I hadn't been out visiting him that night then you could have been with your bit on the side without having to worry. I'd have been in the house. You'd have kept a clear conscience.'

'Get out the way, Sue,' he snapped, gripping one of her arms.

She spun round, her left hand clawing at his face, her nails raking his cheek.

Hacket hissed in pain as he felt his flesh tear.

She struck at him again but he managed to deflect the second blow, gripping her wrists, holding her at bay.

He was surprised by her strength.

'Get off me,' she yelled at him, trying to shake loose of his grip.

She kicked out, catching him a stinging blow on the shin and he winced in pain, pushing her backwards, bolting for the door. She was at him immediately, gripping a handful of his hair, tugging so hard that several strands came away from his scalp.

Again he swung round, this time managing to pin her arms behind her back. He lifted her bodily and carried her back into the sitting room.

As he was about to drop her onto the sofa she spat in his face.

Hacket looked at her, both surprised and horrified by the savagery of her reactions.

He pushed her away from him as if she had some kind of contagion.

Then, as she struggled to get up he sprinted for the front door, opened it and hurried up the path towards the waiting car.

'You stay away from him,' Sue shrieked from the door, watching as the car pulled away, its tail lights swallowed up in the darkness.

She was weeping madly, tears of rage pouring down her cheeks. She stepped away from the door and slammed it, walking through into the sitting room, her fury unabated.

302

She crossed to the window and looked out into the night then she turned and glanced at the clock on the mantelpiece.

9.46 p.m.

She looked to the phone.

Should she warn Curtis?

She was moving towards the receiver when the first stab of pain tore through her.

Seventy-nine

Ronald Mills looked at his watch.

9.54 p.m.

He picked a piece of meat from between his front teeth and spat it onto the carpet of the room then he crossed to the bed and pulled the .38 from beneath the pillow.

He sat on the edge of the bed, dug his hand in his jacket pocket and took out six bullets. He flipped the cylinder out then carefully loaded the pistol. That done, he snapped the cylinder back into place and spun it, holding the gun at arms length, peering down the sight.

Not that he would need to aim.

He intended getting close.

And then there was always the knife.

He wanted to be near to Hacket, and to the woman as well.

Wanted to see their pain, feel their agony.

Just like he had done with their child.

The thought of the act he had already committed and that he was about to commit caused the beginning of an erection which he savoured, smiling as he felt the stiffness growing.

Perhaps he would gag them in case their screams were heard, but that, he reasoned, would deprive him of one of the most pleasurable parts of the exercise. Hearing them beg for their lives.

He would take off the woman's breasts.

He had already decided that.

Cut deeply and sever them both.

He would make Hacket watch while he performed the act, slicing each mammary in turn. Then he would cut her. Five, six, seven. A dozen times. He wanted her to die slowly. He wanted Hacket to see it.

Then he would kill Hacket.

He would carve the man's eyes from their sockets.

'If thine eye offend thee, pluck it out,' he chuckled.

He looked again at his watch then he headed for the door, locking it behind him, feeling the gun in his pocket, the knife wedged into his belt.

The drive to the Hackets' house would take him about fifteen minutes.

It was 10.01.

Eighty

The Renault skidded slightly on the road as Hacket spun the wheel and guided the vehicle into the driveway which led towards Curtis' house. The smoothness of tarmac was replaced by the loud crunching of gravel as Hacket drove on.

A powerful wind was gusting across the large open front garden bending a number of topiary animals to such extreme angles it seemed they would be uprooted.

Hacket heard the strong gusts hissing around the car but his attention was on the house itself.

The place seemed to be growing from the night itself. Only the dark outline showed that there was a building there at all, its frontage finally illuminated by the lights of Hacket's car.

There wasn't a light to be seen inside the house itself.

The teacher brought the car to a halt outside the front door, noticing immediately that Curtis' car was not in evidence. No lights. No car. *Nobody home?* He swung himself out of the Renault and crossed to the front door, the powerful wind buffeting him, blowing through his hair. He almost overbalanced, such was the force of the gusts. But, eventually he reached the large oak door and knocked hard, the sound dying away rapidly beneath the persistent howl of the wind.

There was no answer.

Hacket knocked again, harder this time.

Still no response.

He stepped back from the door and looked up at the windows. What little natural light there was reflected back off them and it reminded Hacket of staring into blind eyes. He looked around, wondering if there was access to the rear of the house.

To his right was a path which curved around one corner of the ivy-covered building. The teacher headed towards it. As he turned the corner the wind seemed to hit him with increased ferocity and he steadied himself against the wall of the house for a second before walking on. The path, sure enough, led to the back of the building but, as with the front, Hacket found it devoid of light.

Perhaps Curtis was out on a call, he reasoned. Well, if

305

that was so he'd wait for him. He'd wait as long as he had to in order to speak to the other man, to find out what the hell he was up to, to find out what he'd been pumping into Sue.

Hacket found the back door and pummelled on it angrily as if expecting his outburst to elicit some kind of reaction.

He stepped back, passing along the path, peering into a couple of the windows close by. He could see nothing through the gloom. His frustration and anger growing he turned away from the house, glancing out over the similarly well-kept back garden. The rockery close by, the lawn which sloped down towards the high privet hedge.

Hacket frowned, narrowing his eyes in an effort to see through the gloom.

Down by the high privet hedge something moved.

He was sure of it.

Maybe the wind had disturbed one of the well-kept bushes down there, he thought at first. Maybe.

He took a couple of steps onto the lawn, his eyes fixed on the spot ahead of him where he was sure he'd seen the movement.

Whatever he'd seen before stirred again.

Hacket froze for a moment, not sure whether to advance or remain where he was. He swallowed hard, his initial anger now tempered slightly by the realisation that he was trespassing. If Curtis chose to, he could prosecute.

The doubts vanished from Hacket's mind as quickly as they'd come. What the hell did he care about trespassing? He had more important things to worry about than that. Besides, if Curtis had nothing to hide then he would not object to this visit.

Fuck him, thought Hacket, heading for the bottom of the garden and the area where he'd seen the movement.

As he drew closer to the high privet hedge he heard a

high pitched squealing sound, carried to him on the blustery wind.

He squinted through the darkness once more and saw, a couple of feet ahead, a rusty metal gate set into the hedge.

It was a kind of entrance, he reasoned, the gate swinging wildly back and forth, flung helplessly by the wind.

Hacket paused as he reached the gate, gripping it in one hand to stop the maddening squeak of the hinges. He looked beyond into the area shielded by the high hedge.

Just a simple square of slightly overlong grass, a few flowers.

The flowers were scattered over the ground, tossed wantonly by the breeze.

He saw the piece of flat stone at the centre of the square.

Hacket let go of the gate, pulling it shut behind him as he moved towards the flat stone, finally glancing down at it. Even from so close it was difficult to read the words upon the marble. He knelt and fumbled in his pocket for his lighter. However, no sooner had he coaxed a flame from it than the wind blew it out. Cursing, Hacket leaned closer in an effort to read the words on the stone, realising, as he did, that it was a gravestone.

He ran his fingers across the stone, almost like a blind man, picking out each word carefully.

MARGARET LAWRENSON
BELOVED WIFE AND MOTHER
DIED JUNE 5th 1965

Hacket frowned.

'Lawrenson,' he murmured. He didn't see the connection.

He was still pondering this anomaly when he heard the sound of a car approaching from the front of the house.

Hacket got to his feet and sprinted across the rear lawn towards the house.

The sound of the engine grew louder, tyres were crunching on the gravel drive.

The teacher pressed himself against the wall and peered round into the drive.

Doctor Edward Curtis brought his car to a halt outside the house, switched off the engine then swung himself out from behind the wheel.

Hacket watched. Waited.

Curtis glanced across at Hacket's car but seemed to pay it little heed, something which puzzled the teacher. Instead, the doctor crossed to the front door and unlocked it, then he returned to the car and fumbled with the bunch of keys, selecting one and pushing it into the lock of the boot.

Hacket watched, unaware that he himself was the target of other eyes.

The figure watched.

And waited.

Eighty-one

'Bastard.'

She muttered the word under her breath, clutching her stomach with one hand, wincing with each fresh stab of pain. But it was not the pain to which she directed her anger. She glanced at the phone, wondering once again, if she should warn Curtis. Tell him that her husband was on his way. She looked at the clock. No, he'd have arrived at the house by now, surely.

Sue exhaled deeply, her mind turning over all the poss-

308

ible scenarios. A row. A fight even. She tried to push the thoughts from her mind.

Why was her husband so obsessed with the treatment she'd received? Why wasn't the gift of a child enough for him?

She felt another stab of pain. One which reached from her vagina to her naval and she sucked in a laboured breath, getting to her feet as if the movement would relieve the pressure on her belly.

The swelling there was only slight, as if she'd just eaten a heavy meal but it felt heavy. Sue felt bloated. Replete. As if the child she was carrying was growing not by the day but by the minute. Its progress to maturity accelerated beyond comprehension.

She walked across to the phone once more, her hand hovering over it for a moment.

Should she call Curtis?

She was still trying to decide when she heard the knock on the front door.

Sue froze for a moment, glancing down at the phone then at the door.

Could it be her husband? Had he finally seen the stupidity of his reactions? Perhaps their night would end in reconciliation instead of anger. She sucked in a deep breath and moved towards the door.

As she opened it she realised that if it had been her husband out there he would have used his key.

Ronald Mills stood on the doorstep, smiling.

Sue saw that he had a hand dug into his jacket pocket but, before she could speak he had pulled it free.

The .38 looked huge as it was pushed into her face.

'Don't scream,' snarled Mills. 'Just step back inside the house.'

She obeyed and he pushed her before him, stepping over the threshold.

The door swung shut behind them.

Eighty-two

The boot of the car opened like a large metallic mouth and, as Hacket watched, Curtis leant forward and scooped something up from within.

Something large.

Something which he struggled to carry.

The object was about five feet long, perhaps larger, thought Hacket. Wrapped·in a blanket.

Curtis stood still for a moment, the wind swirling around him, as he braced himself to carry his heavy load.

His large load.

Hacket squinted through the gloom once more.

It was big enough . . .

'Jesus Christ,' he murmured.

Big enough to be a man.

Curtis crossed to the front door of the house and entered, bumping one end of the object he carried against the frame as he entered. Hacket stepped back around the side of the house, pressing his back against the cold stone of the wall, sucking in deep breaths. He stayed there for long seconds then peered around into the drive once more. There was no sign of Curtis, he had not returned to shut the car boot, obviously more intent on depositing his cargo inside the house first.

Hacket realised what he must do.

He scurried towards the open front door and paused by the threshold, enveloped by darkness. Curtis had not bothered to turn on any lights when he'd entered.

From inside the house Hacket heard movement.

He entered, pulling the door closed but not shutting it, momentarily silencing the wild howling of the wind. He stood in the hallway, looking around in the gloom.

To his right there was a wide staircase which looked as

310

if it had been plucked from some baronial mansion. It rose into even more impenetrable darkness.

To his left was a door.

It was slightly ajar.

Hacket advanced slowly towards it, hearing sounds from beyond. Another door being opened. The occasional bump.

He found himself in what he took to be Curtis' reception.

The door marked 'SURGERY' was open.

He moved through it, slowing his pace slightly as he came to the corridor which linked the doctor's office to the waiting-room. He moved slowly, trying to minimise the sound of his footfalls on the polished floor.

It was like being blind in the narrow passageway. No light to guide him.

It was then that he noticed the smell.

Hacket froze, his throat dry, aware of the pounding of his heart.

He recognised the smell.

Strong and coppery.

As he moved another step forward his foot slid in something wet and he almost overbalanced.

He stepped back, looking down at the spot which had caused him to slide.

He pulled the lighter from his pocket and flicked it on.

Illuminated by the sickly yellow flame was a puddle of blood about three inches across.

There were drops of it all along the corridor – they led to the door of Curtis's office.

Hacket flicked off the lighter and moved on, his initial anger now gradually turning to anxiety and something a little stronger.

Fear, perhaps

Why question it? he told himself. It *was* fear.

As he stood with his hand on the doorknob of the doctor's

office he felt the hair at the back of his neck rise. He pushed the door gently.

It swung open to reveal yet more darkness.

And more blood.

It had dripped onto the carpet. Hacket could see it glistening in the natural light which flooded through the study window.

Outside the wind battered against the windows as if trying to gain entry, its banshee wail rising as Hacket glanced around the room, his gaze eventually coming to rest on yet another door.

It was like a maze inside the house.

He moved towards the last door and peered through it.

This time there was light beyond.

Beyond and below.

He realised that he was looking down into a cellar, lit from overhead by banks of powerful fluorescents.

Of Curtis there was no sign.

Only the drops of blood which spattered the stairs leading down into the cellar.

Hacket waited and watched, backing off slightly when he saw the doctor struggle into view, still carrying the blanket covered form. He finally laid it on a trolley and stepped back, wiping his hands on a paper towel which he then screwed up and tossed into a bin.

Hacket was mesmerised by the tableau before him, his eyes fixed on the blanket-swathed shape.

The wind continued to scream, its cries masking Hacket's low breathing.

If not for the wind he might have heard the heavy footfalls on the wide staircase, descending slowly from above him.

Eighty-three

She knew she was going to die.

It was just a matter of when.

But the inevitability of it made it no more acceptable and her fear grew by the second.

Sue Hacket sat on the chair in the classroom looking at her captor.

Ronald Mills glared back at her, the knife held in one hand, the .38 laying on a nearby desk-top.

She had been surprised at how easily he had gained access to the school, pushing her before him, expecting alarm bells to sound when the main door was eased open. But only silence had greeted her wish. There had been no bells. No panic.

No rescuers.

Mills had dragged her through the deserted school, up and down corridors, up a flight of stairs, finally pushing her into a classroom, hurling her towards a chair.

Then he had pulled some rope from his pocket and tied her to it, pulling so hard on the hemp that it had cut into her wrists and ankles. She could see blood running onto her feet when she glanced down. It looked black in the gloom of the classroom.

'I suppose you wonder who I am,' he said, speaking the first words since he'd brought her to this place.

She tried to swallow but her throat felt constricted.

'Well, don't you?' he hissed.

She nodded.

He moved towards her, the knife pointing at her face. He touched the point to her cheek, drawing it gently, almost lovingly, towards her eye.

She closed her eyes, gritting her teeth against the agony she knew must come next.

He pressed the point of the knife against the corner of her eye.

'Open,' he whispered.

She couldn't. Her eyes remained tightly shut, as if the thin flesh of her eyelids would protect her from the razor-sharp point of the blade.

'Open your eyes,' Mills snarled.

Sue opened them slowly, tears beginning to form, to trickle down her cheeks.

'That's better,' he said, smiling. 'I mean, don't you want to see the face of the man who killed your daughter?'

She felt her stomach contract and her body felt as if it had been wrapped in a freezing shroud.

She stared at him through tear-filled eyes, the knife still pressed against her cheek.

'Now we're going to sit and wait,' he told her, trailing the knife down towards her mouth where he ran the tip across her bottom lip. 'Sit and wait for your husband.'

Eighty-four

Hacket took a step forward as he saw Curtis reach for the corner of the blanket. From his position at the top of the cellar steps, Hacket was hidden from the view of the doctor but still able to see what was happening. He looked on, his heart thudding against his ribs.

Curtis took hold of the blanket and pulled it free.

Hacket had to stifle a gasp.

Lying on the trolley was a man, he guessed in his mid-

314

forties, dressed in a pair of trousers and a shirt, both of which were spattered with blood.

The long doubled edged stiletto blade still protruded from the dead man's right eye.

As Hacket watched, Curtis took hold of the blade and pulled, removing it from the eye with infinite care. He laid the knife on a table beside him, wiping some blood from it with a towel, then pulled off his own jacket and hung it on the back of a chair.

That simple task done he returned to the body and, using all his strength, turned the body over so that it was lying on its stomach.

Blood from the ruptured eye dribbled onto the trolley.

Curtis then pulled another, smaller, trolley towards him and Hacket could see the dozens of medical instruments laid out upon it. As he watched, the doctor reached for a scalpel; then he carefully pushed the hair away from the neck of the corpse and pressed the point of the scalpel to the nape of the neck, close to the base of the skull.

The razor-sharp blade cut effortlessly through flesh and muscle. More dark blood spilled from the incision.

Hacket gritted his teeth as he saw Curtis reach for a larger blade.

Hacket couldn't see but, from the vile sawing sounds which came from below he realised the blade had a serrated edge.

Curtis worked expertly with the tool, finally removing a piece of the occipital bone about two inches wide and three inches long. He discarded it into a metal tray close by.

Even from his high vantage point Hacket could see that the base of the victim's brain was exposed, and it took all the willpower he could muster to prevent himself vomiting. He gripped the door more tightly, hiding behind it, part of him wanting to run, to be away from this scene of butchery, the other telling, forcing him, to remain. Mesmerised by what he saw.

Using a pair of what reminded Hacket of pliers, Curtis cut through the spinal cord.

The snap of breaking bone echoed around the cellar like a gun-shot and the head of the man on the table seemed to collapse forward now, unsupported by the brain stem.

Hacket watched as blood oozed from the open skull, some of it covering Curtis' hands as he worked, but he seemed oblivious to the crimson weepings.

He reached for a small pair of tweezers and another scalpel, pushing the twin prongs deep into the thick grey-pink tissue of the brain, seizing something within its bloodied folds.

Curtis smiled as he gently gripped the pituitary gland between the prongs of the tweezers. One swift nick and the gland came free. He held it before him like some kind of trophy, admiring the swollen, dripping gland for a second before dropping it into a jar filled with clear fluid.

Hacket could stand no more.

He spun round and bolted back through the doctor's office, his only thought now to be away from this place, to tell the police.

To tell his wife.

Sue. Sue. What had Curtis done to *her*?

Hacket slipped on the carpet, fell but dragged himself upright again, not caring if Curtis heard him. He crashed through the door and out into the corridor, heading for the reception then the hall beyond.

If he could reach his car.

He heard footsteps behind him, heard Curtis hurtling up the cellar steps.

Hacket wrenched open the door which led out into the hall, glancing back, convinced that he could outrun the doctor. He was half-smiling when he blundered into the hall.

He collided with the figure.

It stood before him, blocking his path, barring his way to the front door.

Hacket had but one reaction as he looked at the figure.

His eyes bulged madly in their sockets, he fell back and, as he did, he screamed until he thought his lungs would burst.

Eighty-five

'I don't understand,' Sue Hacket said, quietly, tears spilling down her cheeks. 'Why are you doing this?'

Ronald Mills picked a piece of the scab from his left hand and rolled the hardened flesh between his thumb and forefinger.

'Why did you kill Lisa?' Sue persisted.

'Does it matter?' he asked, smiling, thinly. 'It's done now.' He moved closer to Sue, touching her shoulder, gripping it firmly for a second as if he were about to begin massaging it. Instead he pushed the knuckle of his index finger into the hollow beside her collar bone, digging hard until she winced in pain.

'She was pretty, your little girl,' Mills said. 'And so quiet too.'

Sue could not fight back the tears as he began to rub her neck, stroking his hand somewhat clumsily through her hair.

'When I went into her bedroom she didn't make a sound,'

he continued. 'Not even when I climbed onto the bed beside her.

'Please,' Sue said, softly, not wanting to hear.

'I asked her what her name was and she told me. Lisa. Such a pretty name.' He began to tug on Sue's hair then allowed his free hand to slide down the front of her blouse towards her breasts.

'Stop it,' Sue sobbed.

'She started to make a noise when I got out the knife,' Mills said. 'I thought she was going to cry then. That was why I had to put my hand over her mouth.'

The tears were pouring down Sue's face, dripping from her chin, some falling onto the back of Mills probing hand. He gripped one of her breasts hard and squeezed until she groaned in pain.

'She tried to scream when I used the knife on her,' he said, softly, his erection now throbbing against the inside of his trousers. 'But I kept her quiet.' He smiled. 'I pushed the knife into her throat. You should have seen the way her eyes opened up. It was like there was some kind of spring inside her head. I pushed the knife in and she opened her eyes wider. The further I pushed the wider they got. I thought they were going to fall out of her head.

Sue was sobbing uncontrollably now, Mills' hand still roughly kneading her breasts.

'And when I fucked her,' he sighed, wistfully. 'She was so tight. So beautifully tight.'

'You're fucking mad,' Sue wailed, her exhortations dissolving into racking sobs.

'Am I?' he asked, stepping back slightly. 'Could a madman have done what I've done? Tracked you and your husband to this place, planned revenge the way I have done?'

Sue merely shook her head, her cheeks burning, her eyes blurred.

318

'I'm going to kill your fucking husband,' he told her. 'Do you know why?'

She continued to cry.

'Do you?' he roared at her.

'No,' she yelled back, her body shaking violently.

Mills took a step forward, the knife held before him. He pushed it beneath Sue's chin, pressing just hard enough to puncture the skin. A tiny dribble of blood ran down her neck.

'Because he killed my friend. The only friend I ever had. Your husband killed him. Made him fall under a train. And I saw it all. I saw what he did and now he's going to pay.'

'Haven't you done enough to us?' she sobbed.

Mills smiled crookedly.

He began unbuttoning Sue's blouse.

'Done enough?' he hissed, a slight smile on his face. 'I've only just started.'

Eighty-six

Hacket was sure that his sanity had gone.

He was mad, that was the only answer.

A sane man would not have seen what he saw now.

He pushed himself back along the floor as the figure took a step towards him.

The teacher tried to pull himself upright but it seemed as if all the strength had drained from his body. He felt his bowels loosen, and the hair at the back of his neck stood up sharply. He shook his head slowly, wondering now if he was truly encountering madness.

The figure which faced him was not like those of a nightmare. No mind, however diseased, could conjure up an image like that which now confronted the teacher. No nightmare could be that bad.

It was fully six feet tall, about fifteen stone, perhaps more. A large man. *Man?* Hacket's tortured mind corrected itself. The monstrosity which stood before him was no man.

Supported on two legs the torso seemed much too broad, too heavy to be carried on even limbs as thick as those Hacket saw.

Its skin was pale, darkened only on the forearms by black hair. And there was power in those arms. Hacket could see each muscle clearly defined. Hands like ham-hocks swung from arms which looked a little too long, not quite simian but only a few steps removed. The torso seemed to widen as it reached the chest, and here, beneath the gauze-like shirt which the figure wore, Hacket could see several bulging growths. One on the right breast, another on the left shoulder.

It was the head which caused him to moan aloud as he stared at it.

Head?

Not one but two. Joined at the temple.

Four perfectly formed eyes fixed him in a freezing stare. The mouths opened simultaneously and, had Hacket been in a position to reason, he may well have realised that the body was controlled by just one brain. The scalps were bald, graced only with fine whisps of gossamer like the hair of old men.

A growth the size of a fist swelled from the right cheek of the left head. Another from the other cranium. The flesh around the eyes was puffy, almost liquescent, as if it were filled with fluid waiting to burst. The growths looked like massive boils, replete with pus and ready to erupt.

The figure took another step towards Hacket who had

320

managed to drag himself up onto his knees into what looked like an attitude of prayer.

He watched as the figure advanced, its piercing gaze never leaving him. His mind was still reeling, but somewhere inside the madness a note of reason told him that he was looking at a Siamese twin. Two bodies supported by just one pair of legs. Two entities in a single body.

The twin reached for him, one powerful hand lifting him to his feet.

'What do you want?'

The two mouths moved in perfect unison, the words not slurred and laboured but crisply spoken, eminently understandable. Coming from such a monstrous source it made them sound all the more incongruous.

Hacket could not reply. His entire body was shaking.

A door behind him opened but he was scarcely aware of it.

Curtis dashed into the hall, slowing his pace when he saw that the teacher had been stopped.

The doctor nodded and the twin hurled Hacket to one side.

He crashed heavily against the wall and lay there as Curtis stood over him.

'You're trespassing, Mr Hacket,' said Curtis, calmly. 'You realise that?'

'What the fuck is going on here, Curtis?' Hacket gasped, his gaze drawn once more to the other figure. 'What is *that*?'

The twin moved forward angrily but Curtis stepped in front of it.

'*That*, Mr Hacket,' the doctor said, angrily. 'Is my brother.'

Hacket laughed uncontrollably. Was this the beginning of madness, he wondered, his eyes beginning to fill with tears. This was the laughter of the insane.

Curtis looked on impassively.

Hacket wiped his eyes and glared up at the doctor.

'One of your fucking experiments don't you mean?' he snarled. 'The product of your treatment. The same treatment you gave to my wife. Is that what she'll give birth to?' He pointed at the twin.

'I ought to kill you now,' the figure said, quietly.

Hacket swallowed hard, stunned once more by the figure's voice.

'Kill me like you killed that poor bastard in your cellar?' he hissed, looking now at Curtis. 'Who is he? Why did you kill him?'

'Call him a donor,' said Curtis, smiling.

Hacket looked vague.

'I couldn't expect a man of your limited perceptions to understand, Mr Hacket. Perhaps I at least owe you the privilege of some kind of explanation. Although I doubt it will mean much to you.'

Curtis glanced at the twin. 'Bring him.'

Hacket rose, but as soon as he was on his feet the other figure grabbed him, one powerful arm snaking around his throat the other hand clamping onto the back of his head.

'If you try to struggle,' the figure said, softly. 'I'll break your neck.' As it pulled him backwards, Hacket felt the heavy growths on its chest rubbing against his back.

Curtis set off for the cellar, followed by Hacket and the twin.

'Time for you to learn, Mr Hacket,' said Curtis, smiling. 'You should feel honoured.'

'And when I *have* learned?' Hacket said, struggling to speak because of the pressure on his windpipe.

Curtis didn't answer.

They began to descend into the cellar.

Eighty-seven

The stench from the body made Hacket feel sick, but held as he was by the twin he could not pull away. Instead all he could do was gaze helplessly at the corpse, his eyes drawn to the gaping hole in the back of its skull, and also to the small gland which still floated in the jar of clear liquid.

'From death comes life,' said Curtis, smiling, gesturing first to the body then to the gland. 'To coin a cliché.'

'What are you talking about, Curtis?' asked Hacket, wearily.

'I'm talking about hope, Mr Hacket. Something which you and your wife didn't have until *I* came along.'

'What have you done to her?' Hacket rasped, trying to pull away but finding himself restrained by the powerful hands which held him.

'I've done what she wanted me to do. I've given her hope. Her and dozens of women like her over the years. Women who couldn't have children. Women who now, because of me, are mothers.' He lifted the jar. 'And all because of this.'

'What is it?'

'The pituitary gland. Source of the body's growth hormones. I'll try to keep this simple Mr Hacket, otherwise I'll end up sounding like some kind of mad doctor.' He smiled. 'They belong in bad horror films.'

'And you belong in prison you murdering bastard,'

Hacket snarled. 'What about that poor fucker lying there? What about him? Where's *his* hope?'

'I said I'll keep this simple. I'll also keep it brief. My father began this work over forty years ago, on the directive of the British government. The project was called "Genesis". That name, I know, will mean nothing to you.' Curtis smiled. 'Except perhaps in its Biblical sense. The name was apt. Genesis describes the creation of life, and that was what Project Genesis was designed to do. My father perfected a fertility drug, refined from human pituitary glands. Given in the right doses it would cut the gestation period from nine months to three. In larger measures perhaps even to four weeks. And it worked.' The doctor's tone hardened. 'He did what *they* told him to do. The government, Churchill in particular, knew that the Germans would invade after Dunkirk. They also knew that there weren't enough men to combat an invasion. They needed my father and his work. Once the women had given birth the children would be regularly injected with the drug, their growth outside the womb would be as rapid as it had been while they were gestating. A child could grow into a man in less than two months.'

'You're mad and by the sound of it, so was your fucking father,' Hacket said.

The twin twisted his head sharply and Hacket felt excruciating pain in his neck and skull. He opened his mouth to scream but no sound would come.

'Another inch and I'll break your neck,' said the twin, leaning close to his ear, both mouths moving slowly.

Curtis held up a hand for the other to release the pressure and Hacket felt the force diminish somewhat. White stars danced before his eyes, and for a second he thought he was going to black out, but he kept a grip on consciousness, listening as Curtis continued.

'There was no madness, Hacket. Only supreme intelligence. But *they* couldn't see that. The men who had wanted his expertise were frightened by the success of his experiments. Some of the children were born deformed. Like my brother. Mentally they were perfect but their physical appearance was unacceptable.' He spoke the last word with sarcasm. 'They told my father to stop his work. He refused, so they had him murdered.' The knot of muscles at the side of the doctor's jaw throbbed angrily. 'My mother was left alone. She was pregnant at the time, carrying myself and my brother. She brought us up alone. Protected my brother, paid for me to go through Medical school. When the time was right she passed on our father's notes. I continued with his work. And, if people have had to die during the course of that work, then too bad. A few human lives are drops in the ocean. Besides, for every one that's died there's been another to take their place. A child where there would never have been one. Hope where there was only misery.'

'The grave in the back garden,' Hacket said, quietly. 'Who is it?'

'Our mother. Margaret Lawrenson. After we were born she gave us her maiden name. Curtis. Better for her to lie there than with others like those who had my father killed. The hypocrites and the doubters.'

'And she supported you? She knew what you were doing? Knew you were killing people?' Curtis asked.

'She knew that sacrifices had to be made if my father's work was to see true fruition. She believed, Hacket. Believed in *him*, believed in *me*.'

'And the children that were born by using your '*treatment*'? What happened to them?'

'All well. All thriving. There is one minor side-effect however. The introduction of so much growth hormone into their systems seems to stimulate other parts of their brains. Without regular treatment they revert to cannabilism.'

325

'And their parents *know* this?' Hacket gasped.

'Know it and accept it, Mr Hacket. How does the cliché go, love conquers all? Even the knowledge that your child may kill.' He smiled again.

'How come the police haven't found you by now?'

'If I told you that the wife of the local Inspector was one of my patients would that explain why?' Curtis smiled. 'They really do have the most beautiful young daughter. She's almost fifteen now.'

Hacket shook his head, his eyes screwed up tight.

'You *are* mad,' he murmured. 'This whole thing is insane. Weller thought so too, didn't he? The man who lived at the house before me. He knew didn't he?'

'Very astute, Mr Hacket. Unfortunately Weller wasn't prepared to live the kind of life necessary to protect his son. He was ungrateful. And he was a fool. He's better off dead. I gave him what he wanted and he destroyed it.'

'I won't let that happen to my wife. I'll stop her having that child.'

Curtis shook his head and sighed.

'I'm afraid you have no choice, Mr Hacket,' he said, his tone darkening. 'Besides, it's far too late to stop it now.'

Eighty-eight

The pains were growing worse.

Each fresh contraction caused Sue Hacket to wince. It felt as if someone were pulling her intestines out through her navel with red hot tongs. The burning sensation had spread to her vagina too and she shifted as best she could on the chair in order to try and alleviate the growing pain.

Ronald Mills walked up and down the darkened classroom agitatedly, glancing alternately out of the window then at his watch. He swore under his breath then strode across the room towards Sue.

'Where is he?' he hissed. 'Where's your fucking husband?'

She gritted her teeth as a fresh wave of pain swept through her.

'I don't know,' she grunted.

'Lying cunt,' he snarled and lashed out at her.

The blow with the back of his hand caught her across the left cheek. A blow so powerful it almost knocked her over.

'Where is he?' Mills repeated.

'I don't know,' Sue wailed, helplessly, the pain from her lower abdomen eclipsing that from her cheek. She tasted blood in her mouth as she licked her tongue across her bottom lip.

Mills gripped the knife before him, pressing it to her chest, prodding her bare breasts with the tip. He brushed it against her left nipple which stiffened with the cold touch of the steel. Mills grinned, feeling the first stirrings of an erection. How easy it would be to cut that fleshy bud off, he thought. The idea excited him even more. No. He wanted Hacket to see it. Wanted him to see his own wife in agony, bleeding. He wanted to hear her pray for death.

And then it would be Hacket's turn.

Mills had waited a long time for the moment and he intended savouring it.

He watched as Sue doubled over, a fresh jolt of pain filling her. Mills grabbed a handful of her hair and wrenched her upright, so that he was staring into her face. Tears were flooding down her cheeks once more.

'I want to know where your husband is,' hissed Mills.

'And I told you I don't know,' Sue sobbed. 'Why don't you believe me?'

Mills took the knife and carefully slashed the waistband of her skirt, tugging aside the material, leaving her in just her panties. Then he slid the blade under the elastic at the side and pulled them from her.

She continued to cry, now exposed to his leering stare.

'I don't think I can wait any longer,' said Mills, smiling, running approving eyes over her naked body. He could feel the erection pressing almost painfully against the inside of his trousers.

'I think I'll have to start without him.'

Eighty-nine

Hacket knew he had to break free but the task seemed impossible.

The pressure on his neck and throat reminded him of that.

Curtis regarded the teacher silently for a moment.

'What did you hope to gain by coming here tonight?' he said, finally. 'If it was the truth you wanted, then at least now you know it.'

Hacket's arms dropped to his sides, he didn't struggle against the pressure on his neck, merely stood there, half leaning, half-supported by the immense strength of the twin.

'And now I know?' he asked. 'Are you going to kill me?'

'What choice do I have?' Curtis snapped. 'I offered you

something more precious than you could have imagined, you *and* your wife, but you couldn't be content with that.'

'How many more people will you have to kill, Curtis, to carry on this fucking insanity?'

'As many as it takes. It's people like *you* who are mad, not me,' Curtis said, jabbing an accusatory finger at the teacher. 'What I do I do for the good of others. As I said to you, sacrifices have to be made.'

'Very noble,' Hacket chided, his hand brushing against the twin's leg. 'What about the families of the people you kill, do you ever think about what they must feel? You cause pain, Curtis. It's all you're any good for.'

So much pain.

Curtis glanced at the twin and nodded.

Hacket felt the pressure tighten on his neck.

It was then that he reached back and fastened his hands on the twin's testicles, squeezing as tightly as he could, gripping them in a vice-like hold which made the twin shriek in pain.

Hacket gritted his teeth and squeezed harder, pushing backwards.

The twin screamed again and the two of them fell to the ground.

Hacket felt the pressure on his neck released.

He struggled to his feet, turning swiftly to drive a powerful kick into the groin of his fallen captor. He turned back to face Curtis who had lurched towards him, his hand clasping the stiletto blade.

The doctor lunged at Hacket and the teacher shouted in pain as the blade sliced through his shirt, cutting into his forearm. Blood burst from the wound and Hacket jumped back, avoiding the twin's large hand as it grabbed for him. The monstrosity was raising itself up, trying to block his path.

Hacket lashed out again, kicking it in the chest this time but the impact had little effect.

Curtis struck at him once more, the blade carving through his shirt at the back this time.

Hacket screamed in pain as he felt the blade scrape his shoulder blade. The wound opened like a mouth, spilling more blood onto the already damp material of his shirt. He fell forward, crashing into a tray of instruments. Scalpels, forceps and syringes were sent skittering across the floor of the cellar and Hacket gripped one of the scalpels, turning to face the twin as it bore down on him.

He struck out wildly but the blow was effective.

The twin shrieked as the razor sharp blade cut through its calf. It staggered for a second, blood pouring from the wound, some of it spattering Hacket, who was now trying to reach the cellar steps.

He dragged himself to his feet and slashed at the twin once more.

Both mouths opened simultaneously to shout their pain as the blade sliced effortlessly through an outstretched hand. The palm was laid open to the bone, the thumb nearly severed.

Hacket edged backwards, Curtis and the twin advancing on him, blood from his own wounds dripping on to the floor. His left arm was beginning to go numb where Curtis had cut him, but he gripped the scalpel in his right hand, glancing from one attacker to the other, waiting for the inevitable rush.

Before it could come he took his chance and turned, running as fast as he could for the stairs.

He had reached the fifth one when the twin caught him.

Hacket felt a huge hand grab his arm, jerking him back but, as he fell he brought the scalpel around, driving it deep into the side of his attacker.

More blood spurted from the wound and onto Hacket,

who again struggled free, looking up to see Curtis preparing to strike.

The stiletto blade hurtled down, nicking Hacket's cheek. He felt warm fluid running down his face and knew that the cut was deep. As he sucked in a breath he could feel the cold air hissing through the wound.

Curtis pressed his advantage but Hacket ducked beneath the next swipe, striking upwards, catching the doctor in the thigh, burying the scalpel so deep he felt it scratch against Curtis' femur.

The blade remained embedded, quivering there as Curtis dropped his own knife and tried to pull the scalpel free.

From the amount of blood jetting from the wound he thought for one fearful second that his femoral artery had been severed. For fleeting moments he forgot all about Hacket, intent only on ripping the blade from his leg. It finally came free and Curtis screamed in pain.

Hacket, his throat now filling with blood from his slashed cheek, scrambled up the steps and managed to reach the cellar door. He tore it open and crashed through, feeling sick, his head spinning.

The twin, bleeding from the wound in its side, followed.

Curtis remained at the foot of the steps, using his handkerchief to stem the flow of blood from his thigh.

Hacket staggered on through the house, knowing his only hope was to reach his car, to get out of this house, away from this madness.

He blundered through the waiting room and out into the hall.

The twin followed.

Hacket ran for the front door and tugged on it.

It was locked.

He beat frantically against it, as if trying to smash his way free.

The twin reached the hall a second later.

Hacket turned to face it, watching as those two mouths turned upwards simultaneously in a grin of triumph.

'You should have stayed away,' the twin told him, clutching its injured side.

Hacket stood close to the door, the scalpel held before him, his breath coming in gasps, hissing through the savage gash in his right cheek.

As the twin advanced slowly, Hacket glanced to his left and saw another door.

He suddenly turned and bolted for it, crashing through into what, he guessed, was the sitting room.

The twin followed, shouting something after him.

There was a large bay window in the room and Hacket knew what he must do. There was no time for thought, no choice.

He ran towards the window and launched himself at it.

He screamed as he leapt at it, covering his face with his arms, hitting the glass like some kind of human projectile.

The window exploded outwards, huge shards of glass bursting into the cold night air.

Hacket hit the driveway outside with a sickening thump, dazed both by the impact and by the collision against the glass. He was close to unconsciousness, but the cold wind rapidly revived him and restored his senses. He rolled over in time to see the twin clambering through the remains of the window.

Hacket felt for the scalpel but he'd dropped it.

The twin was practically free of the window, ignoring the jagged pieces of glass which scratched it.

Hacket got to his feet and ran for his car, dragging open the door, jamming the key into the ignition.

The twin was pulling its bulk clear now, about to drop down onto the driveway.

Hacket twisted the key.

Nothing.

He gripped it harder and turned again.

The engine roared once then faded as his foot slipped off the accelerator.

The twin was lumbering towards him now, blood spilling not only from its hand and side but also from both of the mouths.

Hacket turned the ignition key again, the twin now less than twenty yards from him.

The engine roared into life.

Fifteen yards.

Hacket jammed the car into gear.

Ten yards.

The twin roared in defiance and ran at the car.

The Renault shot forward as if fired from a cannon.

It slammed into the twin, the impact so great that the figure was catapulted into the air, slamming down on the roof of the car before flying off. It crashed to the ground behind the Renault.

Hacket saw it in the rear-view mirror and reversed at top speed.

The second impact knocked the twin flat, the rear wheels running over the huge head.

It seemed to burst under the weight and pressure.

A vile flux of blood and brains exploded from the riven skull, some of the seething mixture flying up around the car as the back wheels spun impotently on the gravel drive for a second, then Hacket jammed the car into first and swung it around, heading for the main road.

Had he looked in the rear-view mirror he would have seen Curtis emerge from the house to see his dead brother then to bellow something after the fleeing car.

As it was, Hacket gripped the wheel as tightly as he could and pressed his foot down on the accelerator.

The car skidded violently as it reached the main road but the teacher kept control of it, guiding it towards Hinkston.

He seemed to forget his pain, even the horror of what he'd just experienced. It was all pushed to the back of his mind.

For now, all he could think of was his wife.

And the monstrosity she might be carrying inside her.

He drove on.

Ninety

12.08 a.m.

Hacket brought the car to a halt outside his house and glanced at the clock on the dashboard.

He swallowed, fighting back the nausea as he tasted blood. As he swung himself out of the car the wound in his back began to throb mightily, an accompaniment to the pain he was feeling from his gashed forearm. But fighting the pain as best he could he hurried to the front door and selected the appropriate key.

The house was silent as he walked in.

No TV.

Not even any lights.

Maybe Sue was in bed, he reasoned.

Hacket made his way up the stairs, his breath coming in gasps.

Half way up he called her name.

No answer.

As he reached the landing he stood against one wall, feeling a wave of pain wash over him, and for a second he thought he was going to faint; but the feeling passed and he moved into the bedroom, calling her name again.

The room was empty.

Hacket didn't even bother checking the other rooms, he hurried back downstairs, slapping on lights as he went, calling her name once again.

It was in the hallway he saw the blood.

There was more on the kitchen door.

He pushed it open.

The back door was open, banging gently against the frame as each fresh gust of wind blew it. The table and two of the chairs had been overturned. The room was a wreck.

He whispered her name under his breath, his eyes finally alighting on the piece of paper propped up on the draining board beside the sink.

He strode across and snatched it up, examining the large, almost child-like, letters. As he read the words he felt his body beginning to quiver.

COME TO THE SCOOL

COME AND GET YOUR

FUCKING WIFE

Ninety-one

Why hadn't the alarm gone off?

It was a curious thought, but one which nevertheless occurred to Hacket as he paused by the main door of the school, peering through the glass into the gloom beyond.

He could see smashed glass inside where his wife's kidnapper had broken in, but the alarm obviously hadn't gone off. He must have disabled it first, the teacher reasoned, pushing the door tentatively, wincing as it creaked slightly on its hinges. He slipped inside and stood in the entryway, ears alert for the slightest movement. The silence was chokingly oppressive. Like the darkness through which he moved, the solitude seemed almost palpable, holding him back from his quest.

Sue was in the building somewhere, along with the man who had abducted her. At least Hacket assumed it was a man. Just who it could be he didn't know. All he wanted to know was that she was alive. The questions could come later.

He gripped the carving knife he'd taken from the kitchen and made his way down the corridor to his left, peering into each darkened classroom in turn.

There was no sign of her.

He paused for a moment, aware of the burning pain coming from his wounds. But then he pressed on, checking the next corridor.

It was also empty.

Sandwiched between the two was the library.

Hacket pushed open one door and stepped inside, glancing around, squinting through the blackness.

He passed through the library quietly, as if preserving the usual reverence for a room normally silent. There was no sign of Sue in there either.

He wandered back up the corridor towards the dining room.

As he wandered around it the questions began to fill his mind.

Why had she been taken?

When?

By whom?

For what purpose?

Hacket leant against a door frame and sucked in a weary breath. There were so many questions. His head was spinning.

Was she still alive?

Was the child still alive? . . .

The child . . .

He shuddered as he thought about it, about what had happened at Curtis' house.

A noise from above him interrupted the whirlwind of questions spinning around in his head.

He pushed open the double doors which led through into the assembly hall. Hacket hurried across the varnished floor towards another set of double doors.

Beyond these were the stairs that led up to the first floor of the school.

He heard the sound again and slowed his pace, gripping the carving knife more tightly.

Hacket ascended slowly, eyes fixed ahead of him. He stumbled as he reached the half-way point, cursing when pain from the wound in his forearm shot through him. He turned a corner, trying to control his harsh breathing and the thudding of his heart.

He reached the top of the stairs and pushed the next set of double doors.

Four rooms faced him.

He checked them one by one.

Through the window in the door of the third room he saw Sue.

She was naked, tied to a chair, a gag stuffed unceremoniously into her mouth.

Hacket tried the door and, to his delight found it was unlocked.

He blundered in, tears filling his eyes.

She looked up and saw him but the look was not one of relief but one of horror.

Her eyes bulged and she shook her head.

'It's all right,' he whispered as he crossed to her.

She continued to shake her head, nodding towards him. Towards him?

Her eyes were not on him but on something behind him.

As he reached for the gag he heard a metallic click.

The sound of a hammer being thumbed back.

'I've been waiting.'

Hacket spun round as he heard the voice.

'Drop the fucking knife.'

Hacket obeyed, watching as Ronald Mills stepped from the shadows, the .38 aimed at the teacher's head.

Ninety-two

'Get over there,' Mills snapped, motioning to the desk opposite Sue.

Hacket did as he was told, his eyes on the large man who held the pistol on him.

Sue moaned beneath the gag as another particularly powerful stab of pain lanced through her.

338

'Who are you?' Hacket wanted to know, watching as Mills moved towards Sue.

The big man removed her gag, pulling it free roughly.

'Tell him who I am,' he snapped, the gun still aimed at Hacket.

Sue hesitated, her words choked away by sobs.

'Tell him,' rasped Mills, pulling her hair.

'You bastard,' snapped Hacket and took a step forward but Mills levelled the pistol at arms length, drawing a bead on a point between the teacher's eyes.

'Tell him who I am,' Mills repeated. 'Tell him what I did.'

'He killed Lisa,' Sue sobbed, tears running down her cheeks.

'Oh Christ,' murmured Hacket, his voice low.

'Does the name Peter Walton ring a bell?' Mills said. Hacket didn't, couldn't answer.

'I'm talking to you, cunt,' Mills snarled. 'Peter Walton. Do you remember him? What happened to him?'

Hacket exhaled deeply, the feelings of frustration, helplessness and fear filling him in equal proportions.

'He was killed. Fell under a train,' Hacket whispered.

'No. You murdered him. I saw you. I saw you chasing him. Saw you push him.'

'He slipped. I didn't touch him.'

'You wanted to.'

'Fucking right,' snarled Hacket. 'And if I could I'd have put you under that fucking train with him, you animal.'

Mills tugged hard on Sue's hair, the gun still aimed at Hacket.

'You better shut your fucking mouth, Hacket,' he rasped.

'What are you trying to do to us? It's me you want. Let my wife go.'

'Fuck you. If she suffers, *you* suffer. You'll get your

339

turn, don't worry but I want you to see *her* die first. Just like I had to watch you kill Walton. He was the only friend I ever had. The only person I ever trusted or cared about. Who cared about *me*.' He shouted the last sentence. 'And you murdered him.'

'The police will come,' Hacket said, desperate for any idea which might save them. 'You'll be caught, perhaps even killed.'

'What do *I* care? At least you'll have died before me.'

'Just tell me one thing,' Hacket said. 'Why did you kill Lisa?'

'She was there. If it hadn't been her it would have been another girl. We broke in to rob you. Finding her was just a bonus.' He grinned broadly and, with his free hand, began unfastening his trousers. 'Now you watch me, Hacket.'

Sue looked imploringly at her husband, realising that he was as helpless as she to stop this madman. If he rushed Mills then he would either shoot Sue or the teacher himself. There was a chance he might just wound Hacket but, from such close range, Sue was as good as dead. Hacket could do nothing but watch as the big man tugged the rope from Sue's legs. He saw the red welts where the hemp had cut into her flesh.

'Open your legs,' Mills told her, unfastening his trousers to reveal a large erection.

Hacket understood.

'She's pregnant for God's sake,' he yelled.

'Shut up, fucker,' roared Mills, moving towards Sue. He grabbed her ankles and pulled her forward. He had to bend at the knees to manoeuvre his penis towards her vagina, all the time keeping the gun pointed at Hacket, who sucked in a painful breath.

Sue screamed as Mills drove into her, his shaft penetrating her deeply.

He began to thrust back and forth.

340

Sue felt him inside her and she sobbed helplessly, looking at the moon face before her but then she felt more contractions, a movement deep within her belly. Movement which seemed to transfer itself to her vagina.

Hacket looked on helplessly, clenching his fists until the muscles ached.

Dear God, just for one second . . .

Just one clear run at Mills.

Sue moaned aloud.

'I think she's enjoying it,' said Mills, still thrusting hard into her. He grinned again but the smile suddenly dissolved into a look of surprise.

Hacket looked more closely at him.

No, not surprise.

It was pain.

Mills thrust deeply once or twice more then tried to pull away.

But he couldn't.

Pain began to grow around his penis, spreading across his groin.

Sue had stopped crying.

She was smiling now as she watched the pain on the rapist's face.

He tried again to pull away and this time he screamed in agony.

His penis felt as if it were being squeezed inside her vagina. As if her inner muscles were contracting, closing like a fleshy vice. But the pain was sharper than that.

Mills pushed against Sue as the pain grew more intense.

Hacket looked on, mesmerised.

Sue merely continued to smile.

Mills shrieked uncontrollably as he felt the grip inside her vagina increase. As if he was being held by small hands.

The hands of a baby.

He felt pain unlike anything he'd ever experienced. An excruciating agony which almost caused him to faint.

Blood began to pump from Sue's vagina but it was not *her* blood. Mills was frantic now, desperate to be away from her, from that grip which was mutilating him. His knees buckled and he began to fall.

He fell backwards.

The scream which he uttered was like nothing Hacket had ever heard before. A bellow of absolute suffering torn from the depths of his soul.

As Mills fell onto his back Hacket could see that where the big man's penis had once been there was now only a spurting stump of shredded flesh. The big man put his hands into the wound as if trying to stem the flow of blood and recover his mutilated manhood.

He screamed and screamed, the sound echoing around the classroom, drumming inside Hacket's head as blood spurted from the savage wound. The teacher felt his own vomit clawing its way up from his stomach as he staggered towards his wife, stepping past the writhing shape of Mills but, as he drew closer, Hacket saw the final act of horror and, this time, he could not control himself.

The lips of Sue's vagina slid open and the torn off shaft of Mills' penis was pushed out to drop onto the floor amidst the puddle of blood which had formed there. Like a child spitting out a distasteful piece of food, the vaginal opening yawned wide to expel the remnants of Mills' manhood.

Hacket swayed then turned to one side and vomited until there was nothing left in his stomach.

Sue continued to smile, gazing down at Mills who was still screaming, his yells becoming fainter as the loss of blood gradually sapped his strength and his life gushed away through his fingers.

Hacket freed her, wrapping her in his shirt which he hurriedly pulled off.

Bloodied and dazed they stumbled past Mills.

'We have to get the police,' Hacket gasped, wiping his mouth with the back of his hand.

Mills' screams had degenerated into low burblings as they staggered out of the room.

Hacket didn't know how long it took a man to bleed to death.

They supported each other down the stairs and out of the school, heading back towards their house, sucking in the cold night air, as if wishing it could wash away the stench of blood and death from their nostrils.

Hacket shivered but he realised that it was not all a product of the cold wind.

Sue, bloodied and barely conscious, looked at him and smiled.

Hacket felt the hairs at the back of his neck rise.

They reached the house and blundered through the back door, Hacket slamming it behind them. Then they struggled through into the sitting room, the teacher slapping on lights as they went.

He froze.

Sitting in one of the armchairs, the stiletto blade held in his hand, was Doctor Edward Curtis.

Ninety-three

For long seconds Hacket couldn't speak, his eyes remained fixed on Curtis.

'My brother is dead, as you may have guessed,' the doctor finally said, his face emotionless.

'It has to end, Curtis,' Hacket said, leaning against the door frame to support himself.

'I agree with you,' the doctor echoed, rising to his feet, the knife held before him.

Sue looked first at her husband then at Curtis.

Then she felt the pain. So powerful she yelled in response to it.

'You've done this to her,' Hacket screamed. 'God knows what she's carrying. Something like your . . . brother? Help her. Abort the baby. Now.'

'No,' Sue moaned, her face twisted into a mask of pain. 'Don't let it die.' She looked imploringly at Curtis. 'Please.'

'Kill it, Curtis,' Hacket snarled. 'It's unnatural.'

Curtis took a step towards Sue, dropping the knife on the sofa.

'I need it,' she said. 'Help it live.' She gripped Curtis' hand and pulled him closer to her.

Hacket stepped forward, pushing the doctor away, slamming him up against the wall, hands clasped around his throat. There was a look of hatred in his eyes. Hatred and something else.

Madness perhaps?

Curtis struggled against Hacket's grip, supported by his hands but dying because of them. His head felt as if it were beginning to swell, and he was fighting for his breath as Hacket dug his thumbs deeper into the doctor's windpipe, lifting him off his feet with the ferocity of his attack.

'You've done this to her,' snarled Hacket, exerting yet more strength on Curtis' throat. 'I'll kill you.' He bellowed the words into the other man's face.

Hacket felt the pain in his lower back first.

Like a punch in the kidneys.

Then it came again. Harder this time and he felt the coldness now.

The third time he realised.

Sue drove the stiletto blade into his back, severing his spinal cord.

He lost his grip on Curtis then dropped to his knees.

As he did she brought the knife down again.

This time it powered into his neck, severing the carotid artery. A huge fountain of blood erupted from the wound, spattering Sue and spraying the wall of the sitting room crimson as surely as if it had been splashed with red paint. Hacket turned and looked at her, tears in his eyes, then he fell forward, his body jerking slightly.

Blood filled his mouth and he blinked hard as his vision began to cloud both with pain and tears.

How long would it take a man to bleed to death?

He would have the answer soon.

Curtis looked down at him, massaging his throat, scarcely able to speak.

Sue continued to sob, the knife still in her hands, crimson dripping from its point like thick teardrops.

'Why did you want to kill it, John?' she sobbed. 'Why?'

Hacket tried to speak but the only sound he could make was a liquid gurgle. Blood spilled over his lips, he felt it run from his nostrils. He reached out towards her, wanting to touch her hand, knowing he was dying. Along with the pain there was fear too.

'The child will live, Hacket,' Curtis said, rubbing his bruised throat.

'My child,' Hacket gurgled, but the effort of speaking only brought fresh pain and a massive heaving within his body. He began to shiver.

Curtis smiled down at him.

'No,' he said softly. 'Not *your* child. *My brother's.*'

Even through her tears Sue was smiling too.

John Hacket closed his eyes.

345

Some wounds never heal. Some pain
is never soothed.

Anon

Hatred shouldn't be forgotten. It
should be nurtured. And self-hatred
is the bloom which responds best.

Anon